**Praise for the Romances
of Amanda McCabe**

"Flawlessly crafted historical romance."   —*Chicago Tribune*

"An enthralling spell of tender romance with a hint of danger,
set against the glittering backdrop of Regency London."
—Diane Farr

"[A] terrific book that kept me engrossed the entire time! A
real winner."   —Huntress Book Reviews

"Amanda McCabe has been delighting readers since her debut,
and this sweetly engaging tale doesn't disappoint. She has a
talent for bringing ordinary characters into soft focus and
making us want the best for them."   —*Romantic Times*

"McCabe is a welcome addition to the ranks of Regency au-
thors. She creates well-developed characters, both primary and
secondary. She re-creates the world of Regency society with a
sure hand. She provides a sweet and moving romance."
—*The Romance Reader*

"Charming [and] deftly humorous."
—Romance Reviews Today (A Perfect 10)

Improper Ladies

The Golden Feather
and
The Rules of Love

Amanda McCabe

A SIGNET ECLIPSE BOOK

SIGNET ECLIPSE
Published by New American Library, a division of
Penguin Group (USA) Inc., 375 Hudson Street,
New York, New York 10014, USA
Penguin Group (Canada), 90 Eglinton Avenue East, Suite 700, Toronto,
Ontario M4P 2Y3, Canada (a division of Pearson Penguin Canada Inc.)
Penguin Books Ltd., 80 Strand, London WC2R 0RL, England
Penguin Ireland, 25 St. Stephen's Green, Dublin 2,
Ireland (a division of Penguin Books Ltd.)
Penguin Group (Australia), 250 Camberwell Road, Camberwell, Victoria 3124,
Australia (a division of Pearson Australia Group Pty. Ltd.)
Penguin Books India Pvt. Ltd., 11 Community Centre, Panchsheel Park,
New Delhi - 110 017, India
Penguin Group (NZ), 67 Apollo Drive, Rosedale, North Shore 0632,
New Zealand (a division of Pearson New Zealand Ltd.)
Penguin Books (South Africa) (Pty.) Ltd., 24 Sturdee Avenue,
Rosebank, Johannesburg 2196, South Africa

Penguin Books Ltd., Registered Offices:
80 Strand, London WC2R 0RL, England

Published by Signet Eclipse, an imprint of New American Library, a division of
Penguin Group (USA) Inc. *The Golden Feather* and *The Rules of Love* were
previously published in Signet editions.

First Signet Eclipse Printing (Double Edition), September 2010
10   9   8   7   6   5   4   3   2   1

The Golden Feather

In memory of my grandmother Roberta McCabe, who always said she just knew I'd be a writer someday.

I wish you were here to see this now, Nana.

Prologue

London, 1810

"Am I dead, then?" Justin Seward leaned back against the cushions of the jolting carriage and reached an unsteady hand up to touch the aching hole in his shoulder. His fingers came away a sticky red.

"Don't be ridiculous, man!" his friend the Honorable Freddie Reed said heartily. "It's barely a scratch. Old Holmes could never shoot worth a farthing. We'll have you home in a trice."

James Burne-Jones, who sat across from them, snickered. "You may not be dead, Justin," he said, "but you'll surely wish you were once your father hears of this. Remember how he shouted the last time!"

Justin groaned again and closed his eyes tightly. Oh, yes. His father, the grand Earl of Lyndon, was sure to ring a mighty peal over him for this, Justin's third duel in a year. After the second one, the earl had threatened any number of dire consequences if he ever heard of his son causing any more such scandals. The very walls had shaken with his wrath.

Justin almost asked his friends to turn back around so that he could ask Holmes to finish what he started. Death was preferable to whatever awaited him at Seward House.

He tried to stay out of trouble, truly he did. For months he had avoided all his usual haunts: the gaming hells, the clubs, the racetrack. How was he to know that Pamela Holmes, who had been sending him provocative, violet-scented letters, had a jealous husband who would be waiting when Justin showed up for their rendezvous—and who would call him out?

Truly, trouble just seemed to seek him out, and had ever since he left Cambridge two years ago.

Unlike his perfect older brother, Edward, Viscount Keir, who never took a step wrong.

The carriage lurched to a halt outside Seward House. It looked quiet, as though all were asleep in the pale early-morning light, but Justin knew better. He knew that divine retribution awaited him in those dignified walls. He had slid neatly out of trouble a dozen times before. This time was different. This time he had used up his last, and probably best, chance.

A deep shame washed over him, burying even the pain in his shoulder and the hot rush of temper he had felt at Holmes's challenge. Shame was a rare emotion for Justin; it was so easy to shrug off his parents' anger, to hurry on to the next adventure. Now he was drowning in it, in the weight of his parents' destroyed expectations, of his own disappointment in himself.

He had gone too far this time, and he knew it. He also knew that not even another horse race, another fight, another woman could ever take away the bitter taste of the ashes of dreams. His parents had expected so much of him, and he had let them down over and over again.

"Here we are now, old man!" said Freddie. "Home again."

Richards, the butler, emerged from the house and hurried down the steps to open the carriage door. "Mr. Seward!" he cried, his eyes widening at the sight of blood. "Oh, Mr. Seward, are you badly injured, then? I shall send for the doctor at once!"

Freddie and James seized Justin between them and lowered him to the ground. His legs buckled, and he would have fallen to the pavement if they had not hauled him upright.

"No need for a doctor, Richards," he managed to gasp. "It is nothing at all. . . ."

His voice trailed away as he looked up the steps to the open door. His mother stood there, leaning heavily against the door frame.

Amelia, the Countess of Lyndon, had not been well for some time. Her face was pale and faded above the neck frill of her dark blue dress, and she looked as if a strong wind could carry her away at any moment. She pressed a handkerchief to her mouth.

Standing behind her, his eyes shining with excitement, was Justin's younger brother Harry. His older brother Edward was, as usual, off on some responsible, respectable task.

"Justin," his mother said softly, brokenly, "you are alive! I was so afraid for you."

The shame that had overtaken him in the carriage was now well nigh crippling. He was glad of his friends' strong arms supporting him. If they did not hold him up, he feared he would fall down at his mother's feet, weeping and begging forgiveness.

And Harry—Harry should not be here to see this. He was far too impressionable already.

Freddie and James helped him up the steps, trailed by the fluttering, fussing Richards. They went past Amelia and Harry and deposited Justin on one of the satin-upholstered chairs that lined the cavernous marble foyer. Then they beat a hasty retreat.

The cowards.

"Of course I am not dead, Mother," he said, as she bent over him to wipe at his shoulder with the handkerchief. "Holmes is a terrible shot. And you should be in bed, asleep."

"How can I stay abed, when I do not know if my son is alive or dead? I had to know."

"Was it a good fight, Justin?" Harry broke in excitedly. "How I wish I could have been there!"

Amelia turned a horrified gaze onto her youngest son.

"It was very dull and stupid, Harry," Justin muttered. "You were well away from it."

"No!" Harry protested. "Next time, I will be there with you, as your second. . . ."

"You will do no such thing, Harold," a voice boomed across the foyer. "Do you want to be as big a dolt as your brother? I will send you away to university in Scotland first!"

Everyone's gaze turned to the shadows at the foot of the grand staircase. A man, tall, erect, silver haired, emerged from them into the murky light from the small windows.

Harry's face turned scarlet. "Sir! I only meant—"

"I know what you meant," the earl said. "Don't be an ass. Take your mother back upstairs, and have her maid give her some of her medicine."

"I want to stay here, Walter," Amelia said quietly.

The earl's face gentled as he came up to his wife and took her hand. "You know the doctor said you should not leave your bed, Amelia. The strain of all this has been too great for you. Please, my dear, go with Harold, and let Minette give you your medicine."

Amelia glanced uncertainly at Justin. Then, under the quiet weight of her husband's command, she nodded and took Harry's arm, allowing him to escort her up the stairs. She only looked back once, lingeringly.

"Richards," the earl said, when they had disappeared from sight, "would you be so good as to fetch Dr. Reynolds? Tell him both Lady Lyndon and Mr. Seward are in need of his services."

"Yes, my lord, right away." Richards bowed, and scurried quickly away.

Justin was left alone with his father.

The earl sat down in the chair next to his and said very softly, "You have gone too far this time, you know, Justin."

Justin bowed his head. Somehow, the quiet resignation in his father's voice was far worse than any thunder or noise. "Yes, Father. I know."

"I paid your debts at that dreadful gaming hell. I paid off the opera dancer who was getting so pushing. I concealed your other duels. Everyone is young and foolish once in their lives. But I cannot go on. You have brought scandal and disgrace onto the Seward name, a name that has been held in highest respect for over three hundred years."

Sharp tears prickled at the backs of Justin's eyes.

He blinked them away furiously. No amount of tears could cleanse the stain of his life.

"I am through with all that, sir," he said roughly. "I promise."

The earl shook his head. "That is what you told us the last time. And the time before that. I fear a change must be made."

A chill of foreboding shivered on Justin's spine. "What sort of a change?"

The earl reached inside his coat and brought out a heavily sealed, deeply official-looking document. "I have purchased you a commission. As soon as you have recovered from your wound, you will go to India, where you will serve in the regiment of my old friend, Colonel Paget."

India. He was being sent off to India. This was almost worse than anything he had imagined on that short but endless carriage ride. India was hot and insect-ridden and very, very far away.

Justin nodded in resignation. It was a dismal prospect, yes, to be so far from home, but perhaps there, in such an alien land, he could bring back to his family a small portion of the honor he had lost them.

"And that, I fear, Mrs. Aldritch, is all that is left."

Caroline Aldritch carefully folded her black-gloved hands in her lap and stared dispassionately across the desk at the sallow-faced attorney.

She should feel *something*, she knew, at the sure knowledge that she was now destitute. Obviously, the attorney expected her to swoon, since he was clutching a bottle of smelling salts in his hand. Or perhaps the salts were for himself, since he was the one who had to deal with the complicated wreckage of her husband's estate.

She should have been weeping or in hysterics, or throwing a fiery tantrum at the fate that had led her to this. Instead, the numbness that held her since she had been told of Lawrence's death still gripped her.

All she could think was, *I knew it.*

Her life with Lawrence could have ended no other way.

"So," she said, "after all my husband's debts are settled, I will be left with twenty pounds. More or less."

"Or perhaps a bit more. If we are careful," answered the attorney.

Caroline nodded. Twenty pounds could keep her in their shabby lodgings a while longer, to be sure. But it would not pay for Phoebe to stay at the privileged Mrs. Medlock's School for Young Ladies.

At the thought of Phoebe, her sweet younger sister, emotion did stir in Caroline's heart. Phoebe was happy at her school; her letters were always full of her lessons and outings and friends. She was meeting people there, young ladies of good family, who could serve her well in her future life. The only good thing Lawrence had ever done for Caroline in their marriage was to pay for Phoebe's schooling after their parents died, though heaven only knew how he did it.

There had to be a way to keep her there, to pay for a fine come-out one day. There *had* to be. Caroline would not see Phoebe end up as *she* had.

She stood abruptly, the folds of her black bombazine dress rustling around her. "Thank you," she said. "You have been very helpful."

The attorney walked with her to the door. "If there is anything else I can do, Mrs. Aldritch, please do not hesitate to call on me."

"I won't. Good day."

Caroline stepped out onto the pavement, shading her eyes against the sudden glare of sunlight. It was not a particularly bright day, but after the gloom of the office it seemed almost tropical. She lowered the veil of her bonnet and looked about for a hansom cab.

Then she remembered the pitifully few coins left in her reticule and decided to walk.

She was very nearly to the rooming house where she and Lawrence had their lodgings when she heard a voice, a man's voice, call out, "Mrs. Aldritch! Mrs. Aldritch, over here!"

Caroline looked over her shoulder to see a tall, vaguely familiar man making his way through the crowds toward her. He was a friend of Lawrence's, she knew; one of the friends he had gone to gaming hells and racetracks with, one of the friends she disliked. However, being rude now was sure to avail her nothing, so she paused, a polite smile on her lips.

"Mrs. Aldritch, thank goodness I have found you! Your landlady said you were out," he said, coming to a halt next to her. Caroline saw then that he held a small, paper-wrapped parcel under his arm.

"I had some business to attend to, Mr. . . . ."

"Burne-Jones. Mr. James Burne-Jones. We met at the Bedford rout last month."

Caroline remembered that rout, given by some of the last members of very minor gentry who still welcomed Lawrence to their home. She remembered standing by the wall, watching the dancers while Lawrence lost desperately in the card room. She did not remember this man, but she said, "Yes, of course."

"Well, I am leaving Town this afternoon, but I could not go without giving you this." He thrust the parcel at her.

Caroline reached out for it slowly. "What? . . ."

"Oh, it is nothing improper at all, Mrs. Aldritch! It belonged to Larry. He left it with me for safekeeping, shortly before . . . before he died."

Died getting run down by a carriage, too foxed to look before he stepped into the street, Caroline thought wryly. The parcel was probably his watch, missing since he died, and maybe a few coins. "Thank you very much, Mr. Burne-Jones. It was kind of you to bring it to me."

"Anything for Larry's widow! We were all so sorry when he died. He was a good 'un, was Larry."

"Indeed," Caroline answered. Then she felt the tiny hairs on the back of her neck prickle. She looked back to see her landlady, Mrs. Brown, watching her suspiciously from between the curtains of her front window.

Caroline sighed. The very last thing she needed was to be tossed out of her already tenuous lodgings on suspicion of being a too-merry widow.

She quickly took her leave of Mr. Burne-Jones and hurried inside the tall, narrow house, clutching the parcel. She sped past the closed door of Mrs. Brown's sitting room and up the stairs, praying that she could avoid another confrontation about late rent payments for just a little longer. Just long enough so that she could think in peace.

Once inside the small suite of two rooms, Caroline shut and locked the door behind her and leaned back wearily against the flimsy wood. It was not even noon yet, but, lud, it felt like this horrible day would go on forever!

She took off her black bonnet and tossed it and her gloves onto the table. Then she sat down on the unmade bed and removed the paper wrappings from the parcel.

It was a box, a small tin box with a little key in the lock. Caroline ran her hand over the cool metal lid and shook the box slightly, listening to the metallic echo.

"Please, let there be enough here to pay the rent," she whispered. Then she turned the key, lifted the lid—and gasped.

Inside there were indeed some coins, along with a few banknotes. Quite enough to keep Mrs. Brown happy for a while longer. There was also a neatly folded piece of paper. Caroline pushed aside the money and took it out to read.

It was a deed. To a gaming establishment called the Golden Feather. It was signed over to Lawrence by the owner, a Mr. Samuels, won the very night Lawrence died. Tucked inside the paper was a heavy key.

How ironic. Poor Lawrence. He had possessed one of his few winning hands that night, but had not lived long enough to enjoy it.

Caroline lifted her gaze from the deed and looked over at where Lawrence's miniature portrait was propped on the narrow fireplace mantel.

The picture had been painted some years before, and the image that looked back at her was not that of her weary, red-eyed husband. It was her young bridegroom, with his clear green eyes full of idealism and honesty.

What hopes they'd had on their wedding day! How impatient they had been, how impulsive and in love. But they had been too young, only seventeen. And their love had not been able to survive their families' obligations and the poverty that had overtaken them. Both the Aldritches and the Lanes had been good families of faded fortunes; they had hoped their children would marry well—not elope with someone equally faded.

Caroline and Lawrence *had* loved each other once, or they thought they did. But not enough to sustain them through all their new and unexpected difficulties. Caroline had tried to make a home for them, but Lawrence had lost himself in the lures of gaming and drink. He had been convinced that if only his luck would turn, just once, if only he could win the next hand, he would be able to take care of them.

Caroline looked down at the deed in her hand. Maybe now, in a strange way, he *was* taking care of her, at long last.

But only if she had the courage to go out there and take care of herself.

Caroline looked at the paper she was holding and then back up at the building. Yes, this was it. The Golden Feather. Lawrence's legacy.

She would never have known it was a gaming establishment from the exterior. It looked like any other nondescript, respectable town house in a row of town houses. Someone had been looking after it; the front steps were swept, the brass door knocker polished, and the heavy curtains were drawn across the windows. The only indication of its true purpose was a small plate affixed beneath the knocker that read THE GOLDEN FEATHER—MEMBERS ONLY.

Caroline took a deep breath, turned the key in the lock, and went inside.

She had to pass through a small foyer, bare but for a desk and chair, to get to the main salon. She pulled back the window draperies of green velvet and looked about in surprised satisfaction. It was very grand indeed, with velvet and gilt chairs clustered about the card tables and the roulette wheel. Fine paintings hung on the silk-papered walls, and a thick green-and-gold carpet covered the floor.

Through an arched doorway she saw a dining room, equally grand. In the corner, a spiral staircase ran up to another floor. Perhaps there were rooms there that could be made into a private apartment.

How prosperous this Golden Feather must be, Caroline reflected, as she gave the roulette wheel an idle spin. She could just envision the crowds of well-dressed gamesters who would flock here, filling the gilt chairs, drinking champagne—spending their money.

She had thought perhaps to sell the place, to pay for Phoebe's remaining years at school from the proceeds. But if she could run it herself, just for a few years, how much more money they could have! Enough for a come-out and a fine dowry for Phoebe. Perhaps even a cozy country cottage for herself.

It would be simple enough to say that Lawrence had lost the deed soon to some mystery lady after winning it. She had come to enough places like this with her husband to know the basics of how they were run. She would need help, of course, but she was a fast learner. It could be done. And then she would never have to marry again, never be at the mercy of a careless, irresponsible man again.

But, oh, then she would have to live every day in a world she hated! A world she had blamed for ruining her husband, her marriage. Ruining the naive, romantic girl she had once been.

Caroline sat down in one of the velvet chairs and propped her chin on her black-gloved hand. She did hate gaming, but what choice did she really have? If she did not make use of this place, she would be utterly ruined. She had no job skills and certainly no matrimonial prospects. She would starve in the streets. Worse yet, Phoebe, her dear Phoebe, would be ruined along with her.

"It will not be forever," she whispered fiercely, convincing herself. "It will not be forever!"

Chapter One

London, Four Years Later

"Justin, you're home! You're home at last."

Justin, now the Earl of Lyndon on the deaths over a year ago of his father and older brother, barely had time to hand the butler his greatcoat when his mother came down the stairs. She enveloped him in her rose-scented embrace, holding him tightly.

"It has been so long," she murmured, her voice muffled against his shirtfront.

Justin rested his cheek against her ruffled lace cap. "Yes, Mother. Too long."

He had thought so many times during the hot, endless days in India that he would surely never be in this place again. Never see his family, never be in his home, never feel the coolness of a sweet English breeze on his face. England had seemed an impossible dream, so distant from the sticky, dusty Indian reality.

Yet here he was. Standing once again in the foyer of Seward House. It all looked the same. The same family portraits hung on the walls; the same faded Aubusson rug lined the floor. Richards was the same, trying to hide his undignified emotion behind a stolid facade. His mother even smelled the same, of roses and sugar cakes.

But she did not look the same, Justin thought as he drew back a bit to look at her. Amelia had been pale and sickly when he left four years ago. Almost like a shadow. Now she had gained some weight; her lavender silk gown lay smooth on her rounded shoulders. Her cheeks were a pale pink, her eyes sparkling with delight at her son's homecoming. She must have ceased taking the "medicine" she used to have.

"I started for home as soon as I received your letter about Father and Edward's accident, Mother," he said. "I'm sorry it has taken me so very long."

"I know, dear. It was so . . . so very difficult, all alone without them," Amelia said, with a rather watery smile. "You are here, though, and that is all that matters. I am certain all will be well now."

All would be well? "Mother, what? . . ."

Amelia shook her head. "Not now. I will tell you everything later, but right now you must be so tired. Come into the drawing room and have some tea. I want to hear all about your journey, and about India! How very brown you have become there, dear."

They were quickly settled in the elegant blue-and-silver drawing room, with a vast tray of tea, cakes, and sandwiches. Justin sat back and watched his mother pour out the tea, listening as she prattled happily about the Season just concluding and her plans for the summer ahead. When at last the final seedcake was eaten and Amelia had paused for breath, Justin said, "I suppose Harry is still at Cambridge, then."

Amelia's bright smile faded, and her gaze fell away from his.

A small chill touched Justin's weary heart. He leaned toward her, reaching out to catch her hand and cease her sudden fussing with the tea things. "Mother? Is something wrong with Harry? Is he ill?"

She shook her head. "No, he is not ill. It is just— oh, Justin! I *am* glad you are home. I simply don't know what to do."

Justin released her hand and sank back in his chair, folding his arms across his chest. "Mother, you must tell me, whatever it is."

"Harry has been sent down from Cambridge."

"Sent down! Well, surely there are appeals that can be made, people to speak to. . . ."

"It is the third time. They will not have him back."

Justin was appalled. Harry had been sent down from Cambridge *three* times? Even he himself, at the height of his mischief-making youth, had managed to stay at university.

Harry must have done something very bad indeed.

"When did this happen?" he asked quietly.

"Not long before your father died. He was livid with Harry, absolutely livid!" Amelia shuddered. "I had never seen Walter so angry."

Justin could well imagine. His father had dealt with one wayward son, only to have another spring up in his place.

He could only shake his head at the desperate foolishness of youth. Wisdom was so hard-won, especially in India. He hoped his brother could be spared a hard lesson like that. Perhaps his hopes

were in vain; he knew how heedless a rakish youth
could be.

And now his mother was looking to him to solve
all their difficulties.

"What is Harry doing now?" he asked.

Amelia shrugged. "Not very much of anything, I
believe. I seldom see him. He is not interested in
going to Almack's with me, or to *respectable* balls
and routs. I think . . . I think he has become quite
a *rake*." Her cheeks flamed as she whispered the
word. "I do hear such stories about him, though I
am sure they cannot be true."

Justin groaned to himself. He had hoped that
once he got home, once he left the strangeness of
India behind, his life would be peaceful. That he
could marry, raise a passle of brats, and be quiet
and respectable at long last.

That was obviously not to be.

"The Season is over now, though," Amelia continued. "Surely things will be better once we are
back in the country, at Waring Castle. There will
be no bad influences for him there."

Justin rubbed wearily at his jaw. "He has agreed
to go to Waring for the summer, then?"

"Not exactly. But I am sure that now you are
home, you can persuade him."

Justin was not so sure. He remembered all too
well the determination of a headstrong boy set on
being a rake. He also knew the terrible consequences of such heedlessness.

"I will see what I can do, Mother," he said.

She nodded, seemingly satisfied. "There is one
more ball before absolutely everyone leaves Town,
and I think we should attend. My friend Lady Bell-

weather has the loveliest daughter who just made her bow this Season. I am sure you would like her. . . ."

Her words faded away as the drawing-room door flew open and Harry rushed in. His hair, a darker brown than Justin's own sun-touched locks, fell in an untidy tangle over his brow, and he was in need of a shave. But it was really his clothes that made Justin's brow raise. Harry wore canary-yellow breeches below a purple—purple!—waistcoat, and a bottle-green coat.

And were those *parrots* embroidered on that waistcoat?

Justin knew then that they had more trouble than his mother thought.

"So you're home at last, eh, Justin?" Harry said, sauntering over to drape himself across the chair next to his mother's. He stuffed the last of the cucumber sandwiches into his mouth and chewed, grinning the whole time. "I see you were too wily for those old natives! Didn't even get stepped on by an elephant."

"Indeed," Justin answered slowly. "It is good to see you again, Harry."

Harry laughed. "I suppose Mother has been telling you all about those toads at Cambridge chucking me out."

"Something of the sort."

"Well, they had no business to do it, I can tell you! It was all a harmless hum. A misunderstanding."

"Your third misunderstanding, apparently."

"Yes, well, *you* know how it goes. These things happen. But it's given me time for more . . . edifying experiences, I can tell you!" He chuckled, leaving no doubt as to the nature of those "edifying" experiences.

Amelia's cheeks colored even further, and Justin longed to box his brother's foolish ears for being such an improper dolt in front of her.

But Harry seemed quite oblivious to any distress or discomfort. He went on. "I say, Justin! I'm going with some friends to the Golden Feather tonight. Why don't you come? It will be a proper welcome home."

"And what might this Golden Feather be?" Justin asked with careful casualness. He knew how much Harry would enjoy disapproval.

"It's a jolly place! My friends and I go there three or four times a week. It's a first-rate gaming hell, really top of the trees."

"A gaming hell!" Amelia cried. "Harry, really."

"Oh, Mother, it's not like that," Harry scoffed. "You can't even really call it a hell. It's perfectly respectable. Members only allowed, and the members are all good *ton*. Nothing havey-cavey. Mrs. Archer wouldn't allow it."

"Mrs. Archer?" Justin said.

"She owns the place. Very lovely, but very mysterious. She always wears a mask." Harry's face softened as he spoke of this mysterious Mrs. Archer. "You *should* come tonight, Justin. I have heard she means to sell the place soon, and it will never be the same without her."

It sounded a perfectly dismal evening. Justin wanted only a bath, a brandy, and his bed. "Harry, I hardly think . . ." he began. Then he caught his mother's eye. She gave him a little nod.

She obviously thought that Harry could not get

into trouble with Justin watching his every move. And perhaps she was right.

So, even though his tired body was shrieking in protest, Justin nodded. "Thank you, Harry," he said. "I would like very much to go with you tonight."

Chapter Two

It was another busy evening at the Golden Feather.

Caroline stood alone in her small office, peering through her secret peephole at the large gaming room. Every chair was filled, every champagne glass glistened, and every table was piled with coins, notes, and jewels. Laughter and the sweet scent of the many flower arrangements floated through the air to her.

Even though the Season was winding to a close, the more daring of society still flocked to the Golden Feather, just as they had every night for four years now.

She gave a small smile. This was perfect. Perfect for one of her last nights in the gaming club. It would be a grand send-off, and no one in London would ever forget the mysterious Mrs. Archer.

Letting the little peephole cover slide into place, she turned back to her office and went over to the desk. The polished mahogany surface was covered with ledgers and papers, but she ignored them and reached for a small, neatly folded letter. She had read it a dozen times since it had arrived a week ago, but it still never failed to make her smile.

Phoebe was soon to finish her studies at Mrs.

Medlock's School for Young Ladies. Her excitement over her girlish plans seemed to spill from the carefully penned words. Caroline couldn't help but feel a bit excited herself. And not just for Phoebe, but for herself as well.

At long last, she was leaving the Golden Feather. The place had served its purpose well. She had a nice, tidy fortune tucked away, and stood to gain even more when she chose a buyer for the Golden Feather. She was a wealthy woman, and she and Phoebe would never have to worry about money again.

And if her soul had shriveled a little more each night as she strolled through the opulent rooms, watching fools lose their money, listening to lechers' suggestive whispers, it was worth it for that security.

Was it not?

Caroline carefully folded the letter and placed it in her locked drawer. Her only escape in these four years had been her annual holidays with Phoebe. Now they could be together all the time, be a true family again. *That* was worth anything, anything at all.

She had already arranged to rent a house for the summer, at the seaside resort of Wycombe-on-Sea, where they had sometimes gone with their parents as little girls. There she could rest at last and wash away the past years in the clean seawater. She and Phoebe could plan how best to introduce Phoebe to some kind of good society. Surely their parents' names still carried weight with someone. . . .

A knock sounded at the inner office door, interrupting these musings.

"Yes?" Caroline called.

"It's Mary, madam."

"Come in, Mary."

Mary was Caroline's maid, and had been ever since she had come to the Golden Feather. Once, in another life, she had been Caroline's nanny. She was the only other person who knew her true identity, and Caroline trusted her implicitly.

Mary bustled into the room, carrying a red wig, a black silk mask, and a small rosewood cosmetics box. "It's almost midnight, madam. They'll be expecting your grand appearance."

The tentative excitement and hope vanished before the prospect of the evening ahead. Caroline sighed. "Yes, of course."

Obviously sensing her melancholy, Mary patted her shoulder comfortingly. "It won't be long now, madam. In two weeks, maybe even less if that buyer comes through, we'll be gone from here."

"You are quite right, Mary. Not long now." Caroline rose from the desk and went around to the small, gilt-framed mirror on the wall. She took the red wig, fashioned into elaborate curls and decorated with ebony and crystal combs, and fitted it carefully over her own short, silvery-blond hair. Over it she tied the ribbons of the black silk mask that covered all her face except her mouth and lower jaw.

"Do you have the lip rouge?" she asked, making sure that no telltale blond strands showed beneath the red.

"Of course, madam." Mary brought the tiny enameled pot of rouge out from the cosmetics box and handed it to her.

Caroline used the little brush to paint her lips crimson, making them appear larger and richer than her usual pale rose bow. Then she slid glittering emerald drops into her earlobes and removed her shawl to reveal a low-cut, deep green satin gown. Long black gloves and high-heeled green satin shoes completed what she thought of as her "costume."

No one who ever encountered her as Mrs. Caroline Aldritch could possibly connect her to Mrs. Archer of the Golden Feather.

"All right, Mary," she said in a voice that seemed even deeper and lower. "I am ready to make my appearance."

Justin stood in the doorway between the dining room and the gaming room of the Golden Feather and looked about in growing boredom.

It was just like all the other gaming establishments he had frequented before he left for India. Fancier than most, perhaps, luxuriously appointed and full of fine flowers and champagne. And the people crowded around the tables were undoubtedly well dressed and well-bred, gentlemen in evening dress and ladies, some masked, in bright silks and jewels. But it was the same.

There was the same look on these people's faces, a mix of desperation and hope. The laughter had the same sharp edge. The same smell of liquor, cigar smoke, and perfume hung in the air.

What had he ever found so appealing in such places? It was appalling, especially after the brutal honesty and the shimmering skies of India. He wanted to run from it all, to breathe in fresh, clean air.

But once he had loved it all with a desperate excitement he saw now on his brother's face.

Harry sat at one of the card tables, avidly studying the hand he had just been dealt. A woman in a blue feathered mask sat beside him. She laid her kid-gloved hand on his arm and whispered something in his ear. Harry nodded and laughed, a sharp, brittle sound.

Justin noted the rather large pile of coins in front of his brother.

He frowned and would have started over to the table, but someone coming out of the dining room bumped into him. Champagne sloshed from the man's glass onto the marble floor, just missing Justin's shoe.

Justin turned around and came face-to-face with his old friend the Honorable Freddie Reed.

It had been only four years since Justin had seen him, on the morning of that fateful duel, but Freddie looked twenty years older. His eyes were bloodshot, underscored by bags and wrinkles. His skin was a grayish pallor, and his ample belly strained at his yellow brocade waistcoat.

Obviously, Freddie had continued on the pathway to dissipation he and Justin had started on so long ago. It was startling to realize that he himself might very well look like this if he had not gone out to India when he had.

Justin quickly concealed his astonishment behind a polite smile. "Freddie!" he said. "How are you, old man?"

"Eh?" Freddie squinted at him, then cried, "Justin! Dem me if it isn't old Justin Seward. Back from India, are you? Must have been very recently—you're as brown as a nut! Quite the pukka sahib." He laughed uproariously at his own weak witticism.

"Quite," Justin answered. "I only arrived in London today. I just came here to accompany Harry."

"Ah, yes. Young Harry. He's been following in his brother's footsteps, so I hear. I often see him about." Freddie turned to the woman at his side, a petite blonde in pink satin who was boldly unmasked. She was obviously as foxed as Freddie was, swaying unsteadily on her feet. "Meet Justin, m'dear. He used to be the boldest rogue in London. Now he's an old, respectable nabob, just back from India, and an earl to boot."

The woman giggled. "Pleased to meet'cha, I'm sure."

"Run along and wait for me at the faro table, sweet," Freddie told her. "I want to talk to Justin." The woman, sped on her way by a tap on the bottom from Freddie, left in a cloud of more giggles. Then Freddie turned back to Justin. "I am glad to see you again, Justin. Town's not been the same since old Larry Aldritch died and James Burne-Jones left. Not the same at all."

"Oh? Where did James go to?"

"Didn't you know? He left the day after your duel with Holmes, sent off to America by his father. I heard he married a rich widow in Boston." Freddie shook his head mournfully. "No, it hasn't been the same at all. But the Golden Feather is jolly good fun. Don't you think?"

Justin looked back out at the crowded gaming room. Harry was still at the same table with the woman in the feathered mask speaking to him quietly. "Indeed."

"I come here at least twice a week."

"The play is that good, is it?"

"Oh, yes. Champagne's not bad, either. And then there's Mrs. Archer." Freddie gave a blissful sigh.

"The owner?"

"Yes. She's a real beauty. At least I think she must be."

Was Freddie so drunk that he couldn't even see the woman straight, then? Justin laughed. "You mean you're not sure?"

"Well, she always wears a mask. But she has a beautiful voice. And a magnificent bosom. Though she is always so secretive; she will never give any man a second look, so they say. Ah, now see, you'll be able to judge for yourself."

A door at the top of a spiral staircase opened, and amid a sudden hush, a woman appeared on the landing there.

She was not especially tall, not above middling height, but she commanded the room just by standing still.

She wore a black silk mask that covered all her face except for her full red lips and an alabaster jawline. Her hair, a deep burgundy-red color, was piled atop her head in curls and whorls. The emeralds in her ears winked and dazzled in the light.

Mrs. Archer was very striking. And she did indeed have a magnificent bosom, its whiteness set off by the low bodice of her green satin gown.

Justin very much feared he was gaping, just as everyone else in the room was. But he couldn't seem to help himself; she was such a terribly striking sight.

"You see?" Freddie sighed. "Beautiful."

Then Mrs. Archer came down the stairs, her skirt held up daintily to reveal green heeled slippers and the tiniest amount of white silk stocking, and moved into the crowd.

Justin could see only the very top of her red head as she walked about, stopping to speak to various patrons and accept a glass of champagne from a footman.

He blinked and turned quickly away, feeling as if he were trapped in some bizarre, terribly attractive dream.

Chapter Three

Caroline had never seen him before. She was sure of it. If she had, she would have remembered him.

He stood in the doorway between the dining room and the gaming room, surveying the crowd with a look of almost-boredom on his face. He did not look contemptuous or disdainful, only as if he wished he were anywhere else.

And he was handsome. Very handsome indeed. His hair, a sun-streaked light brown, was a little longer than was strictly fashionable and brushed back in neat waves from his face. Unlike most of the men who came to the Golden Feather, he radiated good health and vitality. His skin was dark, as if he spent a good deal of time outdoors, and his tall, lean figure obviously had no need of corsets or of padding in his coats.

Beside all the other men who flocked around the gaming room, he stood out sharply, as a beacon of things that were honest and decent. Things like a fresh morning breeze, a brisk ride down a country lane, or a good laugh.

Things Caroline hadn't enjoyed for years.

She smiled wryly, mocking herself for such fanciful thoughts. A beacon of honesty, indeed! Here she had thought herself far beyond having her head turned by a pretty face. If he was here, he could scarcely be so decent as all that. No doubt he gambled terribly, just as Lawrence had. He was just a new patron, perhaps one who had recently come from the country.

Definitely one she should meet. After all, it was her job to make certain everyone who came to the Golden Feather enjoyed themselves.

Just her job.

Caroline made her way slowly across the room toward him, stopping to talk to people, to sip champagne, to check on the dealers at the various tables. All the while, she kept her eye on the stranger, where he stood talking to Lawrence's old friend Freddie Reed.

As she came closer, she felt a most unusual sensation fluttering in her stomach, tightening her throat. Was it . . . could it be nervousness? Nervousness at the thought of talking to a strange man?

Nonsense, she told herself briskly. It was only the champagne.

At last she reached them, and came to a halt to smile up at Freddie. "Good evening, Mr. Reed," she said. "So nice to see you here again."

Freddie blushed at this special attention, and stammered out, "G-good evening, M-Mrs. Archer! You are looking stunning, as always."

"Thank you very much, Mr. Reed." She glanced over at his companion, the handsome stranger, and tilted her head inquiringly.

"Oh!" said Freddie. "Mrs. Archer, I would like you to meet my friend, Lord Lyndon. He is just back from India and has never been to the Golden Feather before."

"How do you do, Mrs. Archer?" Lord Lyndon said, bowing over her outstretched hand. His fingers were warm through her thin glove, his grip steady and sure.

"Welcome to the Golden Feather, Lord Lyndon," she answered. "I do hope you are enjoying your first evening here."

"Of course," he said. "Who could help but enjoy themselves here? You have a lovely establishment, Mrs. Archer." But his eyes, a vivid sky blue in his sun-browned face, still looked bored and perfectly, blandly polite. His gaze slid ever so briefly over her shoulder before focusing on her again.

"Thank you, Lord Lyndon," she murmured, wondering what could possibly be so interesting behind her. Another woman, perhaps?

Her vanity was a bit piqued by this inattention. Unaccountably, she wanted this man's attention; she wanted his gaze to fill with admiration when he looked at her. Usually she disliked male attention and longed to turn away from their flattery, their long, suggestive glances.

"This may be Lyndon's first visit, but his brother is a regular patron," Freddie said, interrupting her jumbled thoughts.

Caroline turned to him in relief, away from Lord Lyndon's mesmerizing blue eyes. "Oh, yes? And who might that be?"

It was Lyndon who answered, in his deep, brandy-rich voice. "Mr. Harry Seward is my brother." He gestured with his champagne glass toward a table.

Caroline looked back to where he pointed. So that was what had caught his attention. His brother, Mr. Seward, was quite familiar to her. He came to the Golden Feather several times a week, sometimes winning, more often losing. He was a bit of a mischief maker, but she had never had any serious trouble with him. Tonight he sat next to another regular patron, a woman who called herself Mrs. Scott, a bottle of champagne between them.

It was hard to believe that the feckless Mr. Seward was the brother of the serious, solemn man who stood before her.

"We do see Mr. Seward often," she said.

"So I have heard," he answered softly. Caroline had the distinct impression that he did not approve of his brother's pastimes.

And that would mean he also disapproved of her.

Caroline glanced at Freddie and saw that his glass was almost empty. "You need more champagne!" she said, half turning to summon a footman. Then she sensed Lord Lyndon's tall figure stiffening beside her.

She followed the direction of his now-cold gaze back to his brother's table. Harry had risen from his chair to face another patron, a Lord Burleigh. They were speaking together, if speaking was the right word, their voices rising sharply. Harry's face was red beneath his untidy shock of hair; his hands were curled into fists at his sides. Mrs. Scott laid her hand on his arm, trying to draw him away.

He shook her off impatiently and whipped back around to face Lord Burleigh. A small crowd was gathering, a hush settling over the room as people noticed the brewing quarrel.

This was not good at all. There was nothing more tiresome than a fight.

Caroline shifted her skirts so that she could better reach the small pistol tucked into her garter, and looked about for the footmen who doubled as guards. Before she could find them, she felt Lord Lyndon's hand on her arm, moving her gently aside as started toward his brother.

"No, please, Lord Lyndon!" She caught his hand, stopping him from taking another step. "Let me handle this."

His eyes were now a stormy gray as he looked down at her. "He is my brother."

"I know. But I deal with this quite often, unfortunately. It will be easier if I speak to him."

Lyndon's jaw tightened, but he nodded shortly. "Damn," he said, "but I knew something like this would happen."

Caroline had just taken one step in Harry's direction when a high-pitched shout erupted from Lord Burleigh followed by a great crash as one of them, Harry or Burleigh, sent the card table toppling. Coins, cards, and champagne flew. There were shrieks and screams as everyone scrambled out of their way. Mrs. Scott sobbed hysterically, stamping her feet and shaking her champagne-splattered skirts.

"Oh, no," Caroline muttered. "This is just what I need on one of my last nights here." She lifted her skirts above her ankles and waded into the fray, closely followed by Lord Lyndon.

It took only seconds for a full-fledged brawl to form. Other people with grievances, seemingly inspired by Harry and Burleigh, broke into smaller fights. Harry himself had knocked Lord Burleigh down and was now planting him a sound facer in the nose. Mrs. Scott was deeply in hysterics.

Caroline picked up a heavy crystal vase, emptied the flowers onto the floor, and tossed the cold water onto the pair of them. It hardly made an impression, but it did thoroughly soak Mrs. Scott's gown, causing the woman to swoon.

It wasn't so good for Caroline's shoes, either.

Lyndon grabbed his brother by the coat collar and hauled him to his feet. Harry flailed helplessly for a moment but instantly stilled when Lyndon said, in tones of steely command, "Harold, you will cease this at once."

Harry quit wriggling and wiped at his bloodied nose with his coat sleeve. "He called Mrs. Scott a-a—"

"It doesn't matter what he said," Lyndon growled. "You should have taken your differences outside. There is no excuse whatsoever for causing a public scene in a lady's house."

Caroline stared at him, more startled by his words than she had been by the whole silly fight. A *lady's* house? She had never heard the Golden Feather—or herself—referred to in such a way.

She had the most unaccountable urge to give a pleased giggle.

"Now, apologize to Mrs. Archer, and we shall take our leave," Lyndon said, giving his brother a shake.

Harry glanced shyly at Caroline, then looked quickly away. "I am sorry, Mrs. Archer. What I did was completely unforgivable."

"Thank you, Mr. Seward," Caroline said, a bit bewildered. "You are forgiven."

"Freddie," Lyndon called to his friend, who was still drinking champagne in the doorway where they had left him, "would you please escort Harry, Mrs. Scott, and your—friend to the carriage and wait with them for me?"

"Of course," Freddie answered, coming forward to offer the sobbing and soaked Mrs. Scott his arm and taking firm hold of Harry with his other hand. "Glad to, Justin."

When they had gone, winding their way through the other, deliciously scandalized patrons, Lyndon turned back to Caroline. He smiled at her ruefully, and suddenly he no longer seemed the remote, polite, bored gentleman. He looked like a young boy, his hair rumpled and his cravat askew.

He swept his hair back off his brow, and said, "I, too, wish to apologize, Mrs. Archer. I hope that my brother does not always behave like this."

"Oh, no," she murmured, quite distracted by one wave of golden-brown hair that would not be tamed. It slid back down over his eye, only to be pushed away impatiently. "Mr. Seward is usually an utter lamb when he comes here."

"I am glad to hear it. I do want you to know that I intend to pay for any damages incurred this evening."

Caroline arched her brow, startled. That was a first. Usually when patrons owed her for damages, she had to threaten to set the Bow Street Runners on them in order to collect. And even that usually did not work.

"Well . . . thank you, Lord Lyndon," she said.

"I shall call on you tomorrow, then, if that would be convenient."

She would get to see him again tomorrow? Caroline's heart gave an unwilling little leap of expectation. She quickly reminded herself that this was strictly business, and said, "Yes, quite convenient. I live here at the Golden Feather, but you will have to knock at the side door."

"Very well." Lord Lyndon looked about at the shambles of the gaming room. The footmen had cleared out most of the quarreling patrons, but tables were upended, flowers and cards thick on the floor, and a couple of gilt chairs were broken. The elegant patrons of the "members only" Golden Feather had behaved as if they were in some pub in Whitechapel.

"Good evening, then, Mrs. Archer," he said. "If I dare call it a good evening."

Caroline laughed, suddenly exhausted and giddy. Perhaps it had not been a good evening, strictly speaking, but it had certainly been a different one. Not the usual evening in the gaming establishment at all. A handsome man and a brawl, all in one night. It was suddenly too much. She longed for her bed, for peaceful sleep.

"Yes. Good evening, Lord Lyndon."

He bowed over her hand again, then turned and left the chaotic room. Caroline watched his tall, dignified figure until the front door closed behind him. Then she knelt down with a sigh and began to pick up some of the rubbish on the floor.

Tomorrow. Lord Lyndon had promised to come back tomorrow.

She laughed again, as silly as a schoolgirl. Oh, this was bad. She should not be all calf eyed over some handsome lordship, not when a new, bright future lay before her. It could only ever lead to trouble.

She still couldn't help but laugh, just once more, as she thought of his lovely blue eyes.

"What were you thinking of, Harry?" Justin looked grimly across the darkened carriage to where his brother huddled in the corner. They had left Freddie and his lady friend and Mrs. Scott at their respective houses, and were now alone.

And it was a long ride back to Seward House.

Harry pressed his handkerchief against his nose and said sullenly, "Whatever do you mean, Justin? You sound as if I just committed murder or something!"

"And you sound as if this evening were just a harmless lark."

"It was! Sort of. That old monkey Burleigh insulted Mrs. Scott. A gentleman would never let such an insult stand."

"A gentleman would never get into a public fight as you did, young pup. You made an absolute cake of yourself in front of dozens of people."

"It was not worse than any number of the hums you got into. At least I've never fought a duel. And remember that opera dancer who actually came to Seward House one night and threw rocks at the windows and shouted for you for hours?"

Justin winced. He did indeed remember those duels and that opera dancer. They had not been his proudest moments. "I was once as young and foolish as you, Harry. But I learned my lesson, and I learned it the hard way. I had thought you might be spared what I went through, that things could be easier for you."

"So send me to India, then!" Harry burst out. "How hard could it be there?"

"How hard could it be? You cannot even imagine, not living this sheltered English life. There are snakes there as long as your leg, venomous enough to fell ten horses with one strike. They curl up in the garden and slip into the house by night; you never know where they might be, where you could fall over them. There are natives who would just as soon kill you as look at you. Bandits who waylay travelers and strangle them with red scarves in the name of their goddess. Mosquitoes whine incessantly at night. The wet heat drains away all energy, all thought. And it is terribly lonely. There are no gaming hells, no racetracks, and very few Englishwomen."

Justin leaned his head back against the leather squabs as he fell silent, drained by his recitation, by the memory of all those things. India *had* been those things, true, and the thought of them made him shudder. But it also held its own strange enchantment. Especially the nights.

He recalled those nights, so warm, so full of the exotic scents of spices and sandalwood and strange flowers. Near his bungalow there had been the ruins of a Hindu temple, filled with bizarre, entrancing sculptures. He remembered how the moonlight would fall like pale, shimmering silk over this temple, how sitar music would echo off the ancient walls.

Mrs. Archer reminded him of India. She possessed that same strange, mysterious enchantment, the same exotic, fragrant allure. . . .

He shook his head fiercely to clear it of such thoughts. Women like Mrs. Archer, as lovely as she was, held no place in his life now. His focus had to be on his family and his proper place in life. He could not be distracted by lovely owners of gaming hells, or the siren song of India and all it stood for.

Harry, who had fallen silent after Justin's outburst, said, "Well, I thought all India teaches is how to be a stuffed-up old prig. You sound just like Father, Justin. And you used to be such fun." The words were meant to sound defiant, but they came out instead sounding uncertain and very, very young.

Harry was scared, Justin could tell. And so he should be.

The carriage came to a halt outside Seward House, and a footman hurried to open the door and lower the steps.

"Go to bed now, Harry," Justin said, so unutterably tired that he could scarce hold up his head. It had been a very long night, and he was carrying the weight of knowing how much he had let his brother down. "We will discuss all this in the morning."

Harry started to climb down from the carriage, then paused, glancing back at Justin uncertainly. "You . . . you won't tell Mother about this, will you, Justin?"

Justin closed his eyes. Lord, had he ever felt this weary before? "That remains to be seen, doesn't it, Harry?"

Chapter Four

It was quite an unseasonably warm day. It was almost summer, but Caroline could not recall it being this warm until July at least. She opened the windows in her small office, letting in the noise from the street as well as what meager breeze there was. She even went so far as to take off her shoes and stockings. Deeply improper, of course, but who was there to see? Far better to be comfortable.

Caroline sat back down at her desk, where the accounts waited for her attention. She had received two good offers to buy the Golden Feather, and she wanted to be sure all her finances were in order before she accepted one and started to pack her trunks. She was in a great hurry to settle the sale and be gone, but somehow her mind would not stay on numbers today.

Her thoughts kept drifting away, to last night—and Lord Lyndon.

With a sigh, Caroline tucked her left foot under her right knee and absently rubbed at the thick scar on her ankle. She had had it for years; she and Lawrence had quarreled rather actively one night. He had broken a vase in his drunken rage, and she had accidentally tripped and cut her ankle deeply on the shards—and lost the baby she carried inside of her. It still itched on hot days or when her mind kept going over and over one subject without ceasing.

Caroline frowned. Why she would be so wrapped up in thoughts of Lord Lyndon she did not know. She had met dozens of men since Lawrence's death. Handsome men, rich men, witty men. Some of them, anyway, mixed among the ridiculous fools. Lord Lyndon was handsome, of course, and rather exotic with his India-dark skin and sad smile. And he was probably quite wealthy, if his large ruby stickpin, his fine carriage, and the way his brother threw money about were any indication. But really, how could he be different from any of those other men?

Oh, but he is, her secret, deepest inner voice whispered.

Caroline sighed again and stretched out her foot to prop it on the desk. Her blasted inner voice was right, as usual. Lyndon was different from the other men she had met, as different as a winter snowstorm from a hot summer afternoon. He had not been just rich and handsome; he had been kind.

He had spoken to her as if she were a person, a lady, who was due courtesy. He had not propositioned her or leered at her or peered ostentatiously down her bodice with a quizzing glass. Instead he apologized for his brother's bad behavior and offered to pay for the damages without any goading or arguing at all.

Most unusual.

Caroline reached out to rub at her scar. Very few men these past four years had bothered to speak politely to her. Manners, coupled with Lyndon's undeniable good looks, were a heady thing.

And that was surely all it was. Probably when he called today, *if* he called, his behavior would be very different. He would resort to typical maleness, would behave as all men did—in their own best interests.

She laid her hand flat against the scar.

Well, she could not afford to be distracted by any man, polite or not, no matter how handsome. She had to look after her sister, to rebuild their family, their lives. In a few short days, she would be respectable again, would go out into the world as Mrs. Caroline Aldritch again. She couldn't let a pair of handsome blue eyes threaten that, not even for a second.

Caroline swung her foot back to the floor and reached for the nearest ledger book. She had work to do, and nearly all the morning was already wasted.

But she had barely totaled up two columns of sums when a knock sounded at the door and Mary stuck her white-capped head inside. She, too, wore a half-mask, as she always did when admitting callers.

"There's a caller, madam," she said. "A *man*."

Despite her resolution of only moments ago, Caroline felt an excitement, an expectation, fluttering in her throat. It was he, Lyndon, it had to be!

She took a deep breath and closed the book. "Did he give his name, Mary?"

Mary handed her a card in reply.

Caroline looked down at the small, cream-colored square. In black print, it read, "Justin Seward, Earl of Lyndon."

Justin. So that was his name. Justin Seward. It sounded rather familiar, as if she had heard it somewhere before. But probably that was only because his brother, or someone else, must have mentioned it in passing. If he had been in India for years, surely he would not have been in the papers recently.

"I told him you never accept callers before luncheon," Mary sniffed, interrupting these ruminations. "But he said that he is expected."

"Indeed he is. His brother was the one who caused such a fuss last night, and he offered to pay for the damages," Caroline answered, carefully laying aside the card.

"Well! That *is* a first, madam."

"Yes, isn't it?" Caroline stood up and went to fetch the wig and mask that lay on a small table under the mirror. "Just give me five minutes, Mary, and then send him in."

After Mary left, Caroline went through the familiar motions of tucking her own cropped blond strands under the red wig, styled today in a simple upsweep. She tied on a blue satin mask and knelt down to retrieve her shoes from beneath the desk.

She debated putting her stockings back on, as any proper lady would, but then decided against it. It would take too much time, and Lord Lyndon would never notice if she remained seated behind the desk the whole time. She stuffed the flimsy bits of silk into a drawer and went to sit down and await the arrival of Lord Lyndon.

"Justin," she whispered to herself, then laughed at her own folly.

*   *   *

Justin followed the black-clad masked maid from the side entrance of the Golden Feather down a long, dim corridor to what he assumed would be a sitting room or office. He looked about in interest, never having been behind the scenes at a gaming house before. The private apartments were not at all the same as the public rooms, and not at all what he had expected. There was very little gilt or velvet, and no marble at all.

Instead, through half-open doors he could see cream-painted walls, old-fashioned furniture upholstered in pastel colors, piles of books, and well-executed landscapes in simple frames. Light, cream-and-gold striped draperies offered privacy from the busy city street but allowed the sun to filter into the small rooms.

It was a cool, pretty, inviting place, as elegant as anything his mother or one of her friends would have decorated. He could have stayed there happily all day.

Justin looked down at the long, pink-and-cream needlework rug beneath his boots.

All last night he had lain sleepless in his bed, thinking about the happenings at the Golden Feather and the mysterious Mrs. Archer. It seemed now that the conclusions he had reached at four in the morning were true. Mrs. Archer was a lady of some sort. Perhaps the ruined daughter of some country squire or a rich man's former mistress set up now in her own business.

Her voice had been educated, though pitched low and quiet, her gestures refined and polite. There was no coarseness about her, nothing that might be expected of a woman living the scandalous life of a gaming house keeper.

But, of course, those had all been impressions gathered in night's mysterious cloak. Darkness could hide a wealth of flaws and sins—as could a mask.

No doubt in the light of day, without the concealing scrap of silk, she would appear very different. Old, maybe, or pockmarked, or simply rude. She could not be what his fevered imaginings had suggested. That was impossible.

Just as he had thought it impossible she would wear a mask in the daytime. Then the maid ushered him into an office, and he saw that Mrs. Archer did indeed wear her concealing mask, even in this hot afternoon.

Her red hair was styled simply today, and her blue silk mask matched her very proper pale blue muslin day dress, but she still looked impossibly exotic in the spartan office.

Justin was seized with the desire, more intense than any desire he had ever known, to see what was beneath the mask.

It seemed that was not to happen, not today, anyway. Mrs. Archer rose behind the large, cluttered desk and held her hand out to him with a smile.

"Good afternoon, Lord Lyndon," she said, in the same low voice he remembered. "Won't you please be seated?" She gestured toward the straight-backed wooden chair situated across from her.

"Thank you, Mrs. Archer." Justin placed his hat and cane on the desk beside the pile of ledger books, and sat down. "I trust you have suffered no ill effects from last night's . . . incident?"

Mrs. Archer laughed. "Certainly not! It would take a great deal more than that little fight, I assure you. I am very glad to see you today, though, Lord Lyndon."

She was glad to see him? He felt an unwilling little frisson of excitement. "Are you indeed, Mrs. Archer?"

"Oh, yes. I have received two very good offers to buy this place, and I am sure I would have to lower my price if the necessary repairs are not made to the gaming room. Your offer of assistance does expedite things greatly."

"So you are really leaving the Golden Feather? My brother said something to that effect." Justin was unaccountably disappointed. Even if she stayed at the place for the next ten years, he could not come back here. Why would he care if she were there or not?

But he found he did care.

"Yes. I hope to be gone from here very soon."

"I am sure all your patrons must be desolate," he said, carefully impersonal.

She shrugged. "The new owner will keep things much the same. No one will notice the difference."

"I know that is not true. My brother calls you 'the incomparable Mrs. Archer,' and says you are the only reason so many flock here."

"Did he indeed? Your brother is very sweet. I trust he is not too ill today."

"He was still asleep when I left the house."

She nodded. "Sleep is the best thing for him. Perhaps when he wakes you could give him a glass of carrot juice mixed with one raw egg. It always helped my hus—" She broke off abruptly, her gaze falling back to the desk. "That is, I have heard many people swear by its efficacy after a night of overindulgence."

Had she been about to say her husband? Justin wondered, with a small jealous pang. Exactly what kind of man was Mr. Archer—or had he been—to deserve a wife like this one? "I wish I had known of such a cure in my younger days."

She smiled at him. "Were you a wild young man, Lord Lyndon?"

"I was terrible. Far worse than Harry."

"But India wrung it out of you, so to speak?"

"Indeed it did. It is hard to play the rake properly when one is laid low by humid heat and snakebite."

The satin of her mask wrinkled a bit as she frowned. "Were you bitten by a snake, then?"

"Twice. After that I learned to be wary. I was lucky to have a servant who knew all about how to treat such things, so I suffered no permanent ill effects."

Mrs. Archer propped her chin on her palm and said in a thoughtful voice, "India must have been very fascinating."

Justin looked at her and noticed for the first time that her eyes were brown. Deep and rich, like a cup of chocolate.

"Yes," he murmured. "Fascinating."

She stared back at him for a long moment. Then she seemed to recall where they were, *who* they were. She shook her head and sat up straight in her chair.

"Here is a list of all the damages," she said briskly, handing him a sheet of paper. "I estimated the cost of the repairs, which you will see here down at the bottom."

Justin dragged himself out of the enchanted circle of her eyes, her perfume, and forced himself to look down at the paper. The neatly printed words refused to come into focus.

He handed it back to her. Their fingers brushed briefly, warmly. The gold of her wedding band, thin and worn, glinted up at him.

That ring, a symbol of things respectable and permanent, seemed to slap him across the face.

He meant to find a proper wife, to do honor by his family. He should not be losing his senses over a pretty gaming house owner!

"It all looks satisfactory," he said quietly.

"Good. If you would like to leave the money with my maid, then, we shall be settled." She rose again to her feet, and Justin followed.

She continued, in an oddly rushed and breathless voice, "I am sure you must be very busy, Lord Lyndon, so I won't detain you any longer." She turned to walk around the edge of the desk. "I will see you to the door. . . ."

Then suddenly half of her seemed shorter than the other half. She gave a little squeak and tottered a bit on her feet.

"Mrs. Archer!" Justin said, coming around the desk and offering his hand to help her regain her balance. One of her shoes, a high-heeled satin affair with brocade ribbons, lay on its side just outside the hem of her skirt. "Are you all right?"

"Oh, I am quite all right!" she said with an embarrassed little laugh. "I just forgot that I did not lace my shoe properly when I put it back on earlier."

"You had your shoes off?" Justin asked, not sure he had heard her properly.

She shot him a haughty glance. "Of course. Doesn't everyone go about in bare feet on a hot day?"

He hardly dared to contradict her. Instead, he knelt down beside her and said, "Let me help you with your shoe, then."

She looked a bit reluctant, but then nodded and slid her foot from beneath her skirt.

He picked up the shoe, noticing with a start that she also did not believe in wearing stockings on a hot day. Terribly scandalous—and terribly attractive. He tried to ignore this, and slid the shoe onto her bare foot, holding the arch of it on his palm for one instant. It was slim and white in his hand, the bones as delicate as those of a small bird. Her toes wiggled, and she giggled a bit as his fingers slid over her sole.

He reached to tie the ribbons, and gasped. "You are injured!" he exclaimed.

Then he looked closer and saw that the gash on her ankle was an old one, not one she had just gotten. Thick, pale pink scar tissue arced across her creamy skin.

She had been badly cut at one time, but not today.

She tugged at her foot, trying to remove it from his grasp. He was almost thrown off his balance by this, and grasped her skirt to steady himself. " 'Tis an old injury," she said. "Not one to worry about."

"But what . . ."

He was interrupted when the office door opened and Mrs. Archer's maid came inside.

"Madam, I just wanted to see if—" She broke into a long scream when she saw him kneeling there, grasping Mrs. Archer's skirt. "What are you doing! Unhand her right now, you brute!"

The fragile-looking older woman grabbed a ledger book off the desk and commenced beating him about the head and shoulders with it. Her mask fell askew, but still she wielded the book.

It hurt like the very devil! Justin feared he would soon be knocked unconscious by the blows, and then what a scandal would ensue.

"Cease, woman!" he yelled, trying to grab at the book. "It is not what you think."

"Not what I think! I know your sort. You leave my lamb alone!"

"Mary, no!" Mrs. Archer reached down and hauled Justin to his feet. "I merely lost my balance, and Lord Lyndon was kind enough to help me. There was nothing improper at all."

"Oh?" Mary slowly lowered the book. "Truly, madam?"

"Truly, He has been the . . . the perfect gentleman."

"Well, in that case . . ." Mary placed the book back on the desk, straightened her cap on her graying brown curls, and her mask over her face and said, "Would you care for some tea, my lord?"

Chapter Five

"Did you conclude your business satisfactorily, then, dear?" Amelia glanced up from her embroidery and smiled as Justin came into the small, sunny sitting room.

"Quite satisfactorily." If one considered getting beaten about the head by an irate housemaid satisfactory. Justin almost laughed aloud at the memory of that chaotic scene. Then he almost groaned as the memory of another scene replaced it—that of holding Mrs. Archer's bare, elegant foot in his hand.

By Jove, but he had been too long without a woman if a naked foot could affect him so.

He sat down across from his mother and reached for a glass of lemonade, wishing it were something a good deal stronger. He needed it after the day he had had.

"There is cake, too," Amelia said.

"No, thank you, Mother. I stopped and had luncheon at the club. It's been years since I went there, but I found I am still on the membership books." He looked about the room again, thinking that it was too oddly quiet.

Then he realized why. Harry was nowhere in evidence.

Justin sighed and took another long sip of lemonade. His brother was probably off somewhere getting into trouble again. Justin had not thought it likely in the middle of the day, but a young man intent on mischief could find it at any time.

"I suppose Harry is out?" he said.

"Oh, no, indeed," Amelia answered. "He is still upstairs asleep."

"Asleep? In the middle of the afternoon?"

His mother gave a little, secretive smile as she plied her needle through the snowy linen. "I gave him a small dose of my old medicine. You remember, from back when the doctor said I had 'weak blood.' I have not taken the stuff since your father died, and I rarely give it to Harry. It is so difficult to give up once started, and it has made all the difference since I made myself give it up. But I felt he should stay home today. You will surely want to speak with him later."

Justin gave a doubtful snort. "My 'speaking to him' hardly seems to make any difference, Mother. The words simply go in one ear and out the other."

Amelia laughed. "Rather like someone else I once knew! I had also thought, though, that he might be more amenable to our summer plans if he had a good night's sleep."

"Oh? And what are our plans?" Justin reached for the crystal pitcher to pour out another glass of lemonade. "Are we off to Waring Castle, the ancestral pile?"

"We can go there if you like, of course. However, my friend Lady Bellweather called on me this morning, and she has given me a much better idea."

Lady Bellweather? She with the eligible daugh-

ter? Justin looked at his mother warily. "What sort
of idea?"

"My dear, you sound as if I am about to suggest
being boiled in oil! It is nothing onerous. Lady Bellweather is taking her children to Wycombe-on-Sea
for the summer, and I thought how nice it would
be to see that town again." Amelia smiled softly.
"Your father and I went there once, when we were
first married. Before any of you children came
along. I thought it was truly lovely, a most amiable
place. But your father preferred Waring or the
hunting box in Scotland."

Justin saw the faraway glint in his mother's eyes
and thought she must hold that long-ago trip to
Wycombe-on-Sea in even greater esteem than she
said. "So you never went back there?"

"Never. But we can go there now, if we so
choose! I know it will not be the same as it was
thirty years ago. Lady Bellweather goes there every
year, though, and she says it is still delightful. There
are assembly rooms and concerts, as well as the sea
bathing. It is not as grand as Brighton, but I do
think the fresh air would be so good for you and
Harry."

"And for you, Mother?"

She laughed. "Perhaps! At least in Wycombe I
shall know that my days of holidays spent standing
about in bogs waiting for the grouse to fly, or whatever it was we were doing, are behind me now.
What do you think, dear?"

Justin thought he would prefer the quiet of Waring to doing the pretty at some sea resort. But he
had never seen his mother looking happier or more
excited, and he didn't have the heart to take that

away from her. "I think that Wycombe sounds a splendid idea."

Amelia leaped to her feet, her sewing falling unheeded to the floor, and rushed over to kiss his cheek. "Oh, my dear, you will not be sorry! We shall have such a grand summer. And just wait until you meet Miss Bellweather. She is truly lovely. Oh, I must go and start my packing! I hope I have the right clothes for the seaside."

With one last kiss, she hurried off, intent on her holiday.

Justin sat back in his chair, sipping at his lemonade, listening as his mother called for her maid. So the price he had to pay for his mother's happiness was meeting this Bellweather girl, was it?

Well, it was a price he was willing to pay. No doubt this girl was just the sort he should be thinking of marrying: well-born, well-bred, and well-versed in all the social graces of being a countess.

But somehow he could not erase the memory of a slim white foot, and brown eyes looking up at him.

Four days after Justin's visit to the Golden Feather, Caroline sat on her bedroom floor surrounded by open trunks and piles of books and belongings. The gaming house was sold, and she was at last truly going to put it all behind her.

She looked at her clothes, carefully stacked into piles. One contained her own dresses, modest muslins and silks meant to be packed and taken to Wycombe-on-Sea. The other was what she considered her "costumes," the brightly colored, daringly cut gowns she wore at the Golden Feather. They were to be given away, as she could never wear them at the seaside assembly rooms.

As she folded a stack of shawls, her gaze fell on a flash of emerald green. She reached out and pulled the gown from the bottom of the pile. The gown she had worn the night Lord Lyndon first came to the Golden Feather.

She spread the soft satin across her lap and examined the small watermarks along the hem. Perhaps she would keep just this one gown, as a memento.

A memento of a man she would never see again.

Caroline laughed and shook her head as she folded the gown. She was not generally prone to sentimentality; she could not afford to be. It must be the prospect of the sea air that was making her so maudlin today.

Beneath the pile of gowns was a silk-wrapped bundle. Caroline unwound it to find the miniature portrait of Lawrence. She held it carefully in the palm of her hand, studying the face painted there. It was almost like looking at the face of a stranger.

He had been gone for more than four years, and she had felt so many things for him in that time. Pity mostly, but anger, too. Anger for his weakness.

A weakness that, ironically, had given her the financial stability she craved, in his last gift of the Golden Feather.

Now all she could feel for him was gratitude and peace.

"Good-bye, Lawrence," she whispered as she re-wrapped the portrait and packed it away.

Mary came in then, freshly laundered linens in

her arms. "Have you decided what to take, madam?" she asked.

"I believe so. These trunks and those hatboxes can go. I do think, though, that I should visit a modiste before we leave. There are quite enough clothes for day, but a distinct scarcity of gowns suitable for the assembly rooms at Wycombe-on-Sea. I shall need a bathing costume, as well."

Mary gave a satisfied smile as she packed away the linens. "It will be very good to leave London."

"Indeed it will," Caroline agreed heartily. If she had her way, they would never see the blighted town again.

"I saw there was a letter from Miss Phoebe in this morning's post."

"Yes. She was so excited to receive the money I sent for new gowns. She also cannot wait to see us next week. I do believe she is very tired of Mrs. Medlock's."

"You can scarcely blame her, madam. She was at the school a whole year after her friends her own age left." Mary considered her longtime position as being sufficient excuse to always speak her mind.

"It could not be helped, Mary," Caroline answered quietly.

"I suppose not."

"Anyway, it has all worked out for the best! Now she is of just the right age to be married. I am sure we will meet a suitable young man in Wycombe. Someone calm and sober, not a wild young rake. Someone who can take proper care of her."

"And maybe a husband for you, too?"

Caroline looked up at Mary, startled. "A hus-

band for me? No, indeed! I don't intend ever to
marry again."

"What, never?"

"Never. Once was quite enough."

"But don't you ever wish for children? A family
of your own? You may be twenty-eight years old,
but there is still time."

Wish for children? Caroline looked back down
at the trunk, staring unseeingly at the books
stacked there. Once she *had* wanted children, very
much. When she and Lawrence first married. She
had grieved mightily at her miscarriage. Eventually,
though, she had come to see their childless state as
a blessing of sorts. Their lives together had been
no place for an innocent babe.

And now . . . now it was out of the question.

"No," she said, too vehement even to her own
ears. "I shall be an auntie to Phoebe's children one
day, and that will be enough."

"But if you should meet someone you really
liked . . . ," Mary persisted.

*Someone with bright blue eyes and a wry, crooked
smile?* "I won't meet anyone again," she insisted.
"Besides, we are not going to Wycombe to meet
someone for me. We are going to find someone
suitable for Phoebe."

Chapter Six

"Caro! Oh, Caro, you are here at last! I've been waiting hours and hours."

Caroline had just stepped down from the carriage outside Mrs. Medlock's School when Phoebe came flying down the front steps and flung herself into Caroline's open arms.

"Silly Phoebe!" Caroline laughed, holding her sister close. "I told you we would surely not arrive before teatime at the earliest."

"Tea was half an hour ago. Though I'm sure Mrs. Medlock would have a fresh pot made, if you like."

"Tea would be lovely. But first I want to look at you." Caroline held her sister out at arm's length for an inspection.

"Have I grown, then?" Phoebe preened a bit, turning her head from side to side so that her curls danced. "Am I taller than when you saw me last autumn?"

Phoebe was not taller, but she did seem somehow older than she had on that last visit. Then her hair had been down, a riot of golden curls to her waist. She had worn the school uniform and giggled and whispered with her friends as any immature girl would.

Today her hair was pinned in a fashionable knot atop her head, and she was obviously trying very hard to contain her natural exuberance and behave like a lady. Her hands were clasped tightly in front of her as she bounced slightly on her feet. She was a bit taller than Caroline, and in Caroline's sisterly opinion anyway, much prettier, with soft violet-blue eyes and pink-and-white skin.

She no longer looked like the baby sister who would follow Caroline all around their childhood home. She looked like a young lady.

A young lady with strange tastes in clothing.

Caroline gazed speechless at Phoebe's ensemble. When she had sent money for new clothes, Caroline had pictured sprigged muslin day dresses and pastel ball gowns. Today Phoebe wore a gown of bright orange lightweight wool, trimmed *à la militaire* with copious gold braid and frog fastenings. A gold lace ruff framed her pretty face, and more lace peeked out at the cuffs.

"Oh, Phoebe," Caroline said quietly, "you look . . . very dashing."

"Do you like it?" Phoebe spun about happily. "I was quite in alt when you said I might have some new gowns. The dressmaker in the village has some lovely fashion plates from London, and she made up such gowns for me. Just wait until you see them! I am sure there can be nothing so fine in Town."

"I am sure not."

Phoebe looked closely at Caroline's own pale gray carriage dress and matching plain bonnet. "Perhaps she could make up something for you, Caro."

Heaven forbid. "Well, dear, I am sure we won't

have the time. We must leave tomorrow, you know, for Wycombe-on-Sea."

"I cannot wait! I have told all the girls about what adventures we shall have. They are quite envious, I assure you. But you must come inside now and have some tea, for you must be vastly tired after your journey! Did Mary come with you?"

"She stayed at the inn with the luggage. You know how she is; she does not trust anyone."

"I can scarcely wait to see her! I'm sure she won't recognize me again."

"I am sure she won't."

Mrs. Medlock appeared then in the doorway, a tall, stern-looking woman in rustling black silk.

"Miss Lane," she said, "I am sure your sister would like something to drink after her journey. It is very warm out here to be kept standing about."

Phoebe smiled at her, dimples flashing prettily. "Of course, Mrs. Medlock."

"Why don't you go ask the maids to lay out the tea again, while I show Mrs. Aldritch where she might refresh herself."

"Oh, yes! I will see if there are any lemon cakes left, since they are your special favorites, Caro." Phoebe kissed Caroline's cheek once more and dashed off to find the dessert, her orange skirts held up to reveal gold-colored stockings and slippers.

"If you would care to follow me, Mrs. Aldritch," Mrs. Medlock said, turning back into the school in Phoebe's wake.

As Caroline followed the headmistress up a winding staircase and along a dim corridor, Mrs. Medlock said, "Miss Lane is very excited about her seaside holiday, Mrs. Aldritch."

"I am rather excited myself," Caroline answered. "It feels I have waited a very long time for her to finish her studies and be ready to make her bow in the world."

"Yes." Mrs. Medlock opened a door and ushered her into a small sitting room, where a basin, towels, and soap were laid out. "You will probably be considering a match for her soon."

"Very likely, if someone suitable appears."

Mrs. Medlock nodded. "She is a very pretty girl, Mrs. Aldritch. I am certain she will have no lack of suitors. But I feel I must also tell you that Miss Lane is one my most, er, *exuberant* students. I realize this is hardly my place to say, but . . ." Her voice faded in hesitation.

Caroline removed her bonnet to look closer at Mrs. Medlock. What exactly was the woman trying to say? "Please, Mrs. Medlock, do go on."

"It is only that I am so fond of your sister, Mrs. Aldritch. I would hate to see any . . . difficulties befall her. And I know that these seaside places are full of all sorts of people, including gentlemen whose behavior is less than respectable. Miss Lane has such an *impulsive* nature."

"So you are urging me to keep a strict eye on her, is that it, Mrs. Medlock?"

The headmistress nodded in relief. "Yes. That is all. Just be vigilant, Mrs. Aldritch. Now, I will leave you to freshen up. One of the maids will show you to the drawing room when you are ready."

With Mrs. Medlock gone, Caroline turned back thoughtfully to the basin of water. Mrs. Medlock, who had always been so proper and reserved on the few times they had met in the past, was urging her to be "vigilant" about Phoebe? What was going on?

Caroline frowned at her reflection in the small mirror above the basin. She had thought it would be so easy to be a chaperon and mother figure. They would go to Wycombe, Phoebe would meet some sober young vicar or squire, and she would marry him and be secure and cozy for the rest of her life.

Oh, Caroline knew that Phoebe was rather high-spirited, as all young girls were. There had been occasional letters from Mrs. Medlock about some small prank or other Phoebe and her friends had undertaken. But those had been ages ago. Phoebe was seventeen now, a young lady of an age to settle down.

Caroline thought very carefully now about Mrs. Medlock's words. She had been so very certain that Phoebe would be eager to listen to her counsel, to meet *nice* young men. She was so intent on making certain that Phoebe did not make *her* past blunders that perhaps she had not seen the obvious.

That perhaps Phoebe was exactly like Caroline was at her age, heedless and romantic, ripe for making mistakes.

At least Mrs. Medlock had seen fit to warn her.

"I *will* be vigilant," Caroline whispered fiercely. "Phoebe will not end up with another Lawrence, that I promise."

Phoebe watched Caroline carefully across the tea table, where she sat making polite conversation with Mrs. Medlock and the music instructor. Her sister was not exactly as she had remembered.

Phoebe always thought of Caroline as being elegant and sophisticated, as indeed she was, though rather plain in her dress for Phoebe's taste. From her childhood, she remembered her sister as being fun, with a ready smile and a merry laugh. She had always been ready for any lark.

The Caroline who sat across from her now, the Caroline she had known for the past few years, always seemed rather, well, worried. Quiet and intense, as if she always had some deep worry lurking in her mind.

Phoebe smiled secretly behind her teacup. Well, *she* would soon have her sister smiling again. And laughing and dancing and wearing bright, daring colors. Making merry was what Phoebe did best; all her friends agreed that she was the very best at coming up with pranks to pull on Mrs. Medlock. And Wycombe-on-Sea sounded like it could be very merry indeed. At least compared with this school.

The sort of place where a determined girl could get up to some grand schemes.

"Why must we go to a sea resort, of all places?" Harry whined for the tenth time in as many minutes. "There will be no one but old ladies and invalids there. If we *have* to go to the sea, we could at least have gone to Brighton."

Justin frowned at his brother. They had been trapped together in the carriage for hours, and Justin had had about all he could take of Harry's complaints. If he had to hear one more, he would surely toss Harry out of the carriage on his gold satin-covered backside.

Their mother, though, didn't appear to notice the squabbling at all. She watched the landscape pass by out the window, humming a cheerful little tune under her breath.

"We are not going to Brighton, Harry," Justin said through gritted teeth, "because there are too many opportunities for you to get into trouble there, with the Prince Regent and his cronies in residence."

Harry crossed his arms over his puce-and-gold striped waistcoat. "I promised you I would not associate with the Carlton House set if we went to Brighton! I would have behaved myself."

Justin snorted in disbelief.

"I would have! There was absolutely no reason for you to drag me off to some old watering place full of matrons and doddering old colonels looking to cure their gout. I would wager there is not a single place where one could get a decent game of cards in the whole town. And no pretty girls, either."

"Harry . . . ," Justin warned, looking at their mother to gauge her reaction to his rude words.

Amelia just laughed. "I do believe you would lose that wager, Harry dear. I gave your father fits the last time we were here, I lost so much at piquet and vingt-et-un." She laughed again, brightly. "Yes, indeed, *fits!*"

Harry looked marginally more interested, but persisted in his sulks. "That was thirty years ago, Mother."

"Things could not have changed that much," Amelia replied, unfazed. "And as for pretty girls, I am sure there will be no shortage of them. Lady Bellweather alone has three daughters, though I fear the youngest two are far from marriageable age. But the eldest will surely gather a crowd of young people around her. So there will be no lack of activities for you, Harry dear, and do stop pouting. It ruins your handsome face and makes you look quite old and crabbed."

"No!" Harry cried, horrified.

Amelia smiled serenely and went back to looking out the window.

Justin, amazed at the sudden silence, took out his book and opened it to where he had left off. But he could not concentrate on the words at all.

He kept seeing red hair and small white feet, kept hearing the low, soft sound of a woman's voice. Mrs. Archer's voice. Without the distraction of Harry's whining, his thoughts constantly went back to the dark-eyed woman.

It was absolutely fruitless, of course, all this ruminating on who she might be, what she might look like beneath her mask. He was not looking for a mistress, and even if he were she was far away.

One thing was certain—he would surely never see her again.

He laughed softly and went back to his book. Mrs. Archer could only be a small, bright memory now, a memory of a woman he had scarcely known but who had interested him, drawn him in.

He could only hope that Miss Bellweather, or someone like her, would be half as intriguing.

Chapter Seven

"Oh, Caro, is it not the loveliest house you have ever seen in your life!" Phoebe ran from room to room in their new cottage, throwing open all the window casements to let the fresh sea air in. "And we have such a grand view of the water. It is just like the Castle Tallarico."

Caroline removed her bonnet and placed it next to her gloves and reticule on a small table. She was quite tired from their journey, but she couldn't help smiling at Phoebe's whirlwind of enthusiasm. The girl had chatted practically nonstop for the whole trip and showed no signs of stopping now that they had arrived in Wycombe. "Castle Tallarico?" she asked.

"From *Contessa Maria's Secret*. Have you not read it?"

"I fear I have not."

"Oh, but you simply must! It is the finest book ever written, I am sure. Contessa Maria comes to live at Castle Tallarico, which is exactly like this place. Well, almost. It is a great, crumbling, medieval stone castle, and this is a red brick cottage. But there is an ocean crashing against cliffs below, and there are secrets and a sinister housemaid and a secretive but fatally attractive prince who is the hero." Phoebe turned wide eyes to her sister. "Caro! Do you think we shall meet a fatally attractive prince here? Perhaps even in that grand house next door!"

Fatally attractive? Lord Lyndon's smile flashed in Caroline's mind, as it had so often, *too* often, in the past days. She pushed it back, reminding herself one more time that she would never meet Lyndon again. "I doubt it, dearest. Though I am sure we will meet many nice young men."

"Nice!" Phoebe wrinkled her nose in disgust. "That makes them sound like spaniels."

"There is nothing wrong with being nice," Caroline chided. "It is far better than being . . . fatally attractive."

Phoebe looked unconvinced. But she just shrugged and went back to peering out the window. "Look, there are people out walking along the shore! Can we go down there, Caro?"

Caroline shook her head. "Not today. It grows late. Perhaps we can go for a stroll tomorrow, or even bathing. Would you like that?"

"Above all things!" Phoebe spun away from the window to give Caroline an impulsive hug. "Are you quite all right, Caro? You look so pale."

"I am just tired, dearest. The journey was such a long one."

"Indeed it was! You should not sit in one place for so long when you are older. You stay here, and I will go see how Mary and the new cook are getting along for supper. Shall I bring you some tea, too?"

Caroline laughed at that "older" comment. "Yes,

please. A cup of good, strong tea sounds just what I need to warm my ancient bones."

After Phoebe rushed out of the room in a flurry of bright pink skirts, Caroline settled herself in a chair by the window. She looked out at the stretch of sandy shore in the not-too-far distance, watching the few people who walked there soaking up the last of the warm afternoon before they went off to their evening's festivities.

Festivities she and Phoebe would soon have to find a way to gain entrance to.

Tomorrow she would look about the town, see who was in residence. Surely there would be someone here who would remember her family, the Lanes; they had summered here so often when she was a child. Someone who would not remember the mild scandal of her elopement with Lawrence Aldritch. Someone who would welcome them. They only had to pay for their tickets to go to the assembly rooms, of course, but that would do them no good without someone to introduce them.

She looked away from the window, and her gaze fell on Phoebe's bonnet, abandoned on a settee. Its pink and gold and green feathers fluttered in the breeze from the open window.

Caroline sighed. Someone would have to give Phoebe some fashion advice, as well.

There was a clatter of carriage wheels in the street below, the last street before the sandy shore sloped down into the sea. They stopped in front of the house next door.

Caroline peered back out, curious to see who had taken the large, white stone structure.

A footman opened the carriage door, and a loud,

querulous voice floated out, ". . . didn't say we would be in such a pokey little place! I vow my old governess must live in a larger house. I told you we should have gone to Brighton!"

A woman's sweet, barely audible voice answered, "Your father and I stayed in this exact same house. It is much larger than it appears, I promise, and it is right on the water. . . ."

One booted foot just emerged from the carriage when Phoebe reappeared, carrying a large tea tray. Caroline turned from the window, closing the casement firmly behind her. She didn't want Phoebe to know yet that their neighbors, far from being "fatally attractive" royalty, were quarrelsome snobs who thought their great mansion too small.

The next day was bright and warm, perfect for strolling along the promenade that ran alongside the shore. Perfect for seeing and being seen.

Caroline just wished that Phoebe chose to be seen in something other than a purple-and-yellow striped muslin walking dress and purple spencer.

More than one passing matron looked at Phoebe with raised brows, then, more often than not, would turn their gaze to Caroline in a most accusing manner. Almost as if they were blaming *her* for the young woman's attire!

Caroline just smiled, sighed inwardly, and fought the urge to dare one of those old hens to try to change Phoebe's mind. She had already taken her sister to see three dressmakers, had pointed out how attractive pale pink and cream were next to golden curls and violet eyes.

Phoebe had just shaken her head, pulled out

bolts of bright blue and sunburst yellow, and said how lovely *they* were for Caroline's dark eyes. She shunned chipped-straw bonnets and pretty pale blue trims. But she begged for a wide-brimmed hat trimmed with yards of red tulle veiling and numerous pink roses.

Caroline sighed again. Now she knew what her mother had meant when, long ago, she had said that one day Caroline would have a daughter just like herself, and then she would know what it felt like.

Phoebe, though, was oblivious to all this. She hurried ahead on the promenade, practically skipping in enthusiasm. She swung her new hatbox blithely by its ribbons and smiled at everyone she passed.

Mary came up beside Caroline, carrying the extra parcels of ribbons and slippers, puffing slightly from the exercise. "I did think, madam, that you said a seaside holiday would be restful after that den of vice in London."

Caroline laughed. "Are you not rested, then, Mary?"

Mary looked ahead to where Phoebe was chasing after some seagulls, and said, "Not just at present."

"Things will settle soon, I am sure. It's just that she is in a new place, and everything is so exciting. She can't stay this energetic forever."

"Hmph. If you say so, madam."

"I do say so. Now, Mary dear, if we just—"

"Excuse me," a woman's soft voice said from behind Caroline, interrupting her words.

Caroline turned and saw a small, slender, pretty older woman. She was obviously Quality, with her soft gray walking dress and fine pearl necklace and earrings. Her only slightly faded blue eyes were hesitant but intent as she looked at Caroline.

"Yes?" Caroline said. "Oh, are we blocking the walkway? I am so sorry!"

"No, not at all. It is just . . . Oh, this is terribly bad-mannered of me to just come along and speak to you like this! But I had to know if you were perhaps related to Margery Elliston."

Caroline looked closer at the woman, startled. "She was my mother."

The woman smiled in satisfaction. "I knew it! You look so very much like her. We were school-mates, you see, back when I was just Miss Amelia Petersham. What larks we did have together then!" The woman laughed softly. "But I don't mean to keep you with my sentimental rambling, Miss . . ."

"Mrs. Caroline Aldritch," Caroline answered with a smile of her own. This was just what she had been hoping for, someone who remembered her family. And this Amelia Petersham, or what-ever her name was now, seemed so very kind. "You are not keeping me at all. I am always happy to meet a friend of my mother's."

"Oh, the stories I could tell you about her! I was so saddened when I heard of her passing. But have you been in Wycombe very long? Are you here with your husband?"

"I fear my husband has also passed away, several years ago."

The woman nodded in sad sympathy. "I am sorry. Widowhood can be so very difficult, as I well know. I trust you are not alone, though?"

"I am here with my sister, Miss Phoebe Lane, who you see just there." Caroline caught Phoebe's eye where she had wandered rather far afield and motioned her to come back closer.

"I am here with my family, as well, my two sons and a friend and her daughters. They are taking tea at that shop, and I fear I abandoned them most rudely. But I saw you out the window, and I simply had to come and see if you had known Margery." She laughed and pressed one gray-gloved hand to her throat in obvious embarrassment. "And now I am being rude again, not introducing myself to you! I am Lady Lyndon; well, I suppose I am the *Dowager* Lady Lyndon now."

Lyndon? Her name was Lyndon? Caroline's breath seemed to stop in her throat, choking her. She stepped back from the woman, staring at her, trying to see some resemblance to *him* in her pretty face.

Surely she could not be related to the Lord Lyndon, Justin, who had come to the Golden Feather? That would simply be too much coincidence, too much like one of Phoebe's beloved silly novels. But there could not be two Lord Lyndons in England.

Oh, what if he was here! How terrible that would be.

But how wonderful, her traitorous mind whispered, if she *did* see him again . . .

"Mrs. Aldritch?" Lady Lyndon said, clearly alarmed. "Are you quite all right? You look rather faint."

"It is just the sun, Lady Lyndon," Caroline managed to gasp.

"Yes, it is rather warm to be standing about. Won't you join us in the tea shop?"

Phoebe came up to them just in time to hear

this. Even though she could have no idea who this woman was her sister was conversing with, she said with great enthusiasm, "A tea shop? Oh, yes, Caro, let's! I am quite famished."

Go to the tea shop, where no doubt this woman's sons, both of whom had met her as Mrs. Archer, were waiting? Caroline did not think that a wise idea. She had to collect her scattered thoughts before she met Lord Lyndon again. "We would not want to intrude," she said.

"Of course you would not be intruding!" Lady Lyndon protested. "Ah, here come my sons now."

Caroline pressed her gloved hand to her suddenly heaving stomach. What if this truly was *him*? What if he recognized her and told all the world the truth about her past?

But a part of her, a part she scarcely dared acknowledge, hoped that it was he.

She turned around and pressed her hand even tighter to her stomach. It *was* he. Justin.

His hair glinted almost a gold in the sunlight, and the lines about his vivid blue eyes deepened as he smiled at his mother. His gaze flickered over Caroline, too, in curiosity.

She reached up, unconsciously trying to tug the wide brim of her bonnet forward even farther, so she could hide beneath it.

Next to her, Phoebe had gone suddenly still, ceasing to bounce on her feet for the first time all day. "Oh, Caro," she whispered, "is he not the handsomest man you ever saw! He should be in a novel."

Caroline looked at her sister, horrified. Phoebe, attracted to Justin? What a nightmare. How could she possibly like him when he was *hers,* Caroline's?

She was even more horrified by that quick, flashing thought. Of course he was not hers; he never could be.

But he could not belong to Phoebe, either. The very thought was absurd!

"Phoebe," she whispered back, "he is above ten years older than you!"

"How can he be? I declare he must be only one-and-twenty at the most."

Then Caroline saw that in her haste to jump to ridiculous conclusions, she had missed the fact that Phoebe was not looking at Justin at all. Her gaze was focused past him, on the man who followed him.

A man in an orange brocade waistcoat and pea-green coat.

Harry Seward.

"Is he not a vision?" Phoebe sighed.

Caroline groaned and closed her eyes against the "vision." Oh, why could the ground not just open up and swallow her whole!

Chapter Eight

"Justin! Have you ever seen such an angel of perfection before?" Harry whispered. He stopped moving forward in midstride and stood frozen as a block of marble, his eyes wide and staring.

Justin, too, looked at the woman who stood talking to their mother and decided that for once he had to agree with his brother's taste. She was as close to an "angel of perfection" as he had seen since . . .

Well, since his afternoon in Mrs. Archer's office.

Not that this lady resembled Mrs. Archer in any way. She was dressed quietly but stylishly in a walking dress of pale yellow muslin and a yellow and white bonnet. Even though her face was half in shadow from that bonnet's wide brim, he could see a small, straight nose, aristocratic cheekbones, and soft, silvery blond hair.

Yes, she was lovely. He would have thought her too subtle for Harry's taste, though.

He glanced at his brother, oddly irritated that Harry had seen her first. "She's not exactly in your style, is she?"

"What are you talking about?" Harry shot back. "She is exactly in my style! Only a true paragon of fashion could have chosen that sublime shade of purple."

Only then could Justin tear his gaze away from the lady in yellow to the girl who stood beside her.

Now, *she* truly was in Harry's style.

She had very pretty golden curls and was obviously young and high-spirited. But she wore a gown that was much too old for her, of bright purple-and-yellow striped muslin topped with a purple braid-trimmed spencer. On her head perched a tall-crowned purple hat ornamented with a band of gold lace. If Justin had been in the habit of wearing a quzzing glass, he would have been groping for it.

"She seems to know Mother, too," Harry said eagerly. "Come on, let's see if she'll introduce us." He came unfrozen then and hurried forward, all his fashionable weariness and whining forgotten in his rush to meet the "paragon of fashion."

Justin followed, more than a little curious himself to meet these new arrivals.

Especially the lady in yellow.

"There you are, my dears," his mother said. "Do come and meet my new acquaintances, Mrs. Aldritch and her sister, Miss Lane. These are my two sons, Lord Lyndon and Mr. Harry Seward."

The lady in yellow looked at them rather coolly, her fair face expressionless as a mask. "How do you do, Lord Lyndon, Mr. Seward?" she said quietly.

Justin had the distinct impression that she was quite underwhelmed to make their acquaintance. As she tilted up her chin a bit, he wondered if perhaps he had forgotten to bathe that morning.

The other lady showed no such reservations. She seemed to bounce on her feet and smiled up at them brightly. "How do you do!" she said, her pretty violet-blue gaze fastening on Harry.

"How do *you* do, Miss Lane?" Harry said, then added hastily, "And you, Mrs. Aldritch. Dashed glad to meet you."

Miss Lane giggled, and Mrs. Aldritch laid her hand on her sister's purple-covered arm, stilling some of that dizzying bouncing.

Justin suddenly realized that he was staring, quite rudely, and said quickly, "Have you been in Wycombe very long, Mrs. Aldritch?"

"Not at all," she answered, still very quiet. She ducked her chin back into the shadow of her bonnet, giving the impression of great shyness or reserve. A reserve he longed to pique. "We only arrived yesterday, and your mother is our first acquaintance here."

"They are the daughters of an old friend of mine," Amelia said happily. "Isn't that the most marvelous coincidence?"

"Marvelous," Justin echoed, watching the quiet Mrs. Aldritch.

"And now you must join me in persuading them to come back to the tea shop with us and meet the Bellweathers," Amelia continued.

Justin almost groaned aloud. The Bellweathers! How could he have forgotten them not five minutes out of their company? He was meant to be paying special attention to Miss Sarah Bellweather.

"Oh, you must!" Harry burst out. "You must join us, I mean. They have the most excellent strawberries."

"I adore strawberries!" Miss Lane said, with another little bounce for enthusiastic emphasis. She looked to her sister inquiringly. Only when Mrs.

Aldritch gave a small nod did she bounce forward to take Harry's arm.

He led her toward the tea shop, both of them chattering happily away. About fashion, no doubt.

"Well, then, Mother. Mrs. Aldritch," Justin said, offering an arm to each of the ladies. "Shall we join them before they devour all the strawberries?"

"And where is your family *from,* Mrs. Aldritch?" Lady Bellweather, a rather buxom matron with suspiciously dark hair arranged in girlish curls about her creased face, sounded as if she strongly suspected Caroline's family came from a cave somewhere. Her eyes were narrowed as she peered at Caroline over her large plate of cake.

Caroline took a slow sip of her tea, acutely conscious of Lord Lyndon seated beside her at the crowded table. The way his shoulder almost, but not quite, brushed against her made it very difficult to concentrate on Lady Bellweather's prying questions. Or indeed on anything at all.

She leaned away from him a bit and carefully placed her cup and saucer back on the table. "My sister and I grew up in Devonshire, Lady Bellweather. Our mother, as you know, was Miss Margery Elliston, and our father was Sir William Lane."

"And you say you were married?" Lady Bellweather's tone implied that that claim was also highly suspect.

Caroline almost laughed. If only Lady Bellweather knew what she had really been doing for the last few years! The woman would surely faint dead away if she heard of the Golden Feather, a

not wholly undesirable thought. "Indeed I was,
though my husband, Mr. Lawrence Aldritch, has
been gone for many years."

"Larry Aldritch?" Lyndon said suddenly. "You
were married to Larry Aldritch?"

Caroline, Lady Bellweather, and Lady Lyndon
all looked at him in surprise. He had been very
quiet ever since they sat down.

Caroline was more than surprised; she was dismayed. He had known Lawrence, had known him
well enough to call him Larry? Only his closest
cronies, the ones he went drinking and gaming
with, had called him by that nickname. But how
could that be? Lord Lyndon seemed such a gentleman, not at all like Lawrence's rackety friends.

Wasn't he?

Caroline looked at him closely for the first time
since they met on the promenade, searching for
signs of dissipation beneath that handsome, pleasant veneer.

Then she realized that now he could see her
fully, too, with her face turned to him and her bonnet's brim no longer in the way. He watched her
steadily, seriously, a bit curiously. Not only that,
but an awkward silence had fallen at the table.
Even the two littlest Bellweather girls stopped their
chatter to watch Caroline's dumbfounded reaction
to his question.

Lady Bellweather gave a smug little smile, as if
she were certain there was some scandal attached
to this "Larry" Aldritch.

Caroline looked away, and said, "Some people
called him Larry, yes. Did you perhaps know him,
Lord Lyndon?"

"Yes. A long time ago, before I went out to

India. May I offer my belated condolences on his passing, Mrs. Aldritch?"

"Thank you," Caroline answered, unsure what else she should say. She wanted to ask what his friendship with Lawrence had been like, what sort of trouble they had gotten into together. If he had been one of the spoiled young noblemen who encouraged Lawrence to gamble far more than he could afford to lose.

Her hands clenched in her lap, hidden by the tablecloth. She didn't want to believe that of Lord Lyndon! She *wouldn't* believe it. His behavior the night he came to the Golden Feather with his brother had not been that of a wastrel.

She carefully looked up at him again and gave him a small smile. "Perhaps you could tell me more of your acquaintance with my husband, Lord Lyndon. One day."

He smiled at her warmly in return. "I should like that, Mrs. Aldritch."

Lady Bellweather put her cake plate down on the table with a loud rattle. "I have never heard of anyone named Aldritch," she pronounced.

"Oh, Mother, please," the eldest Bellweather girl, Sarah, said. She tossed back her dark brown curls impatiently. "We live right next to old Miss Dorothy Aldritch in Grosvenor Square. Wasn't her nephew named Lawrence?"

Phoebe, who had been talking with Sarah ever since they sat down, giggled. The two younger Bellweathers gasped.

Lady Bellweather turned a deep burgundy-purple.

And Caroline, not for the first time that strange afternoon, had no idea what to say. Her mind was too full for any more thoughts just at present. She pressed her fingertips to her aching temples.

It was Lady Lyndon who saved the day. "Well, it does grow rather late, I fear," she said cheerfully. "I do hope, Mrs. Aldritch, that you and your sister can come to my little card party tomorrow evening? There will be a supper before, and it should be quite amusing."

Caroline looked around at all the people gathered about the tea table. Lady Bellweather's expression was most disgruntled as she frowned at her friend. Sarah and Phoebe were whispering together intently, while Harry stared, wide-eyed, at Phoebe. Lady Lyndon smiled expectantly.

And Lord Lyndon watched her intently, waiting for her answer.

Her headache intensified, but she smiled and said, "Of course, Lady Lyndon. We would be delighted to attend."

Chapter Nine

That night, long after the rest of the house was quiet, Caroline sat alone in her bedroom window seat, looking out at the house next to theirs. The house she now knew was occupied by the Sewards.

By Lord Lyndon. Or Justin, as her stubborn, silly mind still insisted on thinking of him.

She sighed and pleated the velvet of her dressing gown between her restless fingers.

Harry Seward she was not so very worried about, despite the calf eyes he made at Phoebe all afternoon. He had generally been inebriated when he met her at the Golden Feather. Justin, though, was another case altogether. He had been all too sober. Certainly a first for any old friend of Lawrence's, if indeed that was what he was.

Why, oh why, did he have to come here to Wycombe? Why could he not have gone to Bath or Brighton, or any one of a dozen other watering places? They were more fashionable.

But no. He was here, right next door in the white mansion his brother had complained was too small.

It would be quite disastrous if he were to recognize her as Mrs. Archer, both for herself and for innocent Phoebe. He seemed like a kind man, but he *was* an earl, with a position in Society to uphold. He would never let his mother associate with a woman who had owned a gaming house, or her sister.

Caroline leaned her aching head against the cool glass of the window, still watching the darkened house across the garden. The most sensible thing would be to stay far away from Lord Lyndon and his family, so that he would have no opportunity for unfortunate recognitions. Yet how could she do that, when Lady Lyndon had invited them for a card party the very next evening?

No, she could not deprive Phoebe of this social opportunity. It had been all the girl could talk of during supper, how charming the Sewards were, how much she liked Sarah Bellweather, and how she looked forward to the party.

Caroline remembered Phoebe's shining eyes and knew she could never disappoint her so.

"He did not remember me this afternoon," she whispered. They sat next to each other in the tea shop for more than an hour, and he had not once shown any flash of recognition or suspicion. Of course, she had been wearing her large bonnet, and she had tried not to look at him too long or speak with him too much.

It might prove more difficult to be evasive if she was seated across from him at a card table, with no sheltering hat. But she had to try, for Phoebe's sake.

Perhaps for her own sake, as well.

She had liked Lord Lyndon in London, had been drawn to him in a way she never had been to a man in the past. Not even Lawrence.

She liked him even more here at the seaside. Not

only was he handsome; he was quite funny, in a wry way. If she had not been so intent on avoiding detection, she would have laughed aloud at many of his observations. He had a quiet, authoritative way with his brother that she wished she could emulate with Phoebe. He was solicitous of his mother, polite with the bevy of Bellweathers, even the obnoxious Lady Bellweather.

Yes, Caroline liked him very much indeed. If things had been different, if she were an ordinary, respectable widow, she would be looking forward to tomorrow night's gathering with great eagerness.

Truth to tell, she still looked forward to it, even if the eagerness was mixed with a healthy amount of dread.

Justin sat alone in the darkened library after everyone else was abed. It had been a rather exhausting struggle to persuade Harry to retire to his room rather than go out and send notes to Miss Lane, but Justin found he was not tired at all. His mind kept going over the rather puzzling afternoon at the tea shop.

The day began as expected. They went to meet the Bellweathers after luncheon for a stroll along the promenade, and he dutifully escorted Miss Sarah Bellweather. She was certainly a pretty girl, with a rather pert air about her, but Justin had not been able to summon up more than a polite interest in her. When she wasted no time in telling him she intended never to marry, he found that that suited him very well, and they thereafter engaged in perfectly polite conversation about the weather.

Then they met Mrs. Aldritch and her sister, the very vivid Miss Lane.

He had felt . . . *something* when he met Mrs. Aldritch. A jolt of attraction, almost of recognition. And he had thought she felt it, too. Her gloved hand had trembled when he bowed over it.

But she was quiet and stiff in the tea shop, especially after she learned he had known Larry. She answered all his attempts to draw her into conversation with soft murmurs. He hardly even got a look at her face; she was always turning away beneath her cursed bonnet. All he had been given were intriguing glimpses of dark eyes and moonlight-colored hair.

Perhaps she was simply shy. Quite unlike another woman of his recent acquaintance, a woman he had also found intriguing. There had been nothing shy about Mrs. Archer.

Justin laughed at the absurdity of it. In all his years in India, there had been only one woman he was remotely interested in, a widow who had soon deserted him for wedded bliss with an elderly colonel. Now, after only a few weeks back in England, he met not one but two lovely, intriguing women.

Perhaps it only meant that after four years of thinking about what he wanted, needed from his life, it was time to start living it.

And tomorrow evening, at the card party, he would have another chance to try to draw out Mrs. Aldritch.

Phoebe lay awake in her bed, tossing and turning, too excited to sleep. It had truly been a most eventful day, everything she had hoped for at dull old Mrs. Medlock's School. She had met what was surely the most handsome man in England. She giggled into her pillow when she recalled Harry Seward's brown curls and lovely hazel eyes.

He had excellent fashion sense, as well; she had never before seen anything so elegant as his orange brocade waistcoat.

He didn't seem to be much of a talker, but that hardly mattered. She had quite enough to say for both of them.

And she was to see him again tomorrow evening! At a card party in his own house. This holiday was turning out even finer than she had hoped it would.

Phoebe turned over onto her side, to look at the wall her room shared with Caroline's chamber. If only she could find someone for her sister, so that she could be just as happy as Phoebe was now. . . .

Of course! Phoebe sat straight up in her excitement. Mr. Seward's brother. Oh, why had she not thought of it sooner? It was so perfect.

Lord Lyndon seemed too serious by half, but Caro appeared to like that. He was very handsome for an older gentleman, *and* he had a title.

"Caroline, Countess of Lyndon," Phoebe whispered. Then she giggled again.

Oh, yes. This summer was just getting better and better.

Chapter Ten

"Isn't it exciting, Caro? Our first party here! I thought this day would last forever and the evening would never come."

Caroline smiled as she watched Phoebe bounce on her dressing table bench while Mary attempted to dress her hair. It had been a very long time since Caroline had eagerly anticipated any social gathering, but Phoebe's enthusiasm infected her. Her nervousness at seeing Lord Lyndon again, her apprehension that he might recognize her, was almost, but not quite, overcome by the pleasurable sense of expectation.

"Now, Phoebe," she warned, "you know that this is not exactly a grand ball. It is only supper and cards."

"That is more than there ever was at school!" Phoebe tried to turn her head to look at Caroline.

"Miss Phoebe, stop that!" Mary said sternly. "If you keep fidgeting about like that your hair will be all lopsided."

"I am sorry, Mary, dear," Phoebe answered, sounding not at all contrite. "I will sit very still now." She finally managed to cease bobbing and face the mirror again, allowing Mary to finish twisting her curls atop her head and fastening them with pearl-headed pins and white ribbons.

Caroline went back to sorting through her own jewel case. She wondered which would go best with her gown, her pearls or the amethyst pendant.

Then, beneath a gold and garnet brooch, she saw a flash of green fire. She reached down and took up the pair of emerald earrings. The earrings she had worn at the Golden Feather the night she met Lord Lyndon.

She held the stones on her palm, turning them a bit so they sparkled in the candlelight. Really, she should have sold them; they were so distinctive in design that she could hardly wear them again.

But she had not.

"Caro, they're beautiful!"

Startled, Caroline looked up to see Phoebe standing behind her. She was so distracted that she had not noticed her sister's coiffure had been completed.

"Can I wear them?" Phoebe continued. "They would go so well with my gown."

Caroline pushed the earrings back into the box and shut the lid firmly. "Certainly not! They are too old for you. You have Mama's locket, and it looks lovely."

Phoebe touched the gold oval hanging on the chain at her throat. "But those earrings would add such dash to my ensemble."

Caroline laughed and stood to hug her sister. "My dear, I am sure you will be the most dashing young lady there!" And indeed she would be. Or at the very least, the most distinctive. Caroline had persuaded her to wear one of her more subdued gowns, a sea-green muslin, but it was trimmed with such copious amounts of lace, so many white satin bows, that Phoebe was sure to be noticed.

"Are you quite certain?" she asked anxiously, fluffing some of the lace on her sleeve. "You do not think the color too . . . pale?"

"Not at all. It is very stylish." Caroline linked her arm in Phoebe's and hurried her toward the door, anxious to have her away before she could decide to change her clothes again. "Now, we must be going, my dear, or we shall be late and miss the supper."

She was not here yet.

Justin paused just out of sight before he entered the drawing room, surveying the guests assembled there. His mother and Lady Bellweather sat talking by the window. Sarah stood behind them, looking pretty in pink silk but rather bored. Harry paced restlessly by the empty fireplace, tugging and smoothing at his waistcoat, a black satin embroidered with copious yellow butterflies.

The rest of the guests, a few friends of his mother's and their sons and daughters, stood about in small groups, talking, laughing, waiting for supper to begin.

Mrs. Aldritch was not among them.

Justin felt a prick of disappointment. He had been looking forward to seeing her again, without the wide brim of her bonnet obscuring her face.

His gaze went to the clock on the fireplace mantel. It was almost time for supper, but not quite. Surely they would be here very soon.

His mother saw him then, and called out "Justin! There you are, dear. Lady Bellweather was just telling me of a concert to be held on Saturday evening that I think we should attend. It is a program of Renaissance songs, which I know you enjoy."

Justin smiled at her and came into the room to stand next to her. "Of course, Mother. It sounds delightful."

"Do you think perhaps Mrs. Aldritch and her sister might enjoy it, as well? I did hear Mrs. Aldritch say that she was very fond of music."

Lady Bellweather gave a loud, disapproving sniff.

Before Justin could answer, the two ladies in question appeared in the doorway, as if summoned by the mention of their names. Mrs. Aldritch was turned away slightly to hand her shawl to a footman, while Miss Lane bounced merrily on her feet, her gaze lightly skimming over the crowd.

Then Mrs. Aldritch faced the room, and he saw that she was even prettier than she had been in the tea shop. Her hair was caught up in soft, pale waves by a bandeau of ribbon and seed pearls. Her gown, a subdued cinnamon-brown silk, was perfectly respectable, but showed off a white throat and sloping shoulders.

A small, polite smile curved her rose-pink lips as she looked around, one kid-gloved hand reaching out to catch her sister's arm and still that bouncing.

Amelia stood and started forward eagerly, tugging an unresisting Justin along in her wake.

But they were not quite fast enough to be the first to reach them. Harry beat them handily, rushing up in a blur of black and yellow to bow politely over Mrs. Aldritch's hand and eagerly over Miss Lane's.

"I do say!" he said breathlessly. "So good to see you, both of you, again. I must say I never . . ."

Justin nudged Harry a bit to get him to cease prattling and release Miss Lane's hand.

"Good evening, Lady Lyndon, Lord Lyndon, Mr. Seward," Mrs. Aldritch said softly. "It was indeed very good of you to invite us, but I fear we are rather late. I do apologize."

"Not at all," Amelia said. "We were only just now thinking of going in to supper, my dear. Justin, would you escort Mrs. Aldritch? And Harry, I do believe you are to escort Miss Bellweather."

Harry blushed a bright, unflattering pink, and frowned. "Miss Bellweather! Dash it all, Mother, I did say . . ."

"Yes," his mother said firmly. "Miss Bellweather, who is waiting for you now. Miss Lane, do allow me to introduce you to your dinner partner, Mr. Allen."

Amelia led Miss Lane away, while Harry shuffled off reluctantly to Miss Bellweather, who looked just as crestfallen to have him for a supper partner as he was to *not* have Miss Lane. This left Justin quite alone with Mrs. Aldritch.

Her dark eyes seemed rather anxious as she watched her sister walk away. Justin tried to smile at her reassuringly.

"I do apologize for my brother's puppyish behavior," he said. "I will speak to him and tell him to cease bothering your sister at once."

She laughed wryly. "I must confess, I fear your brother's . . . botherations are not entirely unwelcomed by my sister. I have spoken to her, but she is still quite young and rather headstrong."

Young and headstrong. Words that described Harry perfectly.

Words that once would have described Justin, as well.

He looked across the room to where Harry stood dutifully next to Miss Bellweather. Harry's gaze was avidly fastened onto Miss Lane, where she stood laughing and talking with Mr. Allen. Every impatience, every passionate emotion was clearly written across his face.

Lud, had he, Justin, ever really been *that* young?

"So you knew my husband, Lord Lyndon?" Mrs. Aldritch said, drawing his attention back to her. She watched him closely, seriously. Her face was as blank and cool as Harry's was open and obvious.

"Larry Aldritch. Yes, I knew him. We were all friends, he and I, and Freddie Reed and James Burne-Jones. Back before I went out to India." He shook his head. "That seems a hundred years ago now."

"Yes. A hundred years at least."

Justin looked down at her. She was so still, so dignified. How had she ever ended up married to such a wild youth as Larry Aldritch? Surely this woman, who seemed such a lady from the top of her pale hair to the hem of her brown silk skirt, had experienced much difficulty tolerating the sort of behavior Larry had gotten up to.

Of course! That must be the reason she seemed so cool to him, so tense in his presence. She remembered him as being a friend of Larry's, and disapproved.

Perhaps that was the explanation for the very odd sense of recognition he felt around her, as well. Maybe he had met her back then and had been too foxed to recall the meeting clearly.

Could he have insulted her in some way?

By Jove, but he hoped not.

"Did we meet before?" he said slowly, half dreading her answer.

She shook her head. "No, Lord Lyndon, not that I recall. I did meet some of my husband's friends, of course, but I seldom went out. I do not remember you, though I do remember Mr. Reed and Mr. Burne-Jones. You will have to tell me of your . . . adventures together sometime."

"So Larry never spoke of me?" he persisted. He had a burning desire to know what he might have done to insult her, so he could make it right.

"No. But then, it was a long time ago. I have long forgotten most of my husband's ramblings." Her delicate jaw tightened.

Justin's stomach unknotted in relief. She *hadn't* seen him at his very worst, then. He forced himself to give a light laugh. "Well, Mrs. Aldritch, I fear you would be quite bored by my tales of adventures, as you call them. They were all very commonplace and dull."

"As the follies of youth so often are," she answered, smiling at him for the first time that evening. "I know that very well. But I am sure that your *true* adventures in India were hardly commonplace at all."

Justin shook his head, remembering the mosquitoes, the heat, and the appalling rain of the monsoons. "Some of them were very dull indeed, I assure you."

"At the tea shop yesterday your mother said you hunted tigers and fought battles with rebelling natives, where you saved a colonel's life and won copious medals. That you survived fevers and plagues. That hardly seems dull to me."

"First of all, they were hardly battles. More like skirmishes," he protested. "And I spent four years in India, Mrs. Aldritch. Of those, perhaps only six months were exciting."

"Exciting or dull, I should like to hear about them nonetheless."

He looked at her, surprised and rather pleased. "Would you really?"

"Of course. I have never left England, and I probably never shall. I would love to hear of other lands. Other lives."

The butler appeared to announce that supper was served.

Justin held out his arm to Mrs. Aldritch, and she slipped her hand softly into the crook of his elbow, allowing him to escort her into the dining room.

"I would be happy to tell you of India," he said, as he seated her at her place at the table. "Some-time soon?"

She seemed to hesitate for a second, then slowly nodded her head. "Soon, Lord Lyndon."

Chapter Eleven

"Has your mother known Lady Lyndon very long?" Phoebe asked Sarah Bellweather. The two of them sat in one of the cushioned window seats after supper, watching the others play cards and whispering together.

"Forever, it seems." Sarah sighed. "They were quite the bosom bows when I came home from school. They expected me to marry Lord Lyndon, you know."

"No!" Phoebe, shocked, looked over to where Lord Lyndon played whist with her sister, Lady Lyndon, and Mr. Allen. He said something to Caroline, who nodded and smiled.

How could he possibly marry Sarah Bellweather when Phoebe had picked him out especially for her own sister!

"But . . . he's so old," she said faintly.

Sarah grimaced. "I know. And I intend never to marry. I want to be an archaeologist."

Phoebe found this even more shocking than the thought of Sarah marrying old Lord Lyndon. Even though she had been widely considered the most daring girl at Mrs. Medlock's School, Phoebe had never thought of doing anything but marrying.

Her esteem for Sarah Bellweather grew by the moment.

"You mean you want to dig about in the dirt for old bones?" she asked, having only the vaguest idea about what archaeologists did.

"Yes, and old treasure, too. I have been reading all about ancient civilizations, and I have corresponded with several members of the Antiquarian Society in London. It is my greatest dream," Sarah said wistfully. "But I fear it will never come true. Mama thinks all a lady should think about are babies and needlework. She's been going on for weeks about how I should be charming to Lord Lyndon."

"You . . . you're not really going to marry him, are you?" Phoebe asked, her gaze still on Caroline and Lord Lyndon. Caroline laughed, actually *laughed*, at something he was saying to her. "You absolutely cannot!"

"I know that. I even told him I intend never to marry, just in case his mother had the same idea as mine. He was really very nice about it, and he agreed that we probably would not suit."

Phoebe smiled in relief. That was all right, then. Lyndon was safe for Caroline.

"Now, though, I fear Mama has set her sights on Harry Seward for me," Sarah continued. "She keeps saying that the brother of an earl is better than no connection to an earl at all."

What! Phoebe almost leaped out of her seat. No, that could not be! Harry Seward was hers; he admired *her*.

Didn't he?

She turned to look at Harry where he sat playing cassino. She had little experience with gentlemen, it was true, but surely she could not have imagined his admiring glances?

"And what do you think of the idea of marrying Mr. Seward?" she asked.

Sarah gave an unladylike little snort. "That is even more absurd than the idea of marrying Lord Lyndon! Why, Harry Seward would not know a first-century amphora if it hit him over the head. No, I just need to disabuse Mama of all her ridiculous notions of marrying me off."

"I see. Yes." Phoebe sat back against the wall, tapping her finger thoughtfully against her chin.

"Oh, my dears, I win this trick!" Amelia cried delightedly, laying down her cards. "That means Mr. Allen and I have beat you most handily, Justin."

Justin laughed. "So you have, Mother! I fear I let Mrs. Aldritch down, after working so hard to persuade her to partner me." He looked sheepishly at Mrs. Aldritch, who smiled as she laid down her own cards.

"It was my own fault entirely, Lord Lyndon," she answered. "I have not played whist for so long, my skills have become quite rusty."

"No, it is Mother's fault for being such a card-sharper," Justin teased.

"Lord Lyndon!" Lady Bellweather cried from the next table. "You should not say such things about your own mother. A cardsharper, indeed!"

"Nonsense, Dolly," Lady Lyndon said, looking rather pleased at the thought of being a "sharper." "I *am* quite a dab hand at whist. Now, my dears, I find myself in need of some refreshment."

"Shall I fetch you some tea, Mother?" Justin said, folding his cards neatly and rising to his feet.

"So good of you, dear! Perhaps you would escort Mrs. Aldritch to the refreshment table, too? I am sure she must be fatigued after sitting for so long."

Justin peered closely at his mother, but she looked back at him steadily, all innocence. Could she possibly have suddenly switched her matchmaking machinations from Miss Bellweather to Mrs. Aldritch?

Of course she could. And Justin found that he did not half mind the idea of being thrown together with Mrs. Aldritch. In fact, he rather liked it.

"*Would* you care to accompany me, Mrs. Aldritch?" he asked her.

"Thank you, Lord Lyndon. I think I would like some tea." As she took his arm and they set off across the room to where the refreshments were laid out, she leaned closer and said quietly, "I would also like to find my sister. I fear I played too intently at the game, and she and Miss Bellweather have quite disappeared."

He looked around the room quickly and saw that she was right. Miss Lane and Miss Bellweather were gone.

And so was Harry. He no longer played at the cassino table where Justin had left him after supper.

"I am afraid my brother is also missing," he muttered.

"Oh, no! You don't think they all would have gone off to get into some mischief, do you?" The fine, fair skin of her forehead wrinkled in a concerned frown.

"With Harry, anything is possible," Justin answered ruefully.

"As with Phoebe. Oh, I am a terrible chaperon! I should have known better."

"Not at all, Mrs. Aldritch. I am certain they have just gone into the library or some such place."

"Phoebe? In a library?"

Somehow, Justin could not picture Harry there, either. "Perhaps not the library. But there are a great many other rooms in this house. I could search for them, if it would make you feel more at ease."

She nodded decisively. "I will go with you, Lord Lyndon. I do not have a good feeling about this at all."

"Mr. Seward! Do be careful. Those rocks look slippery," Phoebe cried, clasping her hands together tightly as she watched Harry climb out on some rocky outcroppings over a small, sheltered cove.

He had claimed there was smugglers' treasure hidden there, just beneath the rocks, when he had come to sit with her and Sarah after his card game ended. When he offered to show it to them, it seemed a fine lark.

Now Phoebe was not so sure. Harry's thin-soled evening shoes slipped and slid on the wet rocks as he inched his way out.

"Oh, do be careful!" she called again.

Sarah Bellweather was more blunt. "You're a silly fool, Harry Seward," she said, pausing in drawing a stick through the sand to watch his hapless progress. "There's probably no treasure there at all."

"There is!" Harry shouted back. "I saw it just last night. Silks, no doubt, and brandy and wine."

"Well, even if there is a treasure, I'm sure the smugglers would not take kindly to your stealing it," Sarah said matter-of-factly. "They would probably shoot you down."

"Shoot him!" Phoebe cried, appalled. "Oh, Mr. Seward, do come back, please."

"Smugglers don't frighten me, Miss Lane," Harry answered stoutly, kneeling down and stretching his hand between an outcropping of two rocks. "I think I just about have something now. Yes, I definitely feel something—" He broke off with a high-pitched scream. "Ahhh!" he shrieked, falling down flat on his face, his hand still caught in the rocks.

"Whatever are you carrying on about?" Sarah called, her eyes wide.

"It bit off my hand!" Harry screamed in reply, flailing his black satin-clad legs about.

Phoebe felt herself tilting swiftly into hysterics. The man she was falling in love with was dying right before her eyes!

It was just like *The Sins of Lady Lydia*.

She turned and fled up the incline toward the Sewards' house, tears streaming down her face. All she could think of was finding Caroline and making her save the day, while Harry flailed and screamed and Sarah called out futile instructions to him to keep breathing.

"They are not in here." Caroline pushed aside the last large plant in the conservatory and fell down wearily onto a wrought-iron chaise. "I feel we have searched everywhere."

"We have, almost." Justin brushed some flower petals from his hair and sat down in a chair next to her. "They were not in the library or the morning room or the upstairs gallery. The servants have not seen them. The only place we have not searched is the attic, and I am sure Harry would not muss his attire by going up there."

"We did not look in the garden."

"You can see almost the entire garden from here."

Indeed she could. One wall of the conservatory was made of windows, and through them was the whole vista of the garden, sloping down to the sea along a gentle incline.

Caroline leaned back to survey the scene laid out before her so perfectly. It was a magical night, with the moon shining down on the manicured gardens and the wild sea beyond. The water shimmered in the silver-capped darkness.

It would be so easy to sit here in silence with Lord Lyndon—Justin—watching the scene of perfect beauty as it shifted and changed all through the night. It had been a delightful evening, and he had lulled her into a dangerous comfort with his presence.

Dangerous because if she lost her wariness, her ever-present knowledge of the secrets she had to keep, she would be so vulnerable to the spell he wove.

The spell he was weaving about her so seductively right now, just by sitting quietly beside her. She was acutely aware of his warmth, of the spicy scent of his soap.

A warm lassitude stole over her, wrought by the

beautiful night, the wonderful normality of the party—and the man beside her. She wanted to turn to him, to put her arms about him and draw his lips down to hers. If she could only feel his kiss, the safety of his arms about her, holding her close. . . .

What was she thinking of!

Caroline sat straight up, trying to shake off the sweet, seductive thoughts that wound around her. Her sister was missing, probably off getting into some mischief, and all she was doing was sitting here, dreaming of kissing the man who could expose her past and cause them ruin.

She stood up quickly, obviously startling Lord Lyndon, who looked as moonstruck as she felt.

"Per-perhaps we should search the garden anyway," she said swiftly.

He rose to his feet, as well, standing next to her. "Of course, if you like, Mrs. Aldritch. I am sure they must be someplace close by."

"I do not know what else to do. What if they—" She was interrupted by the faint but unmistakable sound of a scream coming from outside the conservatory.

It sounded to Caroline's panicked ears like Phoebe. She looked about frantically for a door, but Justin was there before her, throwing open the glass door and hurrying out into the night.

Caroline followed and saw Phoebe running up the slope from the seashore, her pale green gown a flash of light against the darkness.

"Phoebe!" she cried, running toward her sister.

Tears streamed down Phoebe's face, and her hair fell disheveled from its pins and ribbons. One lace ruffle was torn on her sleeve.

Caroline's first, fierce thought was that Harry Seward had somehow hurt her sister, and she was going to have to kill him for it.

Phoebe reached her and threw herself, sobbing, into Caroline's arms.

"Caro!" she wept, her cheek wet where she pressed it against the silk of Caroline's dress. "You have to fix it!"

"Fix what, darling? What has happened?" She looked at Justin over Phoebe's bent head and saw that his face was tight and angry in the moonlight.

Obviously, he was thinking the same thing that she was, and he was utterly furious. Perhaps she would not have to kill Harry after all; his brother would do it for her, most handily.

Caroline shook Phoebe lightly by the shoulders. "Phoebe! Stop this now, and tell me what has happened."

Phoebe shook her head wildly, sending the rest of her curls tumbling free over her shoulders. "He is *dead*!"

Chapter Twelve

"Tell me, Harry. Is your brain still in your head, or did you somehow leave it behind in London?"

Harry, seated across the library desk from Justin, slouched down deeper into his chair and pouted. "Really Justin, I don't know what you're saying."

Justin, completely exasperated, planted his hands firmly on the desk with a loud slap. "I am saying that anyone with a brain, with *half* a brain for that matter, would never have taken two young ladies down to the shore in the middle of the night. Anything could have happened! One of you might have been killed or seriously injured."

Harry held up his bandaged hand. "I *was* injured! And I am in far too much pain for your hectoring."

"Pain! You merely got your hand caught between two rocks, where you had no business putting it in the first place. Then you had such hysterics that you almost frightened poor Miss Lane to death."

"I certainly never meant to frighten her at all," Harry said sheepishly. "I would never hurt such a sweet angel. I merely wanted to show her and Miss Bellweather the, er, smugglers' treasure."

"That part makes it even worse. If that 'treasure' did indeed belong to smugglers', they would have shot you on sight. And God knows what they would have done to the ladies."

Harry's gaze slid away. "Actually, Justin . . ."

Justin sighed. "What now?"

"There never was a treasure of any sort there. There wasn't anything there but seaweed."

"You mean to say you took those girls out there just to show off?"

"I would not put it exactly that way."

"I would. You have hardly been living in a wilderness all your life, Harry. You know how deeply improper your actions were, not to mention dangerous."

"It won't happen again!"

"You are damn right it won't. I intend to watch you very closely from now on, Harry. And if I so much as see you dancing with Miss Lane without her sister's permission, I will send you off to India."

"Now, really, Justin! You can't treat me like I'm in leading strings. I am an adult."

"Show me you can behave like one, then, and I will treat you as one."

"Justin—"

Justin held up his hand in a sharp gesture, stopping the flow of protests. "I don't have time for this now. I have a call to make."

"What sort of a call?"

"Not that it is any of your business, young Harry, but I am going to call on Mrs. Aldritch."

Harry's demeanor cautiously lit up. He slid to the edge of his seat. "Mrs. Aldritch? Perhaps if I could go with you and apologize in person . . ."

"I do not think so. Mrs. Aldritch was very upset

when she found her sister missing, and I doubt she would want to see you today."

Harry looked crestfallen. "Oh."

Justin's anger faded, and he relented just a bit. "Perhaps tomorrow Mrs. Aldritch and Miss Lane would agree to go with us on our picnic with Mother and the Bellweathers."

"Oh!" Harry cried. "Do you really think so?"

"I will ask her."

"I never meant any harm, Caro. I promise!" Phoebe sat next to her sister on the settee, her hands pressed to her tearstained cheeks. "I would not have worried you for all the world."

Caroline sighed. "I know you *meant* no harm, darling. But did they not teach you of the proprieties at Mrs. Medlock's? Of common sense, for heaven's sake! You must know better than to go down to the shore in the middle of the night. Why, there could have been any sort of criminals about! Not to mention what could have happened to your reputation."

"I know, I know! It was silly of me, I know, but when Mr. Seward said something about a treasure, I simply had to see it. It was just like *Secrets of a Windswept Sea.*"

Caroline knew then that she was going to have to go through Phoebe's chamber and dispose of every horrid novel. She pressed a handkerchief into Phoebe's trembling hand, and said, "You must never leave a party, or anyplace else, without telling me first. I was very worried."

"But I was not *alone* with Mr. Seward, Caro! Miss Bellweather was with us." At Caroline's stern glance, Phoebe subsided again, and said meekly, "I promise I will not do it again."

"I do hope not. You know that Wycombe is a very small place, darling. It would never do to have people think you are, well, less than proper. A young lady's reputation is so very important, you know."

Phoebe wiped at her eyes and nodded. "I know you are depending on me, Caro, and I will not fail you. I would never do anything to demean our family."

"I know you would not. Just, please, be very careful in the future. Especially where Mr. Seward is concerned." Caroline leaned over to kiss Phoebe's cheek, then gave her a reassuring pat on the hand. "Now, why don't you go upstairs and wash your face? Perhaps we could go out for ices this afternoon."

Phoebe smiled. "I would like that," she said, and left the room quickly, obviously relieved that the scolding was over.

When she was gone, Caroline tucked her left foot beneath her right knee on the settee and rubbed at the scar on her ankle wearily. How very complicated chaperonage was! Not at all as simple and enjoyable as she had thought it was going to be. Never could she have imagined a scene such as the one she faced last night.

She closed her eyes as she recalled rushing down to the shore with Lord Lyndon and the hysterical Phoebe. The sight of Mr. Seward flailing about with his hand caught between some rocks, shrieking fit to raise the dead, had been so very comical she had had to fight to keep from laughing aloud.

Worse, she had seen the same sort of repressed laughter on Lord Lyndon's face as he worked to free his brother's hand.

She *did* laugh now, alone in her drawing room, at the memory of that absurd tableau.

But she knew very well that it would not have been in the least comical if the entire company had witnessed the scene. No, it would have been very embarrassing, and it would surely have given rise to gossip.

Thank the stars for Sarah Bellweather. She was certainly a cool and calculating thinker, unlike her silly mother. She had concocted a plan for Lyndon to slip his brother up the back stairs and get him tidied up before taking him back to the party, and for Caroline and Phoebe to go back home through the garden. She then told the guests that Phoebe had a terrible headache, and her sister was now taking her home after she had spent an hour in the retiring room with Sarah. Crisis neatly averted.

Phoebe was lucky to have a friend like Sarah, if she was going to insist on being so featherheaded.

But would the next disaster be so easy to avoid?

Caroline rubbed her hand on her ankle. Running the Golden Feather had never been as complicated as this.

Mary came into the room, interrupting Caroline's whirling thoughts.

"There's a caller, madam," she said, waving the silver tray that held one card.

A caller was the last thing Caroline wanted to deal with just then. She had far too many things to worry about as it was without having to make polite conversation over tea.

She supposed she had to be civil, though, if she wanted to be accepted into the center of Wycombe's little society.

"Who is it, Mary?" she asked, swinging her foot back to the floor and smoothing her skirt over her legs.

"It's that Lord Lyndon," Mary sniffed. "The one that came to call in London."

"Mary!" Caroline cried, horrified. "You aren't supposed to even mention London. What if he heard you?"

"He could hardly hear me, madam. He's out on the doorstep."

"You left Lord Lyndon out on the doorstep!"

"Well, where else was I to put him? There's no foyer to speak of in this little place."

"Show him in, Mary, at once. And have some tea sent in, as well."

"Very good, madam."

Mary left in a huff, and soon reappeared with Lord Lyndon behind her. He seemed none the worse for having been left standing on the doorstep. "Lord Lyndon, madam," Mary announced, then promptly ran off again.

Caroline smiled at him, hoping that her hair was not mussed. She had scarce had time to even look in a mirror all day. "Good afternoon, Lord Lyndon. Won't you please be seated?"

"Thank you, Mrs. Aldritch." He sat down in a chair placed directly in a beam of sunlight, and Caroline saw that his face looked rather pale and drawn, as if he had not slept much last night.

He looked as weary as she felt.

"I have come to apologize for my brother's behavior," he said.

"Apologize? Oh, Lord Lyndon, it is hardly your

fault that your brother did something . . . less than advisable."

"I feel that it was. I knew that Harry's behavior of late has been quite unpredictable, and I failed to keep a strict eye on him last night. As a result, your evening was ruined, and things could have ended much worse."

"The evening was hardly *ruined*," she protested. "I had a delightful time at your mother's party. And if you are to blame for not watching your brother, then I am also to blame for failing to watch Phoebe." Caroline realized then that what she was saying was true. After a long night of self-recrimination, she saw that she could not possibly be responsible for every action of Phoebe's. Any more than her parents could have been responsible for Caroline, once upon a time. "We are not their nursemaids."

"That is true." He nodded slowly, obviously still not completely convinced. "I would still like to say I am sorry, though, and promise you that it will not happen again. I gave Harry a scolding this morning. One that I hope he will not soon forget."

"Apology accepted, then, if it will make you feel better. And I also gave Phoebe a few things to think about. I am just glad that the smugglers did not appear last night! Now that would have ruined the party in truth."

Lord Lyndon laughed. "As to that, I can assure you that there was never any danger of smugglers showing up."

"Really?"

"Really. Harry told me he made up the entire corker about smugglers' treasure just to impress the young ladies."

Caroline stared at him, feeling laughter of her own bubbling up. "He . . . made it all up?"

"I fear so."

"The rascal!" She did laugh then; she could not seem to help it. The whole thing was so richly absurd. "Phoebe would be so angry if she knew. She truly feared for Mr. Seward's life."

"Oh, his life was never in any danger, though he certainly carried on as if it were. I hope this entire situation has taught him a lesson."

"I am sure it has." Caroline wiped at her laughter-damp eyes.

"And now I can come to the second, and much more pleasant, reason for this visit."

She looked up at him curiously. "A second reason, Lord Lyndon?"

"Yes. Mother wanted to see the Roman ruins outside of town and is organizing a picnic there tomorrow. The Bellweathers are coming, and Mother and I thought you might care to accompany us as well."

Hmm. Another invitation. Caroline felt a warm, satisfied, nervous feeling blossom deep inside of her. What could it all mean? Was it simply Lady Lyndon being kind to the daughters of her old friend? Or could it possibly be something more? Could the invitation be Lord Lyndon's idea? Could he . . . admire her?"

She forced down a silly giggle, and studied him closely, searching for any signs of admiration at all.

Sadly, he merely looked polite.

"I have heard the ruins are quite picturesque," she said.

"Indeed. I believe they are an ancient bathhouse and villa, or at least parts of them."

"I take it Mr. Seward will be along, as well."

"If he is not sulking in his room, yes. But you need have no fear that he will lure your sister away, Mrs. Aldritch. I promise you that I will tie him to the picnic hamper if I have to."

"Then you do not think he will suddenly discover ancient *Roman* smugglers' treasure?" she teased.

Lord Lyndon gave a startled laugh at her little joke. "Let us hope not."

"Then I should like to go, and I am sure Phoebe will as well."

"We shall call for you tomorrow morning at ten, then, if that would be convenient."

"I will look forward to it."

Oh, yes, I certainly will, her mind whispered.

Chapter Thirteen

Mrs. Aldritch looked most lovely in the afternoon sun. Like a portrait of a fairy queen examining her forest domain.

Justin shook his head ruefully at his fantastical thoughts. He had never been at all prone to being poetical, had always scorned men who went about spouting verses about ladies' eyelashes and such.

But he had to admit that if he *were* to start composing rhymes, Mrs. Aldritch would be a most delightful inspiration.

She sat on a large, flat rock overlooking the villa ruins, watching her sister and Miss Bellweather scurry about, examining the mosaic floor. She held a white, lacy parasol over her head, and the sun filtered through the patterns of the lace, casting shifting shadows on her face and the skirt of her sky-blue gown.

The short waves of her pale hair, though bound back neatly with a wide blue ribbon, shifted and shimmered in the breeze.

But her expression was far too serious for such a beautiful day, such a fetching pose. She was frowning a bit, her gaze far away even as she looked at the girls. She looked as if she did not see the pretty scene before her at all, but something invisible to everyone else.

Something worrisome.

He had the strongest urge to go to her, to take her hand and make her tell him what it was that worried her. He wanted to erase that frown and hear her laugh again, as she had when he told her of Harry's fib. She had a wonderful laugh, warm and rich, though seemingly a bit rusty from misuse.

It appeared that whatever her life had been since Larry Aldritch died, it had not involved much laughter. She usually looked much as she did now, worried and distant.

Justin found it brought out the latent white knight in him. The one with the irresistible urge to make unhappy fair damsels smile.

She looked up and saw him watching her. A smile *did* appear on her lips, albeit a small one, and her brow smoothed.

"Lord Lyndon," she called, "is it not a fine day?"

"Lovely," he answered, coming forward to sit down on the grass at her feet. He stretched out his legs along the ground, enjoying the warmth of the sun.

"I cannot thank you enough for inviting us today. Phoebe looks much better in the fresh air. I feared she would never quit crying yesterday."

"And Harry looks much chastened." Justin gestured toward where Harry sat with his mother, Lady Bellweather, and the two younger Bellweather girls. Harry was apparently meant to be minding the girls while the ladies gossiped, and he held a large wax doll on his knee while one of the girls gave it tea from a tiny cup.

"Well, playing with dolls will do that to a man,

I suppose," she said wryly, whirling her parasol about by its carved handle.

"It is good for him. And those girls are absolute tartars; if anyone can keep him out of trouble, they can."

"Let us hope so." She turned her gaze back to her sister, the frown returning. "Phoebe is so very . . . lively. I do not want to curb her spirit, but I fear what trouble she may run into."

Justin nodded in deepest understanding. He felt exactly the same about Harry.

He glanced over at his brother and saw that Harry was watching Miss Lane again, his face full of longing. Justin knew that Harry fancied himself quite in love with her already, and certainly Justin was tempted to hand Harry and all his problems over to the care of a wife.

The only problem was that Miss Lane appeared to be every bit as prone to flights of fancy as Harry was. With her as a sister-in-law, Justin would not be solving his troubles; he would just be doubling them.

It was the very devil being the responsible one.

Mrs. Aldritch looked at him, her expression startled, and Justin realized with chagrin that he had spoken aloud.

He opened his mouth to apologize, but she forestalled him by saying, "It *is* the very devil, isn't it?"

Justin nodded. "When I was younger, I never dreamed I would be in this situation. Father and Edward, my older brother, took care of everything. Edward was just like Father—always steady and reliable, always getting me out of scrapes. Then they died."

"And you found yourself as the earl."

"Yes. With Harry to contend with. I know Mother wants me to solve everything for her, as Father did—be the 'head of the family.' But I lived alone for so long in India. I am not used to worrying about other people."

He looked down at the grass, suddenly ashamed at his outpouring of words to a near stranger. It was not seemly for an earl to appear unsure, and Mrs. Aldritch must be bored to hear him ramble on of his troubles.

But she didn't look bored. Her dark eyes watched him sympathetically, and she leaned toward him as if to hear all his words. He felt so very *comfortable* with her, felt he could tell her anything, and she would not judge as other people would. He felt as if he knew her.

She nodded. "Phoebe and I also lived apart for a long time. She was at school after our parents died, and I was with Lawrence, and then . . . then with relatives. I fear I concocted a perfect sister in my mind, one who was dutiful and obedient and always cheerful." She laughed humorlessly, mocking herself. "Things have not turned out the way I planned! Phoebe has her own way of doing things."

"That could describe Harry perfectly. His own way of doing things." Justin watched as Harry walked over to where Miss Lane and Miss Bellweather were still exploring the villa, the two little Bellweather girls tripping along behind him. He said something to Phoebe, who nodded, shook her head, then laughed. "My brother obviously admires your sister."

"Yes. But Phoebe is too young yet to be married."

"So is Harry. I wonder if a time in India might not be good for him, as it was for me."

"India?" Mrs. Aldritch tilted her head, looking on as Phoebe hauled one of the children up into her arms and twirled her about, the two of them giggling merrily. "You mustn't say anything about India in front of Phoebe. She would get visions of ivory palaces and rubies as big as hens' eggs into her head, and she would marry Mr. Seward just to go see them."

"At least if they were in India we wouldn't *know* what they were up to," Justin suggested. "Out of sight, out of mind?"

Mrs. Aldritch laughed, the worry fleeing from her face like the clouds from the sun.

Phoebe turned to look at them at the sound of that laughter, and waved. "Caro!" she called. "Do come and see these mosaics Miss Bellweather has been showing us. Those Romans were ever so naughty. Why didn't they teach us this at Mrs. Medlock's?"

Mrs. Aldritch waved back, then looked at Justin, one golden brow arched inquiringly. "Shall we join them, then, Lord Lyndon?"

"Of course." He leaped to his feet and held out his hand to help her rise from the rock. "I confess myself quite fascinated by, er, naughty Romans."

The "naughty" Roman mosaics were indeed fascinating, and quite extensive. Before Caroline realized it, they had left the others behind and found themselves in a quiet glade of trees. The green branches arched over the ruined tile floor, enclosing it in a thick silence.

Only the muted murmur of distant voices, the whisper of the wind through the leaves, and the click of their shoe heels on the tile reminded her that she was still in the real, human world. She felt as if she had fallen into some enchanted realm.

She lowered her parasol and stepped carefully over the cracked mosaic, acutely conscious of Justin close behind her. After their conversation, she felt strangely intimate toward him, bound in silken cords of understanding. She knew she could grow to understand him very well indeed, and he her.

That was a dangerous feeling. She could not afford to let him, or anyone else, truly know her. Truly know what her life had been about. It was a very lonely feeling.

Caroline stabbed at one of the tiles with the tip of her parasol. Well, she had been lonely for many years now; nothing would be different. She would just go on as before.

Justin knelt down beside her to examine part of the mosaic, interrupting her increasingly maudlin thoughts. "I cannot be sure, of course," he said, "but I do believe this scene is not quite as naughty as the others."

Caroline leaned over, pushing some of the tiles into place. "I believe you are right. It looks like a supper scene. See these grapes here. The colors are so vivid! As lovely as if they had been made yesterday."

"Lovely," he murmured. He was so close, his breath whispered coolly across her cheek.

Caroline pulled back, startled. She had not realized she had leaned so near to him.

She looked at him warily, to find that he watched her with equally startled eyes.

"Where did you come from, Mrs. Aldritch?" he whispered.

Oh, dear Lord, he knew. He recognized her; he knew the truth. It could be the only explanation for his astounded look. She fell back a step, away from him.

"C-come from?" she said. "Whatever do you mean?"

He shook his head in a bemused way, as if to clear it. "I am sorry. It must be this place, it seems so . . . otherworldly. You just don't seem quite like everyone else. Not quite human."

Caroline was confused. What did otherworldly glades have to do with gaming hells? "Not . . . human?" she said.

He laughed self-mockingly. "Now I have insulted you. Please believe me, Mrs. Aldritch, that is the last thing I would want to do. It is just that earlier I fancied you looked like a fairy queen, examining her domain. You seem to belong here, with the trees and the sky."

Caroline's tense shoulders slowly relaxed. Did this mean that he did *not* recognize her? She sat down on a crumbling old marble bench. "My mother used to say I was her changeling child. No one else in our family has such pale hair and such dark eyes."

"Perhaps that is it." He sat down next to her on the bench. "You must forgive me, Mrs. Aldritch. I promise you I am not generally prone to such flights of fancy, and I never speak to people I have just met in such a way. I think I must still have some of India in my blood. There *everything* seemed otherworldly, fraught with spirits."

"What is there to forgive?" Caroline answered,

with a small laugh. "Most people see me as a dull old matron now, as Phoebe's chaperon. I would much rather be a fairy queen."

"And that you are," he said, still looking at her with that bemused expression on his face. "That you are."

He looked as if he wanted to say something more, but a burst of chattering voices interrupted them. Phoebe, Sarah, Harry, and the two little girls came hurrying en masse into the glade.

"There you are, Caro!" Phoebe cried. "We feared you had fallen through these old floors or something. Lady Lyndon says we must hurry if we want our sweets."

"Yes," said Sarah, "or my mother will surely eat them *all*."

Caroline gave Justin one last smile, then went to take Phoebe's arm and go with her out of the glade. "Of course, darling. We were just enjoying the cool shade here."

"Oh, my dears," Lady Lyndon sighed, leaning back under the shade of the trees. "I cannot remember when I last had such a splendid afternoon."

Caroline had to agree with her. The afternoon had indeed been splendid. New friends, good food, sunshine—and Lord Lyndon.

She looked over to where he sat with Harry, Phoebe, and Sarah Bellweather, playing a game of Beggar My Neighbor with them. The afternoon breeze kept lifting the cards from the blanket, and he caught at them, laughing. A lock of sun-burnished hair fell across his forehead, and as he reached up to brush it back he caught her watching him.

He smiled at her, and his face, weather lined as it was from the Indian sun, looked endearingly boyish.

She could not help but smile back.

Then he turned away from her, back to the game.

"Would you tell me more about your mother, Mrs. Aldritch?" Lady Lyndon said, reaching for the last of the berry tarts. "After she married your father and I married Lord Lyndon, I fear we rather lost touch. I did receive a letter announcing your birth, and I sent one when each of my boys were born, but that was all."

"Mother was not much of a letter writer," Caroline answered. "We lived so quietly in the country that she feared to bore all her friends with her news."

"Now, that could never have been! Dear Margery was never dull. Your sister rather reminds me of her." They watched as Phoebe won the last of Harry's cards and crowed over her victory.

"Phoebe does look a great deal like Mother," Caroline answered uncertainly. She remembered her mother as being always quiet and proper, not vivid and crackling with energy as Phoebe was.

"As do you, Mrs. Aldritch," said Lady Lyndon. "When I heard of your birth, I must say I harbored a little dream that one day, when you were older, you would come to see me in London. I never had a daughter, you know, and I did so long for one. And you would meet Edward, my eldest, and then . . ." Her voice faded away, and she gave Caroline an embarrassed little smile. "But that was silly of me. I am very glad we have met *now*. Very glad indeed.''

Caroline was surprised, and very touched, by her words. "I am glad we have met, too, Lady Lyndon."

"Then, my dear, perhaps you would like to accompany us to a concert on Saturday evening? It is a program of Renaissance songs. Not to everyone's liking, perhaps, but it should be quite fine.''

Caroline remembered long evenings when she had been alone, Lawrence off heaven knew where, and her only solace was in volumes of poetry by Sir Phillip Sidney and Edmund Spenser. "I adore Renaissance songs.''

"Do you? So does Justin. You will both have to explain the songs to me, then. And the next week there is a large assembly planned. You will have to go with us to that, as well. I intend to enjoy your company as long as I can.''

Caroline glanced back at Justin. An evening of music and then an assembly in his company—this summer just grew better and better.

She let a small, hopeful feeling into her heart, as she had never dared to before.

Then Lady Bellweather came back from where she examined the mosaics with her younger daughters, and the littlest one sat down on Caroline's lap to show her her doll. All romantic fantasies were lost in the immediate practicalities of getting the doll's tiny boot laced up properly.

Chapter Fourteen

Two days after the picnic excursion, Caroline found herself standing on a dock, staring at a large, bobbing boat.

It is a yacht, she reminded herself. *Not a boat—a yacht.*

But no matter what it was called, it looked terribly precarious, rolling with the waves that slapped at its wooden sides. And she was meant to be climbing aboard for a pleasure excursion.

Pleasure? Ha!

Whatever had she been thinking when she agreed to this? She was not a good sailor at all, and just watching the pitch of the boat—yacht—was making her feel a bit queasy.

Of course you know why you agreed to this outing, her blasted, ever-present inner voice whispered. *It is because the Sewards are the ones who invited you.*

One Seward in particular.

Lord Lyndon. Justin.

She had thought about him a great deal since the picnic, gone over all their conversations, every glance that had passed between them. She felt a bit like a silly schoolgirl, prostrate with calf-love for the music master. She wanted to see him again, talk to him some more, maybe have another moment alone with him.

All of which was a very bad idea. The more she saw him, talked to him, the more she liked him. And the more she felt guilty about deceiving him.

But she could not seem to stay away today. Even if it did mean she had to get on the boat.

"Caro, isn't this fascinating?" Phoebe called, coming around a corner with the grizzled captain of the yacht. She looked jauntily nautical in a blue-and-white dress and matching bonnet. "Captain Jones was just showing me how the boat is moored, and he says I can help steer once we are aboard."

"That is very kind of Captain Jones, Phoebe," Caroline answered with a smile. "I just hope you will not run us aground."

"Of course I shan't! Captain Jones says I am a real sea spaniel."

"Sea *dog*, miss," the old captain corrected.

"Yes, of course! Sea dog." Phoebe looked about happily at the boat and the water, completely in her element.

Caroline hoped her sister would not take it into her head now to find some Navy man and elope with him. Or worse, disguise herself and join the Navy in her own right!

These ruminations were cut short by the sound of Harry Seward calling, "Hallo! Mrs. Aldritch, Miss Lane, you are here already."

Caroline turned to see Harry, Justin, Lady Lyndon, and Sarah Bellweather coming toward them, all of them outfitted for a sea jaunt. Harry carried a large hamper, trying to balance it and wave at the same time.

Phoebe rushed over to greet them, and Caroline followed at a slower pace. Her gaze met Justin's, and he gave her a small smile.

Her breath caught at that small, secret curve of his lips, and she smiled at him in return. She could not seem to help herself.

"The water looks calm today," he said.

Caroline glanced doubtfully at the still-lapping waves. "Do you think so?"

Justin laughed. "Not much of a sailor, eh, Mrs. Aldritch?"

"I'm not sure. I have not had much opportunity for sailing."

"Well, I shall help you, then," he said, a teasing twinkle in his blue eyes. "I often went out on the river in India. I won't let you fall overboard."

Was he *flirting* with her? Caroline looked at him, at his half smile. It had been so long since she had indulged in harmless, lighthearted flirtation that she could scarce remember how it was done.

Finally, she smiled, took his proffered arm, and let him help her climb aboard the waiting yacht. They sat down on a bench near the railing and watched as Phoebe, Harry, and Sarah scrambled onto the deck, laughing and chattering boisterously. Phoebe rushed over to climb up on a coiled pile of rope, pointing and exclaiming over something in the water below.

Harry looked at her with a rapt expression on his face.

Lady Lyndon sat down beside Caroline and Justin on the bench, settling her mulberry-colored skirts about her. "Oh, my dears," she sighed, "I feel so very old just watching them. Was I ever so enthusiastic?"

Caroline nodded in agreement. Once she would

have dashed about just like Phoebe, bursting with the joy, the glee, the possibility of life. But years and experience had killed that feeling, had left her feeling numb. Like an old woman.

Now Justin's arm brushed against hers as he leaned forward to retrieve something from the hamper. And the cold, hard knot at the core of her seemed to burst open, releasing that old joyful feeling again. She almost laughed aloud with the delightful surprise of it.

Then the boat began to move, and she was jolted against his arm. She clutched at his sleeve with her hand, catching the smooth wool in her fist.

Justin's other arm came around to steady her, and she found herself in an almost embrace with him. Everything else, the people, the sea, the rocking of the boat, faded around her. She only saw him.

She looked up at his face, so near hers, and wondered dazedly if his lips were as soft as they looked.

Justin wished, as he had never wished for anything before in his life, that he was alone with Mrs. Aldritch.

He was acutely conscious of every move she made, every word she said. He waited eagerly for every time she would tilt up her head and he could see her face beneath the brim of her lavender silk-lined bonnet.

She laughed at something his mother said, her head at a slight angle that caused one pale strand of hair to brush against her cheek.

It made him want to laugh, as well, even though he had no idea what they were talking of.

Then he heard his mother's words.

". . . and there he was, running down the drive without a stitch on, while his nursemaid chased after him."

Oh, dear Lord. Was she telling that old story about the time he was three years old and went dashing about in the altogether again?

She must be. Mrs. Aldritch was looking at him with mirth sparkling in her dark eyes, one lavender-gloved hand pressed over her mouth, holding in her laughter.

His mother continued. "And all the tenants were walking home from the farm at that hour. I would vow that every single one of them saw that tiny dimple just above—"

"Mother!" Justin interrupted desperately, "I am sure you must be boring Mrs. Aldritch with my childhood exploits. Not to mention how improper it is."

Caroline took her hand away from her mouth and said, "I found it to be an extremely diverting story, Lord Lyndon. Extremely diverting, indeed."

"And you are not one to be lecturing about propriety, Justin," his mother added. "That is the *least* of the stories I could tell about you, my dear. Why, there was the time you and young Harry broke into the wine cellar. . . ."

Justin had the unhappy feeling that this talebearing could go on for hours. He wanted Caroline Aldritch to like him, to be impressed by him. Not think he was some wild 'un who always ran about without his clothes as a child.

He stood up quickly and said, "I do believe you expressed an interest in seeing the, er, wheel, Mrs. Aldritch." Is that what they called the steering mechanism of yachts? A wheel? Justin certainly hoped so. He couldn't afford to look any more foolish.

She looked up at him quizzically, with a half smile that said she knew exactly what he was doing. "Did I? Yes. I would like to see the, er, wheel."

With a last word for his mother, she rose and took his arm, allowing him to lead her along the deck. They went past the three young people, who were watching one of the sailors demonstrate knot making, and stopped in the relatively quiet stern.

Caroline leaned her arms on the rail and looked down at the water below. "You are not fooling me one bit, you know," she said, laughter still lingering in her voice.

Justin also leaned on the rail, inches away from her. "Not fooling you about what?"

"I never asked to see any wheels. You merely did not want me to hear any more of your childhood exploits."

"Guilty as charged," he admitted blithely. "They cannot be very amusing to anyone but my mother."

"Oh, no. I found them vastly amusing."

"Then it is not fair. No one is here to tell tales of *your* childhood, Mrs. Aldritch."

"Indeed not. Phoebe is so much younger that she does not recall much. And a good thing it is, too. I had a dull country childhood."

"Nothing about you could possibly be dull," he said, without thinking.

She looked at him from beneath her bonnet, her expression unreadable. "On the contrary. I am very dull, I assure you." Then she turned from him, leaning her back against the railing while she watched her sister.

Justin sensed her drawing away, pulling back inside herself. He wanted desperately to bring her back, to bring back the lightly teasing woman. But he did not know how.

So he said, "My mother told me she invited you to the concert with us on Saturday."

"Yes. I hope that is quite all right?"

"Certainly. I look forward to it."

"Phoebe is very excited. She has already changed her plans for her ensemble four times!"

"And you, Mrs. Aldritch? Are you excited about the concert?"

She turned back to look at him, but before she could reply a chilly wind swept across the deck, pushing back her bonnet. She clutched at the silk brim and looked about worriedly.

Justin only then noticed that the sky, so blue when they set out, had become overcast. He had been so engrossed in talking with Mrs. Aldritch that everything else had faded about him.

Now he saw the captain coming toward them, trailed by his mother, Harry, Miss Lane, and Miss Bellweather. "It looks as if we might be in for a bit of a shower, my lord," he said. "Might be best if you all went below for a while."

"Is it dangerous?" Mrs. Aldritch asked in a tight voice.

"Not at all, ma'am," the captain answered. "We just wouldn't want you to be getting damp."

Justin offered her his arm again and said in what he hoped was a reassuring tone, "I am sure it is nothing at all, Mrs. Aldritch. Let us go down below, and we can have our luncheon."

She nodded and smiled, but her grasp was hard on his arm.

*   *   *

Caroline did not like this one bit.

It was not a real storm, but the soft sound of rain falling on the deck underlay the merry chatter of the party. The boat rocked gently, causing wine and lemonade to slosh against the sides of glasses.

Her stomach wouldn't allow her to partake of the picnic luncheon spread across a table, and she feared her smile at the others' sallies was rather strained. She had no desire to ruin their fine time, so she was very glad when Phoebe suggested a diversion.

Even if that diversion was a game of cards.

Caroline watched warily as Harry dug a pack of cards from the bottom of the hamper and shuffled them deftly. Just the sight of the brightly colored pasteboards brought back unwelcome memories of the Golden Feather.

She steeled herself against those memories now and forced herself to smile as if she had not a care in the world. *You survived Lady Lyndon's card party,* she told herself sternly. *You will survive this.*

But the card party had felt somewhat different. There had been so very many people about, all of them eminently respectable, and there had been no stakes. This was more intimate, just her, Lord Lyndon, Harry, Phoebe, and Sarah seated around a table, while Lady Lyndon watched.

She felt absurdly as if all eyes were on her, judging, waiting for her to slip.

Then she laughed inwardly at herself. No one was watching her at all! Indeed, Harry and Phoebe were so busy giggling at each other that *they* saw nothing else.

Caroline lightly touched the pile of cards, and said, "What shall we play, then? Whist?"

"Oh, no!" Phoebe cried. "That is far too stodgy for being among friends. Let us play Speculation."

"Jolly good!" said Harry. "I shall be dealer." He proceeded to pass out three cards to each player, then put the card to trump faceup in the center.

And, as Caroline looked down at the cards in her hand, the old coolness she had once known when she played dealer at the Golden Feather stole over her again. It was unbidden and unwelcome, but she knew only one thing—she wanted to win.

Justin watched in wonder as Mrs. Aldritch once again produced the highest trump and took the pot. He thought he had never seen a woman so intent on a friendly game of Speculation before, or so good at strategy and winning. She would stop at nothing to secure the trump card!

"Oh, Caro, you win again," Phoebe said with a laugh. "How very unfair! I had no idea what a cardsharper you are."

Caroline froze in the act of collecting her winnings, her hands suddenly still. She looked at her sister as if she had never seen her before.

"What did you say, Phoebe?" she said quietly.

"I said I had no idea what a cardsharper you are! Why, you have trounced us all. I vow I will never play a quiet game of piquet with you in the evening again."

Phoebe's tone was blithe, but Caroline looked oddly stricken. Justin watched, puzzled, as she pulled her hands back as if burned. She stood up suddenly, her face pale.

"What is the matter, Caro?" Phoebe asked, her bright smile turning to a worried frown. "Are you ill?"

"It is very warm in here," said Justin's mother. "Do you feel faint, my dear?"

Justin rose beside Caroline, reaching out a hand to steady her as she swayed a bit. "Let me pour you some wine, Mrs. Aldritch."

She turned to him as if startled to see him there. "Oh, no, thank you. I-I think I just need some air. If you all will excuse me for a moment."

"Shall I come with you?" Phoebe said, laying down her own cards on the table.

"Oh, no, Phoebe dear. Stay here and enjoy yourself." Caroline gave a vague smile and turned to climb the stairs back to the deck.

Amelia came to Justin and whispered in his ear, "Perhaps you should go with her, Justin. She does not look well."

He nodded and went to follow her up the stairs.

She stood beneath the eaves of the cabin, watching the light rain that still fell. She rubbed at her arms, as if chilled beneath the thin muslin of her lavender-and-white gown, but she didn't seem to notice her actions. Indeed, she didn't seem to notice anything as she stared out at the deck.

Justin removed his coat and slid it over her shoulders.

She started a bit, as if surprised to see him. Then she gave him a regretful, grateful little smile and drew the warm wool of the coat closer about her.

"How foolish you must think me," she murmured.

"Not at all," he answered. "It was rather close in there."

"I don't know what came over me. I suddenly did not feel like myself." She closed her eyes and took a deep breath, turning her face into the brisk breeze. Little droplets of water clung to her eyelashes and cheeks.

Justin wanted to brush them away, to touch the ivory of her cheek and see if it was as soft as it appeared. Instead, he took her arm through the layers of his coat and her gown and led her to one of the benches.

As they sat down there, out of the rain, he had a sudden idea as to what had brought on her odd behavior. "It was the cards, wasn't it?" he said.

"What!" She drew away from him, looking at him with wide eyes. "The cards?"

"Yes. I knew Larry, remember? I know he had . . . difficulties controlling his card playing."

"Oh." She sat back again cautiously. "Perhaps that *was* it."

Justin felt like an utter cad. He should have known that perhaps she disapproved of cards and gambling, even among friends.

And he wondered with a pang if her lovely face would cloud with disapproval if she ever found out what a rake he himself had been, so long ago.

He did not know!

For one agonizing instant, Caroline had feared he knew the truth. When he asked her if it was the cards that had bothered her, she had been sure he had guessed.

She had been very silly to get so caught up in the game. At the Golden Feather, winning had been her business, and she took her games there very seriously indeed. Today, for a brief while, she had forgotten that her life was different now. A friendly game of cards was just that.

She looked at Justin, at his handsome, worried, admiring face. It would be terrible to see that admiration turn to disgust at the truth.

She would not be so foolish as to forget herself again.

"Tell me more about this concert we are to attend on Saturday," she forced herself to say lightly. "I am so looking forward to it."

Chapter Fifteen

" 'When Nature made her chief work, Stella's eyes, In color black, why wrapp'd she beams so bright? Would she in beamy black, like painter wise, Frame daintiest lustre, mix'd of shades and light?' "

As the soprano sang out, Justin looked down at the woman who sat beside him, her brown eyes cast down to read her program, and reflected that the words could have been written about her.

As indeed could all the songs, a cycle based on Sir Phillip Sidney's *Astrophil and Stella*. Mrs. Aldritch was very like Stella, the star—beautiful, elegant, remote, and out of reach. Every time he thought he began to understand her, like at the picnic, she slid out of his grasp again. Like on the yacht.

She slowly raised her "beamy black" eyes to look at the soprano, and he was surprised to see that they were suspiciously bright. Her lips moved gently, molding around the words.

The program trembled in her gloved hands.

She was obviously in a world of her own, made of the beauty of the language and the imagery of perfect, elusive love.

" 'Both so and thus, she minding Love should be
Placed ever there, gave him this mourning weed,
To honor all their deaths, who for her bleed.' "

The soprano finished her song amid applause and
stepped back for an intermission.

Mrs. Aldritch wiped quickly at her cheeks with
the tips of her fingers and smiled at him. "Is the
music not beautiful?"

"Exquisite," he said, meaning more than just
the music.

"I have never heard the poems set to music before, but it is very well done. It suits the words
well."

"You know *Astrophil and Stella*, then?"

"Oh, yes! I used to—" She broke off with a
strange little laugh. "That is, when I was younger
I had a great deal of time for reading. Sidney was
a favorite."

Justin grinned at her. "You mean you did not
prefer *Henrietta's Revenge*, as your sister does?"

She grinned back. "I fear not. I have tried to tell
her that Shakespeare and Sidney are full of the
things she loves to read about, but she does not
believe me."

"You mean revenge, curses, and star-crossed
love?"

"Indeed. You are familiar with the Elizabethans,
then, Lord Lyndon?"

"I will tell you a secret, Mrs. Aldritch. I read
them at Cambridge, and adored them. But I did it
secretly. It would never have done for the dons to
know; it would have ruined my reputation as a n'er-
do-well."

She laughed. "Heaven forbid! Then, tell me,

which of the *Astrophil* poems do you prefer? I like 'Some lovers speak, when they their muses entertain.' "

Justin thought for a moment, then, gazing steadily into her eyes, quoted, " 'A strife is grown between Virtue and Love, While each pretends that Stella must be his: Her eyes, her lips, her all, saith Love, do this, Since they do wear his badge, most firmly prove.' "

She watched him with wide, dark eyes, and whispered, " 'But Virtue thus that title doth disprove, that Stella—' "

" 'O dear name that Stella is That virtuous soul, sure heir of heav'nly bliss.' "

They looked at each other in silence, all the chatter and activity around them fading away, leaving them alone on an island of poetry and silence.

Then she broke the spell by giving a small smile, and saying, "Oh, my. You *do* have hidden depths, Lord Lyndon."

"I could say the same of you, Mrs. Aldritch," he answered.

"Indeed you could," she murmured, looking back down at the program. "Indeed you could."

Justin's mother leaned over, from where she sat on Justin's other side. "My dears," she said, "do tell me what is meant when the song says 'Till that good god make church and churchmen starve.' It sounds most unpleasant."

Mrs. Aldritch also leaned forward and launched into a most erudite explanation of Neoplatonic theory. But he heard not a word of it. Her hair brushed against his throat as she leaned forward, and a scent, sweet and exotic at the same time, floated up to him. Jasmine, he thought, breathing it in deeply.

How it reminded him of India! Of warm, thick nights, filled with the rich scent of this same flower and dry earth, and with the sounds of music and chanting.

It suited her perfectly.

Caroline tried to pay strict attention to the singer when the music resumed, but although the song was lovely, her mind kept drifting.

To the man beside her.

His warmth seemed to reach out and curl around her; the scent of his soap was clean and spicy. Every once in a while, as he turned over a page in his program or leaned to whisper a word to his mother, his arm and shoulder would brush against her. The superfine of his sleeve touched, just barely, the half inch of bare skin between her glove and her puffed muslin sleeve; then it slid away.

Caroline opened her painted silk fan and waved it in front of her face, disarranging her carefully made curls. Really, they should ventilate the concert rooms better!

And she should stop mooning over Lord Lyndon. She was far too old to be behaving like a love-struck schoolgirl; she had more important things to concern herself with.

Such as Phoebe. She looked about until she found her sister, seated at the end of the row with Harry and Sarah. The three of them were whispering and giggling, obviously paying no attention to the music or anything else.

As Caroline watched, Phoebe peeked up at
Harry from beneath her lashes and gave him a flirtatious little smile. Harry blushed and grinned.

Caroline frowned.

When she had hoped for a match for Phoebe in
Wycombe, Harry Seward was not at all what she
had in mind. Far from being a quiet, respectable
vicar or squire, Harry was young and wild. She remembered the fight on her last night at the Golden
Feather, and grimaced.

Life with Harry would not be the secure one
Caroline wanted for her sister.

But then, Phoebe was not exactly quiet herself.
Perhaps no calm squire would have her.

"You are frowning, Mrs. Aldritch," Lord Lyndon
whispered in her ear, his warm breath stirring the
curls at her temple. "Do you disapprove of the
song?"

"Not at all," Caroline answered, with one last
glance at Phoebe. Then she turned back to smile
at him. "It is quite fine."

"But you feel you must keep a stern eye on
your sister."

"Can you blame me?"

"Not at all. I have also been watching Harry. But
I think we need not fear that they will run away
to the shore again. Not after the scoldings we
gave them."

"Indeed not! Phoebe was all that was contrite."

Lord Lyndon gave a small sigh. "As was Harry.
But it is very wearing, is it not, Mrs. Aldritch, to
always have to be the responsible adult?"

Indeed it was. Caroline reflected that if she were
still the reckless, romantic girl she had been before
she wed Lawrence, she would not be sitting here

so quietly. She would be trying to lure Lord Lyndon to the shore.

But that girl was no more. She was buried under the weight of the years of a difficult marriage and the Golden Feather. She had to make certain that Phoebe did not follow the same reckless path she had, and that was all that was important now.

So she just nodded and smiled sympathetically.

Chapter Sixteen

The next several days passed in an idyllic whirl. Caroline and Phoebe spent a great deal of time with the Sewards and the Bellweathers, but they also met many other people in Wycombe for the summer. There were venetian breakfasts, teas, more card parties, a play, a dance, and another, sunnier boating party. There were also warm, convivial afternoons bathing in the sea, and mornings looking in the shops.

There was scarcely time to pause for thought.

But when Caroline *would* have a quiet moment, when bathing or dressing or in bed about to fall asleep, she would think of Justin.

He had been very attentive, sitting beside her at suppers or playing cards at the same table with her (fortunately, there were no more flashbacks to card-playing days at the Golden Feather!). Justin was a charming companion, funny and interesting and always polite.

But he was that way with everyone, from the littlest Bellweather girl to the ancient Lady Ryce. She felt rather foolish wishing, hoping, that his attentions were a mark of admiration for her specifically. Even if they were, she could scarcely afford to encourage them.

That did not mean, though, that she could not dream and imagine, all alone in her room.

And wonder if he would ask her to dance with him at the grand assembly.

The evening of the grand assembly was a very warm one. All the windows in the high-ceilinged assembly rooms were open to admit what little breeze there was, but still the mingled scent of perfumes, flowers, and warm people hung heavy in the air.

Caroline stood close to one of the windows, fanning herself and wishing that her gray silk gown was a little less weighty. She watched as Phoebe, partnered with Harry, moved blithely through the figures of the dance, seemingly immune to the heat in her bright yellow muslin gown. Phoebe's curls, piled fetchingly atop her head and caught with ivory combs, were still crisp, while Caroline feared that her own locks were quite wilted beneath her opal and seed pearl bandeau.

She supposed she really ought to move about, greet the many people she had met under the auspices of Lady Lyndon these last weeks. But the heat, combined with her sleepless night and the thoughts of Justin that caused it, made her feet feel leaden in their satin slippers. Her mind was dull and languid.

She leaned back against the window frame and wished she could go outside and search for some fresh air.

"Would you care for some lemonade, Mrs. Aldritch?" a familiar voice said. The voice that had echoed in her mind all the night before, keeping her awake.

Caroline turned to see Justin standing there, two glasses of the pale yellow liquid in his hands.

He smiled at her tentatively. "I do hope I didn't startle you."

"Oh, no. I was just . . . thinking," she answered, managing to summon up a small smile in return. She took the offered glass and sipped at the cool lemonade gratefully. The tang of it seemed to help clear her mind a bit. "Thank you. This is delicious."

He leaned against the wall beside her, drinking from his own glass. "I always thought that the seaside was meant to be cool. But if I closed my eyes now, I might almost imagine myself in India again."

"It does seem rather foolish of us to truss ourselves up in silk and go out dancing on such an evening," Caroline said with a laugh.

"I do not see you dancing," Justin teased.

"Nor I you. It must be because we are too sensible."

"Unlike our siblings, you mean?"

They watched as Harry and Phoebe skipped down the line of the dance, ending their set with a bow and a curtsy. Phoebe was quickly claimed by her next partner, and Harry went off to sit with his mother and watch Phoebe. The music for the next set, an old-fashioned minuet, struck up.

"I suppose, then," Justin continued, "that since we are so sensible, it would be futile for me to ask you to dance."

Actually, despite the heat, Caroline could think of nothing she would like better. To feel his hand on hers, his grasp at her waist, would be everything she longed for.

Well . . . almost everything.

And it would be so dangerous.

"I fear I must decline," she answered, hoping her tone was light and teasing. "Not that you would make such a poor partner, I'm sure! But I can summon little enthusiasm for the exercise this evening."

"How about a stroll on the terrace, then? Perhaps we could find a breeze out there."

The thought of fresh air, not to mention the thought of Justin at her side, almost alone, was too much temptation to bear.

She gave in to that temptation and nodded. "I would like that, thank you."

Justin placed their empty glasses on a table and offered her his arm. Caroline glanced over to make certain Phoebe was well-occupied, then slid her hand over the soft cloth of his sleeve. She seemed to have no control over her feet; the satin slippers led her inexorably out the doors into the night, even as she told them how foolish they were being, in light of her feelings for Lyndon. It seemed the height of folly to be alone with him in the night.

But they were not entirely alone. A few other couples had come outside in search of a cool breeze and stood along the marble balustrade talking and looking out at the sea. Justin and Caroline walked along until they came to the end of the terrace, where it was quiet and dark, except for the bars of light and faint music that came from the window.

Caroline stepped into the shadows and turned her face to the light breeze from the sea.

"Mother has been saying we should go soon to Waring Castle," Justin said softly.

Caroline looked at him. His face was half in shadow, and he watched the water.

"Your country estate?" she said.

"Yes. She does not want to go; she is quite loath to quit Wycombe. But I have not been to Waring since I returned to England, and it is past time to see to my duty."

"Of course. Will you go soon?"

"Perhaps in a fortnight; not sooner. The Bell-weathers are thinking of going to Brighton then, and Mother won't want to leave while they are still here."

A fortnight. Caroline closed her eyes against the sudden rush of ineffable sadness. In only fourteen days the idyllic summer of picnics, boating, concerts, and suppers would be at an end. Justin and his family would be gone, vanished into their world of duty, and she and Phoebe would be at loose ends again.

She did not want to lose it all, she realized with a fierce pang. She didn't want to lose that feeling of respectability, of belonging that the summer had brought. She didn't want to lose dear Lady Lyndon's friendship, or the chance to laugh at Harry's ridiculous antics, or play at dolls with the little Bell-weather girls.

Above all, she did not want to lose Justin. Their conversations, the times she was in his company, had come to mean so much.

They meant all the world.

She had done what she swore she would never do—she had fallen in love. With Justin. Lord Lyndon. The one man who could expose her for the terrible fraud she was.

"Phoebe and I will . . . will miss you terribly,"

she managed to choke out, when all she really wanted to do was run away and hide, to cry alone like a wounded animal.

"I know that Harry will miss your sister. To be honest, I think he means to make her an offer before we go. But I have been thinking he should go to oversee another estate of ours, Seward Park, and grow up a bit before he takes on such responsibility."

Caroline nodded. "I did fear that. Not that you would send him away, that he would make her an offer."

"Feared?"

"Yes. You are being honest, Lord Lyndon, so I will be as well. Once, all I could have wished for Phoebe would be to marry someone from a family like yours. It would be a great honor for her. But I see now that even though she is of an age to wed, she is too young in her feelings. I would be doing her a great disservice to let her make the same mistake I did."

"You married too young?"

"Oh, yes. So I think you are wise to give Harry some task far away. Phoebe and I will travel for a year, maybe come to London for the Season. Perhaps then, if your brother were to meet us again, things would be different. If you had no objections?"

"How could I? Harry would be lucky to win your sister. Miss Lane is charming." He paused, then went on in an oddly thick voice. "But not quite as charming as you."

Caroline looked up at him, confused. Could he possibly? . . .

No. He could not be feeling the same way she was.

But his gaze was intense as he looked at her, his eyes almost silver in the meager light.

Inside, the orchestra began a waltz, and its lilting strains floated out to them on the night wind.

"Would you care to dance?" he asked.

Wordlessly, Caroline nodded. The heat of the evening no longer seemed to matter, for she craved the warmth of Justin's touch.

He slid his arm about her waist, warm and secure through the silk of her gown. She made the automatic motions of sweeping up her short train in one hand and sliding the other into his.

His fingers closed about hers tightly, and they began to move. Unmindful of anyone who might be watching, they swayed and turned about their small patch of marble.

Closer than was strictly proper, their bodies moved together as if they had been dancing thus for years. His legs brushed against the silk of her skirts, and the fabric clung to him, as Caroline longed to do herself.

Slowly, they twirled to a halt at the edge of the terrace, alone in the darkest shadows. Caroline stared up at him, as breathless as if she had run a mile. Her heart was full, so full she feared it might burst.

He looked down at her, his lips parted as if he were about to say something but could not find the words. Then he *did* find the words.

"Mrs. Aldritch," he whispered, "I do believe I love you."

And Caroline's heart *did* burst. She could feel the tears welling up in her eyes and falling down her cheeks, but she could not let go of him to brush them away. She had been alone, lonely, for so long. She needed his closeness, his touch. Only his. Justin's.

"I think," she whispered back, "that you should call me Caroline."

Caroline, Justin's mind sang. *Caroline, Caroline.* He looked at her in the moonlight and thought he had never seen a more beautiful sight. She almost glowed, as if she were made of the finest marble, the most expensive alabaster.

"Caroline," he whispered. Only that. But all his heart was in that one word.

Caroline.

She must have heard all the ache, all the longing in his voice, for her lips parted in an expression of wonder. "Justin," she whispered. "Justin."

He glanced quickly behind them. Everyone who was on the terrace had gone back inside to join the waltz, but the windows all stood open.

"Walk with me in the garden," he urged.

"I . . ." She looked around uncertainly. "I should look in on Phoebe."

"My mother is no doubt watching her. It will only be for a moment. Please."

She nodded and walked with him down the terrace steps into the small garden adjacent to the sea. Once they were outside the light, he slid his arm about her waist. She leaned against him, her pale hair brushing against the shoulder of his coat.

They stopped beneath the sheltering branches of a tree, and Caroline turned to face him.

"Did I shock you with my words of love?" he asked.

She shook her head. "It has been a long time

since I was shocked by anything. Though I was rather surprised. We have not known each other very long."

"Does that mean that you do not return my feelings? You know you need only say the word and I will bother you no more."

She gave him a little half smile. "Bother me? Silly man. Don't you know that I love you, too?"

Joy unlike any he had ever known blossomed in Justin's tired heart. Joy and another unfamiliar emotion.

Hope.

Hope for the future, for a happy life, a family of his own. With this woman, who was so unlike anyone he had ever met before, all things seemed possible.

In a burst of emotion, he pulled her closer to him and lowered his lips to hers.

Her mouth was soft and cool, and it yielded so sweetly, so perfectly beneath his. He felt her rise up on tiptoes and slide her arms about his shoulders, her fingers tangling in his hair.

The kiss, so gently begun, caught fire. Justin drew her even closer, urged her lips to part under his passion.

She responded, clinging to him, mingling her sighs, her soft moans, with his.

Suddenly, he knew that if they went on this way he would not be able to stop with a kiss. He would not be able to let her go all night.

He pulled away from her slowly and dragged in long, ragged breaths of warm night air. Her forehead fell to his shoulder, and he felt her slim frame tremble under his hands.

He held her away a bit and saw tears on her cheeks, shimmering in the moonlight. "Caroline!" he cried, shocked at this reaction to his kiss. Was he so terribly out of practice, then? "What is wrong?"

She shook her head and wiped away the teardrops with her gloved hand. "It is just that I am so happy. I have never felt this way before, ever. It is too wonderful. Too wonderful to last."

He drew her back against him, holding her very tightly. So tightly he could vow he felt her heart beat against his chest. He rested his cheek against the silk of her hair and closed his eyes.

"Of course it will last," he said firmly. "Of course it will."

Her grip tightened, crushing the fabric of his coat. "Justin, promise me that, no matter what, you will always remember this night, this perfect, perfect night. And remember that I love you with all my heart."

"I shall have to remember it, won't I? To tell our grandchildren someday."

She gave an oddly hysterical little laugh and answered, "Yes." Her voice turned suddenly sad, as if she knew a secret that he did not. "Yes."

Late that night, after the assembly was over and everyone else was abed, Justin sat in his library, staring out the window at the waning moon.

The same moon he had kissed Caroline Aldritch under.

It had been a glorious kiss, the most wonderful, the most intimate of his life. It had felt almost as if he held the very essence of her in his arms and shared himself with her in a way he had never done with anyone else.

And she had seemed to feel it, too. But then she had pulled away, her face sad and strangely bitter.

She said she loved him. But did she then change her mind?

He longed to see her again, right that moment. The wild boy he had once been would have gone to her house and climbed up to her window, demanded to know the truth of what was in her mind, in her heart.

The respectable earl he was now knew he would have to wait until the next day to see her, to talk to her. But it felt like a hundred years until daylight.

Caroline also lay awake in her bed, listening to the distant sounds of the sea whispering through her open window. Her scarred ankle itched, and as she reached down to rub it she thought about the moments in the garden, going over each one carefully, minutely.

They had been the most perfect moments of her life, and she wanted to memorize each one, tuck them close, and hold them forever. For she knew it could not last.

Justin truly loved her. She did believe that. He understood her, understood her struggles, as she understood him. But she could not be with him. Once he knew the truth about the Golden Feather and Mrs. Archer, he would look at her very differently. He might understand the forces that had led her along that path, but he had a family, a title, and a position to uphold.

Yes, he might now be talking about the grand-children they would have together, but he would not be after he found out about her past.

And she knew, as surely as she knew she loved him, that she would have to tell him. Soon. .

Chapter Seventeen

"What shall we do today, Caro?" Phoebe asked, stretching out on a chaise set in a patch of morning sunlight. She looked like a satisfied little cat, lazy after the dancing and talking of the night before.

Caroline looked up from the book she was ostensibly reading. In truth, she had not turned a page in fully fifteen minutes; she was too caught up in thoughts of Justin to concentrate. "Whatever you like, I suppose, dearest. We have no engagements until the Westons' supper this evening. Would you want to go to the shops?"

Phoebe wrinkled her nose. "It is too warm to shop. Last night I thought I would faint for lack of air in the assembly rooms."

"You seemed to be having a fine time."

"Oh, I was! Anytime I can dance is a fine time." She slid Caroline a sly glance. "I noticed you quite vanished before the supper."

Caroline looked back down at her book. "I was in need of some air."

"Ah, yes. Apparently so was Lord Lyndon." Phoebe leaned forward eagerly. "Is there anything you want to tell your sister, Caro? Anything at all?"

Tell Phoebe that she kissed Lord Lyndon in the moonlight, but she couldn't marry him because she had once been the proprietor of a gaming hell? Caroline thought not.

"I did happen to stroll with him on the terrace for a while," she answered carefully. "But there is no need to act like this is scene from one of your novels, Phoebe. There were many other people there, and . . . and nothing of any consequence happened."

"Nothing at all?"

She just lost her heart, that was all. "Nothing."

Phoebe fell back with a disappointed little huff. "How very vexing. I was hoping this would be a *romantic* summer."

Caroline laughed at her pouting expression. "I believe you have enough romance for the both of us. This house is flooded with bouquets from your admirers every day."

Phoebe tried to shrug carelessly, but she looked too pleased for it to be effective. "But that is not really romance!"

"It isn't? Then what is?"

"Grand emotion! Passionate declarations! Embraces under the stars!" She peered closer at Caroline. "Did you and Lord Lyndon embrace under the stars?"

Caroline laughed harder. "Phoebe!"

"No? Well, you should have."

Caroline decided that a small fib might be in order. "We did not 'embrace under the stars.' And you and young Mr. Seward had best not have done so, either."

"Oh, Harry Seward. All he has talked of these last few days is 'making a name for himself' and 'having adventures.' Nothing romantic at all. I don't know what has gotten into him."

Caroline nodded. She remembered Justin saying he wanted to send Harry to manage one of the family's smaller estates, but she would have thought Harry would not be very enthusiastic about it. Perhaps she had been wrong, and he liked the idea of his independence.

"Are you disappointed in him, then, Phoebe?" she asked.

Phoebe shook her head firmly, but her violet-blue eyes looked a bit sad. "What is there to be disappointed in? He is a silly young man, not at all like the Count Enrico in *The Sins of Madame Sophie*. Beside, I have adventures of my own to have! Starting today." She gave a dramatic little pause. "Let's go bathing."

Caroline closed her book, glad to have a purpose for the day besides brooding over Justin. "An excellent idea! But I am sure everyone else in town will want to do the same. Perhaps I should send Mary to reserve a bathing house."

"No need for that! Sarah Bellweather showed me the most delightful cove, just outside of town. It's very quiet there; not many people know about it. If we went there to bathe, we wouldn't have to worry about bathing houses and crowds. We would be all alone." Phoebe giggled. "We could even take off our stockings!"

"I hardly think *that* would be appropriate," Caroline murmured. But a quiet swim, just the two of them and the sea and the sky, with no crowds, sounded just what she needed. "We could go there, though, and take a picnic."

"Wonderful! I'll just go change into my bathing

costume, then." Phoebe rushed off, calling for Mary to come and help her dress.

Caroline set aside her book with a pang of guilty relief. If she was bathing with Phoebe all day, she couldn't call on Justin with her tale of the Golden Feather until tomorrow. Or the next day. Perhaps that was just as well. She needed time to gather her thoughts, prepare her words very carefully. She didn't want to hurt him, or herself, but he deserved the truth.

"I think, my dears, that I will not go with you to Waring," Lady Lyndon announced at breakfast the morning after the assembly.

Justin turned to his mother in surprise. "I thought you *wanted* to go to Waring, Mother."

"Oh, I do, and I *will* go there, in the autumn perhaps. But Lady Bellweather has asked me to accompany them to Brighton for the remainder of the summer. I would like that, I think. It has been a long time since I went to Brighton." She touched her napkin to her lips and smiled at them. "But you must go to Waring, of course. You have been away too long, Justin, and the country air will be good for you."

Harry swallowed his bite of eggs and said, "If Mother isn't going to Waring, then neither am I."

Justin looked at his brother. "And what are you going to do instead? Stay here to dangle after Miss Lane?"

Harry's face took on a rather comically serious expression, and he tilted up his chin. "Certainly not. You mentioned the possibility of my going to manage Seward Park."

"I did, but you hardly seemed enraptured at the possibility."

"Well, that was then. I have given it some thought. I do . . . like Miss Lane, but you were quite right when you said I don't have very much to offer her. If I managed Seward Park very well, then it would prove to her and her sister that I'm not just a useless fribble."

Justin regarded his brother with near shock. For once there was no pouting, no whining on Harry's part. He looked earnest and worried and very, very young. "Harry, that is the first sensible thing I have heard you say since I returned to England."

Harry looked down at his plate, his cheeks reddening. "Yes, well, Miss Lane is a very special young lady. I want to be worthy of her."

"Then you can go to Seward Park. If you make a go of it, then I will give it to you as a wedding present," Justin answered.

"Would you?" Harry cried, his eyes shining with new hope. "You *are* a good 'un, Justin."

Amelia beamed at her sons. "You see, my dears, I knew all would be well!"

The butler came into the breakfast room, carrying a note on a silver tray. "This just came for you, my lord."

"Thank you, Richards." Justin broke the wax seal and read the scrawled words quickly.

"What is it, Justin?" Amelia asked worriedly. "Bad news?"

"Not at all," Justin said with a smile. "It is from next door."

Amelia gave a sly, satisfied smile. "From Mrs. Aldritch?"

"No, from the young lady we were just speaking of. Miss Lane."

"Miss Lane!" Harry cried, half rising from his chair. "Why is she writing to *you*?"

"Now, don't get all upset, Harry. You've been doing so very well this morning. She simply wants to invite us to a picnic at the cove just outside of town."

Harry settled back warily. "Both of us?"

"Of course. She says her sister and Sarah Bellweather will be there, as well."

"That's all right, then. Sounds like jolly fun." Harry popped another bite of eggs into his mouth and chewed happily. "I can wear my new waistcoat, the one embroidered with tulips. She's sure to admire that!"

Justin folded the note back carefully and tucked it beside his plate. It *did* sound like "jolly fun," but he couldn't help the nagging feeling of doubt that crawled inside of him. Why would Miss Lane write the note, and not her older sister? And why the cove, not the more public shore area?

Very strange, indeed. But he would go, of course. He couldn't stay away from Caroline.

He smiled as he remembered their embrace in the night-dark garden. It had been sweet and fiery and perfect. So perfect. Not even her strange sadness after could mar the memory.

He wanted to see her again, to hold her in his arms, to talk to her and tell her all he was feeling.

Why, then, did he have the nagging thought that he should not go on the picnic today?

Chapter Eighteen

"This is wonderful! I feel just like a mermaid." Phoebe splashed about happily in the cool water, her blond hair sleek in the sunlight. She had long ago removed her cap, and now she and Sarah were frolicking like two little seals.

Caroline, perched on an outcropping of rocks with her stockinged toes dangling in the water, laughed when Phoebe splashed her. "You look like a monkey! You will catch a chill without your cap."

"Of course I won't! The water is quite warm. Why don't you come in, Caro?"

"I will in a minute. I want to enjoy the sun first."

Phoebe nodded and went back to swimming in circles with Sarah.

Caroline leaned back on her elbows and closed her eyes to bask in the warm light. She knew she should not; the sun was sure to make her quite brown since she wasn't wearing a hat. But somehow she felt too languid to even worry about her complexion.

The sun, the sounds of the sea and the girls' laughter, and the late night at the assembly all conspired to make her drowsy. She closed her eyes, letting the peace of the moment, so precious and transitory, steal over her.

She was startled into full awakening by the sound of a man's voice calling out.

She looked over her shoulder to see Justin and Harry coming toward them. She sat straight up, automatically tucking her legs beneath her to hide the stockings of her bathing ensemble.

Whatever were *they* doing here, in this out-of-the-way spot? Surely Phoebe would not . . .

"Hello, Lord Lyndon! Mr. Seward!" Phoebe called out, waving her hands from the water, confirming Caroline's sudden suspicions. "There you are at last."

Caroline gave her a stern glance, but Phoebe just smiled blithely and swam over to snatch her cap and stockings up from where she left them on the rocks. She donned them beneath the water and came out onto the shore, Sarah behind her.

Caroline stood up and caught Phoebe's arm as she walked past. "Did you invite them here?" she whispered.

"Of course," Phoebe answered innocently. "I thought they might enjoy a picnic. Did I do something wrong, Caro?"

Caroline watched as Justin came closer and closer. He was dressed casually today, in a blue coat, buckskin breeches, and a plain, simply tied cravat. He wore no hat, and the breeze ruffled his sun-touched hair.

He smiled at her and waved.

Caroline thought he was the loveliest sight she had ever seen.

As he came ever closer, she reached up nervously to make certain her hair was still tidy and smooth beneath her cap.

"Good afternoon, ladies," he said, handing Caroline a small parcel. "Mother sent some of her raspberry cordial, since she couldn't be with us today."

Caroline stared up at him and heard herself saying, as if from a long way away, "Thank you, Lord Lyndon. We are very glad you and Mr. Seward could come."

"I got the distinct impression earlier that you were rather startled to see us. Did your sister invite us without your knowledge?"

Caroline's hand tightened on Justin's arm. They were walking along the shore after the long and very merry picnic luncheon, watching the three young people where they dug about in the sand up ahead. Looking for smugglers' treasure, no doubt. Then the three of them ran off behind a small hill, out of sight.

"I confess she did," she answered. "But that does not mean that your presence was at all unwelcome. It has been a delightful day."

She realized that these were not just polite words. It *had* been a delightful day, full of laughter and good cheer. She felt warm and happy, with the cordial in her veins, the sun on her head, and Justin beside her.

It was a perfect day, almost as perfect as the night in the assembly rooms garden had been. A day she wished could go on forever and ever.

But she knew it could not.

She turned to face Justin, walking half sideways. "Lord Lyndon—Justin—there is something we have to talk about."

He smiled at her, so sweetly that she felt her resolve to be honest and truthful melting away beneath it until it was almost gone.

Almost.

"I know," he said: "We have many things to talk about. What would you care to start with?"

She tried to steel her resolve against his teasing. His casual, happy manner only made her fear what she must say even more.

She didn't want to lose this, his smile, his laughter, his admiration. She closed her eyes tightly, hoping that not seeing his face would help her to say what she had to say.

Unfortunately, shutting one's eyes while walking is not the wisest thing to do. Her slippered foot caught on a clump of driftwood, and she fell with a thud to the hard-packed sand.

For one moment, she lay there absolutely stunned, unable to move or breathe. She felt sick to her stomach.

Then she felt absolutely mortified. When she finally caught her breath, reality returned, and she realized she was lying like a beached fish at the feet of the man she loved.

She groaned and pressed her forehead harder into the itchy sand. So what if she had been about to destroy his faith in her forever with her confession? That didn't mean she wanted his last vision of her to be *this*. A small part of her, the part that had once been young and foolish and read cheap novels, had wanted him to remember her as tragic, self-sacrificing, and nobly alluring, even as she gave him up.

Well, now she could bid farewell to nobly alluring. He would surely always remember her as awkward and dirty with wet sand.

She moaned softly.

Then she noticed that he was kneeling beside her, calling her name frantically. Her ears must be full of sand, too.

"Caroline!" he cried. "Caroline, can you hear me? Are you conscious?"

She slowly turned her head to look at him, or rather at his arm as he reached for her. She still couldn't bring herself to look at his face. "I am . . . conscious," she murmured.

"Thank the Lord! Are you in pain anywhere? Can you sit up?"

She did ache a bit, but she knew she could not just go on lying there forever. The sand was beginning to prickle. She nodded, and he slid his arms about her, pulling her gently upright.

A sharp pain shot up her left leg, and she cried out.

"What is it?" Justin asked, his blue eyes slate-gray with worry.

"My ankle," she gasped through the throbbing ache. "I must have twisted it when I fell."

"It could be broken."

Caroline shook her head and reached into the tight sleeve of her bathing dress for a handkerchief to wipe her face with. She might be crippled now, but she wanted to be a cripple with a clean face.

"No," she said. "I don't think so."

"We should make certain. Then we will get you to a physician. Where are those blasted children at? They're never about when you actually need them." He reached for her foot and started to draw the heavy woolen stocking down from her knee.

At first, Caroline was too busy scrubbing at her face to truly realize what he was about. Then she felt the soft, tantalizing brush of fingertips against her calf and looked down at him.

For one long moment, time seemed suspended. She could still feel the touch of him on her skin, the sunlight beating down on her head, the piercing ache of her ankle. But she could not move or speak. She was frozen.

Only one image kept replaying itself in her mind. The image of her standing in her office at the Golden Feather while he held her scarred ankle in his hand.

It was an image eerily like the one she was living now. Only now it was so very much worse, because she knew all that she was losing.

And the only thing she could do was watch and wait.

He rolled the stocking to her ankle, then glanced up at her. She made her face as cool and expressionless as she could, and gave him a small nod.

If this was how it was fated to be, then so be it. Perhaps it would be easier if he hated her as a deceiver, after all.

He drew the stocking the rest of the way off and pressed his thumbs to the delicate bones of her foot. They moved gently over the arch, pressing lightly. Closer his touch came, ever closer, until his thumb brushed over the rough, raised scar on her ankle.

Then he stilled. He became as frozen as she herself felt, and even his hands felt chilled against her skin.

He lifted her foot a bit and stared at the pink scar. Caroline fought the urge to yank her foot away, to scream and cry out and run away. She made herself sit there, as still as ice, her face the

cool mask she had learned to don in her lonely
years at the Golden Feather.

She only wished she had one of her cloth masks
to hide behind, as well.

He raised his gaze to hers. His eyes were bewildered and dazed. "How could? . . . Is this? . . ."
he said hoarsely. His grasp tightened.

Caroline swallowed hard. "Yes. I am, or was,
Mrs. Archer."

Justin slowly placed her foot back onto the sand.
Caroline caught up the stocking and pulled it
quickly back over her leg, wincing as it passed over
the swollen ankle.

The pain was as nothing compared to the pain
in her heart.

Justin sat back against the driftwood. The
stunned look on his face ripped at her soul. "Tell
me," he said.

"What is there to tell? Lawrence died without a
farthing to his name. His only legacy to me was the
deed to a gaming establishment, a place called the
Golden Feather. He won it, you see, in a game of
chance the very night he died. So he did not have
time to lose it again."

"And you took the place over?"

Caroline nodded wearily. She found she could not
go into all the reasons for that action now. She was
tired and in pain, and all that seemed so far away
now. As if it had all happened to another woman.

Besides, to Justin, a gentleman, her reasons
would not matter. A true lady would have chosen
genteel poverty over ill-gotten riches.

As indeed she would have, for herself. But not
for Phoebe. Never for Phoebe.

And now they were both ruined.

"Why did you not tell me?" he said, his voice tight with anger. "All these weeks, we have spent so much time together, and you never said a word."

"Why do you think I did not tell you? Because then you would have given us the cut direct and made your mother and brother cut us, too. All of Society would have followed your example, starting with the Bellweathers. I could not have borne that for Phoebe, never!"

Caroline feared she was about to start weeping. She turned her face away from him, refusing to look at his furious, wounded eyes any longer.

He stared at her in the heavy silence, his gaze like a hundred knives stabbing at her heart.

Then the dark spell was broken by a piercing shriek.

Caroline looked up to see Phoebe running toward them, closely followed by Harry and Sarah. She had lost her cap again, and her hair fell down in unruly curls. Her hands were bunched into fists, and she was frowning most fiercely. She looked like a vengeful little Valkyrie.

"Once again your guard comes to your rescue," Justin muttered. "First your maid and her book, and now this, Mrs. Aldritch. Mrs. Archer." He raked a shaking hand through his hair, leaving it sticking up in wavy tufts. "Whoever you are."

"I am Caroline," she whispered. "I am me."

But he did not hear her. Phoebe was upon them, shouting, "What have you done to my sister? Why is she sitting in the sand like that? Did you knock her down?"

Justin stared at Phoebe unseeingly. Then he said, "Pardon me. I must . . . go. I am sorry. Harry, please see the ladies home."

Then he stood up and walked quickly down the shore, out of their view.

Caroline watched him until he disappeared, and at that moment she could no longer help herself. The tears she had choked back, making her throat ache, came out in a great salty flood. They fell off her chin and dripped onto her clenched hands.

They were not ladylike, diamondlike tears. They were great, gulping, ugly sobs.

She had not cried like this since she was a little child. Now she could not stop, even though she knew she was creating a scene.

Phoebe and Sarah knelt beside her, patting her and murmuring soothing words. Sarah pulled out a bottle of smelling salts.

Harry fluttered about helplessly, offering handkerchiefs and saying in a quavering voice, "Oh, I say! Do let me see you ladies home or send for the physician. Or something. Anything!"

Phoebe glared up at him. "It was *your* brother who caused this, Mr. Seward!"

"No, it wasn't," Caroline protested through her tears. "I caused it. Every bit of it."

"Of course you didn't," Phoebe soothed. "It was Lord Lyndon. Men are such beasts."

"I beg your pardon!" Harry cried.

"Beasts!" Phoebe repeated loudly. She put her arm around Caroline's shoulder and said, "Come, dear, let me take you home."

"*I'll* see you ladies home," Harry offered again.

"We have our own carriage, thank you, Mr. Seward." Phoebe and Sarah helped Caroline up between them and supported her on her injured ankle as they left the sandy shore.

Harry trotted along behind them all the way.

Chapter Nineteen

Justin hardly knew where he was walking. He only knew he had to get away, to escape from the nightmare his life had suddenly become.

He walked blindly down the shore, unaware of the waves lapping at his boots or the birds wheeling overhead. He rubbed his hand hard over his brow, but he could not blot out the vision of Caroline, Mrs. Aldritch/Archer, staring at him with wide, dark eyes in her pale face.

What a blasted, stupid fool he had been not to see what was right before him all these weeks! Of course he recognized Caroline when he first met her, but not because of some mystical union of souls. It was because he had called on her once in her very own gaming house.

She must have laughed at him so behind her hand. The fool who didn't recognize her, who hung about all the time like a love-struck puppy. How easily he had fallen in with her, let her use him for her social ends.

Justin sat down on a large chunk of wood to stare out at the sea, at the white-capped waves that danced and flowed endlessly. He knew it had been insufferably rude of him to leave her and the others alone on the shore, but he *had* to get out of there, to be alone. To think.

He had thought of himself as much changed by his years in India—older and wiser. In truth, he was as silly as Harry, taken in by a pretty face and a sad air.

What a fine actress she was. Her talents were wasted in owning a gaming house, and especially in matronly respectability. She should be treading the boards.

He picked up a stick of wood and tossed it into the water, watching it sink beneath the waves. He should have been thinking of the future all these weeks. He should have followed his mother's original advice and courted and married Miss Bellweather, even if she did prefer digging about in the dirt to matrimony. She never would have made him feel this way, angry and hollow inside.

Because he had truly fallen in love with Caroline, whoever she was. He had never given his heart to any woman like this before, but she touched him with her quiet grace and understanding. He had wanted to take away the sadness in her eyes, to make her life full of nothing but happiness.

It had all been false. All a lie.

But even as he castigated himself for a fool, he could not forget the way she had looked under the moonlight while he kissed her.

"Tell me, Caro, please! Tell me what happened," Phoebe beseeched. She sat on a chair in Caroline's bedroom, watching helplessly as her sister lay in bed, tears still trickling down her cheeks.

Caroline shook her head. She didn't want to talk about what had happened, or anything else. She just wanted to stay here in bed and forget. As if she would ever be able to forget at all. She would see Justin's shocked, betrayed face in her mind forever.

She rolled onto her side to stare out the window. She could just barely see the edge of the house next door.

"At least let Mary and me help you into your nightdress," Phoebe said desperately.

Caroline looked down at herself to see that she still wore her sandy bathing costume. She sat up and reached down to pull at her stockings, taking them off and throwing them onto the floor.

Her scarred ankle was still there. It hadn't been erased.

Phoebe gasped. "Caro, you're hurt! Did Lord Lyndon do that?"

"Of course not. It is an old scar." Caroline rubbed at it furiously with her palm, wishing that it would vanish, and with it all the past.

Her fingernails scraped across the swollen skin there, making it bleed.

Mary, who had just come into the room with a glass of brandy-laced milk, cried out, "Stop that, madam! You are making your injury worse." She rushed over to pull Caroline's hand away and look at the scratches.

"It cannot get any worse," Caroline murmured. "It's all over."

Phoebe's eyes were as wide as saucers. "Caro, you are scaring me. You are acting just like that Lady Macbeth."

Caroline looked over at her, a faint beam of surprise penetrating the fog of her mind. "Lady Macbeth?"

"Well, don't look at me like that. I do sometimes read things other than novels, you know. I am not completely ignorant."

Caroline laughed at that, and Phoebe and Mary exchanged relieved glances.

"Miss Phoebe, go and fetch some warm water and bandages," Mary instructed. "And you, madam, will change out of those dirty clothes and drink every drop of this milk. It will help you rest."

Caroline obediently stood up and unbuttoned the top of her bodice. "I can't rest now. We have to start packing."

"Packing? Where are we going?"

"I don't know. Italy maybe, or America. Somewhere far away." Caroline dropped the last of her clothes and turned back to look at her reflection in the mirror. She looked thin and pale in her chemise, almost like the ghost she felt. "Something terrible has happened, Mary. We are ruined."

And her heart was shattered.

"Ruined, madam?" Mary's voice held only mild curiosity. After four years at the Golden Feather with her mistress, she could hardly be shocked anymore. She dropped a clean nightdress over Caroline's head.

The soft cotton folds enveloped her, sheltering her. "Yes. Justin—Lord Lyndon—discovered the truth about Mrs. Archer."

Now Mary *did* look shocked. Her hands froze on the pearl button she was fastening at Caroline's throat. "Oh, no, madam. Did he threaten to expose you?"

"Not exactly." He had not said much of anything. That was the worst part. If he had shouted, she could have shouted back. But he had just walked away. "You know he *will* tell, though. We will no longer be accepted into the Sewards' house, and people will want to know why."

"Oh, madam!" Mary cried, her lower lip trembling. "I thought we were going to be *normal* now."

"I thought, so, too. But it seems my life is doomed to drama, no matter how much I might wish it otherwise." Caroline pulled a valise out from under the bed and limped to the wardrobe, not even noticing the pain in her ankle as she reached in for an armload of clothes. "I want Phoebe to be affected by this as little as possible, so we must leave at once. Tonight, if possible."

She balled up a lacy petticoat and thrust it into the valise. Then she picked up a pink silk spencer.

"Here, let me do that! You are wrinkling everything." Mary caught the spencer out of Caroline's trembling hands and folded it neatly. "If we have to leave, then we have to leave. You know I will follow you anywhere. Though I must say I do like it here in Wycombe."

"So do I, Mary," Caroline answered wistfully, sitting back down on the bed.

She had never been so happy anywhere in her life before.

Phoebe appeared with a basin of water, which she almost dropped when she saw the open valise. "What are you doing? Where are we going?"

Caroline turned to her sister and held out her hand. "Phoebe, darling, come over here and sit down beside me, so we may talk."

Phoebe backed up, water sloshing from the basin onto her bright green muslin gown. "It's Lord Lyndon, isn't it? He hurt you, and now we must leave to get away from him! How vile he is. I should not have invited him to our outing; then none of this would have happened."

"It isn't like that at all." Caroline had thought to make up some tale for Phoebe about why they were leaving Wycombe. But now, as she looked into her sister's desperate eyes, she knew she had to tell her the truth. She was done forever with lies and half-truths. All they had ever brought her was pain.

Caroline took the basin from Phoebe and placed it carefully on a table. Then she drew her over to sit down on the window seat. She pulled the curtains against the sight of the Sewards' house.

"Now, Phoebe," she said, taking Phoebe's trembling hands in her own, "I must tell you something. We *are* leaving because of Lord Lyndon, but it is not his fault. It is mine."

"Yours, Caro? How can that be?"

Caroline took a deep breath and plunged ahead. "After Lawrence died, I told you I was working as companion to his elderly aunt. Remember?"

"Yes. That is why we could only see each other a couple of times a year."

"I fear I lied to you."

Phoebe looked confused. "Do you mean you were not working for Mr. Aldritch's aunt?"

"No." Caroline closed her eyes so she could not see her sister's reaction to her words. "I-I owned a gaming establishment, called the Golden Feather. Lawrence won it in a game of chance right before he died, and I took it over."

She steeled herself for the storm, for Phoebe to rail at her for her lies.

Instead there was . . . silence.

Caroline cautiously opened her eyes. Phoebe was watching her, a rapt and fascinated look on her face.

"A gaming establishment," she breathed. "Truly, Caro?"

Caroline nodded. "I fear so."

"Oh! It is just like *A Gamble on Love*. You must tell me all about it. What fascinating people you must have met!"

Relief swept over Caroline. She should have known her sister better; Phoebe did not have a condemning bone in her body. But she was far too curious for her own good.

"I certainly will not 'tell you all about it.' The people were generally most unfascinating, too drunk to walk straight, let alone converse. It was a dreadful life, and we are well away from it here."

Phoebe's face, so avid and shining only a moment before, darkened. "Only we will not be here much longer. All because of Lord Lyndon. I suppose he came to your . . . your place frequently, and that is how he knew you. Though I must say it took long enough for him to recognize you."

Caroline shook her head. "I always wore a mask, so no one could recognize me. And it was actually Harry Seward who was a frequent visitor. I only saw Lord Lyndon there twice, once when he came with his brother right after his return from India and then the day after."

"Why did he come then?"

Caroline hesitated. The story of Harry Seward and his fight was so very inappropriate for a young girl's ears. But then, she had already told this particular young girl the rest of the sordid story.

"Mr. Seward had a . . . a disagreement with another patron, which resulted in some furniture breaking."

Phoebe nodded sagely. "A brawl. That sounds like something Harry Seward would do."

"You are not disappointed, dear? I know you are rather fond of him."

"Perhaps I was, once. Now I am through with him and all his family. I suppose Lord Lyndon paid off his brother's debts on that second visit?"

"Yes. When he was there, I tripped." She looked down ruefully at her swollen appendage. "Much like today. He came to my assistance and saw the scar."

"So that is how he knew you," Phoebe murmured. "Oh, my poor, poor Caro! And now we must go away."

Yes. They had to go away. "You can see why, can you not? We will be ruined if we stay."

"Like Mary, I will go with you anywhere you like. You are the best sister in the world, and I have been such a trial to you!" Phoebe threw herself into Caroline's arms, crying contritely, "I will never be any trouble to you again, I swear."

Caroline kissed the top of Phoebe's head and held her close. "You could never be a trial to me, Phoebe. You are all my family now, and I love you."

"I love you, too. And I will help you, I promise. I will make everything better."

"You make things better just by being here."

Phoebe hugged her once more, then stood up and walked toward the door. "I will just go and start my own packing now. I'm supposed to have tea with Sarah later, and I can tell her good-bye then. You just rest, Caro." She smiled and ran off.

Caroline looked after her suspiciously. "Do you believe she is just going to pack, Mary?" she asked.

Mary just pressed the glass of milk and brandy into her hand and said, "Drink this, madam. It will help you feel better."

Chapter Twenty

"I am here to see Lord Lyndon," Phoebe said stoutly, facing down the prune-faced butler with her hands on her hips. "If you please."

The butler's lips flattened even farther, and he kept a firm grip on the door, leaving Phoebe on the doorstep. "His lordship is occupied at the moment, Miss . . ."

"I am Miss Lane."

"Miss Lane. His lordship is occupied at the moment with important business and is not accepting visitors."

Phoebe felt a hot flare of temper in her stomach spreading up until it threatened to burst forth in a torrent of screaming, shouting, and generally unladylike behavior. Her sister was in despair, all because of Lord Lyndon, and he sat smug in his house, guarded by this elderly dragon of a gatekeeper.

She stamped her foot. "*I* happen to have 'important business' with his lordship, and I will see him right now!"

With that, she burst past the shocked butler and through the front door. She dashed down the corridor, looking quickly into the doorways she passed, the butler hard on her heels. For such an old man, he was incredibly quick.

But not quick enough for Phoebe.

She finally found Lord Lyndon in the library, sitting behind a large desk with a decanter of what looked like brandy.

Phoebe marched up to the desk and planted her hands flat on the cool wooden surface. "How dare you, you wicked man!" she shouted.

Justin had been sitting alone in his library with his brandy for about two hours, feeling more and more guilty over his behavior toward Caroline, trying to drown the image of her white, stricken face in the amber liquid's warmth, when he heard the commotion in the foyer. Loud, raised voices, Richards's and a woman's.

Justin shook his head. He hoped it wasn't someone Harry knew, come to cause trouble. He had enough trouble of his own without dealing with Harry's messes.

Then the voices came closer. He heard a rather familiar one insist, "I *will* see Lord Lyndon!"

Miss Lane's voice?

He put the glass carefully back down on the desk. Surely he had not drunk enough of the stuff to be hearing things! His head did not feel in the least bit fuzzy. But not even Miss Lane would come to a gentleman's house and shout at his butler.

Would she?

Then the library door burst open, and Phoebe did indeed stand there. She had changed from her bathing costume into a somewhat respectable bright green gown, but her hair fell down in a mass of curls that positively writhed with indignation.

She strode across the carpet, arms akimbo, then leaned across the desk and shouted, "How dare you, you wicked man!"

Justin just stared up at her frowning face. He had never been called a "wicked man" by a young miss before, and he hardly knew what to say. Should he ask her to sit down? Offer her a brandy? Let her pummel him thoroughly, as she so obviously longed to do?

This was all completely outside his realm of experience. All he could seem to do was stare at her rather stupidly.

Richards appeared at the door, puffing to catch his breath. "My lord," he gasped. "I am so sorry! The young lady . . . she pushed past me. . . ."

Justin rose slowly to his feet. "That is quite all right, Richards. You might fetch my mother, and have some refreshments sent in." Yes. His mother would know what to do.

"Very good, my lord." Richards bowed and gratefully retreated.

Justin turned back reluctantly to face Miss Lane. She stood with her fists planted on her hips, glaring at him. "This is not a social call. You needn't have ordered refreshments."

Justin propped his hip against the desk and crossed his own arms over his chest. He knew it was quite improper to be in his shirtsleeves, but he didn't want to risk pushing past Medusa to retrieve his coat. "You look as if you have been running a long way. I thought some tea might be in order."

"I don't want anything from you! You are a wi—"

"I know," he interjected dryly. "I am a wicked man."

"You are. A very wicked man. Caroline says we must leave here and go abroad, all because of you. We were happy here, and you ruined everything."

Justin rubbed wearily at his jaw. She was leaving. Leaving. His mind repeated that one word over and over.

"So you knew, too?" he muttered. "Everyone knew the truth but me."

Phoebe shook her head. "I did not know. All these years I thought she was companion to Mr. Aldritch's old aunt. She just told me this afternoon, to explain why we have to leave so quickly."

"And you were not angry that your sister lied to you?"

She looked shocked. "Of course not! Caroline is the very best of sisters. She always has been." Phoebe bit her lip, her eyes suddenly swimming in tears. One drop spilled free, and she wiped it impatiently away. "It was all my fault."

"Your fault?" Justin said sharply. "Why? Were you the one who concocted this scheme to run a gaming establishment, to fleece young men like Harry of their money? To go about in disguise?"

"There is no need to be sarcastic, Lord Lyndon. And Harry is hardly some poor lamb to the slaughter. He practically begs people to take money from his pockets; even I can see that. I am not the stupid little girl everyone thinks me." Phoebe sat down, dropping heavily into the chair beside the desk. "And you are trying to distract me, but it will not work."

This conversation was getting more and more bizarre. Justin wondered if he had fallen asleep at his desk and was having a brandy-induced dream. "Trying to distract you from what, Miss Lane?"

"From my purpose in coming here."

"Which is?"

"To tell you what a looby you are, of course. A wicked looby."

Justin choked. "A—what?"

"A looby." Phoebe shrugged. "It is a word I heard your brother use. And I am sure you are one. You were mean to my sister. She is an absolute angel, and you were cruel to her!"

He *had* been cruel. Justin knew that and was ashamed of it, though, truth to tell, he remembered little of the scene on the shore. He had been in a fog of shock and dismay. "Was I?"

"Caroline would never have done what she did if not for me." Phoebe stared past him, obviously in her own world of recriminations, regrets, and memories. "She hated that Silver Plume place. I could see the revulsion on her face when she spoke of it."

"Golden Feather," Justin automatically corrected.

Phoebe went on as if he had not spoken. "I am sure she would have gone to be a companion to her husband's aunt when he died. But Mrs. Medlock's School, dull as it was, was very expensive. And my clothes, my gewgaws, my pin money." She seized a handful of her green skirt, as if to tear it away. "If I had known, I would not have taken any of those things! I would have left school and taken a position with some other old lady. I would not have let her do that!"

Justin sensed that she was going into hysterics, and looked frantically to the door. Where the deuce *was* his mother?

When Amelia didn't appear, he did the only thing he could think of. He poured a small measure of brandy into a glass and pressed it into her hand.

She sniffled and looked down at it with interest. "Is this brandy?"

"Yes. It will help you calm down."

"I've never had brandy before," she said. Then she gulped it all down.

And promptly began to choke.

"Miss Lane!" Justin thumped her on the back until she stopped wheezing. "You must sip it slowly if you are not accustomed to it."

"You might have told me that before." She eyed the decanter. "May I have some more?"

"Certainly not." Relieved that the coughing, as well as the hysterics, had passed, Justin sat down in a chair across from her. "So Lawrence left your sister no money at all?" he asked, going back to their previous conversation.

Phoebe shook her head. "Not a farthing. Just that . . . that place, which he won in a card game. And, as I said, Mrs. Medlock's was expensive. I would have left there in an instant if Caroline had come for me, but she did not. I am sure she never even considered it. She has always tried to protect me, even when we were children. That is why I have come here today."

Justin was not sure he followed her reasoning. "Why is that, Miss Lane?"

"Because Caroline has always done everything for me. For four years she worked and sacrificed so that I could have a future." Phoebe looked down at where her fist was balled in her skirt. "And today, when I saw how in despair she was, how you hurt her, something inside of me just . . . broke." She smoothed out her skirt and raised her gaze to meet his. "My sister is a lady, Lord Lyndon. The finest lady who ever lived in England, I am sure. I could not allow you, or anyone, to treat her as anything else."

Justin sat back in stunned silence. He had thought Miss Lane to be a rather flighty young woman. But she spoke the truest words he had ever heard, solidifying the vague thoughts that had been floating around in his confused mind all afternoon.

Caroline Aldritch was a true lady. And he had been too blind to see that.

He had thought himself a fool for not seeing that she was Mrs. Archer. Now he knew, like a flash of clarifying light, that he had not really been a fool until the moment he walked away from her on the shore.

The woman he had known these past weeks in Wycombe, the graceful, intelligent, understanding woman he talked to, danced with, and kissed was the real Caroline. And it had been even when she wore the mask of Mrs. Archer.

She was a woman who would live a life she disliked, even hated, for four long years for the love of her sister. If Justin could understand anything, he understood that. Harry was obnoxious at times, yes, but Justin would do anything to keep him safe, to make certain that his future was happy and secure.

Caroline had done the same thing, and he had condemned her for it, abandoned her. Now she was leaving. He had lost her.

Justin groaned and turned his face away from Phoebe, who was crying softly again. In one afternoon, his life had swung in so many different directions he hardly knew where to go.

But he did know that Phoebe was right. He *was* a wicked man, a hypocritical one, who had almost carelessly smashed the lives of the two sisters.

"Caroline says we have to go abroad, because you will tell everyone about the "Copper Quill" and we will be ruined. Not even Sarah will talk to me anymore if I am ruined," Phoebe sobbed. "I don't want to go abroad!"

"You will not have to, Miss Lane. I will never tell anyone."

Phoebe looked up, cautiously hopeful. "Do you promise?"

"I promise, on my father's grave."

She looked as if she wanted to say something else, but his mother came into the room, with Harry close behind her.

"Justin, what is this nonsense Richards says about Miss Lane being in here with—" Amelia broke off when she saw the young lady actually sitting there. "Oh. Good afternoon, Miss Lane."

Phoebe gave a long sniffle. "G-good afternoon, Lady Lyndon."

Harry looked about, bewildered, at Phoebe's tearstained face, the brandy on the desk, and Justin in his shirtsleeves. His youthful face hardened. "You utter cad!" he shouted. "Taking advantage of an innocent lady!"

Before Justin could even guess what he was about, Harry leaped forward, grabbed him by the cravat, and dragged him to the floor.

Justin tried to seize his brother and push him off,

but Harry had the strength of his anger behind him, and clung with terrierlike tenacity. His fist flew out and caught Justin on the cheekbone.

"Dash it, Harry!" Justin shouted. "Get off me, you fool, and I will explain."

"Explain what, you despoiler of virgins!"

"Stop it, boys!" Amelia cried, running around them in a flurry of pale gray skirts. "Stop it this moment!"

Phoebe threw herself into the fray, pummeling Harry with her small fists. "Mr. Seward, no! He was *not* despoiling me. I came here myself." She pulled at his hair.

Harry looked up at her. "Do you mean to say that . . . that you *like* him? My brother?"

"Of course not. He is much too old for me! I came here to talk to him about my sister."

"Oh." Harry released his grip on Justin and stood up. "I am sorry, Justin."

Justin also stood, and tried to rearrange his rumpled attire. His cheek ached like the very devil, and he was sure a nice bruise was forming there. "I suppose you were only defending the lady. But do not let it happen again."

Amelia picked up the brandy from the desk and poured herself out a generous measure. "I must say I am heartily ashamed of you both. Fighting in our own home!" She tossed back the drink with a deep sigh, her shoulders visibly relaxing. "Now see what you have driven me to? Drinking spirits in the middle of the day! I was going to ask you to come to the tea shop with me for strawberries and cake, but now I think Miss Lane and I will go by ourselves. Shall we, Miss Lane?"

Phoebe jumped up eagerly, her earlier tears obviously forgotten in all the excitement. "Oh, yes, please, Lady Lyndon!"

But as Amelia ushered Phoebe out the door, she turned back to level one last stern glance at her sons. "This is not over, Harry, Justin. I will want a thorough explanation of this scene when I get back."

"Yes, Mother," they murmured in a chagrined chorus.

Chapter Twenty-One

The shore was deserted at that time of day; all the bathers and strollers had gone home for their tea. Justin relished the quiet as he stood there on the sand, waves reaching for him but not quite catching him. There, in the silence and the sweet sea air, he felt like the fog that had shrouded his brain was finally lifted, and he could see his way clear.

He loved Caroline. He loved her as Mrs. Aldritch, or Mrs. Archer. Hell, she could call herself Mrs. Tiddlywinks if she liked and he would *still* love her.

He could slap himself for being such an idiot after hearing Phoebe's story, which only confirmed what he had known, deep inside, to be true all along. If Larry, who Justin well knew had not been the most reliable of men, had only left his wife a gaming establishment and a handful of debts, what choice did she have? Would he rather she starved to death in some genteel garret and her sister with her?

"Never," he whispered to himself.

Instead of starving, she had shown herself to be a resourceful and shrewd businesswoman. She had run the Golden Feather with a flair and a panache

that no man could ever have matched; she had
made it the most successful gaming house in all
London.

And she had not done it out of some perverse
desire to be shocking, as Justin's first, irrational reaction had been on hearing the truth. No woman
with Caroline's innate seriousness and dignity
would do that, and he had been an idiot to think
so for even an instant.

She had done everything she did out of love, so
that her sister could have a happy, respectable life.

He turned his back to the sea to look at her
house in the distance. He was on his way there, to
apologize, to grovel on his very knees if necessary.
But now that the moment was upon him he was a
coward. He had no idea what to say, what words
might bring her back to him. He was afraid he
would forget everything he wanted to say, and just
fall on the floor and sob at her feet.

Getting her shoes all wet would hardly endear
him to her.

He sensed that this was the most important, the
most vital conversation he would ever have in his
life. And he had to have it now, before she left
Wycombe, her sister and her luggage in tow, and
he never saw her again.

Justin smoothed down his windblown hair,
tugged his cravat into place, and walked toward
her house.

A knock sounded at the door.

Caroline, tucking a stack of chemises into a
trunk, looked up impatiently and blew a stray lock
of hair out of her eyes.

"Oh, who could that be?" she muttered. "I don't have time for callers, with all these clothes still to be packed."

She listened for Mary or the new housemaid to answer the door, but there was no sound. They must still be in the kitchen, arguing with the cook over supper.

Then there was another knock.

Caroline pushed the rest of the garments into the trunk, reached for her makeshift walking stick, and stood up to go answer the blighted thing herself. The sooner she sent whoever it was away, the sooner she could finish her packing.

And the sooner they could leave Wycombe.

She was halfway down the stairs when Mary came hurrying across the small, trunk-filled foyer, murmuring and shaking her head.

The maid opened the door, and shouted, "You! We don't want to see the likes of *you* here! Go away."

She started to slam the door, but a booted foot was thrust between the stout wood and the frame, preventing it from closing.

"Please, Mary," a deep voice said. "I know I am not your favorite person at the moment, but I must see Mrs. Aldritch."

"You *must* go away!" Mary pushed her slight figure against the door, but he was well wedged.

Justin. Justin had come to see her.

Caroline pressed her hand against the sudden fluttering at the base of her throat. What could he want? To shout at her, threaten her? To warn her to stay away from his family before she tainted them with the stench of the Golden Feather?

She knew she should send him away, that she

should not subject herself to any more of the pain his condemnation brought. But her curiosity—and the wild desire to see him just once more—won out over self-preservation.

"Mary," she called, coming the rest of the way down the stairs, "it is quite all right. You can let Lord Lyndon in."

Mary looked up, her cap askew over one eye. "But, madam . . ."

"I will deal with him," Caroline said.

"Please, Caroline!" Justin called. "I only want to talk to you."

Mary stepped suddenly away from the door, causing Justin, whose entire weight was against the wood, to tumble ignominiously onto the foyer floor. He sprawled most inelegantly on the black-and-white tile.

Mary looked down at him and sniffed. "Talk, then, your lordship," she said scornfully. "But don't expect any tea."

Then she stalked off, back to the kitchen.

Caroline bit her lip uncertainly as she watched Justin scramble to his feet, his elegant attire all in disarray. She didn't know if she should laugh at the sight, or cry. So she just said, "Shall we go into the drawing room?"

Justin nodded, as dignified as he could be with his hair all tumbled about. "Thank you."

Caroline drew her shawl about her shoulders and limped her way into the drawing room, closing the door behind them against any prying ears. As he moved past her, she smelled the warm sun caught on the wool of his coat, a spicy scent, and a tang that was only Justin. And . . . something else.

Brandy? Was he foxed, and that was what made him come to her?

"Have you been drinking?" she blurted before she could catch herself.

He turned to look at her, a rueful half smile on his lips. "Just a bit. Have you?"

Caroline felt an equally rueful expression steal across her own face. "A bit. Mary put brandy in the milk."

"Good. Then we will be equally incoherent."

Caroline sat down on the settee beside the window, holding herself stiff and still. "Why have you come here? I thought we said everything there was to say this afternoon."

Justin shifted on one foot, looking every bit as uncomfortable as she herself felt. "I had a visitor this afternoon."

"Who was it?"

"Miss Lane."

"Phoebe?" Caroline cried. Phoebe had gone alone to Justin's house? She knew her sister was rather, well, *impulsive*, but this was the outside of enough. "She told me she was going to tea with Miss Bellweather."

"I daresay she *is* at tea now. My mother took her to the tea shop for cake and strawberries. But on the way she made a small stop in my library."

Caroline looked down at her lap, twisting and smoothing the pale blue muslin of her skirt. Now he would think her a terribly irresponsible chaperon on top of everything else. "I do apologize."

"There is no need for that. She taught me a very valuable lesson."

She gaped up at him in surprise. "A lesson? Phoebe? What could that have been?"

"That I am a wicked looby, of course," he said in a strangely blithe tone.

"A—what?"

"A wicked looby. Those were her words."

"Oh, Justin—Lord Lyndon—she should not have done that." Caroline could have sunk to the floor in profound embarrassment.

"Of course she should have. I heartily deserved it for . . . well, for my loobyish behavior. If there is such a word." He came over to her and knelt beside her settee. His hair brushed silkily against her fingers, his fragrance and warmth wrapped around her. "She also taught me the value of true loyalty. And that brings me to what I came here to say."

Caroline linked her fingers tightly together to keep from twining them in his hair. "What did you come here to say?"

"That I am sorry. So very sorry, Caroline."

Were her ears deceiving her? Or maybe she was dreaming. Surely he, the Earl of Lyndon, could not be kneeling here on her floor, telling her he was sorry.

"You . . . are sorry?" she managed to whisper.

His eyes were ablaze with the blue heat of a summer's sky as he looked up at her. "I was so . . . so shocked when I saw the truth. My damnable Seward pride was hurt. I was convinced that you had set out to deceive me, to make a fool of me."

"I did not!" Caroline cried. "I wanted so many times to tell you the truth these last weeks. But I didn't. I couldn't."

"You had your sister to protect."

"Yes. If I had told you, we would have been ruined. I don't mind that so much for myself; I would like a quiet country life, away from society. But Phoebe is innocent, and she deserves to decide her own fate." She shook her head. "Even that would not have held me back much longer, I'm afraid. Once I realized how . . . how very serious things were becoming between us, I determined to tell you the truth. I tried to this morning, before I fell."

"You did. But then I saw that scar, and I reacted like a complete idiot. I did not see the obvious."

"I never set out to use you or your family," Caroline said. "I just liked your mother so much, and even Harry, too, began to grow on me."

"And me?" he said, his voice boyishly hopeful. "Did you like me?"

"Oh, yes," she answered softly. Then she gave in to her yearning to touch him, placing her hands softly on either side of his face, framing his beloved features. The prickle of his afternoon whiskers tickled at her palms. "How could I help but like you? You were everything I ever dreamed about but thought could not possibly exist."

"Do you like me still?" he whispered.

"Justin," she whispered back, "I love you."

He raised up on his knees and kissed her, his mouth moving softly, sweetly against hers. Then she wrapped her arms around him, and he pressed closer, his lips parting to meet hers.

Eventually he drew back, his eyes heavy with desire as he looked at her. Both of them were gasping for breath, and Caroline slid off the settee to sit on the floor beside him. He rested his head in her lap, clutching at her skirts as if he feared she might escape him.

"Oh, Caroline," he murmured. "Why could I not have met you years ago?"

Caroline stroked the hair back from his brow and laughed softly. "You would have had to come to Devonshire. Were you ever in Devonshire?"

"Not that I know of."

"Well, that is where I was."

"But if I had met you then, I would never have gone to India. You never would have married Larry. We could have sixteen children by now."

"I do not think it works that way. We were not the same people then that we are now. I was very young and silly when I married Lawrence. I did not make a good wife."

"Will you tell me about it?"

Caroline let her head fall back against the edge of the settee, reluctantly remembering. "My family was a good one, an old one, but they had little in the way of . . . of material comfort. We lived quite shabbily in the country, and I knew that my parents expected that I would improve their fortunes with a good marriage. They were trying to scrape together enough money for my Season."

"But you wed Larry instead."

"His family, whose estate was very near ours, was much in the same situation as ours. They had a good name, but little money. Lawrence's father had problems with gaming, and I think his mother did, too. They wanted, needed, an heiress for their son. But we were in love. Or thought we were. We often met in secret. It felt very thrilling."

"And what happened?"

"We eloped, of course. Made a dash for Gretna Green. When we came back, our parents were furious. All their plans were ruined, and not even my mother, who really was fond of me in her own way, could help. They disowned us, so we went to London. Lawrence had some vague idea of getting work of some sort."

"How long was it before you realized Larry had the same . . . the same problem as his parents?"

"Gaming, you mean? Not very long. He would often go out at night, leaving me alone in our shabby little lodgings. I suppose he was with you and his other friends."

Justin winced against her skirt. "He said his wife did not mind that he was out so late."

"I *did* mind, but I did not say anything. I was still silly and in love."

"When did things change?"

"We had been married a little over a year. I was *enceinte*, and Lawrence was drinking heavily. Losing money heavily, too. I had to hide coins from him so I could buy food and coal. Then, one night, he found out what I was doing. We quarreled, shouted. Lawrence was never physically violent with me, but that night he had been drinking. He broke a vase, and I fell. I cut my ankle open on the shards, and I-I lost the baby."

She closed her eyes tightly. It still hurt, the memory of that long-ago night.

Justin reached out and touched her ankle, laying his palm flat against the raised scar beneath the silk stocking.

"I am so sorry," he said simply.

"It was for the best, really. That was no life for a child. And certainly the Golden Feather would not have been!"

"Did you hate the place so very much?"

Caroline thought about this question carefully, her mind winding around the past. "I hated men trying to grab my backside as I walked past them, and drunken people getting loud and angry when they lost. But I did not hate the place itself. It meant independence and the possibility of a future for Phoebe and myself. It was Lawrence's last, best gift to me. No, I did not hate it."

As she suddenly realized that truth, she felt freer and lighter than she had in years. She could acknowledge the past, and let it go. Lawrence, the lost baby, the Golden Feather—it all flew away.

She looked down at Justin, lying in her lap.

"The Golden Feather brought me you," she said lightly. "How can I hate it?"

He turned his face up to her and kissed her quickly on the chin. "I think you are the bravest person I have ever met."

Caroline felt herself turning pink. "Brave? Certainly not. I only did what I had to in order to survive. *You* were brave to go to India and face tigers and snakes. I never could have done that, not even for Phoebe."

He laughed ruefully. "I went to India because my father sent me there after I fought three duels."

"You fought three duels? Never! I can't believe it."

"Oh, believe it. I was quite the young hellion. I put Harry to shame. My father didn't know what else to do with me, so off I went." He fell silent for a moment, stroking a bit of her soft muslin skirt between his fingers. "I hated India at first, and I hated my father for sending me there. But now I am deeply grateful to him. It made me stronger, more independent. It made me see what is truly important in life."

"And what is that?"

"Family. And true honor. And love." He reached up and drew her head down to his for another long, lingering kiss. "Especially love."

"Umm, yes," Caroline murmured with a smile. "I do see what you mean."

"So I suppose it was a good thing we did not meet years ago."

"No. We would have been too careless to see what we had."

"And now that we are older, our marriage will be stronger."

Caroline, who had been leaning down for another kiss, froze. "Marriage?"

Justin laughed. "Of course marriage! You did not think I was offering you *carte blanche,* did you? After all the groveling and apologizing I have done?"

"No. I did not think that." Caroline carefully moved him aside and got up to sit back down on the settee. "But I did not think of *marriage,* either. Not seriously, anyway. To be your countess . . ."

Justin sat up, a fierce, puzzled frown on his face. "Then what exactly were you thinking?"

That was a very good question, and it was not one that Caroline had an answer for. Truly, she had not been thinking at all. She loved Justin, longed for him, but she had thought that with her secret they could never wed. Now all was revealed, and he wanted to marry her anyway.

She looked at him and saw that he offered everything she had ever wanted. Love, family, a title, a home, respectability. He held it out to her on the palm of his hand, and all she had to do was reach out and pick it up.

She wanted, more than she had ever wanted anything, to be selfish, to reach out and take it, and damn the consequences.

But she loved him too much. Too much to marry him, to risk someone else finding out the truth, and spreading it far and wide that the Countess of Lyndon was once the owner of a gaming hell. The Sewards were an old and proud family. She would not destroy them, or the man she loved.

A sharp pain clawed at her belly as she thought of the life, the children they could have had. But looking after others before herself was too deeply ingrained.

She closed her eyes and shook her head. "I cannot marry you."

"What!" He leaped to his feet. "Then what is this all about? I love you, Caroline. I thought you loved me."

"I *do* love you!" she cried. "That is why I cannot marry you."

"I do not understand."

"What if someone discovered the truth? The scandal would be a hundred times worse if I were the Countess of Lyndon than if I were just plain Mrs. Aldritch. Don't you see?"

A pulse ticked in Justin's jaw. He was obviously furious, more furious than Caroline had ever seen him. "No, I do not see."

"I will not be the cause of scandal for your family. I care about all of you too much."

"You are being ridiculous," Justin said tightly. "No one knows of this but you, me, and your maid and sister. I hardly think *they* will go gossiping about it."

"*You* found out! Someone else could as well."

"I only found out because I saw your scar. Did you go about flashing it at everyone?"

"Of course not!"

"Of course not. And not even Harry, who met you on several occasions as Mrs. Archer, has recognized you."

"I cannot take that chance."

Justin looked as if he would very much like to say something else. His mouth opened and closed again.

Finally, he said, "All right, then, Caroline. Be all self-sacrificing if you want to. But this is not the end. I will come back, again and again, until you agree to marry me."

Then he turned on his heel and left. The front door closed with a loud snap behind him, and Caroline was all alone in the echoing silence.

"I am *not* self-sacrificing," she muttered, hitting at a cushion with her fist. "I am *sensible*."

Chapter Twenty-Two

"It was awful!" Phoebe whispered to Sarah and Harry. The three of them were huddled together on the last row of chairs at Mrs. Stone's musicale, whispering and murmuring beneath the loud screech of Miss Stone's violin solo. "I was just going up the walkway to our front door when Lord Lyndon came bursting out. His face was all red, and he was muttering to himself. He walked right past me without saying a word. I would vow he did not even see me."

Harry squirmed uncomfortably in his seat, but Sarah's brown eyes were wide with interest. "What did you find when you went inside?" she asked.

"My sister was in the drawing room, just sitting there all quiet. But I could see she had been crying." Phoebe sighed. "I thought I was helping by going to speak to Lord Lyndon. It seems I have only made things worse. Something tragic has happened to separate them!" She shot a sharp glance at Harry. "If only *someone* had not lost his temper and started a fight. I know I was getting through to Lord Lyndon, given just a bit more time."

"Me!" cried Harry. Several people looked over

at them, and he quickly lowered his voice. "Me? I was only coming to your rescue."

"I did not need to be rescued. I was just starting to make some progress." Phoebe turned her gaze to where Caroline sat, ostensibly listening to the music. She never moved her eyes from Miss Stone and her violin. Then Phoebe looked at Lord Lyndon, sitting with his mother and Lady Bellweather on the opposite side of the room from Caroline. He, too, pretended great interest in the terrible music, but he kept darting little looks at Caroline.

"Now it is all ruined," Phoebe continued. "Caro gave up the scheme of leaving Wycombe the very next day, but she says we will go at the end of the week." Phoebe did not want to leave, or at least she did not want to go back to Devonshire as Caroline was talking of doing. She wanted to go to Brighton with Sarah, or maybe to London.

And she wanted her sister to be happy. It hurt her heart every time she saw Caroline drifting about the house, pale and sad. She wasn't certain what had happened between Caroline and Lord Lyndon three days ago, but she was sure there must be something she could do to make things right. The two of them so obviously cared for each other. It was ridiculous and tragic for them to be apart, just like in *Lady Lucinda's Passion*.

"Did your brother say anything to you about what happened?" she asked Harry.

"Not a word," he answered. "But Justin has been an absolute bear ever since. I spilled some tea at breakfast, and you would have thought I burned down the house from the way he shouted!" Harry sighed. "I vow I will be glad to rusticate at Seward Park after this."

Phoebe tapped her finger thoughtfully on her chin. "There must be *something* we can do to help, since they are too bacon brained to do it themselves. Come, help me devise a scheme."

The three of them bent their heads together.

Harry and Phoebe and Sarah were up to something, Justin could tell.

In between stealing glances at Caroline, he watched them. They had been whispering, thick as thieves, at the back of the room ever since the music (if one could call it that) began. After the smugglers' treasure contretemps and all the little mischiefs since, Justin did not trust them one whit.

But he did wish he still had some of their aptitude for scheming. If he did, he could come up with a plan to get Caroline to marry him.

Not that he had even tried. In the three days since the scene in her drawing room, he had lain awake every night, devising wild and unlikely plans to win her. In the clear light of day, they all looked extremely ridiculous. Caroline's mind was made up; she was obviously doing what she felt was right, and all the letters and bouquets he sent would not move her.

If only he could make her see that nothing mattered, nothing but her! No one would ever find out about Mrs. Archer, and even if they did it would not matter. He would just take her and all their family to stay at Waring Castle, and the scandal would die the natural death of a nine days' wonder.

What he needed was a really good plan, something romantic, something that would prove to her his sincerity. . . .

His gaze snapped back to the whispering young trio.

As the violin piece ended and relieved applause broke out, Justin rose from his chair and went to the back row where the three of them were sitting.

Their alarmed glances and sudden silence proved to him that he had indeed been the subject of their conversation.

"Harry, ladies," he said, sitting down beside them, "I wonder if I might beg your assistance. . . ."

Oh, Lord, would this evening never end?

Caroline sat very still, her hands folded in her lap, her eyes aimed forward to the young lady and her violin, a polite mask on her face. But she was all too aware of Justin watching her, trying to catch her attention, and her mind was racing wildly from one thought to another.

She longed to go home, to shut herself away in her room, alone. Maybe there, in the quiet, she could sort out her thoughts.

Then again, maybe not.

She had been trying to sort them for three days, three days of steadfastly avoiding Justin, and they had insisted on remaining in chaos.

She told herself over and over that she was doing the right thing. If she gave in to her selfish desires and agreed to marry Justin, they would be happy for a while. But eventually he would come to resent her past, especially if it caused a scandal. He would become cold, would turn to other women, maybe to drink as Lawrence had. She had seen such things over and over among the *ton*nish patrons of the Golden Feather. Men who gambled until the wee hours to avoid going home, masked women with wedding bands on their fingers who drank and laughed with forced gaiety.

A life of that sort would kill her. It would be more painful to have a life with Justin and lose it than any pain she was going through now could be.

At least that was what she told herself. Repeatedly.

If only he would cease sending her flowers and notes, reminding her of his presence! If only he would accept that what she was doing was for his benefit, and go away to his castle.

A burst of applause broke out around her, and she realized with a start that the music was over. She looked about, and saw that Justin was gone from his seat.

Caroline rose to her feet, relieved, and was about to go seek some refreshments when she saw her sister and Sarah Bellweather coming toward her. Phoebe had one gloved hand pressed dramatically to her brow.

"Oh, Caro!" she cried. "May we please go home now? I have such a dreadful headache."

"A headache?" Caroline said in alarm. Phoebe was never ill; she was always far too busy for fits of the megrims. She took off one glove and laid her fingers against Phoebe's forehead. "You *are* rather warm, and your cheeks are flushed."

"It came upon her very suddenly," Sarah offered. "She could hardly rise from her seat."

"Miss Stone's violin and this heat are enough to give anyone a headache," Caroline said. She even felt one throbbing at the back of her own head now. "Let us just say good-bye to our hostess; then we can be off. Mary will know of a posset for you."

"And can Sarah come, too?" Phoebe said, leaning weakly against Caroline's arm.

"It is quite all right with my mother," Sarah said. "We already asked her."

Caroline peered at Phoebe closely. "You felt well enough to walk across the room and speak to Lady Bellweather before coming back here to me?"

Phoebe gave a pitiable little smile. "It would make me feel *ever* so much better to have Sarah with me."

Caroline was too tired to argue. "Oh, very well, then. Come along, girls."

Phoebe's chamber, unlike Caroline's, had a window that faced the street. When Caroline and Sarah went to tuck her up in her bed, she insisted that the curtains be left open.

"But you will be disturbed by the noise from the street," Caroline protested. "That is not good for a headache."

"I-I like the light," Phoebe said, leaning back against her pillows.

"All right, then." Caroline, who had been in the process of closing the satin curtains, reopened them, and went to give her sister a kiss. "I will leave you and Sarah to retire, then."

Phoebe's gaze darted past her, toward the small clock hung above her fireplace mantel. "Oh, no!"

Caroline drew back to look at her. "What do you mean no? Phoebe, you are acting very oddly." She was surely up to something, Caroline could tell. Her cheeks were red with a hectic flush, and Sarah

Bellweather's brown eyes were far too wide and innocent.

They were most assuredly up to some mischief.

"I, well, I just mean don't go yet," Phoebe said with a little laugh. "I would like some . . . some warm milk. To help me sleep."

"I will ring for Mary, then," Caroline said, reaching for the embroidered bellpull.

"But you make it ever so much better!" Phoebe said beseechingly. "You make it much better than Mary does."

Caroline regarded Phoebe with narrowed eyes. Now she *knew* something was afoot. The minx could not be planning to elope with Harry Seward, could she? Perhaps she meant to climb down from her window and jump into a carriage with him as soon as Caroline's back was turned. To make a run for Gretna Green, as she had done herself so long ago.

Well, they would just see about that.

"Very well," she said. "I will go fetch the milk. But you had best be here when I return."

"Why, Caro!" Phoebe cried, all innocence. "Where would I go?"

Caroline gave her one last warning glance, then hurried downstairs, sending Mary back up to keep a sharp eye on the girls while she made the milk. It took longer than expected to heat the milk and find cinnamon and cloves to grate into it while avoiding the cook's irate questions about why she was in the kitchen, so it was fully fifteen minutes before she returned to Phoebe's chamber.

There she found the window overlooking the street wide open, and Phoebe, Mary, and Sarah all leaning over the sill looking down.

And floating up to them was a sound egregious enough to rival even Miss Stone's violin playing.

The strains of some stringed instrument, a lute or a mandolin perhaps, were discernible, and above them rose a voice of unimaginable unmusicality.

" 'When Nature made her chief work, Stella's eyes, In color black, why wrapp'd she beams so bright?' " the voice warbled. " 'Would she in beamy black, like painter wise, Frame daintiest lustre, mixed of shades and light?' "

Caroline put the glass down on a table and went over to the window, hardly aware of her own feet moving, carrying her forward.

Surely this could not be what she thought.

The three women parted at her approach, hovering at either side of the window with silly, giggling grins on their faces. Caroline leaned over the sill and looked down.

Justin stood on the pavement outside the house, singing as loudly as he possibly could and gesturing broadly with his arms. Behind him stood Harry, strumming inexpertly but enthusiastically on a lute.

They had gathered quite a crowd of interested onlookers about them, as well, some of them people Caroline recognized from the musicale. Perhaps they thought this was merely a continuation of the party.

Against her will, Caroline felt a silly grin spreading slowly across her own face. Then a laugh rose up in her throat, and another and another. She could not help it; he looked so very comical, and so dear.

And so scandalous. Everyone in Wycombe would know of this scene by morning, and it would be greatly exaggerated as well. Earls simply did not sing beneath respectable women's windows, causing scenes. It just wasn't done.

Perhaps he was foxed, and Harry, too. But Caroline only remembered a weak claret cup being served at the musicale, and they had not been gone long enough to go to some tavern.

" 'Both so and thus, she, minding Love should be Placed ever there, gave him this mourning weed, To honor all their deaths, who for her bleed.' "

His song at an end, Justin fell silent.

"Whatever are you doing, Lord Lyndon?" Caroline called, trying to sound stern despite her helpless laughter.

In answer, Justin fell to his knees, one hand clasped over his heart. Harry laid down his lute and reached into a basket at his feet for a handful of flowers, which he tossed up to her window. Some fell back to the ground and some hit her in the face.

She clutched at the blossoms, her gaze never leaving Justin's face.

"Can't you see, Caroline?" he called back. "I am willing to cause any scene, any scandal, for you. If you refuse my proposal again tonight, I will just come back tomorrow, and the night after that, and the night after that, until you hear me out. I do not care about anything but you, and I never will."

The collective gaze of the gathered crowd swung from him up to her window. Phoebe, Mary, and Sarah were all happily crying against each other's shoulders.

"It is just so romantic," Mary sobbed.

"Like *The Romance of the Ruby Chalice*," Phoebe sniffled.

Caroline saw and heard none of this. The stares, the whispers—it was everything she feared, everything she had hoped she left behind at the Golden Feather. But somehow she didn't care about any of it.

She only cared about Justin and what he was doing for her. Earls were meant to be dignified and elegant, and he acted the abject clown right in the middle of the street. All for her, to gain her attention.

She had been a fool, she saw that so clearly now, to ever hold propriety above love. A silly fool, so blinded by her past that she could not see the truth that was right there before her.

Justin had faced down scandal in his own past, and he was not afraid of it. He was too strong for that, and she had underestimated him.

She would never do that again.

Tears were falling warmly, silently down her cheeks. She buried her face in the fragrance of the flowers she held.

"Well, Caroline?" she heard Justin say. "Shall I sing again? I only know the one song."

Caroline looked up and laughed. "Certainly not! We do not want poor Sir Phillip Sidney to rise from his grave in protest."

"I will only not sing again if you will let me come in and talk to you."

Caroline looked at his beloved face, bathed in moonlight and hope. Yes, she *had* been a fool to think she could ever leave him.

She was a fool no longer. "I will do more than that," she answered. "I will marry you."

All the onlookers burst into applause, while Phoebe and Sarah danced a little happy dance, waltzing each other around the room.

Justin rose slowly from his knees. "Say that again," he said in a strangled voice.

"I will marry you!" she shouted happily.

Justin ran up the front steps then and through the door that Mary had gone down to obligingly hold open for him.

Caroline spun about and dashed out of the room. They met halfway up the staircase, and Justin caught her against him in a kiss that no woman could be foolish enough to leave again. He lifted her off her feet, and she wound her arms about his neck, clinging as if she would never let go.

Justin pulled back and leaned his forehead against hers. "I just want to be certain I heard you correctly. Did you say you would marry me?"

"I did, and I will."

"When?"

"Tomorrow?"

"A dash for Gretna Green?"

Caroline hesitated, but then nodded. "If you like."

"Of course I would like it! To have you as my wife within days would be heaven. But I could not do that to you. Your first wedding was an elopement. This time you should have all the gewgaws."

"Like cake!" a voice cried. "And champagne."

"And rose petals!"

They looked up to see Phoebe and Sarah hanging over the banister, watching them with avid young eyes.

"And we want to be bridesmaids," Phoebe added. "In orange silk."

"No, blue," said Sarah.

"All right, then. Blue." Phoebe sighed happily.

"It will be just like *Lady Arabella's Royal Wedding*."

"You see, now, Caroline dear," Justin said. "We must have a grand wedding. We could never disappoint two such lovely, and helpful, young ladies. Could we?"

"I suppose not. A grand wedding it is, then."

"In the autumn? At Waring Castle?"

Caroline nodded and actually giggled in her soaring delight. "Autumn. And not a day later!"

Then she leaned her head against his shoulder and closed her eyes. Safe. She was safe at last. After all the years of searching, of loneliness, she would never be alone or fearful again.

Epilogue

October, Waring Castle

"It is all so lovely," Phoebe said, her voice rhapsodic. "Just like . . ."

"*The Sins of Madame Evelyn?*" suggested Harry.

"I would wager it is *The Enchanted Vale,*" said Sarah.

"You are both wrong," protested Phoebe. "I was going to say it is just like a . . . a fairy tale. Like the ones Caro read to me when I was very little."

Indeed it was. The three of them stood at the edge of the grand ballroom at Waring Castle, watching the dancers swirl and twirl in the figures of a waltz. Bright silks and satins and flashing jewels created a kaleidoscope of color and motion. Music soared to the sky blue–painted dome above, and the scent of flowers hung sweetly in the cool autumn air.

It *was* like a scene from a fairy tale, a royal ball on the eve of a glorious wedding.

And at the center of it all were a prince and princess, or rather an earl and a countess-to-be.

Phoebe watched her sister dancing in the arms of her almost-husband, looking radiant and happy in a gown of emerald green silk, and she gave a smug smile. Without her help, things would not have reached this most satisfactory conclusion, and she was feeling quite smart indeed.

Surely there were other people who could benefit from her help. She would just have to look about for them, after her wedding duties were concluded.

"I suppose we will not see each other again until Christmas, Phoebe," Harry said to her quietly.

She turned and smiled at him. Dear Harry. How very dashing he looked tonight, in his red-and-gold striped waistcoat and red coat. It went so well with her own coral-colored ensemble. "I suppose we will not," she answered lightly. "You are off to take charge of Seward Park, and I will be staying with Sarah and her family while my sister is on her wedding trip to Scotland."

Harry shifted on his feet, uncharacteristically shy. "But . . . well. Dash it, that is, will you write to me, Phoebe? While I am gone?"

Phoebe laughed and tucked her hand in the crook of his elbow. "Of course I will write to you, Harry! We are family now."

"Are you happy tonight, Caroline dearest?" Justin swung his bride-to-be in a wide circle, making her skirts shimmer in an emerald fire.

She tightened her grip on his shoulder and laughed merrily. For the first time in many, many years she felt free. Free and light and young. In his arms, she knew she could soar. "Happier than I have ever been."

"And this is only the beginning."

"Oh, yes! Only the beginning."

The Rules of Love

Chapter One

"*O*h, Allen. What have you done *this* time?"

Though she'd spoken softly, Rosalind wanted to groan the words, scream them out, even throw something at her brother's head as he lounged so casually in his chair across from her. She could not, of course. That would be highly improper, and it would never do if one of the teachers or, heaven forbid, one of the girls heard her make a fuss. So she folded her hands on the mahogany surface of her desk, clasping her fingers together until the knuckles turned white.

Besides, even if she *did* throw something at Allen, it would scarcely make a dent in his thick skull. This was a scene they had played out dozens of times, and it always ended the same way.

"Oh, now, Rosie, really that is unfair," Allen protested. He crossed his booted foot over his buckskin-covered knee and jiggled it impatiently. Rosalind frowned as flakes of mud showered from the boot's sole onto the freshly polished floor. "I have done nothing untoward! A man must pay his gaming debts, after all. It is a point of honor."

Honor? Rosalind's head pounded as if a hundred

drummers were tattooing that word inside her brain. She should show him *honor*, the ignorant young pup!

Be calm, she thought, pressing her fingertips to her temples. *Remember how your parents asked you to look after him.*

Remember the rules. Breaking his skull was assuredly against the rules.

She reached out for the frighteningly official-looking letter. "So you borrowed money from a bank?"

"It was only until I receive my allowance. I needed to pay Carteret right away, you see, or I could not have shown my face at the club. They were never supposed to bother *you*, Rosie. It's dashed embarrassing to have them go to one's sister! What if Morley, or one of the others at the club, found out?"

Morley again. Always the blasted Viscount Morley. Even the very name made Rosalind silently curse, which usually she would never dream of doing. Cursing was also against the rules. Morley was the one who led Allen, and no doubt other impressionable young men, into folly. Morley, and his club, were a terrible influence on Allen.

But Rosalind did not say that. Any time she tried to talk to Allen about Lord Morley and his questionable activities, to warn him, he cut her off. It was futile— as futile as urging him to concentrate more on his studies and less on the lures of Town.

"Your allowance would never have covered this amount," she told him. "Not in a year. And the interest . . . !" Rosalind took a deep breath. "Allen, banks have ways of compelling people to pay. This is a legal debt. Do you have any idea what you have gotten yourself, not to mention this school and me, into?"

Allen's face, so bored and careless-looking ever since he had come into her office, flushed a dull red. His foot slid off his knee to land with a loud thud on the floor and he pointed a shaking finger in her direction. "Now, see here, Rosie! I am eighteen now. I can't stand for having my sister ring a peal over my head. I must live my own life, as a man."

Rosalind had had just about all she could take of this scene. Her head was pounding as if it would explode, and she knew that nothing she could say or do would persuade Allen of the truth. These days, only *Morley* could do that.

"I must remind you that I am your guardian until you are twenty, along with Uncle Silas, though truly I do everything since he lives in the wilds of Yorkshire. Our parents wished it this way, and in any case they left neither of us much money. It is *your sister* who pays for your schooling at Cambridge, as well as your allowance, and it is *your sister* who pulls you out of the soup every time you fall in. Which has been more and more of late!" Her voice rose dangerously on those last words. Rosalind took another deep breath and folded her hands together again. She would *not* let this get the better of her. "We are not wealthy people. This school allows us to be quite comfortable, but we cannot be extravagant as Mo—as some of your friends are."

Allen crossed his arms across his chest, still mulishly stubborn. "I am not *extravagant,* Rosie! I only need the necessities."

"Such as gaming debts? Coats from Weston? New boots every week?"

"I told you, it was the—"

Rosalind held up her hand to stop his endless flow of protests and explanations. "I know. It was for your club."

"Well—yes. It was. You must agree that a man must maintain his good name at his club."

Rosalind sighed, and resisted the almost overpowering urge to sink back wearily in her chair. She wished she could take a tisane and crawl into her bed, to sleep and forget all this. But she could not. It was too early in the day, and she had far too many responsibilities. The parents of her pupils would be arriving soon to take their daughters home for the spring holiday, for the beginning of the Season in London.

"I cannot think about this right now, Allen," she

said. "Most of the students are leaving today, and I must see them off."

Allen nodded, obviously deeply relieved. He never liked quarrels, even when he was the one who started them. "Of course, Rosie. I'll just come back tomorrow, then, or the day after."

Two days. That would give him plenty of time to run up even more debts, Rosalind thought. He would never learn. She just nodded, though, and watched him gather up his hat and greatcoat and hurry to the door.

There he turned back and gave her an uncertain glance, a flicker of a pleading smile. "Er, Rosie, about that letter from the bank . . ."

Rosalind stared down at the letter beneath her clenched hands. The stark black signature stared back, like an accusation. An accusation that she was failing in her duties to her family. Her parents, her flighty, social mother and her distracted vicar father, had always relied on her to look after Allen. Now that they were gone, she owed that to them even more. She was all Allen had. "I will write to them, and see what can be done. I will take care of it." *As always.*

Allen gave her a relieved smile, and came back to kiss her cheek. "You *are* a brick, Rosie. I knew you would see that it could not be helped."

She answered his grin with a stern frown. "I do not see any such thing. All I see is that banks must be dealt with. But I have no time to talk about this now. Just go, Allen."

Rosalind closed her eyes, and did not open them again until she heard the click of the door closing.

Alone at last. Her office, her sanctuary, looked the same as it always did. The lovely, restful lavender and cream draperies and chairs and settees, chosen to be feminine and soothing, were the same. The small mahogany desk she sat behind, the painting of pink and white roses that hung above the fireplace, the porcelain shepherdesses and vases on the tables—all the same. This room was where she could come to be alone, to be quiet, to do what she loved most in the world—write, and run her school.

Yet after such meetings with her brother, such futile, ridiculous meetings, nothing could soothe her.

"If only I wasn't a lady," she murmured, "I would have a whiskey."

Just as her late husband Charles had when things became too contentious. It had always soothed the few rough patches in their marriage.

But she *was* a lady. She had standards—high standards—to uphold. And the parents of her pupils would be arriving soon to fetch their precious daughters for their holidays. It would simply never do to greet them with *whiskey* on her breath!

She would have to content herself with a cup of tea in the drawing room, with those very parents.

Rosalind stood up and crossed the room to the small mirror hanging on the wall between two bookcases. She feared her reflection would show her inner turmoil, with wild eyes and straggling hair. Aside from a pink flush in her cheeks, however, she looked the same as she always did. Her bright red curls, the bane of her life, were drawn tightly back and covered with a lace cap. The frill of her chemisette was spotlessly white, tucked neatly into the square neckline of her green and gold striped silk afternoon dress. Her blue eyes *were* brighter than usual, sparkling with the force of suppressed anger, but other than that she was the perfectly proper Mrs. Chase.

She opened the little hidden drawer in one of the bookcases and took out a small pot of rice powder and one of lip color. She dusted the powder over the faint golden freckles that splashed across the bridge of her nose. Not for the first time, she wished she had Allen's smooth chestnut locks and clear complexion, instead of the red hair and freckles that came from their grandmother.

The thought of her brother made her eyes narrow again, and pink spread across her cheeks and down her throat into the ruffle.

"Not now," she murmured. "I cannot think of this now. Allen will just have to stew in his own soup for the moment."

There was a knock at the door. It was probably Molly, the housemaid, come to tell her that the first of the parents were arriving. Rosalind pushed the powder and lip color back into the drawer, and called, "Come in."

It was not Molly's face that peeked around the door, though. It was Lady Violet Bronston.

Rosalind couldn't help but smile at the sight of Lady Violet's golden curls and merry green eyes. She was one of the best students at Mrs. Chase's Seminary for Young Ladies, adept at music, watercolors, and French. She was sweet, and friendly with the other girls, a great favorite of the teachers. And of Rosalind, too, if truth be told. Violet's conversation was always cheerful, despite the fact that her family life was not entirely happy. Rosalind would miss her when she graduated and went on to her first Season next year.

Yes, Violet *was* a dear. Even if she was the sister of Viscount Morley.

"I am sorry to disturb you, Mrs. Chase," Violet said shyly. She glanced around quickly. Usually only Rosalind and the teachers came into this office.

Rosalind smiled at her, and gestured for her to enter. "Please, do come in, Lady Violet. You are not disturbing me at all. I was just going to come and be sure that everyone is packed. Is your father here to fetch you already?" She said this most pleasantly, even though her lips wanted to twist bitterly at mention of Violet's father. The Earl of Athley was certainly an important man indeed, but also a most unpleasant and arrogant one. He was assuredly one of the most difficult of the parents to deal with. Fortunately, she seldom saw him.

Rosalind also thought Lord Athley could use a thorough lesson in manners.

Violet shook her head, a relieved smile on her rosebud lips. "No, indeed! Papa could not come today.

My brother, Lord Morley, is going to fetch me and take me into Town."

Morley again. Could not an hour pass that she did not hear that name? Rosalind covered her chagrin by turning away to pick up her shawl and drape it over her shoulders. "Your brother? We have not seen him here in quite a while." Not since that one disastrous visit last year. That had not gone well at all.

Violet sat down on one of the brocade settees, happily oblivious to any possible strife in her small world. She smoothed the skirt of her stylish, pale lilac carriage gown. "He came to see me last month, when you had gone to Bath. He says he will take me to have ices at Gunter's when we are in London, and to the theater, and Astley's Amphitheater, so that—well, so that I do not have to spend *all* my time with Father at Bronston House."

Rosalind sat down beside Violet, surprised to hear of such generosity from such an annoying man. "That sounds lovely for you."

Violet nodded, and stared down at her lace-gloved hands folded in her lap. "Yes, of course. But I *will* miss the school so much! And you, and Miss James, and the other girls. I wish . . ." She paused and swallowed hard before she went on in a softer voice. "I wish I could stay here."

Rosalind nodded. She had had this discussion with Violet before, had listened to the girl when she spoke of her unhappiness at home. It made Rosalind's heart ache that she could do so little for her. "Some of the girls *do* stay here for the holidays, of course," she said carefully. "But most of them have family homes that are far away, not nearby as yours is."

Violet nodded. "I know, and Father would never hear of my staying here." She gave Rosalind a brave, bright little smile, and said, "But I promise you, Mrs. Chase, that my time in London will not be wasted! I will work on my watercolors, and my French verbs. And Miss James has assigned us to read *Hamlet,* which is very good since my brother has promised to take me to see the play at Drury Lane." She opened her reticule and pulled out a small book, handsomely bound in dark blue leather. The embossed silver letters on the cover read *A Lady's Rules for Proper Behavior*. "And I will always be very careful to follow the rules. A true lady is known by her manners, is she not? That is what you always say, Mrs. Chase."

Rosalind laughed. "Yes, of course. And a true gentleman, too. Manners are what raise us above the animals in their forests and barnyards. They are the mark of true civility."

Violet nodded eagerly. "I read it every night." She ran her fingertip over the silver words, *By an Anonymous Lady*. "Do you think we shall ever know who wrote it?"

"Perhaps not. But that is not important, Lady Violet. What *is* important is the content of its pages."

Violet tucked the book carefully back into her reticule. "Perhaps I should get a copy for my brother?"

I doubt it would do him much good, he is so far gone, Rosalind thought wryly. But outwardly she just nodded, and said, "I am sure Lord Morley would appreciate that. Now, my dear Lady Violet, tell me what else you have planned for your holiday."

She half-listened as Violet talked of tea parties and museums. Yet in her mind she saw the most distracting image of *A Lady's Rules* in the philistine hands of Lord Morley.

For Rosalind had a secret, an even greater one than the rice powder that covered her freckles. She herself was the anonymous lady who wrote the very popular *Rules*. And the sales of this slim volume, so dependent on its interest among the *ton,* helped pay her own, and her brother's, bills. Fortunately for her, Lord Morley and his ilk were in the minority in Society at the moment. *A Lady's Rules* had become all the crack among the *haute ton*. Everyone was eager to buy the book and show how very civilized they were.

That tiny book was Rosalind's very life's blood.

Chapter Two

"Young ladies are particularly impressionable, and look to their families for a fine example. Proper behavior and language, while always important, should be especially observed in their presence"
—*A Lady's Rules for Proper Behavior*, Chapter One

*M*ichael Bronston, the Viscount Morley, drew his phaeton to a halt on the gravel drive outside Mrs. Chase's Seminary for Young Ladies, and sat there for a moment, studying the surroundings. The Seminary was only a few miles outside London, but it might as well have been on another continent, so different was it from the rush and noise of the city. Situated in its own green, tidy park, surrounded by a high wall, it had almost the hush of a monastery.

The school building itself was of red brick, faded by time to a rose pink, with neat white shutters at the windows and white pillars lining the portico. Heavy draperies hung inside all the windows, shutting out the light.

Michael frowned at its terribly tidy, terribly proper appearance.

A fitting prison for my poor sister, he thought. Then he had to laugh at himself. It seemed the whole "poet persona" he took on himself in Society was beginning to tell on him. He was becoming melodramatic.

And, prison though the Seminary might be for Vio-

let, it was far better for her than being at home. Their
father was a more accomplished jailer than Mrs. Chase
could ever hope to be.

Ah, yes. *Mrs. Chase.* The beauteous Mrs. Chase,
who tried to hide her glorious sunset-colored hair
under hideous caps, and whose disapproving moue
made her seem far older than she surely was. Michael
had met her only once, on one of the occasions he
came to visit Violet, but her cool glance had almost
frozen him where he stood.

There was something *about* her, though, something
in the pale depths of her ice blue eyes that made him
want to bait her, to tweak her maddening propriety—
to make her show some emotion. So he, perhaps child-
ishly, had acted even more the "poet" around her,
lounging indolently in the dainty chairs of her drawing
room, quoting suggestive verse to her.

Mrs. Chase had merely raised her chin even higher,
and stared at him as if he was an insect on her polished floor. And Violet had berated him for his lack
of manners for hours afterward. It had not been his
proudest moment. He had been deeply relieved to find
Mrs. Chase gone to Bath on his next visit to Violet.

But now here he was again, and there was very little
hope that Mrs. Chase would not be on the premises.
He vowed that this time he would act his age, and be
impeccably well-mannered. He had even brought a
sort of peace offering, a volume of his newest collection of poems, though he doubted it would thaw any
of Mrs. Chase's frostiness.

A footman in the school livery came to take the
reins of the phaeton, and Michael jumped down to
the gravel drive. No sooner had he placed one booted
foot on the front steps than the white-painted door
opened and Mr. Allen Lucas came barreling out.

The young man was scowling, distracted, until he
saw Michael, and a grin lit up his face.

"Lord Morley!" he cried happily, and caught Michael's hand in a hearty shake. "Fancy meeting you
here, of all places."

Michael remembered then that Lucas was Mrs. Chase's brother. It was hard to remember that when he saw the young man at their club every week; his behavior and demeanor were so very different from hers. Allen Lucas was one of a group of young men, newcomers to the Thoth Club, who had literary and artistic pretensions and who spent most of their time trying to outdo one another in hell-raising.

"I've come to fetch my sister home," Michael said, pulling off his leather driving gloves.

Lucas gave a lopsided grin, which he obviously considered sardonic, and leaned against one of the pillars. "And I've just left *my* sister."

"Your sister is Mrs. Chase, is she not?"

"The very same." Lucas heaved a deep sigh, full of exasperation. "I vow I will never be able to fathom females! Rosie has become such a dry stick, and I don't know when it happened. She was always laughing, always game for a lark, when we lived at my parents' house."

Mrs. Chase, of the icy blue eyes and tilted chin, game for a lark? Mrs. Chase, called *Rosie*? Somehow, Michael could not envision it. But then, he very often could not fathom females, either. "So you are leaving, Lucas?"

"Indeed, and the quicker the better, before Rosie finds me and rings another peal over my head. See you at the club on Thursday? I heard Lord Waverly and Mr. Gilmore are going to race their curricles!"

"Not in the club, I do hope."

Lucas guffawed loudly, far more loudly than the light jest deserved. "Certainly not! The road to Brighton, I daresay. But it will be on the betting books."

"Ah. Well, then, I will see you there. Good day, Lucas."

"Good day, Morley!" Lucas bounded down the steps to where a footman held the reins of his horse.

Morley gave him a farewell wave, and then turned back to the front door. Lucas had left it ajar on his exit, so Michael just pushed it open and went in.

The foyer was crowded with piles of trunks and valises, with girls in fluttery pastel travel gowns, who called to each other, and giggled, and cried as they tied their bonnet ribbons and draped shawls over their shoulders. Footmen and teachers moved between them, carrying bags away or just shifting them about. Michael glanced back to the door he had just entered. It seemed to be a portal back to sanity, out of bedlam.

But he was too late. Miss James, one of the teachers, saw him before he could make his escape.

"Lord Morley!" she called. She handed one of the girls a pink bandbox and made her way over to him, wending past the obstacles of luggage. "How good it is to see you again. Lady Violet has been asking every five minutes when you would arrive."

"Hello, Miss James," Michael answered. He pushed away his doubts about all the feminine fuss, and gave her a polite bow. "I must say I am quite eager to see my sister again, too. It has been far too long."

"Such brotherly devotion is most touching, Lord Morley." Miss James smiled at him rather mistily. "Lady Violet is in the drawing room. Mrs. Chase is serving tea in there, as well. I am sure you must be in need of refreshment after your long drive."

"Thank you, Miss James." Michael bowed to her again, and made his way toward the door that led to the drawing room, trying not to knock over any scurrying young misses or fall over any errant trunks on the way.

It was slightly quieter in the elegant pale green and cream drawing room. There was no luggage piled about, only the usual chairs and tables and bibelots. Parents, and a few daughters, gathered in clusters and groups, chatting and laughing in perfectly civilized tones. On one large, round table was an array of tea things—cups, pots, tiered trays of tiny sandwiches and cakes.

There was a small, barely perceptible lull in the conversation when Michael appeared, and a few female glances turned his way. He was not entirely thrilled to meet the dark gaze of Lady Clarke. They had flirted casually at a ball or two, but she had soon spread the word that Michael's poem, "Alas, fair cruelty," was about *her*. It most decidedly was not. She gave him a little wave of her dainty fingers.

Michael acknowledged her greeting with a brief nod, but his own gaze was caught by the woman who stood next to the tea table—Mrs. Chase. She had not seen him yet, and was talking to one of the parents. She nodded at whatever the other woman was saying, and tilted her head thoughtfully to one side. Her hair was smoothed back beneath an ugly lace cap, but one flame red curl had fallen from its confines and tangled with a pearl drop earring. She reached up absently to brush it back, and the curl twined around her slender finger before she managed to confine it.

Then, unexpectedly, she laughed. Really laughed. The sound reached all the way across the room to him, wrapping around him silkily, as her hair had caught on her finger. It was sweet and rich, surprisingly dark, like a Spanish sherry. It transformed her entire being, making her face, usually so pale and distant, glow with an incandescent radiance.

"Aurora, the dawn . . ." he whispered.

As if she heard him, though that was impossible from across the room, she looked up and saw him standing there. The laughter faded as if it had never been. Her eyes turned from sky blue to ice, and her lips thinned.

Michael wanted her laughter back—more than wanted, he *needed* it. He could not have said why he mourned the loss of this woman's merriment. She was a person he hardly knew, did not even *like*. But there it was. He found he would do anything to hear her laugh again.

As if in some sort of a trance, a daze, he took a step toward her, then another.

The invisible cord that pulled him to Mrs. Chase snapped when he heard his sister's silvery voice call, "Michael! Here you are at last."

Michael blinked, as if awakening from some dream, and rubbed his hand roughly over his eyes. That—that *whatever* it was that had come over him dissipated, and he found himself still in the school drawing room. He glanced quickly over to where Mrs. Chase had gone back to her conversation, half turned away from him. She was hardly an Aurora; she was just a stern schoolmistress.

"I am sorry I was delayed, Vi," he said, catching his sister's hands in his and leaning down to kiss her dimpled cheek. "There was a great deal of traffic on the road from London. It was all coming here, I see."

"Oh, yes, indeed! It is always crowded before holidays." Violet smiled up at him, those dimples flashing. "It is very good to see you again, Michael."

"And it's good to see *you,* Vi. It has been far too long." His sister was looking very well, he thought, as he held her away from him so he could study her. She had always been a pretty girl, the very image of their late mother with her golden curls and grass green eyes. But she had always been rather quiet, too, lost in her own world. Here, away from their father, she seemed more confident, more a part of the world around her.

If only she would learn to follow her own way in that world, and not follow in the paths of others so much.

"Oh, Vi!" he teased. "When did my baby sister grow to be such a grand lady?" He caught her up in a hug, until her little feet left the floor.

"Michael!" she squealed, pushing him away. "There are people watching."

He laughed. "So, since people are watching, I am not allowed to greet my sister?"

Violet frowned up at him, her pink and white forehead puckering, her lips drawn together in a perfect imitation of Mrs. Chase. She opened the reticule that dangled from her wrist and drew out a small, blue leather-bound book. She flicked through the pages until she found what she was looking for, and she read aloud, " 'A gentleman shall never be overexuberant when greeting a lady, even one nearly related to him. Bowing over the hand, or, if closely related, a kiss on the cheek, will suffice.' "

Michael laughed again, thinking she could not be serious. But Violet's frown deepened, and she even tapped the toe of her kid half-boot against the floor.

"Michael!" she scolded. "The rules are not to be mocked. They are important. Manners are what make us *civilized.*"

"What on earth are you spouting about, Vi?" Michael asked, and grabbed the book out of her hands.

A Lady's Rules for Proper Behavior.

Michael almost groaned aloud. So the insidious "rules" had spread out from Town into the Seminary. And his own sister was an adherent.

He should have known that Mrs. Chase, of all people, would read and espouse this book.

Violet took the volume back, and tucked it into her reticule. "You should read it, Michael. It is really most edifying."

"Edifying, eh?" Michael couldn't resist reaching out to tweak one of his sister's sunshine curls. "They *do* teach you big words here."

Violet drew back with another frown. "You see, Michael? You *do* need to read the rules. A gentleman should never pull a lady's hair. But come and say hello to Mrs. Chase now! I have told her all about our plans for the holiday."

"Did you, indeed?" he muttered. He politely offered Violet his arm, and led her across the room toward Mrs. Chase. He pasted an amiable smile on his lips, but inwardly he hoped he could just keep himself from throttling Mrs. Chase. She was turning his sweet sister into a rule-following stick—just like their father.

Chapter Three

"A gentleman must never seat himself on the settee beside his hostess, or any lady not related to him, unless invited."
—*A Lady's Rules for Proper Behavior,* Chapter Five

*R*osalind watched Lord Morley's exuberant greeting of his sister—and almost laughed when Lady Violet pulled out *A Lady's Rules* and proceeded to read her brother a portion of it. She did not know which rule it could be, but it must be a good one to cause the dark frown on Lord Morley's face. He stepped back from Violet, his hands planted on his hips, leather driving gloves dangling carelessly from his curled fingers.

Lady Violet, usually the mildest of young ladies, looked like a fierce little Valkyrie, swooping down to avenge wrongs done to decorum.

Rosalind thought again what a very fine student Lady Violet was.

"Ah, I see Lord Morley is here!" said the woman Rosalind was talking to, Lady Stone-Smythe. She reached up to pinch some color into her plump cheeks, and straightened her pink and green confection of a bonnet. "Such a treat to get a glimpse of him. He is invited simply *everywhere,* you know, but is so unpredictable in which invitations he will accept. I have hopes he will come to the literary evening I have planned." She half-turned toward where Lord Morley stood, displaying her ample charms in a tight green carriage costume to better advantage. "Imagine seeing him at a ladies' seminary."

Rosalind thought of one or two rules Lady Stone-Smythe would be well-advised to follow, but she resisted the urge to say so. Lady Stone-Smythe had three daughters in the school, and was one of her finest patrons. Even if she *was* a bit of silly goose.

"Lord Morley is the brother of one of my pupils, Lady Violet Bronston," Rosalind said. "She told me he was going to escort her home today."

"Of course! Lady Violet. Such a lovely young lady. And she is such good friends with my Imogen. I must go and say hello to her." With nary another glance at Rosalind, Lady Stone-Smythe sailed off across the drawing room to greet Lady Violet, clutching at the young woman's hand with great enthusiasm.

Violet stared at her, obviously bewildered, while her brother looked on, one corner of his lips lifted in amusement. Rosalind realized with a start that those lips were really quite handsome, narrow but sensual. She shook her head hard. What was she doing, thinking of his *handsome* lips! Ridiculous.

When Lady Stone-Smythe turned her effusions onto him, the quirk became a charming smile, and he bowed over her outstretched hand in its bright pink glove.

Rosalind could not fault his performance. His expression was interested, but not *too* interested, as she listened to Lady Stone-Smythe, leaning slightly closer as if to better hear her words.

Lady Stone-Smythe's performance, on the other hand . . .

Rosalind sighed, and poured a bit more tea in her cup. Some people, no matter how often they read the rules, simply never learned.

"Mrs. Chase," a voice said, interrupting her musings on Lord Morley, Lady Stone-Smythe, and proper behavior.

Rosalind turned to see Lady Clarke walking toward

her, her daughter Emmeline in tow. Lady Clarke was one of the reigning Diamonds of the *ton,* tall, willowy, with dark, glossy hair and perfect snow-white skin, set off elegantly by her dark red pelisse and tall-crowned hat. Sir Walter Clarke, whom Rosalind had met only once and who was not present today, was also quite handsome, a perfect match for his wife. Rosalind wondered what *he* would think of his wife's attention to the poet.

For Lady Clarke's gaze, like that of Lady Stone-Smythe, slid irresistibly to one magnetic object—Lord Morley.

Lady Clarke smiled charmingly at Rosalind, but kept sending tiny, surreptitious glances across the room. "Mrs. Chase, it is time Emmeline and I were leaving for Town, but we could not go without saying good-bye to you first. Emmeline has so enjoyed her time here, and is looking forward to returning next term."

Rosalind turned to Emmeline, who was a tall, dark girl, not yet revealing any beauty she might have inherited. "I am so glad you have enjoyed your time here, Emmeline. You have certainly been a fine addition to the school."

Emmeline murmured something and dropped a quick curtsy before hurrying off to join some of her friends.

"Your daughter is very talented musically, Lady Clarke," Rosalind told Emmeline's mother. "Her performances at the pianoforte are very pleasing."

"Oh, yes? How—very nice," Lady Clarke answered, without much interest. She still stared across the room, and reached up to finger the stiff lace trim of her pelisse. "I see that Lord Morley is here. Imagine encountering him at a girls' school."

Her words were almost exactly what Lady Stone-Smythe's had been, and Rosalind gave her the same answer. Lord Morley was here to fetch his sister.

"Indeed?" Lady Clarke said. Her touch moved from the lace to the ruby drop in her earlobe. "I—that is, we see him quite often in Town. We do try to support literature and music, and he is such a fine—poet. Have you read his work, Mrs. Chase?"

"No," Rosalind answered. "I have not had the privilege."

"Oh, you really should. A lady with a school should always be au courant, don't you agree? Well-versed in poetry and such."

"Indeed yes, Lady Clarke," Rosalind answered stiffly. "A girl cannot truly call herself a lady until she has attained accomplishments such as music, languages, and proper demeanor." Chapter One, *A Lady's Rules for Proper Behavior.*

Lady Clarke gave her one final, dismissive nod, and moved on to find her daughter. Before she reached Emmeline, though, she took a small detour to Lord Morley's side. As Rosalind watched, Lady Clarke laid an elegant hand on his sleeve, and said something quietly into his ear. He grinned at her, and she gave his arm a tiny, nearly imperceptible squeeze before moving away.

Oh, really, Rosalind thought wryly. Her school was not a place of assignation for Lord Morley! It was not a *harem.*

She turned away to place her empty cup back on the table. As she did so, she remembered that she had a small gift for Lady Violet in her office, and she should fetch it before the Bronstons left. She excused herself to the parents and teachers around her and left the drawing room.

Her office was quiet and peaceful after the milling throng of people, the early afternoon light a pale gold where it fell from the high windows. Rosalind fetched the little package from her desk drawer, but then, rather than return immediately to the drawing room, she sat down in her chair. Her earlier headache was still there, lurking behind her eyes, and she rubbed at her temples and closed her eyes.

She loved the girls who went to school here; she loved teaching. But she was also so glad when they all left for their holidays, and she had days and nights of perfect quiet all for herself. It was—peaceful.

Peaceful, except for worrying about Allen.

She groaned at the reminder of Allen and his debt, and a new pain stabbed above her left eye.

"Mrs. Chase?" someone said. A *masculine* someone.

Rosalind pressed hard one more time at her temples, before she dropped her hands and opened her eyes, a polite smile automatically forming on her lips.

The smile died before it had even truly been born when she saw the man that voice belonged to. Lord Morley stood in the doorway, watching her with a concerned frown.

"Lord Morley," she said, lacing her fingers together atop the desk.

"Mrs. Chase, are you quite all right?" he asked, moving farther into the room. He stopped in the middle of her lavender and cream carpet, and glanced about almost as if he was surprised to find himself there. He totally ignored the mess of dried mud Allen had left behind. "You look pale."

Rosalind stared at him, her voice frozen in her throat. He seemed a mirage here in her frilly, feminine sanctuary. He was tall and dark, overpowering the dainty gilded furniture, his deep blue greatcoat spreading like the wings of some bird of prey.

He *was* handsome, she had to admit, even if he was a blackguard. Worthy of the stares and simpers of Lady Clarke and Lady Stone-Smythe—worthy in a physical sense, anyway. He was tall, slim but not emaciated. Lean, in the way horsemen and swimmers were. His black, curling hair, overlong in the poetical tradition, was brushed back from his forehead and tumbled over the collar of his coat. His nose was a bit crooked, as if it had once been broken, but his jaw was firm, and his eyes—his eyes were dark as a starless night, dark as sin.

Rosalind almost groaned, and she closed her eyes again. What was wrong with her? She had drunk no spirits today at all, yet she was staring like a wide-eyed, moonstruck schoolgirl. Staring at the man who was leading her brother to perdition! Was there a rule against this? She was too tired to recall for certain, but if there was not there *should* be. *A lady will not stare at the rogue who is intent on ruining the prospects of silly young men.*

She opened her eyes and stared down at her hands.

She realized she had not said anything for too long when he took another step toward her and said, with mounting alarm in his voice, "Mrs. Chase! Do you feel faint?"

"I am quite well, thank you, Lord Morley," she managed to say. She reached up to make certain her cap was firmly in place.

"Nonsense! You are as white as milk. I will be right back."

Rosalind opened her mouth to protest, but Lord Morley had already spun around on his heel and left the room.

Oh, now where had he gone? Rosalind stood up, bewildered and even a bit frightened. This situation was spinning beyond her control, and she did not even know how it had happened.

And if there was one thing Rosalind *hated,* it was not being in control of every situation. Before she could stumble to the door, though, Lord Morley returned, a cup of tea in his hand. The fragile, pink-flowered china looked tiny and absurd in his long, elegant fingers.

"Here," he said. "You should sit down, and drink this." With his free hand, he clasped her arm and led her to the nearest settee.

"It is nothing, Lord Morley," she protested, and tried to draw away from his strangely disturbing touch. He was too strong for her, though, and did not let go until she was safely seated. "A mere headache."

"It is no wonder your head aches," he said. "Listening to those clucking women all morning is enough to give anyone the megrims!" He handed her the cup of tea, and went on in a perfect imitation of Lady Stone-Smythe's fluting tones. "'Oh, Mrs. Chase, my dear Harriet is *so* fond of playing the harp! You *must* allow her more time with the music master, she is *so* fond of him—I mean, fond of *music*.'"

Rosalind nearly choked on the sip of tea she had just taken. She knew she should not laugh at him, not find him funny in the least—it would only encourage his outrageous behavior, and it was surely rude to poor Lady Stone-Smythe. Yet she could not seem to help herself. She pressed her fingers to her lips to hold in the inelegant giggles.

"You see? Your color is better already, Mrs. Chase," he said, and knelt down beside her. He grinned in an infuriatingly satisfied manner.

"None of Lady Stone-Smythe's daughters is named Harriet," was all Rosalind could think to say.

"Ah, but you knew it was meant to be Lady Stone-Smythe. It must have been a worthy effort on my part."

"Yes, indeed, Lord Morley," Rosalind said tartly. Her dizziness was subsiding, and she felt a bit more like herself. Not like a woman who stared at rakes, thinking how handsome they were. "You ought to be treading the boards."

"So I think, but my family would simply not hear of it. I must content myself with poetry."

"Yes, your poetry." Rosalind swallowed the last of her tea, grateful for the strength of the smoky brew even if it was a bit cold by now. "Did Lady Stone-Smythe manage to lure you to her little literary evening?"

"She has been trying to for at least a month." As he shook his head in exasperation, his black raven's wing of hair fell over his brow, and he impatiently pushed it back.

Rosalind stared down at him, kneeling there on one knee beside her. "It is most improper for you to be there on the floor, Lord Morley," she said, yet there was not as much heat in the words as she would usually have put there. For once, she did not feel like scolding on a point of etiquette. She *did* want to touch that wave of hair, to see if it was as satiny as it appeared.

She curled her fingers tightly around the cup, and said, "It is not proper for you to be in here at all."

"You were ill, Mrs. Chase. Would it have been proper for me to leave you alone with your pain?"

"You could have fetched one of the teachers."

"They were all conversing with the parents of your pupils. I thought it best not to interrupt them."

Rosalind suspected that perhaps he had just not wanted all the ladies in his harem snatching at his sleeves again.

Her lips tightened at the thought.

Lord Morley moved up off the floor, but only to sit beside her on the settee. Rosalind, shocked by the sudden movement, slid back as far as she could against the arm of the settee. His heat still reached out to her, curling around her, beckoning her closer.

She turned away from it, away from *him*, pulling her skirts to the side so they would not brush against his boots. This was the man who was encouraging Allen in his wild ways, she reminded herself. This was not a man to be friends with, to sit close to. "Why were you in my office in the first place, Lord Morley? Was there something you wanted?"

His gaze slanted toward her, dark, surprisingly intense. "Wanted, Mrs. Chase? I suppose you could say that."

He said it as if—as if— She had not meant it in *that* way! Really, this man was maddening, twisting a simple word about until she hardly knew *what* she had been thinking. "Was it something concerning Lady Violet?"

The mention of his sister seemed to recall Lord Morley back to himself. He looked away from her. "Violet. Yes. She seems to like it here very much."

"I hope she does. We like *her* very much. She is one of our best students."

"Thank you, Mrs. Chase. I wanted to see you before I left today, to tell you how much I appreciate your kindness to Violet. I brought this for you, as a small gesture of thanks."

From inside his greatcoat, Lord Morley withdrew a small, tissue-wrapped package.

"A—a gift, Lord Morley?" Rosalind said, eyeing the harmless-looking package almost as if it could reach out and bite her. "I am not sure I should accept it."

"Really?" He raised his brow at her inquiringly, turning the tissue invitingly in his hand. "It is not a great deal, Mrs. Chase, surely not improper. It is for your library here."

Rosalind's curiosity got the better of her. She took the package from him, careful not to touch his fingers as she did so, and folded the tissue back. It was a book, bound in brown leather, decorated with gold gilt designs and lettering. She opened the cover to read the title page.

Songs to Athene, by Michael Bronston.

"Your—your poems, Lord Morley," she said. She did not know what she had been expecting. Rubies? Silken scarves? Though this was almost as disconcerting as those would have been.

"Violet tells me that you enjoy poetry," he said. He sounded a bit uncertain at her reaction.

"Yes, of course." She *did* enjoy poetry—Shakespeare, Donne, Spenser. The newfangled romantic, wild poetry of the sort Lord Morley wrote, it—well, it *disturbed* her.

But it was kind of him to bring it for their library, even if it was not the sort of thing the girls ought to be reading. She should give him something in return.

And there was only one thing she could think of that he needed. Needed in a most dire way.

She stood up and crossed the office to one of her bookcases, and extracted a volume from the shelf. Lord Morley had also stood, and followed her.

She held out the book. "Thank you for your gift,

Lord Morley," she said. "I would like to give you this in return."

"A *gift,* Mrs. Chase? I am shocked." He smiled at her, with that quirk at the corner of his lips. Then he looked down at the book—and the smile faded. *"A Lady's Rules for Proper Behavior."*

"Oh, yes," Rosalind answered firmly. She *did* feel more like herself, more like sensible, practical, proper Rosalind Lucas Chase. The strange spell Lord Morley had cast over her had obviously been a fleeting thing, brought about by their solitude in the office and her headache. "It is the one book that no one should be without. I believe that you in particular are most in need of it, Lord Morley."

Chapter Four

"The only proper gifts between unmarried ladies and gentlemen are flowers, sweets, or small books."
—*A Lady's Rules for Proper Behavior,* Chapter Seven

A Lady's Rules for Proper Behavior. She had given him a blasted book of etiquette!

Michael still could not cease thinking of it, even as he drove the phaeton out the Seminary gates and turned down the road toward London. Fortunately, Violet, on the seat beside him, was too preoccupied in studying the small silver locket Mrs. Chase had given her to notice his silence.

It was not so much that Mrs. Chase had given him the book, Michael thought. After all, she was a schoolmistress and would naturally advocate proper behavior, even of the extreme sort promulgated in that book. It was that she implied he was so greatly in need of it. What was it she had said? Oh, yes. "I believe that you in particular are most in need of it, Lord Morley."

As if he was an ape of some sort! A bumbling monkey with no idea of how to behave in a proper home.

It was true, he grudgingly admitted, that on his first visit to the Seminary he had not been all he should have been. He had needled Mrs. Chase and her deep propriety. He had spent his entire adult life striving against just such rigid mores, such shallow emphasis on conduct. And her stiff attitude had near driven him mad.

But he was sorry for his previous behavior, his boorishness. Had he not apologized to her, tried to make up for it? It was Mrs. Chase's home, and her guests had a duty to behave according to her—he winced to think the word—her *rules*. And he had mended his ways today, striving to behave within proper gentlemanly boundaries. Aside from his exuberant greeting of Violet, he had been everything that was proper. Even the Anonymous Lady who wrote *A Lady's Rules* would have approved of him. He had even given Mrs. Chase a book of his poetry!

What more could the woman want of him? What could ever erase the pinch of disapproval from her pretty—*too* pretty—lips?

And why was he thinking of her as pretty, anyway? Her caps were an absolute fright, and her eyes were frozen. There was nothing behind that ice blue façade—nothing but manners.

"Michael, why on earth are you driving so fast?" Violet cried, her voice edged with alarm.

Only then did Michael realize the great speed he had urged his horses to. They practically barreled along the road, dashing past the other now-gawking travelers into Town. The wheels clacked and whirred as if he was in a race.

He immediately drew back on the reins, slowing to a more moderate pace. "Sorry, Vi," he said, and threw his sister an apologetic smile.

She stared at him with wide, wary eyes. "Whatever were you thinking of? You looked a million miles away."

He sought quickly for a believable answer—anything but the truth. He could hardly tell her that he was thinking her teacher was a priss. "I was wondering which waistcoat I should wear to Lady Clarke's rout on Friday."

"Hmph." Violet folded her hands daintily in her lap, her mouth pursed. Michael saw that she had fastened the locket about her neck, the silver oval lying against the lace frill of her collar. He wondered if the gift from Mrs. Chase had somehow magically imparted some of that lady's qualities into his sister. "I think you should keep your thoughts on the road when you are driving."

Michael just laughed at her prim attitude, and reached out to tweak one of her curls again. He had often done that when she was a child, and it had always made her giggle.

Now she pushed him away, and said, "I also think you should keep both hands on the reins. Your horses look most unpredictable."

"Yes, Your Highness," Michael answered, in a mock-obsequious tone, and returned his gaze again to the road. When had his giggling sister turned into an elderly duchess? "But I would have you know that Nicodemus and Beelzebub are perfectly well-trained, and as gentle as lambs."

"Of course they are, with names like that." Violet turned her head away to study the passing landscape, so that all he could see of her was the brim of her white straw bonnet.

Silenced, he too watched their surroundings. The green expanses of the countryside were giving way to the edges of London. The grass was sparse, turning to pavement and gravel, the trees more stunted, the air heavier. The peace of the Seminary's grounds seemed a different world than that of the shouts and calls of the people—farmers going to market with their carts, racing aristocrats, workers on foot. On the road, they had been a trickle—now they became a flood. Michael had to slow the horses even further as they turned toward the rarefied air of Mayfair.

"I wish it did not take such a short time to get here," Violet murmured, so softly that Michael almost could not hear her. "I wish it took days and days. I wish the Seminary was in Scotland, or—or America."

She looked at Michael, and he saw that her eyes were misty with unshed tears. The prim duchess was again just a scared young girl.

"I know," he said, hating the damnable helpless feeling in his heart. "But it will not be so bad, I promise. You will be back at school next month, and in the meantime there are many things we can do."

She swiped her gloved hand over her eyes. "Gunter's, and the theater?"

"Of course. And I am sure Aunt Minnie will give a musicale or a Venetian breakfast or some such for you. You will probably just be at Bronston House to sleep."

"I wish I could stay with you."

Michael laughed, still trying to cheer her up. "You would not like that at all, Vi, I assure you! My lodgings are not at all up to the standards of *A Lady's Rules*. You would be most appalled."

She giggled, a good sign. "I am sure it is *horrid*. Tell me about it, Michael."

For the rest of their drive, Michael regaled her with exaggerated tales of the decrepitude of his rooms. His descriptions of piles of dirty laundry and thick dust on the bookshelves made her laugh. By the time they drew to a halt outside Bronston House, her eyes were clearer and her cheeks pink.

Her laughter faded as she stared up at its forbidding gray stone façade, and she reached up to touch her locket. "Will you stay for tea, Michael?" she asked quietly.

"Of course I will, Vi," he answered. He handed the reins to a footman, and jumped down to come around and help her to the ground. "And I will take you to supper at Aunt Minnie's tonight, too, if you want."

"Oh, yes!" she agreed enthusiastically. "I would like that very much."

Michael offered her his arm, and together they climbed the front steps to the door of Bronston House—or, as Michael chose to think of it, the portal of doom.

The Seminary was so quiet with all the girls gone, Rosalind thought. A bit *too* quiet, perhaps. For the first day or two of a holiday she was never quite sure what to do with herself.

She sat alone in her private sitting room after supper, with a tea tray on the table beside her and an open workbasket at her feet. Miss James, the only teacher still at the school, had taken supper with Rosalind, but then retired to pack for her own holiday.

So Rosalind was alone, with only the crackle of the flames in the grate to break the silence. Usually, in the evenings, she would listen to the girls play the harp or the pianoforte, or examine their watercolors and needlework. She tried to make the Seminary a home atmosphere for them, a place where they could be comfortable and happy.

Why could the home atmosphere not be here for *her* as well, even when they were gone? Why was it so very *silent*?

Nonsense, she told herself. She was just being maudlin. This happened every time a holiday commenced. Of course this was her home, the finest home she had ever known. And there were many things she could be doing. Things such as working on a new edition of *A Lady's Rules,* which her publisher had requested.

Thinking of *A Lady's Rules* made her remember that scene in her office, where she had presented a copy to Lord Morley. The expression on his face had been mocking, arch—after a flash of what, on another person, might have been hurt. It had been gone in an instant, yet Rosalind still felt the vague stirrings of regret when she remembered it.

Did she herself not have a rule against making guests feel uncomfortable in her home? Yet she had practically accused the man of uncouth rudeness, which was *not* the done thing.

"Even if it *is* true," she whispered, staring into the flames.

The first time she met Lord Morley she *had* been appalled by his manners. But she had to admit, today he had behaved better. Much better. There had been no lolling in the chairs, no suggestive poetry, no winking at housemaids. This afternoon, aside from lifting his sister off of her feet when he greeted her, he had been a picture of the *Rules*. Almost. He could never be completely.

And he had been truly kind when she felt ill. She had repaid his kindness by thrusting the book at him and practically accusing him of being a baboon.

"What has become of you, Rosalind?" she asked herself, not caring that it was ridiculous to be talking to an empty room in such a manner. "You are only thirty years of age, but you act worse than your grandmother ever did."

She sighed when she recalled their cheerless childhood visits to Grandmother Allen, their mother's mother who had been the sister of an earl and never let anyone forget it. Grandmother Allen insisted children sit perfectly straight and still and silent. How she and her brother had hated those calls!

Was she now *becoming* their Grandmother Allen?

Rosalind shuddered, and stood up to walk over to the fireplace. Of course she was not becoming her grandmother. She merely placed a great importance on manners, on proper deportment, and there was nothing wrong with that.

She braced her hand on the carved wooden mantel, and studied the miniature portrait displayed there on its silver stand. Her late husband, Mr. Charles Chase, stared back at her with his frank blue gaze. "There is nothing wrong with that, is there, Charles?"

She fancied that his smile widened. Charles, a very proper village attorney, had also believed in the importance of propriety, despite his occasional whiskey or card game. It was what had brought them together, had sustained them through their too-short three years of marriage before Charles succumbed to a fever.

A perfectly proper three years. They had been friends, even if theirs had not been a romance for the ages.

Rosalind's gaze shifted from the portrait to the book she had laid on the mantel before supper.

Lord Morley's poetry.

Rosalind reached for it, wrapped her fingers around the rich brown leather cover. She should have left it downstairs in the library, but some compulsion had made her bring it up here before she ate. For some light, before-bed reading, perhaps?

She opened the volume to a random page, and read, "Her lips, two roses touched with morning dew . . ."

Rosalind snapped the book shut. The fire felt so warm, *too* warm. She turned away, still holding the book, and went to the window.

She had not yet drawn the draperies, even though it was full dark now. The moon was almost full, and cast a greenish silver glow over the garden. The grounds looked lovely, just as they ought to.

Rosalind rested her forehead against the cool glass of the window, letting the blessed familiarity of the scene into her heart. This was what she wanted, what she had always wanted. The familiar, the known, the proper.

Why, then, did her fingers close so tightly about the book she held? So tightly that its corner bit into her palm?

She closed her eyes for a moment. When she opened them, the scene in the garden was the same—except for a new shadow falling from behind one of the trees. It flickered and moved, not a part of the tree's own solid shadow at all.

But when Rosalind blinked and peered closer, it was gone.

"Now you are seeing ghosts, in addition to everything else," she muttered. She stepped back and pulled the draperies firmly closed.

No sooner had she settled the yellow taffeta draperies than the door opened, and Molly, the housemaid, came in. Rosalind was deeply grateful for her cheerful smile, her bob of a curtsy—it made the evening seem *right,* somehow, after poetry and ghosts.

"Have you finished with the tea things, ma'am?" Molly asked.

"Oh, yes, thank you, Molly. I am done with them."
Rosalind watched the maid as she gathered up the
tray. "Molly?"

"Yes, ma'am."

"None of the gardeners are still here, are they?"

Molly seemed surprised by the question, as well she
might. Why would anyone be asking about gardeners
at nine o'clock at night? "No, ma'am. It's just you and
me and Miss James now."

"Oh, yes, of course."

Molly lifted up the tea tray. Before she turned back
to the door, she said, "I'll come right back, ma'am,
and help you with your gown, if you're ready to
retire."

"Yes, thank you, Molly." Rosalind rubbed her hand
over her eyes. She *was* ready to retire—obviously, she
was in need of some sleep. Exhaustion was making
her fanciful.

She had been reading one of Mrs. More's edifying
epistles before she went to sleep. But perhaps tonight
she might take a peek at some more of that poetry . . .

Chapter Five

"Parents and other elders should always be respected."
—*A Lady's Rules for Proper Behavior*, Chapter Seven

"So, here you are at last. I thought that with the harum-skarum way *you* drive, Michael, that you would have been here hours ago."

The Earl of Athley's voice, stentorian as a brass gong, rang through the cavernous drawing room as Michael and Violet stepped inside the door. Michael squinted through the gloom of the room, until he saw his father seated by the fire.

As usual the drawing room, indeed the whole house, was dark and stuffy, the air thick with smoke and the overpowering sweetness of the rose and orchid flower arrangements. Heavy green velvet draperies, hung with swags of gold fringe, covered all the windows. More green velvet upholstered the dark, old-fashioned furniture, and gloomy landscapes hung on the paneled walls.

It was overpowering, suffocating. Michael felt his chest tighten painfully, his throat close as if gasping for a breath of clear, true air.

He felt this way every time he entered the house. And that was why he stayed far, far away, unless his duty to his sister pulled him back. At least he could leave—she could not.

He reached up to loosen his cravat slightly, as Violet's hand slipped from his arm and she crossed the room to their father's side. Her lilac-colored carriage gown and white bonnet were like a flash of springtime dropped into the gloom.

She leaned down to peck a dutiful kiss onto the earl's wrinkled cheek. "It was my fault we are late, Father. I stayed too long at the school, saying good-bye to everyone."

The earl scowled. "Who at that pitiful Seminary could have been worth your taking all that time? Some parson's daughter or merchant's niece?" He banged his stout walking stick on the floor, the hollow thud of it echoing up to the rafters. "I was a fool to ever send you to that school, Violet. I should not have listened to your aunt's blandishments. Associating with people of all sorts has obviously made you forget your position. You should be here, learning to prepare for marriage. What else are girls good for?"

Violet turned panicked eyes onto Michael.

Michael came toward her, breathing a bit easier now that he had somewhat adjusted to the dimness. He understood Violet's panic—the Seminary, as fusty as it was, was her refuge from this place. But he was not as worried as she. Their father often ranted about the school, about Violet's "forgetting her position" there, getting too educated and not being able to find a suit-able husband because of it. Yet the truth was, the earl would rather not have the trouble of his daughter being underfoot. So her school was safe—for now.

"Father, you know that the Seminary has only stu-dents from the finest families enrolled there," Michael said, gently taking Violet's arm and leading her to a chair away from the overpowering heat of the fire. "Violet has only the most suitable friends, who will be of great help to her when she makes her debut next Season."

Michael had almost said "use" rather than "help," since that was all the earl truly cared about in peo-ple—how he could use them to his advantage. How they were placed on the social scale. "I understand,

Father, that the Duke and Duchess of Wayland are sending their own daughter there in few years."

"Wayland, eh?" The earl's dark eyes narrowed shrewdly as he absorbed this. The Waylands were assuredly at the pinnacle of Society. "Well, that at least is something. Though I do not know what they are thinking to send their daughter there so early. There is no telling what odd notions the gel might absorb there. But then, the Waylands are odd people. The duchess is an *artist*." His lips curled with disdain on the word *artist*—it might as well have been *courtesan*.

As their father went on, dissecting the peccadilloes of the Waylands and their "disgraceful" set, Michael sat down in the chair next to Violet's. He leaned back, trying to get comfortable in the heavily carved piece of furniture, stretching his legs out before him. Violet was rubbing her fingertip over her silver locket, staring at the floor. She was the very picture of a dutiful daughter, but Michael recognized the misty look in her eyes as one of faraway thought. She was lost in some daydream, so Michael tried to follow her example and think of something else.

Their father's conversation seldom required more of a response than a nod, or an "Oh, yes?" or a "You are quite right, sir." So distraction was fairly easy. His gaze moved over the half-hidden footman standing in a shadowed corner to await the earl's command, to the large stone coat of arms over the fireplace. It had the Bronston insignia of a hand holding a sword and a lion, with the motto *Semper Officiosus.*

Duty Always. Perhaps, Michael thought, it should have been *Dullness Always.* He almost wished he could trade places with that footman.

His musings were interrupted when he heard his name.

"Michael," the earl barked, "is that a *pink* cravat you are wearing?"

Michael grinned. "Indeed. Though the correct name is 'maiden's blush.' Quite evocative, wouldn't you say? It is all the crack."

Violet made a suspicious choking sound, and bent her head down until her expression was entirely concealed by the brim of her bonnet.

The earl turned a deep red color, one that would never earn a moniker like "maiden's blush." "Miser's apoplexy," perhaps.

"Insolent!" the earl shouted, and banged the stick against the floor again. "I have put up with your deplorable behavior thus far, your 'poetry,' your 'club,' the tittle-tattle I hear from every quarter. Even your ridiculous notions about fashion! But I will not stand your disgraceful behavior any longer. You are a viscount, and one day you will be the earl . . ." He broke off, gasping for air. The footman hurried forward to pour out a glass of some clear liquid, which the earl gulped down.

"Father!" Violet cried, and started to rise from her chair.

"Sit back down, gel!" her father choked. "I am not finished with what I have to say."

"But you are ill," Violet dared to say.

"A mere shortness of breath. I am not dying, which is a very good thing, considering the disgraceful state of the next generation. The family will be ruined before I am cold in the ground."

Violet's face crumpled with hurt at those words. She sank back into her chair.

Michael's hands tightened onto the arms of his own chair until his knuckles whitened. His father had always been cold, hateful, haughty to those not of his own station—and even to his own children. Ever since his wife died bringing Violet into the world, he had revealed no hint of human feeling. But age had brought a new venom to him, a deep anger.

Michael had never met a man more in need of a good thrashing. But his father was indeed an old man—it would not be at all honorable for Michael, with all the strength of his twenty-eight years, to beat him.

Really, he thought, all he would have to do now was steal the earl's walking stick. Even *that* could not be done, but one day Michael would tell him every last truth he had coming to him. Every last hateful thought that Michael harbored in his own heart.

Not now, though, with his sweet Violet looking on. Michael would never do anything that could possibly hurt his tenderhearted sister.

Before the earl could launch into another diatribe, Michael stood up and said, "I am sorry to cut short this cozy family moment, but I fear I have errands I must perform. I told Violet I would take her to Aunt Minnie's house for supper, so you need not share your dried-out lamb cutlets and overcooked peas with us. Good day, sir."

"I will just see you out, Michael," Violet said hurriedly. Together they left the room as quickly as dignity would allow, their father's sputterings chasing them out the door.

"How absolutely horrid," said Violet, shuddering, once they stood safely on the front steps. "He becomes worse every time I see him!"

Michael kissed her cheek, and she curled her hands into the folds of his coat, holding onto him in defiance of her precious rules.

"It will be all right, Vi," he said reassuringly. "Do not go back to the drawing room. Go up to your chamber, and send your maid for some tea. Father will settle down now that my infuriating presence has been removed. I will be back in only a couple of hours, and we will have a lovely supper with Aunt Minnie and her friends. Does that sound nice?"

"Very nice." Violet nodded, and stepped back to give him a brave little smile.

"Now go inside. It is becoming chilly out here." Michael tapped Violet on the tip of her nose, and climbed up into his phaeton.

At the corner of the street, he glanced back to be sure she had gone inside. She had not. She still stood there on the steps, her arms wrapped around herself.

She gave him a wave, and another smile—and Michael's heart ached. He wanted so very much to go back to her, to sweep her up and carry her away from that gloomy house.

Carry her all the way back to the serenity of Mrs. Chase's drawing room. Mrs. Chase would be able to comfort Violet. And what was even odder, he wished *he* could be there, as well. That he could sit in that small office again, and tell Mrs. Chase all the things that ached in his soul. Not the stern, stiff schoolmistress Mrs. Chase, but the one he had glimpsed so briefly. The one with rich depths to her sky-eyes, and soft hands and sunset hair. That Mrs. Chase had hints of gentleness and understanding in her.

Instead, all he could do was keep driving into the gathering London night.

The townhouse of Lady Minerva Fielding, better known as Aunt Minnie, was as different from Bronston House as day was from midnight. She was their father's sister, but she had lived a very different life from his, as evidenced in the spacious, pastel airiness of her rooms, the fine paintings on her walls, the constant merry sparkle in her green eyes.

She was one of the last people Michael would ever have expected to follow *A Lady's Rules,* but there the volume was, in a place of honor on the round table in the middle of her foyer.

As Violet hurried off to greet some of Aunt Minnie's other guests, Michael picked up the book, riffling through its gilt-edged pages. Their aunt had marked certain "rules" with ticks of dark green ink.

" 'A gentleman must never seat himself on the settee beside his hostess . . . unless invited,' " he muttered.

"Michael!" Aunt Minnie cried. He looked up to find her sailing out of the drawing room doors toward him, the tall feathers in her rose pink turban waving jauntily. She went up on tiptoe to kiss his cheek. "My most handsome nephew."

Michael laughed, and kissed her in return. "I am your only nephew."

She waved this away with an airy gesture of her gloved hand. "If I had a hundred nephews, you would still be the most handsome. You are becoming quite the heartbreaker, so I hear."

"Exaggerations, I assure you, aunt."

"Hmm," she murmured, clearly unconvinced. "Exaggerations, perhaps. But obviously it runs in the family, as Violet is also becoming a very pretty figure. It is obvious that Mrs. Chase's Seminary agrees with her. She is blooming."

Michael glanced over to where Violet was chatting with an elderly colonel and his wife. She was smiling, and as bright and pretty as her yellow muslin gown. It was reassuring that she had emerged unscathed from their meeting with their father—at least for now. "It was thanks to your persuasions that our father agreed to send her there."

Aunt Minnie gave an inelegant snort. "Oh, my brother is terrible, and has been ever since we were children! But Violet seems to be weathering the storm, as do you, my dear."

"Violet will *always* be fine, because she has inherited your beauty and good heart. As well as your literary taste, I believe?" He held up the copy of *A Lady's Rules*.

She laughed, and snatched the volume out of his hand. "It is all anyone is reading of late! I haven't seen a craze to equal it in years, not since I was a girl and everyone had to wear heart-shaped patches. To be au courant now one must be *polite*. Such a bore, not at all like the great fun we had in my youth. Wigs a foot tall, high heels, card games that lasted a week, not to mention those patches. But the *Rules* are really quite amusing to peruse. I can loan you my copy."

"No need, Aunt Minnie. I was recently given a copy of my very own." Michael remembered the expression on Mrs. Chase's face as she held the book out to him. *"You in particular are most in need of it, Lord Morley."*

Aunt Minnie gave him an arch glance. "Oh, yes? And may I venture a guess that it was a gift from a lady?"

Michael gave her a *look* of his own. "You may venture as many guesses as you like, Aunt Minnie. A gentleman never tells. Is that one of the rules?"

She laughed again. "If it is not, it should be! But come with me, young rascal. We have been standing here for too long, and there are guests I would like you to meet."

As she took his arm to lead him into the fray of her company, Michael took another glance at the book before tossing it back onto the table. *A Lady's Rules*— they were everywhere.

Chapter Six

"A lady should always try to avoid discussing such matters as finances and politics."
—*A Lady's Rules for Proper Behavior,* Chapter Two

"*T*he morning post has come, ma'am," Molly announced, putting a small silver tray down on Rosalind's desk.

Rosalind glanced up from her writing, automatically sliding a blank sheet of vellum over her notebook. It was not that she didn't trust Molly—it was simply instinct. She was working on the new edition of *A Lady's Rules,* which her publisher had been trying for weeks to get her to begin. She had to preserve her anonymity as A Lady.

"Thank you, Molly," she said, and reached for the sheaf of letters.

"Would you like your luncheon in here, ma'am, or in the dining room?" the maid asked.

Rosalind did not need very long to make *that* decision. It was much too gloomy to eat all alone in the spacious dining room. During the term, it was full of people, students practicing their table manners under the watchful gaze of the teachers, their talk and laughter ringing out. During the holiday, it was silent.

"In here, please, Molly. I am going to try to work through the afternoon."

"Very good, ma'am." Molly bobbed a curtsy and left the office, closing the door behind her.

Rosalind sorted through the post. There were a couple of missives from her teachers, on their holidays in Bath and Lyme Regis. A few notes from parents inquiring about future places at the school for their daughters. A scribbled, blotted note from Uncle Silas at his country home.

And one frighteningly official-looking letter from the bank in London. The one Allen had borrowed money from.

Rosalind stared down at the green blob of wax on the heavy white vellum. As she stared, the wax shifted, twisted, until it looked like a yawning, gaping, *biting* tiger's jaw. Poised to swallow her, and her comfortable world, whole.

She slid a letter opener under the wax wafer, popping it open, and unfolded the sheet.

It was short, polite, and to the point. Mr. Richards, one of the managers of the bank, would very much appreciate an appointment with her and Mr. Silas Lucas, to discuss recent loans made to Mr. Allen Lucas. Sincerely hers, etc. . . .

Rosalind dropped the letter to her desk. The skin around her eyes tightened painfully at the thought of having to meet with some *bank manager*. It sounded, well, less than respectable. Not something a lady should have to face. It reeked of financial ruin. She took off her wire-framed spectacles and rubbed at the bridge of her nose.

Blast Allen anyway. He had no right to put her through this. This was the fault of Lord Morley, and others of his reprehensible ilk. If not for their influence, Allen would be quietly studying, not running up debts.

What was she going to do about this mess?

The Thoth Club was crowded on this Wednesday night, thronged with gentlemen freed at this late hour from their duties of escorting wives, sisters, and sweethearts to the dreaded Almack's. Brandy was liberal, the billiards room full, the card tables surrounded by players and observers.

Michael sat in one of the comfortable wingback chairs by the fireplace, a glass of port cradled in his hands, watching the hum of activity. He himself had just passed an evening in respectable society, escorting Violet and Aunt Minnie to a small musicale. Not, thankfully, to Almack's—Vi was still too young for its hallowed portals—but still heavy with propriety. Now Violet was left with Aunt Minnie and her cronies in Minnie's drawing room, and Michael was here, in this masculine sanctuary.

Sanctuary? Strangely, it felt like a mere extension of the outside world.

Michael sipped at his port, and tried to decipher why this place, which had always been a place of enjoyment and escape for him ever since he helped to found it, should feel so cold tonight. He had always enjoyed the Thoth Club. It was full of members with an artistic or literary bent, not like politically minded Whites and Brooks, or sporting-mad Boodle's. There was always discussion of Byron's latest volume or Turner's newest canvas to go along with the cards and drink. Even the food was not half bad.

Tonight, though, he felt oddly—restless. He did not want to play cards, or talk about poetry, or do any of the things that usually sufficed to while away a pleasant evening. Ordinarily it was all amusing enough, even if not profoundly satisfying. Tonight, though, it was just not enough. He briefly considered visiting the home of a most obliging golden-haired courtesan, but not even that appealed to him.

He should leave, go back to his lodgings and write. In his own world of words and fantasies, time could often fly past on silvery wings. That was sometimes the only thing that could satisfy him, the ephemeral zone of art. It was far, far beyond the shallow pastimes of gaming, horse races, balls—even blond courtesans. Tonight, though, he felt that even poetry could not fill the hollowness at the very center of his being.

So he just sat there, sipping at the glass of port, watching the activity of the club swirl past him.

The front doors opened, letting in a burst of cool evening air and a flurry of new arrivals. They were laughing brightly, talking too loudly—obviously, they had begun their carousing long before coming to the club.

Among them was Allen Lucas.

"Morley!" Lucas cried upon seeing Michael. He handed his cloak and hat to the footman, and staggered across the room to collapse in the chair next to Michael's. He paid no attention to Michael's obvious solitude, gesturing for a port of his own.

"How are you this evening, Lucas?" Michael asked, and put his half-empty glass down on the nearest table. Apparently, alcohol was going to be of no use to him this evening.

"Very well indeed. Haven't seen you since that day at m'sister's school." Lucas tossed off his first drink, and poured out another from the decanter. He loosened his elaborately fashioned cravat. "I didn't know your sister attended the Seminary."

"Oh, yes. Lady Violet enjoys it there very much."

Lucas snorted. "I daresay she does. All the girls just *worship* Rosie."

"Hm," Michael murmured noncommittally. He really did not want to think about Mrs. Chase this night. Lately, every time he closed his eyes he saw her disapproving face, her blue eyes watching him with disappointment. He did not know why that should be; he had only met the woman twice in his life. And neither encounter had been what could be called auspicious. But there it was—he *had* been thinking of her, and he wanted to escape it.

And now here was the woman's very own brother, sitting down right across from him. *I need a distraction,* he thought.

Fortunately, he was saved from hearing any more about "Rosie" by the arrival of two of Lucas's cronies, Lord Carteret and Mr. Gilmore.

"Good evening, Morley!" Gilmore said, helping himself to the port. "Damn shame you didn't come out with us earlier."

"Oh, yes? Where did you go?" Michael replied, not deeply interested in the answer. But as long as the silly puppies were here, they might as well keep him entertained.

"We were at Lady Lovelace's rout," Carteret said, with a small hiccup. "And she threw us out!"

Now, that *was* a bit interesting, Michael thought. Lady Lovelace was not a woman generally known for being a high stickler, so this trio must have done something rather naughty indeed. "She threw you out?"

"Tossed us right out on our ears," Lucas said, laughing into his port.

"Why?" Michael asked. "What did you do?"

Carteret leaned his elbow lazily on the edge of the mantel. "She said we were breaking the rules."

The rules! Of course. Michael gave a bitter little laugh. Only something as ridiculous as "the rules" could get three such harmless pups expelled from the Lovelace rout. They were spreading like a virulent weed over Society, choking out any trace of individuality, any spark that could possibly enliven dull *ton* events.

"She said that the rules forbid a gentleman from being intoxicated in front of a lady," Lucas said indignantly. "We were hardly *foxed*! How could one be, on that weak stuff Lady Lovelace serves?"

"And when I tried to tell a simple joke to Lady Lovelace's daughter, the silly gel squealed like an affronted mouse, and ran off to tell her mama," added Gilmore. "It was just the one about the opera dancer and the clock at St. Sebastian's . . ."

"Lady Lovelace pulled out a copy of *A Lady's Rules* and spouted off something about tasteless anecdotes," said Lucas.

"Tasteless!" Gilmore cried. "That was my very best joke. It always gets a laugh."

"Hm." Michael studied the flames leaping in the grate, as the three young men went on muttering about their "shabby" treatment at the hands of Lady Lovelace.

It was true that their behavior had not been all that it should have been, Michael admitted. Drinking too much and telling questionable stories to young ladies was *not* the done thing. But they were harmless young men, and had meant nothing by it. Their behavior had surely warranted their being taken outside by Lord Lovelace into the fresh air to sober up, but *not* being tossed publicly out of the soiree.

"It is those blasted rules," Gilmore said, echoing Michael's own thoughts. "Ever since Lady Jersey and the other patronesses started touting them all over the place, everyone is wild to follow them to the exact letter."

"It's dashed hard," Lucas complained. "I can never remember all of them at once, so I'm always bound to break at least one."

"But one *has* to follow them," said Carteret gloomily. "If one wants to be accepted. As dull as all those routs and balls are, I want to be able to attend them. That is where all the pretty girls are, and my father would cut off my allowance if I didn't do my duty there."

"We just have to try harder to remember the rules," said Lucas.

Here was the distraction he sought, Michael realized.

They all fell into a maudlin silence, broken only when Michael said quietly, "Not necessarily, gentlemen."

The three of them turned in concert to stare at him, three pairs of eyes wide.

"What do you mean, Morley?" asked Lucas.

"Well, you say that a person cannot be accepted in Society unless he follows all these rules," Michael said, and tapped thoughtfully at his chin with his steepled fingers. "Yet it seems to me that the people who have commanded the most attention, indeed the adulation, of the *ton* have been anything but rule followers."

The trio brightened, leaning toward Michael avidly to hear what he might say next. "You mean like you, Morley?" Lucas asked.

Michael laughed. "I was thinking more of Byron, or perhaps Beau Brummell, who made his own rules and everyone followed *them*. These men, and others like them, would never have slavishly followed any rules in some book. Why, this lady will not even put her name on her own book! How much importance can her rules truly have, if she won't even own up to them?"

Gilmore appeared most confused. "You mean we should write our own book of rules and get people to follow them?"

"I don't think I could write a book. Not bright enough, y'know," Carteret added doubtfully.

Michael almost groaned in exasperation. No wonder he was restless, if these bacon-brains were the only people he had to converse with! But somehow he felt he had to persuade them, to save at least three helpless souls from more mindless rule-following. "No, I do not mean write your own rules. I mean forget about rules entirely. If we follow common courtesy, and our own instincts, we will be fine. If you go a step beyond, and follow a different path, you will be admired."

"Like you, Morley," Lucas insisted again. "The ladies love it that you never do what is expected."

"They *did* love it," Gilmore said, his voice slurred from the great quantity of port he had consumed. "But I haven't seen you out much of late, Morley, and you weren't at the Lovelace rout tonight."

"That is because he did not *choose* to waste his time at such a dull place as Lady Lovelace's rout!" Lucas cried. "She would have given her right arm to have him there, as would every Society hostess. Morley is right. Some people are above the rules."

Michael had rarely had champions in his life, and never one as unlikely as Allen Lucas. But it was rather touching all the same.

"The lady who wrote the book says *no one* is above the rules," Gilmore insisted.

"No one is above courtesy, perhaps," said Michael. "But no one should slavishly follow someone else's commands."

"I would wager that not even *you* can flout the rules and still be accepted, Morley," argued Gilmore. "They are too popular."

Lucas leaped to his feet to face Gilmore, his face flushed a deep red. "And I would wager that Morley will *always* be accepted, no matter how many rules he breaks! I wager fifty pounds."

"Done!" Gilmore answered.

Carteret glanced between them, laconically gleeful at the quarrel.

Michael studied the three of them in silence, tapping his fingertips on the arms of his chair. The wager was completely ridiculous, of course; Michael had outgrown betting on such silly matters years ago. But the rules had irked him, probably more than they should have. He hated seeing everyone, especially his sweet sister, behaving like such wooden soldiers, marching in the cause of rigid etiquette. It reminded him too much of his father.

Plus, this would give him a chance to get—and keep—his thoughts off of Mrs. Chase.

"Very well, gentlemen," he said. "I will take that wager."

Chapter Seven

"Correspondence is a private matter, and one must never read another person's letters without being invited."
—*A Lady's Rules for Proper Behavior*, Chapter Six

"*T*here is a caller, ma'am."

Rosalind glanced up from her embroidery to see Molly in the doorway of the sitting room. "A caller?" she said, puzzled. It was early on a quiet morning, and Rosalind had been enjoying the time to make some progress on her needlework while she pondered Allen and some new expenses at the school. She had not heard from her brother for several days, and it was beginning to worry her. Also, the roof had begun to leak in the east wing, and the funds would have to be found to repair it.

She always thought more clearly with a piece of embroidery in her hands. But today, no solutions were occurring to her. She was almost grateful to be interrupted, even if it was not the usual time for callers.

"Who is it, Molly?" she asked, and tucked her embroidery away into her workbasket.

Molly came to her and held out the silver tray, where one stark white card reposed. "He says his name is Mr. Richards. From the bank."

Rosalind's hand froze as she reached for the card. *Mr. Richards*. The one who had been writing her letters about Allen's stupid loan. Now he was here, in person. He must be quite serious if he took all the trouble to come out here to the school.

She grasped the card, and folded it into her hand until it bit into her palm. "Tell him I will be down momentarily, Molly."

Molly bobbed a curtsy, and left the room with her empty tray.

Safely alone now, Rosalind took a deep breath of air. She hated dealing with finances, except for paying bills with the local tradesmen at the end of the month. Those were simple, straightforward, necessary transactions. Her experiences with Allen's creditors in the past had proved to be anything *but* simple.

And this was the first time she had had to face a banker from London.

Rosalind straightened her muslin cap and smoothed the skirt of her gray morning gown. He would not go away if she just kept hiding in here. She had to meet him, work out some sort of payment plan for Allen's loans.

Oh, she was just going to *strangle* her brother when next she saw him!

She squared her shoulders and marched down the stairs to the drawing room.

Rosalind had never given much thought to what bankers should look like, but if she *had*, it would be much like this man. He was very tall, very thin, and very pale—pale skin, pale blond hair. He wore a plain dark blue coat, and a stiff white cravat tucked into the front of a black waistcoat. He stood across the room, examining a collection of small porcelain figurines and boxes arrayed on a tabletop.

"Mr. Richards?" she said, drawing herself up to her full, tall height and walking toward him, her hand outstretched. "I am Mrs. Rosalind Chase."

Mr. Richards straightened from his examination of the bibelots, a monocle falling from his eye. "Mrs. Chase," he said, and bowed briefly over her hand. "I was really hoping to speak with both you and Mr. Silas Lucas."

"My uncle is quite elderly now, and not in the best of health. He seldom leaves his home in the country. But I assure you that, as co-guardian of my brother, I have the authority to speak to you myself. Please, won't you be seated?" She gestured toward a pair of chairs.

"Of course, Mrs. Chase," Mr. Richards said, clearly still reluctant. He sat down, and placed a large black leather portfolio across his lap. From it he withdrew a stack of papers. At the bottom of the top sheet Rosalind saw, with a sinking of her heart, the bold slash of Allen's signature.

"These are the documents pertaining to Mr. Lucas's loan," Mr. Richards began. "As you see here, Mrs. Chase . . ."

He went on in this vein for some time, spouting different legal terms and quoting figures.

A suspicious throbbing began above her left eye, until she had to say, "Please, Mr. Richards. Could you please just tell me what I must do to repay this loan?"

Two hours later, when she collapsed onto the settee in her office, Rosalind was very sorry she had asked that question. She had indeed worked out a repayment plan with Mr. Richards and his bank, but it was not going to be quick or simple. The school was prosperous, yes, but it could not long support such debts. The building and grounds of the Seminary also required upkeep, not to mention the wages of the teachers and servants.

Her head ached in earnest now, as it had so often of late. She pressed the heels of her hands against her temples.

"Oh, Allen, Allen!" she groaned. "What were you thinking of? Where did I go wrong?"

But she knew in her heart that it was not her fault. She had tried hard to teach him the values of education and thrift. He had fallen in with a bad example of behavior in London.

He had fallen in with Lord Morley and his crowd.

At the thought of that name, her head pounded harder. She could *not* think of him now! She had to conserve her energy for what truly mattered—finding a solution to her financial dilemma.

She pushed herself up off the settee and went over to the desk to pull out her ledger books. One detailed the school's finances, the other the profits from *A Lady's Rules*.

"I will just have to write more books," she murmured, and reached for her pen and ink. "A Lady's Rules for Fashion? A Lady's Rules for Garden Design?"

As she sharpened the tip of the pen, her gaze fell on the new pile of letters on the edge of the desk. The morning post. Molly must have left it there when Rosalind was in the drawing room with Mr. Richards.

She did not really want to face correspondence on top of everything else, but the missive on top appeared to be a letter from her school friend, Georgina Beaumont, now the Duchess of Wayland and cutting a dash in London. Georgie would surely have gossip to cheer her! Reading of her adventures always lifted Rosalind's spirits.

Rosalind pulled the post toward her, anticipating a respite from her woes. But the letter just beneath Georgina's was a missive from her publisher.

"Oh, thank heaven!" she whispered, breaking the wax with her letter opener. "There is sure to be a bank draught."

There *was* a draught—yet it was not nearly large enough. It was only half what her previous payments had been. Appalled, she put aside the bank draught and read her publisher's letter.

"We apologize for the unexpectedly small sum," it read. "Unfortunately, sales of *A Lady's Rules* have inexplicably dropped. We would be very happy to look at any other manuscripts you may have to offer. Yours, etc. . . ."

"What!" Rosalind screamed out, and dropped the paper as if it burned. "Sales have dropped? What can this mean? *Everyone* wants to read *A Lady's Rules*."

Did they not? They had become so very popular.

This was the worst possible time for something of this nature to happen. She was counting on that money—she *needed* it. She had known that the popularity of *A Lady's Rules* would one day wane, but not so very soon. Not *now*.

Lights exploded in her brain, pounding at the inside of her skull. Rosalind pushed the letter away, not caring when it fell to the floor. She felt so—trapped. Unable to break out of this dilemma. It was even worse than it had been when her husband died, and she discovered that his estate was far smaller than she had thought.

She needed some air.

Tucking Georgina's letter into the pocket of her morning gown, Rosalind stumbled out of the office, across the empty foyer. She pulled open the front door and walked blindly out into the garden.

At first the pale sunlight hurt her eyes, made her headache worse. But the breeze was cool and clear, the garden an early spring pale green. Slowly, as she filled her lungs with its country freshness, she felt calmer. More in charge of herself.

She sat down on a marble bench beneath a spreading oak tree, and pulled Georgina's letter from her pocket.

Her hope for distraction was not in vain. Georgina's usual effervescence, which had carried them through some difficult school days, came across in her words. Rosalind soon found herself smiling at Georgina's stories of her young daughter and baby son, her sister-in-law's come-out, gossip about her friends, including their fellow school friend Elizabeth Hollingsworth, who was traveling in Italy with her husband and twin daughters. Rosalind even laughed aloud at a particularly spicy tale of a certain Lord Bunberry and Mrs. Brown-Perkins, even though she knew she shouldn't.

Her laughter faded at Georgina's final paragraph, though.

"And, in closing, my dear Rosie, something most odd is happening. You know of *A Lady's Rules for Proper Behavior,* that amusing little book everyone has been so wild to follow of late? Even *I* have improved my etiquette! Well, Lord Morley and some of his cronies have been behaving just so badly of late. It is as if they are trying to break every rule. Everyone is absolutely agog to see what they will do next. I will write more of this later, for I think it will grow even more interesting."

Morley! Rosalind wanted to scream that name to the wind. It was always Morley, popping up whenever she was most vulnerable. Ruining all her plans, her good work. He was becoming the bane of her life, setting himself up against every civilized tenet that Rosalind stood for.

She tightened her grip on the letter, crumpling it into her fist. There was just one thing to be done. She had to go to London.

Chapter Eight

"A crowded ball is not the proper sphere for private conversation."
-A Lady's Rules for Proper Behavior,   Chapter Three

*T*he Portman ball was quite the crush. People thronged along the silk-papered walls, lined the staircase to the ballroom, jostled across the corridors in order to greet Lord and Lady Portman and proceed into the soiree. The crème de la crème of Society was arrayed in all its glittering, silken splendor.

And they all turned to stare when the butler announced, "Viscount Morley."

There was a tiny pause, a sort of collective murmur before talk resumed in one great rush. Lady Portman and several of her friends rushed forward to greet him.

It was slightly disconcerting. Michael was used to a certain amount of attention, as any unmarried heir to an earldom would be, but not *this* much attention. It was gratifying, too. At least he knew his wager was going well. People still associated with him, indeed fawned on him, even though he tried to break all of *A Lady's Rules* whenever possible.

Well, not *all* of them. There were still two or three he had not gotten around to. But it was early days yet. Surely, given time, everyone would see how absurd such rules were. Even Violet, who had been watching him with narrowed, disapproving eyes of late. Ever since his rule-breaking had begun in earnest.

His sister, his sweet, pliant sister, was clinging tenaciously to every strict tenet that she had learned at that blasted school. Every conversation, it was Mrs. Chase this, and Mrs. Chase that, Mrs. Chase says this, Mrs. Chase does that.

Always Mrs. Chase. The rule-following Mrs. Chase.

He frowned as he thought of her again. The memory of Mrs. Chase came into his mind at the most inopportune moments, ever since that strangely intimate scene in her office. He would be at the theater, and an actress's red hair would remind him of the ringlet that had escaped from Mrs. Chase's cap. He would be riding in the park, and a whiff of some springtime scent would make him think of her perfume, so green and fresh when he leaned close to her. He was even at a prizefight, and—well, he was not sure *what* had reminded him of her at that violent scene, but he had thought of her nonetheless.

It was absurd. Ridiculous. Mrs. Chase was a stern, cap-wearing schoolmistress, who looked at him with the highest disapproval. She had even given him a copy of *A Lady's Rules*! She was not at all the usual sort of woman he was drawn to—blond, giggling, vivacious, petite. Mrs. Chase was a tall, redheaded Valkyrie.

Yet there it was. He could not cease thinking about her—even now, at a grand ball, surrounded by females. Her ice blue eyes lingered in his mind. It was almost as if she watched him across the miles, disapproving of him.

He shook off the thought of Mrs. Chase, and turned to Lady Portman. "Good evening, Lady Portman," he said, bowing low over her gloved hand. He lingered over it just an instant more than was proper, mindful that the rules required the merest airy salute. "You have quite outdone yourself this evening. Your ball is the event of the Season."

Lady Portman gave a gay little trill of laughter, and tapped him on the arm with her folded lace fan. "You flatterer! I am sure it cannot be *the* event of the Season, but it has surely moved closer because you are here, Lord Morley. Perhaps you could read us one of your new poems after supper?"

"Oh, yes!" Lady Portman's friend Mrs. Eastman cried. She laid a beseeching hand on his other arm. "I so admired 'The Onyx Vase.' It was so—evocative."

Lady Clarke, whom Michael last recalled seeing in the drawing room of Mrs. Chase's Seminary, slid up to them in a flurry of orange silk and fragrant plumes. "I am still partial to 'Alas, fair cruelty,' myself," she said, with a secretive little smile.

Lady Portman moved closer to him, tightening her clasp on his arm. She gave a glare to the other women surrounding them. "Right now, though, Lord Morley, let me introduce you to some of the other guests. So many of them are literary-minded, and are so eager to greet you."

She led him farther into the crowded ballroom, while Lady Clarke stared after them with smoldering dark eyes. In truth, Michael was rather glad to be borne away from the woman. She was becomingly annoyingly persistent of late, sending heavily scented missives to his lodgings. Ever since he had begun to break the rules, in fact.

He stopped to speak to various acquaintances, to talk of other balls, routs, plays, and exchange *on dits* about people who were not here. As Lady Portman and her circle spoke of a certain Madame Varens who was performing at Drury Lane, Michael took a glass of champagne from a passing footman's tray and gazed about him at the throngs of people.

As he was taller than most of the crowd, he could see over the ocean of dancers, the sea of potted palms. Near the invitingly half-open French doors was another knot of people, much like the group that had greeted him on his arrival, with one great difference.

Most of this gathering were men, and they clustered about two tall, redheaded women.

One of them had her back to him, but the one who faced him he recognized as the Duchess of Wayland, and he immediately understood the draw for those men. The Duchess of Wayland, nee Mrs. Georgina Beaumont, was a vivid beauty, a famous artist in her own right, and, since her exalted marriage, a leader of Society. Michael had talked with her about art and writing before, and liked her very much, even though he had been oddly unmoved by the renowned "green fire" of her eyes. Tonight, she was like a brilliant, exotic bird of paradise amid pastel sparrows with her bright blue gown and sparkling sapphires.

The woman who was turned away from Michael looked as if she could prove to be no less beautiful, even if she was less colorful. Her hair, a river of red ringlets, was piled atop her head and anchored with a bandeau of pale sea green silk twisted with seed pearls. Her tall, slender figure was set off perfectly by a gown of pale green satin that just barely skimmed her waist and the long length of her legs. She tilted her swanlike neck as one of her companions spoke to her, and one long curl slid over her shoulder.

Michael was drawn to her, this mysterious, sea-clad woman. She seemed an oasis of serenity in the over-crowded ballroom, a poised, elegant, gardenia-like blossom that promised sanctuary from all the empty chatter, the high-pitched laughter, the hands pulling at his arms.

He murmured some excuse to Lady Portman, and made his way across the room, drawn by the woman in green. It was not an easy endeavor; he was stopped numerous times, obliged to make polite conversation. Yet finally he was able to break free, to skirt around the edge of the dance floor. He was very nearly to the crowd by the French doors, when the woman turned.

Michael almost dropped his champagne glass. Standing not fifteen feet away from him in the Portman ballroom, clad in that shimmering satin and pearls, was—Mrs. Chase.

For one off-guard instant, he was filled with a deep flush of pleasure—pleasure at seeing her again, when she had been so much in his mind of late. And she was more beautiful than he remembered, her hair a glory when released from those hideous caps.

Pleasure was quickly swept away by cold shock, and Michael impatiently shook his head, certain he was hallucinating. Mrs. Chase could not be here. He must be dreaming, hallucinating.

He closed his eyes quickly, and opened them again. She was still there, and she was undoubtedly Mrs. Chase. She was watching him, her head tilted quizzically as if she could not believe *he* was there, either.

Then her gaze narrowed, and her lips pinched together.

Yes. It was assuredly Mrs. Chase. Michael pushed away his bemusement, and pasted on a wry half-smile. He could do nothing but go forward. "Mrs. Chase," he murmured to himself. "Fancy meeting you here."

Whatever was she doing here?

Rosalind stared around her at the teeming ballroom. Once, long ago, when she had been a young girl, she had daydreamed about such scenes. Had imagined herself in beautiful gowns, surrounded by handsome swains who flattered her and flirted with her.

The tableau she found herself in now was indeed very close to those old dreams. Her sea green gown was exquisite, and there were more handsome gentlemen than she could count. When she first stepped into the ballroom at Georgina's side, she had felt giddy, dizzy, almost overcome by the color and noise of it all—so very different from her daily life.

But too much time had passed since her girlhood dreams; too much had happened. The dreamy daughter of the local vicar had grown up, married, been widowed, struggled to build up her own school. She was no longer as starry-eyed as she had once been.

She saw this crowd for what it was, a seething cauldron of gossip and decadence beneath a veneer of frothy glamour. For a brief while, though, rules—*her* rules—had held them in check, at least outwardly.

She was not here to make merry, she reminded herself. She was here merely to discover what had made the popularity of *A Lady's Rules* wane, and to set things right. When she had done that, she would leave her borrowed finery behind and return to the quiet life of the Seminary.

That was truly all she wanted. *Truly,* she told herself, even as she sipped at the sinfully delicious champagne and listened to Georgina relate a scandalous *on dit* to her gathered friends. London life had no interest for Rosalind, really it did not.

She told herself this even as she scanned a gaze over the dancers, trying to detect any infraction of the rules that could be causing diminished sales. She saw nothing there—everyone was wearing gloves, and holding their partners at the prescribed distance. When she had first entered the Portman mansion, she had noticed one or two tiny things—a couple laughing too loudly, a man who had had a bit too much to drink—but nothing to give any alarm.

She had not yet seen Lord Morley or any of his cronies, though. That might explain all the good behavior this evening.

"May I fetch you another glass of champagne, Mrs. Chase?" the gentleman beside her asked.

Rosalind looked down with surprise to see that her crystal flute was empty. However had that happened? She *never* overimbibed. Then she noticed that she was indeed a bit light-headed. "Oh, no, thank you," she answered, with a small measure of regret. It *was* very good champagne. "Perhaps a lemonade, though."

"Of course! I shall return forthwith."

Rosalind wasn't sure he *could* return "forthwith" in such a crush, but she smiled at him gratefully, and half-turned to watch him thread his way through the crowd. She handed her empty glass to a footman, and resumed her inspection of the dancers and the crowds that clustered about the edges of the room.

Her gaze skimmed over a couple strolling arm in arm; a group of young misses, one of whom was Georgina's sister-in-law Lady Emily; a tall gentleman in a midnight blue velvet coat . . .

Her gaze veered back to that gentleman. As she saw who it was, she knew he could surely not be called a "gentleman"—gentlemen did not go about trying to ruin ladies' livelihoods! They did not flaunt themselves and their so-called poetry, as Lord Morley did.

And it was Lord Morley who stood only a few feet away from her, watching her as if he had never seen her before in his life. Almost as if—as if he *admired* her.

But that could not be. She was not some dashing, daring titled lady, the sort who Georgina said clustered about him. Perhaps he meant to mock her, then, by watching her so intently. To poke fun at her for being in a ballroom where she so obviously did not belong.

She frowned at the thought, and her head gave a warning pang. She started to turn away from the sight of him, to try to immerse herself again in Georgina's conversation, but she stopped when she saw Lady Clarke come to Lord Morley's side.

As Rosalind watched, Lady Clarke, the mother of one of Rosalind's very own pupils, laid her hand on Lord Morley's arm and stepped up close to him. Far too close for propriety. Lady Clarke went up on tiptoe and whispered into his ear, her ample white bosom displayed in a tiny orange silk bodice. Lord Morley placed his hand—his *ungloved* hand—on her waist. It was unclear if he was pushing her away or holding her there.

Rosalind found she could scarcely tear her gaze away from the ridiculous spectacle. But when she finally managed to look elsewhere, she saw that the people around them, far from being aghast, watched with smirks and smiles of scandalized satisfaction. No one cared at all that Lord Morley was breaking at least four—no, five!—rules.

Much to Rosalind's shock, however, she found that it was not entirely the rule-breaking that pained her. She also felt a sharp pang of something that felt suspiciously like jealousy in her heart.

Her head throbbed in earnest as she watched Lord Morley's hand slide from Lady Clarke's waist to her arm. He said something quietly to her, and her red lips curved up in an enticing smile. Lady Clarke began to turn away from him, but Rosalind turned first, unable to bear the disgusting sight a moment longer.

She needed to be alone. The noise of the ballroom had risen to an infernal din, and even the orchestra was too loud and clanging.

"Do excuse me for a moment," she murmured to Georgina. "I must go to the ladies' withdrawing room."

Georgina's emerald eyes, so bright and laughing only an instant before, turned dark with concern. She laid her hand on Rosalind's arm, her sapphire bracelets tinkling. "Is something amiss, Rosalind? Shall I come with you?"

Rosalind managed to give her a smile. "It is a slight headache only. I think I just need a quiet moment. You must stay here and enjoy the party, keep an eye on Emily. She is such a sought-after young lady."

"Are you certain? I can make Alex leave his discussion of new farming techniques and watch his sister while I am gone. My husband needs to remember his social duties anyway! He *is* a duke, after all, even if he would rather just be a gentleman farmer!" Georgina laughed, but the soft glow on her face spoke volumes of her love for her "gentleman farmer."

Rosalind felt another twist of envy, and she did not like it at all. How *could* she be envious of anyone, least of all Georgie, who so richly deserved her happiness? Or of Lady Clarke, whose impropriety was legendary? To be envious at all was horribly unladylike.

It was *not* envy, Rosalind told herself. It was simply fatigue. She was not accustomed to the social whirl.

"Oh, no," she said. "Leave His Grace to his conversation. I will just go sit down for a moment and will be quite well soon."

She gave Georgina what she hoped was a reassuring smile, and turned to make her way through the ballroom. Since she was of little importance in the grand *ton* scheme of things, it did not take her very long to make her escape—no one stopped her to talk, aside from one or two of Georgina's friends. She slipped out the ballroom doors and past the butler, who waited to announce any latecomers.

The ladies' withdrawing room was down the staircase from the grand ballroom, and along a quiet, dim corridor. The long expanse was lit only by a couple of branches of candelabra, and only the faintest echo of music and voices could be heard from the party.

Already Rosalind could feel the tight band of her headache loosening. She leaned back for a moment against the papered wall, and closed her eyes.

So it is true, she thought. Lord Morley *was* the one responsible for the diminished popularity of the rules. He was using his dash, his reputation as a rogue and a poet, to break the rules of good conduct, and others were following him. Not just young nodcocks like her brother, either, but people in polite society.

She did not know why she should feel such a sourness of disappointment at the realization. Surely she had known all along. Yet it was one thing to know; it was another to *know,* to see it with her own eyes.

Morley *was* a care-for-nothing, a slapdash poet who squandered the benefits and duties of his high position. She had always known that. And yet—and yet, he had been so kind to her that day in her office. He had brought her tea, had made her laugh.

She could scarcely reconcile that man with the one who had stood so intimately with Lady Clarke in the ballroom.

She was such a fool to feel so disappointed.

As Rosalind reached up to rub at her temples, a voice came echoing down the empty corridor.

"Good evening, Mrs. Chase. What an unexpected pleasure it is to see you here."

Lord Morley. Rosalind's eyes flew open, and she turned to see him standing there, half in the shadows. He looked mysterious, almost insubstantial, with a single flickering beam of candlelight falling over his dark hair, his high cheekbones. She could almost have fancied that he was a ghost, the spirit of a wild pirate of old, come back to claim his treasure—his woman.

Unfortunately, he was all too real. And he had caught her yet again at her most vulnerable.

Drat the man.

Chapter Nine

"A gentleman must never approach a lady uninvited at a soiree."
A Lady's Rules for Proper Behavior, Chapter Five

*R*osalind pushed herself away from the wall, staring dazedly at Lord Morley. She knew she was gaping like the veriest lackwit, but she could not seem to help herself. He was like a mirage—or a nightmare—standing there in the shadowed, quiet corridor. She had known she would see him here in London sooner or later; that was really one of the purposes of her visit, was it not? To somehow stop him from his rule-breaking.

The difficulty was, her plan was only half conceived, and she had no clue what to do with him now. She had not thought beyond arriving in Town, and doing *something* to save her situation. What, she was not sure, but she had imagined that a plan would occur to her once she saw Lord Morley.

She had not imagined she would meet him like *this,* however. Alone, in the half-dark. She thought herself a self-possessed woman, a woman of social poise. Of good sense. All that sense had fled, though, and she did not know what to say.

She straightened her shoulders, and reached up to be sure her hair was smooth. "Good evening, Lord Morley. I did not see you standing there."

"No. I can see that." He moved closer to her still

in the shadows. The gold threads embroidered on his cream-colored waistcoat glinted in the candlelight. "I did not mean to startle you."

"Indeed? Then what are you doing here, Lord Morley, lurking in the shadows? I was under the impression that this was the direction to the ladies' withdrawing room." Or perhaps she had taken a wrong turn? There appeared to be no one about in this part of the house at all. Rosalind tried to draw in a deep breath, but her chest felt tight, constricted—and not from her light stays or silk chemise. It was from this man's very presence. He made her feel unsure; he seemed to take up all the air in the narrow corridor.

It was just because she loathed him, she told herself sternly. Because he was a wastrel, who squandered his life in shallow, careless ways.

That was all it was. That was the only reason she felt her face burn, her fingertips and toes turn icy. She just wanted to be out of his presence.

"I believe the withdrawing room is the other way," he answered lightly, with a shrug of his wide, velvet-covered shoulders. "Yet I could not believe my eyes when I saw you in the ballroom. You are one of the last people I would expect to see here. I had to assure myself that it was you, Mrs. Chase."

He could not believe it because she was of such lowly station, perhaps? Rosalind frowned. She would have thought that men who flouted their position by writing poetry would not think of such things. But then, he *was* of the *ton*—she should not be amazed that he was like everyone else. She remembered the shifting of peoples' gazes, the smirks, when they discovered she owned a school.

She was past caring about all that now. She had always done what she had to do, to take care of herself and her family. Why, then, did it sting so when *he* implied as much?

"Oh, Lord Morley?" she said, with a forced, careless little laugh. At least, she hoped it sounded careless. "And why is that? Because I am a mere schoolmistress?"

He gave her a smile, a knowing grin that made her cheeks burn hotter. "Not at all. Because it seems as if Town would be too wicked for you, Mrs. Chase. Too full of temptations. Sins."

Temptations? Such as a pair of fathomless dark eyes that seemed to see into her very soul? A heady whiff of some citrus soap? Oh, yes. Apparently Town, or at least Lady Portman's corridor, was full of those. She stepped back from him, until she felt the edge of a marble-topped table against her hips.

He just took another step toward her, so close she could see the faint blue-black shadow of whiskers along his jawline.

"It is not safe here, Mrs. Chase," he said softly, tauntingly. "Not like it is behind the high walls of your school."

Rosalind's gaze flickered past him to the painting on the wall, but she still sensed him there. Sensed his warmth. She did not see the indifferent seascape at all. "Ah, but Town has become much more civilized of late, has it not? Since people have found a source of manners, of good behavior."

"You mean *A Lady's Rules,* do you not?" he said, with a rich chuckle. That sound seemed to vibrate deep inside of her. "Do you truly think of them as a simple guide to manners? A gentle suggestion of how to be—civilized?"

She looked back to him, unable to break her gaze away from the velvet of his eyes. He watched her intently, leaning toward her, as if he truly cared about her answer. "Of course. What else could they be?"

"Oh, now, I do not know. A way to keep people in line? To make them conform to someone else's views of how things should be?" He leaned one hand against the wall, carelessly, as if he was not aware of his action. The soft fabric of his sleeve was near—so near—her neck, her bare shoulder.

"C-conform?" she choked out. She tried to edge away from his arm, but the table blocked her path. "Conform to what?"

"Society has always been constrictive in certain ways," he said. "Yet there has also been room for a degree of freedom for people who, shall we say, have a different way of looking at things."

"People such as you, perhaps?" she asked. "People who behave in wild ways, not caring what boundaries they cross, or who they hurt by it."

Something flickered in the sherry brown depths of his eyes, a flash of anger or maybe even pain. But it was gone in an instant, and he glanced away from her with a laugh. "I would never knowingly hurt anyone, Mrs. Chase. I only try to enjoy my life; it is far too short to do otherwise. How can that harm people?"

Rosalind didn't know what he was saying, what he meant. Her head was spinning, her ears ringing. She wanted to move away from him, to run away, but she was frozen to the spot. "How have the rules hurt anyone?" she cried, more passionately than she intended. Her voice echoed along the corridor.

He seemed startled by her vehemence, and studied her closer. His hand, as of its own volition, moved to her hair, to the long curl that lay along her neck. It twined like a twist of red silk around his finger.

Rosalind forgot to breathe. She could not move away, she could not do anything but stare at her hair twined about his long, elegant finger.

"Oh, Mrs. Chase," he whispered. "They hurt people in ways far too complicated for me to explain. They are hurting *you*, if you could only see it."

Hurting her? *No!* They were the only thing that was saving her—the only thing that could begin to help her brother. *Morley* was the one who was hurting her. She had left the safety of her school to come here and stop him.

But it was hard, indeed almost impossible, to remember that now. She reached up to grasp his wrist, to push him away, but she could not seem to. Her fingers curled around his velvet cuff, and she leaned closer to him . . .

"Well, well," a voice said. "What is all this?"

Rosalind jerked away, as if she was burned, and almost tripped over the table. As she righted herself, clinging to the cold marble, a hot, red rush of shame flooded through her. What was she doing, standing here in the dark, practically *embracing* Lord Morley? Morley, of all people! She had broken at least six— no, seven—of her own rules in just those few seconds.

Moon madness. That was the only explanation. Or perhaps the spell of the city, the unfamiliar social whirl, that made her lose her head. Made her forget what was truly important.

She peered down the corridor to see Georgina standing there, her famous sapphires glittering like a blue fire in the candlelight. Georgina watched her with no hint of condemnation—that would never be Georgina's way. There was speculation in her eyes, and a hint of amusement.

That amusement was almost worse than condemnation. It was like a splash of icy water, bringing her back into reality. Rosalind slipped past Lord Morley and hurried down the corridor toward her friend.

"Georgina," she said, and was dismayed to hear the breathlessness of her voice. "I was just—just coming to find you."

"Oh, yes? I trust your headache is better." Georgina's gaze shifted past Rosalind to Lord Morley, who had moved away from the wall and stood in a flickering beam of candlelight. "Viscount Morley, is it not?"

"Indeed it is, Duchess." Aside from a faint thickness in his tone, there was absolutely no change in his demeanor. It was as if he was completely unaffected by their brief, strange, unsettling scene. He pushed the waves of his dark hair back from his brow, and came forward to bow over Georgina's hand.

"I was not aware you knew my friend Mrs. Chase,"

she said, tilting her head as she looked up at him speculatively.

"My sister attends her excellent Seminary," he answered, and glanced over at Rosalind. There was a plea in his eyes—perhaps an apology?

But Rosalind could not bring herself to look directly at him just yet. She could scarcely even think.

"Lady Violet, yes," said Georgina. "I have met her. She is a lovely girl. My friend's school obviously agrees with her. No doubt you were chatting about her education just now?"

"Among other things," Lord Morley murmured.

"*Fascinating* things, I am sure," Georgina said. "I would love to stay here and chat with the two of you, but I fear we have no time for that at the moment. Rosalind, I came to find you to tell you there is something in the ballroom you *must* see."

Something in the ballroom she had to see? Rosalind could not imagine what it could possibly be. More dancers? More gossiping dowagers? But she found she longed for the crowded ballroom, for the noise and distraction of it. At least there Georgina could not question her about this scene, as Rosalind could see her friend longed to do. There, she could not think about all this nonsense.

That could wait for tonight, when she was alone in the quiet opulence of Georgina's finest guest bedchamber.

"Of course," she said. "I will come at once."

"Good. Though I fear you will not be at all happy when you see it." Georgina took Rosalind's hand and started to turn away, back to the staircase to the ballroom. Then she glanced back at Morley. "Lord Morley, we would be happy to have you call at our house at any time that is convenient. My husband and I so enjoyed your last volume of poems."

Lord Morley bowed. "That is very kind of you, Your Grace. Thank you."

Georgina nodded, and drew Rosalind along with her up the stairs.

"Why did you invite that man to your house, Georgina?" Rosalind whispered.

Georgina turned to her, auburn brows arched in surprise. "I thought you liked him, Rosie! Why else would you be standing there alone with him? He *is* very handsome."

Rosalind just shook her head. She had no words, not right now. The usually unflappable Mrs. Chase was—flapped. She felt like an unsure young girl, not like the thirty-year-old widow she was.

"We must speak more of this later," Georgina said, as they reached the closed ballroom doors. There was a strange rumbling noise from behind those inlaid panels, a crash, a roar. "But for now, my dear—you must brace yourself."

Blast! What was he thinking of?

Michael turned away as Mrs. Chase and the duchess hurried off, and closed his eyes to suck in a large breath of air. It did no good, though—the corridor was still filled with the fresh, green scent of her perfume.

He braced his fists against the wall, and restrained the fierce impulse to drive them through the painted silk paper.

He knew what he had been thinking of. He had been thinking of Mrs. Chase's bright curls, her white skin above the silken line of her bodice. The look in her blue eyes as she watched him. Once he had thought of them as ice. But tonight, they glowed as brilliant as starlight.

Brilliant with dislike, mayhap? Or a deep, hidden desire? The same desire that sparked inside him when her hair curled about his finger. As he looked at that one red curl, he had envisioned the wealth of her hair spread over her shoulders, over his chest and arms, the whiteness of linen pillows . . .

He pounded against the wall, until a painting hanging above him rattled perilously. He had been having those lustful thoughts about Mrs. Chase! *Mrs. Chase,* of all people. The woman who wore ugly caps, and trumpeted the rules to all and sundry. She would not know a free moment, a spontaneous act, if they reached up and snatched one of those caps off her head.

And yet she was beautiful tonight, in her fashionable gown, her chic coiffure. She almost appeared like a normal female. Yet what he had forgotten was that beneath that pale green satin beat the heart of a true rule-follower.

But she had not been thinking of the rules when they stood there, so close together in the near darkness. And neither had he, despite their words to each other about manners and etiquette. He had thought only of tasting her kiss, breathing in the scent of her.

Her lips were surprisingly lush and pink when not pinched together disapprovingly. Her eyes were wide and wondering, so young for just that moment.

There was more to her than what she showed the world. She went to great pains to appear cool, prim, proper, always so very in control. And she was quite successful—even he had seen only that façade. Now he suspected there was something else, something hidden there. Perhaps so hidden that not even she herself could see it.

And *that* was what drew him to her, he realized. He wanted to discover her hidden heart, the free soul she buried beneath her manners and her ugly gowns. He had glimpsed her for the merest instant tonight, he had even held her, felt the trembling inside of her.

Then she was snatched away, and he had watched the veil of her propriety fall over her again. There was a hectic red flush on her fair cheeks, the freckles she tried to hide standing out in golden relief. She would not even look at him, and seemed appalled at her friend's invitation to him to call.

It was deeply saddening to see. He wanted to go after her, to catch her in his arms and *demand* that she give him back the woman he had seen so fleetingly. But he had not, of course. That would only have driven Mrs. Chase further away, made her retreat deeper beneath her careful façade.

Now that he had glimpsed her inner secrets, he wanted to know more of her. He *had* to know.

He would accept the Duchess of Wayland's invitation to call. Very soon, before Mrs. Chase had time to scurry back behind the high walls of her school.

Perhaps he would even go tomorrow.

Michael pushed himself away from the wall, and straightened his coat and his cravat (not pink tonight, but sky blue—much like Mrs. Chase's eyes). As he turned away, he glimpsed a flash of something pale against the dark carpet runner. He bent down and picked up a fan. A pale green satin fan, edged in white lace and scattered with tiny, glittering beads.

Mrs. Chase's fan. She must have dropped it when they were standing here together. The soft pleats still smelled of her perfume.

Michael tucked it inside his coat. Now he had the perfect excuse to call at the Wayland house, if the duchess's invitation was not enough.

With a smile, he strolled to the staircase leading to the ballroom. Halfway up, he became aware of an odd noise from the party, a rush of wild laughter, a crash, a shriek. He hurried his steps, along with the other stragglers from the ball who lingered on the stairs—and stopped abruptly in the doorway.

He could scarcely believe what he was seeing!

Chapter Ten

"When dancing, a proper distance must be kept between partners at all times."
A Lady's Rules for Proper Behavior, Chapter Three

osalind could hardly believe what she was seeing. The ball was not quite the crush it had been when Rosalind left; no doubt many people had gone on to other soirees or home to their beds. But there were many people remaining, and several of them— nay, most of them—were riveted on one spectacle.

Rosalind froze as she stepped into the ballroom. This could not be happening. This was just a nightmare. Obviously, she had not yet awakened from her dream-scene in the corridor with Lord Morley. Her face, her hands, her whole being froze with the hot-icy feel of sheer humiliation.

Sprawled out flat in the middle of the parquet dance floor was Allen, dressed in a most outlandish Pierrot costume. The loose black and white satin of his baggy pantaloons and tunic spread about him in a shimmering puddle, and his black velvet cap fell drunkenly over his eyes. He slowly sat up, pushing the cap back, and the observers gathered in a ring around him stepped back—all but a large, buxom matron in purple satin, who menaced Allen with her reticule, and a petite, sobbing miss.

Laughter and titters rose as an inexorable tidal wave

through the crowd, audible even over the lovely music that still played.

Rosalind rubbed her gloved hand over her eyes, but it did not make the surreal scene disappear. Another young man, whom Rosalind did not know, went to help haul Allen to his feet. This man, too, wore a costume, the garb of a Roman centurion with a clanking brass breastplate.

She turned to Georgina, who was trying, not very successfully, to hide her smile behind her fan.

"What happened here?" Rosalind demanded.

Georgina lowered her fan, and used it to tap thoughtfully at her chin. "I am afraid I could not say exactly. I was over there, talking with some friends, when we became aware of some, er, disturbance. People running about, girls shrieking. Then—this." Her voice ended on a tiny hiccup that sounded suspiciously like a giggle.

Rosalind sighed. She could not really blame Georgina for laughing. It *did* look so oddly comical. Yet, somehow, she could not quite laugh herself. Not with her cheeks burning and her head pounding. There was probably no chance she could just pretend not to know Allen. Everyone in the *ton* knew everything about everyone else—even such insignificant sprigs as Allen and Rosalind.

As Rosalind turned and prepared to wade into the fray, Georgina's sister-in-law Emily rushed up to them. Her china blue eyes sparkled with excitement. She was in her third Season now, but had obviously never seen anything like *this* at the many, many balls she attended!

"Oh, Georgie!" she cried. "Isn't it just too funny? And I was right there when it happened!" Then her gaze fell on Rosalind, and some of the sparkle faded. "I'm sorry, Mrs. Chase. I did forget that Mr. Lucas is your brother."

"That is quite all right, Lady Emily," Rosalind said. "But what exactly *did* happen here?"

Emily glanced back over to Pierrot and the Roman,

who had now been joined by Louis XIV in powdered wig and high-heeled shoes. The matron in purple still shouted incoherently at them, and swiped at Allen with her beaded reticule. "Well, I was dancing with Mr. Elliott, and we were very near Miss Anderson and her partner, Lord St. Regis. Miss Anderson is Lady Anderson's daughter, you know." Emily gestured toward the matron and the sobbing young lady hidden in her shadow. "It was all quite ordinary. Then, all of a sudden, Miss Anderson screamed! And Lord St. Regis hit poor Mr. Lucas."

Rosalind was completely bewildered. "But what was Allen doing here at all? He was not invited to this ball, and even if he was this is *not* a fancy-dress event." The cabbage-head was not even supposed to be in London, but hard at his studies at Cambridge.

"I do not know," Emily said. "Miss Anderson was saying he just grabbed her and kissed her! And when he was on the floor, having been planted a facer by Lord St. Regis, Lady Anderson came up and hit him with her reticule. I have heard that she carries a very large vinaigrette in that reticule." She lowered her voice confidingly, and added, "I do believe, Mrs. Chase, that Mr. Lucas is quite foxed. He smelled rather—pungent."

Foxed. Oh, wonderful. That was just what this situation required. Not just an idiot, but a drunken idiot.

"Thank you for that information, Lady Emily," Rosalind said. Her tone was surprisingly calm, considering the roiling turmoil in her heart. She curled her hands into fists, and marched across the ballroom, Georgina and Emily hurrying behind her.

Fortunately, before they reached the violent scene Georgina's husband, Alexander, the Duke of Wayland, joined them. He had apparently just returned from his farming conversation, and seen his wife and sister being drawn into a scandalous scene. He took Georgina's arm, and whispered, "What have you done now, Georgie?"

Georgina looked at him indignantly. "Why do you

assume that just because there is a disturbance *I* had something to do with it?''

He grinned at her. ''Because, my love, you usually do.''

She laughed. ''Well, I did naught to cause it this time. It is poor Rosie's brother.''

Alexander looked to Allen, and his handsome face darkened as Lady Anderson landed another blow on Allen's head. ''So I see. Well, ladies, shall we discover what can be done?''

The gathered crowd parted for the duke and duchess, allowing them to walk unimpeded to Allen's side. As Alexander spoke quietly to the red-faced Lady Anderson, Rosalind turned to her brother.

Do not hit him, she told herself sternly. *Be calm. Remember the rules. Surely there is one about not pummeling gentlemen in public places.* Even foolish younger brothers.

''Rosie!'' Allen cried. For one instant, relief flashed across his face. Perhaps, Rosalind thought, he supposed his big sister had come yet again to his rescue. But the relief was quickly replaced by chagrin, and then bluster. ''What the deuce are you doing here?''

''What am *I* doing here?'' Rosalind said, trying to keep her voice quiet. She was all too aware of the many people watching them with avid interest—including parents of some of her pupils. ''*You* are meant to be at university, not gallivanting about London making an absolute fool of yourself—and of me.''

''Ah, Rosie, you are making too much of it,'' Allen insisted. He sighed, releasing a wave of that ''pungent'' odor Lady Emily had mentioned. He pulled off his battered cap and twisted it between his hands. ''It is nothing. A mere wager.''

''A *what*?'' Rosalind's voice rose dangerously as she felt her temper slipping out of her control. She felt a soft touch on her arm, and glanced over to see Georgina's reassuring smile.

''Lady Portman says we may speak privately in her library,'' Georgina said. ''Perhaps that would be better than staying here? Alex and Emily will smooth things over with the others."

Rosalind turned to Alexander. Indeed, he had already smoothed the ruffled purple feathers of Lady Anderson and her sobbing daughter. The indignant matron was even smiling, and much of the crowd was wandering away as the spectacle faded.

"Ah, young men," Alexander said to the general gathering, with a handsome, rueful smile. "What can one do?"

There was a knowing ripple of laughter, and Rosalind began to think—to hope—that all might not be lost after all. A faint ray of relief pierced the gloom of her anger and humiliation. But it did not entirely eradicate them—they still simmered in the depths of her mind.

She and Allen would not always have a duke to rescue them, and Allen had to come to understand that. Even if he understood so little else—like how precarious their livelihood was at the moment. She had this bank loan to pay, and not enough to pay it. The money from *A Lady's Rules* that she had counted on was dwindling away. If pupils abandoned her school due to a scandal attached to her family, she and Allen would be entirely lost.

"Yes," she said to Georgina. "We should retire to the library." Then, not giving Allen a chance to argue, Rosalind took one of his arms and Georgina the other, and they marched him out of the ballroom. Behind them, the music resumed, and Alexander led Lady Anderson into the dance.

Rosalind was still not entirely certain what had just happened here, but she was quite sure it had *something* to do with Lord Morley.

When Michael returned to the ballroom, many of the guests had departed. But there were still a great many people dancing, sitting in the white brocade chairs lining the dance floor, and taking turns about the room. Everything appeared just as a ball ought

to—except for the two men huddled in the shadows
by the door.

Mr. Gilmore and Lord Carteret, dressed incongru-
ously as a Roman centurion and a fop from the last
century.

"Morley!" Gilmore cried, his voice hoarse with relief. "You are here."

"Yes," Michael answered, as they pulled him into
the shadows with them. "I am here. What, though, are
you two doing here? And dressed like that?"

"It is that wager," Carteret said, flicking at the deep
lace of his cuff. "We thought Lucas would see he cannot win if we brought him here tonight. So we made
a sort of secondary wager."

Carteret seemed faintly amused by the whole thing,
while Gilmore looked pale and shaken. Michael
glanced from one to the other of them, a strange, sick
feeling growing in his stomach. Something had obviously happened while he was lingering with Mrs.
Chase in the dark corridor, something involving that
very lady's brother.

Something else she could hate him for. Because he
knew, deep down, that she would surely blame him for
whatever trouble young Lucas had wreaked tonight.

He swept a quick glance over the ballroom, and did
not see Mrs. Chase, Mr. Lucas, or the Duchess of
Wayland anywhere. Lady Emily, though, stood not
very far away, watching their little group with far too
much shrewdness for such a young miss. Michael gave
her a rakish grin, hoping she would blush and turn
away. She just laughed, but she *did* leave, crossing the
room to her brother's side. The duke was talking with
a very buxom lady in bright purple satin, whom Michael recognized as Lady Anderson, mother of the
prettiest debutante this Season.

Michael turned back to Gilmore and Carteret.
"Now tell me exactly why you three came here in
costume."

Carteret gave him a resentful scowl. "You are not
our father, Morley, to be taking us to task."

"Carteret . . ." Gilmore said nervously.

"But," Carteret continued, "since you *are* our friend, we will tell you. We were at a masquerade at Vauxhall, with the loveliest little bits o'muslin you ever saw. There was a bit too much wine and brandy, too, and so we conceived the idea of coming here."

Michael stared at them through narrowed eyes. "That cannot be the entire story."

"It is *almost* the entire story!" Gilmore said. "Except that Carteret dared Lucas to steal a kiss from Miss Anderson, then dash away before he was caught. Miss Anderson is the Diamond of the Season, y'know."

"It would have worked, too, if the chit hadn't sent up such a fuss," said Carteret. "Then Lord St. Regis and Miss Anderson's mama laid Lucas low."

Miss Anderson "sending up a fuss" was surely exactly what Carteret had been hoping for, Michael thought. Public humiliation was probably the only way Lucas was going to be persuaded he must follow the rules, and thus allow Carteret to win the silly wager. "Where is Lucas now?"

"His dragon sister and the Duchess of Wayland marched him out of here, quite smartishly," said Gilmore. "And the duke calmed everyone down in here. Even Lady Anderson."

"So you see?" Carteret said languidly. "There was no harm done."

No harm done? Could these—these *loobies* truly be so very ignorant? Their prank had very nearly humiliated a young man and ruined his sister's business. Michael knew very well how unforgiving people in Society could be if they felt they had been embarrassed, and these boys' escapade had involved the loveliest debutante in London and her snobbish parents. Only the intervention of people as influential as the Waylands had saved the entire ridiculous situation. And now this smirking bacon-brain was prating about no harm done.

Michael could not stop himself from reaching out

to grab Carteret by the lace of his cascading jabot—his anger blinded him, burned white-hot behind his eyes. Carteret's eyes widened in shock, and he made ineffectual little jabs with his beringed hands as Gilmore, looking on, gave an incoherent cry.

"Don't you realize what could have happened here tonight? Lucas's *sister* was here. Her reputation was at risk as well as his, if your 'harmless' prank had not ended where it did. The Waylands saved all of your hides this time, but next time you will not be so fortunate, you brainless pups."

Carteret's face was turning red beneath his layer of rice powder, and his hands clawed ever more insistently at Michael's arm. Michael loosened his grip, but still held onto the lace.

"You were the one who claimed we could break all the rules and still be accepted," Carteret gasped. "Are you so quick to change your mind, just because Lucas got taken to task?"

Michael had never meant his words like *this*. Yes, following all of *A Lady's Rules* was absurd, was soul-killing. But their behavior this evening, that of all three of them, had been beyond the pale. Michael himself would never do anything so rash, so ill thought out. He would never actually damage anyone.

Would he? Certain youthful indiscretions flashed through his mind, pranks every bit as ridiculous as the one this trio had tried tonight. Yet that had been long ago; he had learned from those mistakes, as one day these boys would have to learn from theirs. That sort of wild, pointless rule-breaking was far behind Michael.

Then another vision flowed through his mind—himself, pulling Lady Clarke close to him and putting his arm about her waist. All in this very ballroom, not three hours ago—and under the gaze of Mrs. Chase.

A heat that felt uncomfortably more like regret than his previous anger flowed through his veins. He released Carteret, who fell back a step and reached up to rub at his throat.

"You are far more dangerous than we are, Morley," Carteret said weakly. "People pay far more attention to *your* infractions than they ever would to ours. And I think the ladies over there would agree with me."

Michael, still trembling with the force of his anger and uncertainty, glanced back over his shoulder.

Mrs. Chase and the Duchess of Wayland stood in the doorway of the ballroom, with Allen Lucas nowhere in evidence. The duchess paid them no attention; her gaze was scanning over the crowd, no doubt looking for her husband.

But Mrs. Chase was staring right at them—at *him*. Her posture was perfectly straight, her expression completely composed. Her eyes, though, burned with a freezing, pale blue light, even more vivid than the duchess's sapphires. She watched him, unblinking, for a long, still moment, the force of her disdain clear. She then slowly turned her back to him and moved away into the sea of people.

It was as if their moment in the corridor had never happened at all. As if he had never glimpsed the heat that lay beneath her serene, proper exterior.

He felt as if he had just lost something precious, something he had not even realized he could desire so much until this very moment—something as beautiful as Mrs. Chase's smile.

He had the strongest urge to rush after her, to apologize, to beg for her understanding. He could not, though. It would do no good, not when her eyes were as cold as they were right now. She had drawn back into herself, after shyly peering forth when they were alone. She was again the self-contained Mrs. Chase. And how could he ask her to understand something he could not yet understand himself?

He should talk to her, and he would. But not here. Not now, with all these people about. He strode away from Gilmore and Carteret, down the staircase toward the Portman's front door. He reached inside his coat and touched the satin and lace fan—Mrs. Chase's fan. Tomorrow, he would take it to her, would talk to her.

Chapter Eleven

"Be very careful whom you choose to confide
in—be certain they are true friends."
A Lady's Rules for Proper Behavior,   Chapter Ten

"*G*ood heavens, what an evening!" Georgina collapsed onto a settee in her own sitting room, and
kicked off her satin slippers before propping her feet
on a low footstool. "I cannot recall a more diverting
soiree, can you, Emily?"

"Not at all," Emily replied, settling herself in an
armchair. "There was that jug-bitten young man who
tried to slide down the banister at the Eversleys' ball
last Season, but I would say . . ." She broke off, and
cast a guilty smile in Rosalind's direction. "Not that I
enjoyed seeing *your* brother get into trouble, Mrs.
Chase."

Rosalind gave her a small smile in return. A small
one was all she could manage, she was so very tired.
She wished she could kick off her shoes like Georgina,
but it did not seem proper. Not in front of people. "It
is quite all right, Lady Emily. Allen *did* look ridiculous
there, and it was entirely his own fault." His—and
Lord Morley's, for encouraging such silliness among
impressionable young men. "I wonder if I should go
up and see how he fares?"

"Oh, no, Rosie," Georgina said, scratching the ears
of her spoiled white terrier Lady Kate. "Alex will have
him tucked away in a trice. He knows exactly how

to deal with drunk young men, after all his years in the army."

"It was very kind of you to give him a chamber for the night," said Rosalind. "When you invited me to stay with you, you could hardly have expected to put up my entire family."

"Oh, pooh!" Georgina answered, with a careless wave of her hand. Her ruby betrothal ring flashed in the firelight. "We must have a hundred guest chambers in this place, and no one to fill them. Mr. Lucas is welcome to stay as long as he likes."

Rosalind's lips tightened. "He will not stay long. Tomorrow, he will be going back to Cambridge, where he belongs."

Georgina laughed. "Rosie dear, I fear he will not be in any shape to travel tomorrow!"

Emily, who had been staring thoughtfully out of one of the windows, turned serious eyes to them. Rosalind wondered what she was thinking of; usually, Rosalind was adept at reading young ladies, but she found Lady Emily to be a mystery. Emily, in her third Season, was older than most of the misses on the Marriage Mart, and had seen far more of life than they had. She might look like a china shepherdess, with her golden curls and china blue eyes, but she was shrewd and did not miss much around her.

Her words showed that. "I am of the mind that Mr. Lucas could never have conceived of such a prank alone. He is too good-hearted, and was far too foxed."

"Do you suppose it was that silly Mr. Gilmore?" Georgina asked. "Or perhaps Lord Carteret. I saw them both there, in their costumes. They must have had a part in it."

Rosalind sat up with interest. She remembered Allen saying the original gaming debt had been owed to someone named Carteret at his club. "I fear I know little of Allen's friends in Town. He does not care to confide in his *sister* about them. What are these young men like?"

"Oh, they fancy themselves quite the rogues,"

Georgina said. "But really they are just mutton-heads, causing nuisances. They are often racketing about Town in the phaetons their fathers bought them, racing and throwing things."

"They belong to the same club as Mr. Lucas," Emily said. "The Thoth Club."

Oh, yes. Rosalind *had* heard of that club. The blasted club where Allen went to run up debts he could ill afford. "Is it a popular club?"

"Quite," Georgina said. "And now becoming harder to gain a membership, since so many have joined. Some would say your brother is very fortunate to be a member."

Rosalind gave an inelegant snort.

Georgina and Emily laughed and Lady Kate barked. "I quite agree," said Georgina. "Men and their clubs! I have sometimes thought of starting one myself, a sensible one for women only."

"Or one for artists?" Emily suggested. "But I do believe they have artists in the Thoth Club."

"Allen is not an artist," commented Rosalind. She would be glad if he *did* show an interest in art, or in anything besides carelessness.

"One can be of any sort of artistic bent at the Thoth Club—painting, music, literature, or even just possess an appreciation of such things," Emily said. "It was begun by Viscount Morley and Sir William Beene, another Society poet."

Of course. Rosalind remembered the particulars about that club now. She also remembered, with a hot flash of shame, how close she had been to Lord Morley in that dark corridor. If he had made another movement toward her, if Georgina had not appeared when she had . . .

Rosalind shivered to think what might have happened. Why, she might even have let the rogue *kiss* her!

She closed her eyes tightly to try to block out the memories, the images. When she opened them, she found Georgina watching her speculatively.

"Morley is quite handsome," Georgina commented. "Quite popular with the ladies."

"Oh, yes!" said Emily. "Did you see the way Lady Clarke was throwing herself at him tonight? Very scandalous. And that sort of thing happens everywhere he goes."

"I did not notice," Rosalind said, trying to sound careless and bored. To *feel* careless and bored. She certainly did not want to beg Emily to tell her more.

"How could you not notice, Rosie?" asked Georgina. "He certainly seemed to notice *you*."

Emily stared at Rosalind with avid wonder. "Did he, Mrs. Chase? What did he say to you? What did he *do*?"

"He did nothing, Lady Emily," Rosalind said tightly. "Your sister-in-law exaggerates. But it does not matter, for I fail to see Lord Morley's fabled charms." *Liar!* her mind screamed at her. "He may be handsome, but he has no manners. No man can be truly attractive without those."

Emily laughed. "Who cares about manners when a gentleman has such a handsome . . ."

"Emily!" Georgina cried, laughing. "You are meant to be an innocent young miss. Such a scandal you are."

Emily just shrugged. "I may be young, but I am not blind."

Even Rosalind had to laugh. "Right you are, Lady Emily. And such a handsome, mannerless man could have no interest in a woman such as me."

"You underestimate yourself, Rosie," Georgina argued. "You always did, even when we were in school."

"Indeed you do, Mrs. Chase," agreed Emily. "You had so many admirers tonight. I can't count the number of people who asked me about you."

"Only because they were trying to ingratiate themselves with *you*, Lady Emily," Rosalind said.

"Emily is quite the belle of the Season," Georgina said. "And she was last Season, and the Season before that, as well!"

Emily laughed, and pushed herself up out of her chair. "That is now my cue to retire, before Georgie starts hinting that it is about time I accepted one of my suitors."

"I did not do any such thing!" Georgina protested.

"Oh, of course not. Not *you*, never," answered Emily, still laughing. "Good night, Georgie. Good night, Mrs. Chase. Be careful, or she will start matchmaking for you, too."

"Good night, Lady Emily," said Rosalind. "Don't worry—I would never let her."

When the door had closed behind Emily, Georgina fell back onto her settee with a sigh, Lady Kate clambering up onto her lap. "I do sometimes worry about her, Rosie."

"Worry? About Lady Emily? She seems quite well to me."

"Oh, yes, she is. But this is her third Season. She has turned down at least two dozen offers." Georgina sighed. "I fear she will never find a man to love as I love my Alex. As you loved your Charles."

Charles. Yes, once Rosalind *had* thought she loved him. Not in the same way Georgina loved her duke, but with a quiet affection. He had been so well-mannered, so thoughtful. Now, sometimes, she had a difficult time recalling his face. Or the sound of his voice.

She shook her head sadly. This was no time to be maudlin! She was just tired—tired, and worried.

"Oh, Georgie," she said, with a weak little chuckle. "I would much rather worry about marrying off a duke's beautiful sister than try to convince my cabbage-head of a brother to behave sensibly."

Georgina leaned forward to squeeze Rosalind's hand reassuringly. "It is true that Mr. Lucas behaved badly tonight. But he is young! We were all young and foolish at one time. After a day or two, no one will speak of this incident at all. Something new and more scandalous will take its place."

"Yes, I know. But then he will do something else,

and then something *else*, and then . . ." And then—
they would be ruined. No one would trust their daughters to her care; her publisher would not buy any
more books.

It was all suddenly too much. Too much to bear
alone. Her exhaustion, her strange, unruly feelings for
Lord Morley, her brother's bad behavior—it was overwhelming. She covered her face with her hands, and
choked back a sob. But it would not be choked back;
it broke free, followed by another and another.

"Rosie!" Georgina cried. She put aside Lady Kate
and knelt down beside Rosalind in a rustle of silk.
"Oh, my dear, what is it? It must be more than what
happened tonight. I have never seen you so set-to.
Tell me what is wrong, please. Let me help you, if
I can."

Her friend's kindness was simply too much for Rosalind. Everything poured out of her—the book, the
school, the loans and debts Allen had accrued. Everything—everything, that is, except for Lord Morley. She
could not bring herself to tell even Georgina about
that. Whatever it was.

When it had all drained from her in a torrent of
tears and incoherent words, Rosalind fell back, de-
pleted, into her chair. She slumped down, forgetting
even the rules of proper posture.

Georgina stared up at her with wide, shocked green
eyes. Rosalind thought vaguely that this must be a
moment to remember. She had never seen Georgina
shocked before.

"*You* wrote *A Lady's Rules*?" Georgina whispered.
"You, Rosie? And you never told me?"

"I have told no one," Rosalind answered. "I must
be discreet, for the sake of my school, and I feared
that even something so harmless as an etiquette book
could bring unwanted attention."

"But you are famous!" cried Georgina. "Or at least
A Lady is. Everyone adores your book."

"Or they did—until recently. My publisher says that

sales are falling, and they do not want to publish a planned second edition."

Georgina sat back on her heels. "So that is why you came to London. To investigate."

"I did hope perhaps I could discover something that might be of use," Rosalind admitted.

"And you found it is Lord Morley who is breaking your rules!" Georgina's eyes sparkled, and her lips curved in a grin. "And that is why you were with him in the corridor. To make him confess."

Rosalind could see she just had to nip this in the bud. Georgina was much too fond of intrigues, schemes, and romances. She read too many horrid novels. She was quite capable of making all of this into some grand drama. "Now, Georgina, listen . . ." she began.

"Here you are, ladies!" the duke's voice interrupted. Rosalind turned to see Georgina's husband standing in the doorway, a tray with a bottle of fine brandy and some glasses in his hand. "I thought after such a strange evening a brandy might be in order."

"Alex, my darling, you are an angel," Georgina said. She sat back in her chair, but tossed Rosalind a glance that promised this discussion was not finished. "You have read my mind yet again."

Rosalind usually did not imbibe brandy. But tonight, it sounded exactly what she needed. "Thank you, Your Grace," she murmured, and accepted the glass of lovely amber liquid.

"Now, Mrs. Chase, I have asked you many times to call me Alexander," he said, and sat down on the arm of his wife's chair.

"Of course—Alexander," Rosalind said, though it still did not feel quite right to call a duke by his given name!

"Very good," said Alexander. "And you will be happy to know that your brother is safely asleep in the Green Room. No worse for wear, though he will have a demon of a headache in the morning."

Rosalind gave him a grateful smile, and sipped at her brandy. For now, for this one moment, it felt so very good to let someone else help her, to let at least a tiny portion of the burden drop away.

She would have to pick it up again soon enough.

Allen was already tucked up in bed when Rosalind looked in on him as she made her way to her own chamber. He looked exhausted and wan against the clean white linens, but he sat up smartly enough when she entered the room, pulling the blankets up to his chin.

"Rosie!" he cried. "For heaven's sake, I have retired. You shouldn't be in here!"

Ordinarily, Rosalind would agree. It was against the rules for a lady to enter a man's chamber, even that of her brother. Tonight, though, after everything that had happened, such niceties seemed faintly ridiculous. She had to talk to Allen, and she had to do it now.

She waved away his sputtering protests and sat down on a chair by the bed. "Allen, please do not be missish. I watched the nursemaid change your nappies when you were two months old; it scarcely matters if I see you in your nightshirt now."

"Oh, Rosie," Allen muttered miserably, sinking down against the pillows.

"I wanted to talk to you now," Rosalind went on, "but I promise I will be quick. I am very tired, as no doubt you are. It was a most *turbulent* evening."

Allen looked even more miserable, if that was possible. "I never meant for you to find out about that. If I had known you were there . . ."

"I know you are sorry now, Allen. And I am sorry, too."

Allen's bloodshot eyes widened in surprise. "*You,* Rosie? What are you sorry for?"

"I have only just now realized something, and that is that I still think of you as that baby in nappies, and not as the young man that you are. I was so much older than you, eleven years old when you were born, that I have always felt I had to look after you. Now I see that I need to help you look after yourself."

"What do you mean?" Allen appeared profoundly confused, and really, Rosalind thought, who could blame him? He had never had to take care of himself before, as Rosalind had always swooped in to do it for him. But she was tired now, so very tired. She could be his caretaker no longer.

"I mean that I have done you a disservice. I have lectured you about your careless behavior, and exhorted you to cease your gaming. But I have not told you of our true situation, which would have helped you to see the right path for yourself."

Rosalind closed her eyes, took a deep breath—and told her brother the truth of their financial situation. She told him about *A Lady's Rules,* the expenses of the school, the letters from the bank. She told all this in the shortest, sparest language she could find, but when she was done she still felt drained. She slumped back in her chair and opened her eyes.

Allen had left the bed in silence and knelt on the carpet beside her chair. He looked so very young, with his overlarge borrowed nightshirt and tousled hair. But his eyes—his eyes glowed with a faint light that was years older.

"So you see, Allen, that there is enough money for your education," she told him. "Indeed, I am happy to give you that. But there is not enough for any more debts. It cannot go on, or we will be ruined. That is as plainly as I can say it."

Allen shook his head, his jaw working as if he *wanted* to say something but could not find the words. Then he said, "I am sorry, Rosie. So sorry. I should have realized—should have known. You always said . . ."

"I tried to protect you, as our parents wished."

"You do not need to *protect* me! I am a grown man now. I should be protecting *you.*"

"All I want is for you to return to school, to prepare for a career. That is all I ever wished for."

Chapter Twelve

"Never make a glutton of yourself in public. Sip daintily at tea, and only take small nibbles of the lightest of foods."
A Lady's Rules for Proper Behavior, Chapter Eight

*M*ichael drew his phaeton to a halt outside the Waylands's townhouse, and stared up at its white marble façade. In its way, it was even more grand than Bronston House, with its classical pediments and multiple chimneys and sparkling windows. By all rights, it should be twice as forbidding, since it housed a ducal household. But the bright green draperies at the first floor windows, the potted topiaries that lined the front walk, and the redheaded moppet of a child who peered down from one of the upper story windows, gave it a life, a welcoming air, that Bronston House could never hope to possess.

He feared that one of the residents of the house would not be nearly so welcoming, though. In fact, he would be quite fortunate if Mrs. Chase did not toss him down those front steps on his backside. He was not her favorite person in the world—he knew that from the cold stare she had given him in the Portmans' ballroom last night, but that did not change his own feelings. He wanted to see her; he *had* to see her, no matter in what state he found her this morning, even if she shouted at him and *did* throw him out.

The image of the dainty, proper Mrs. Chase pushing

him onto the pavement like some avenging etiquette goddess made him smile. That smile faded when the front door opened and a black-coated butler appeared. Michael would *have* to go in now that he had been spotted.

He handed the reins to a footman who appeared beside the phaeton, and jumped down to the walkway to enter the house.

"Good morning, sir," the butler said, holding out a small silver card tray.

"Good morning," Michael answered. He dug out a card from inside his coat and deposited it properly upon the tray. Even Mrs. Chase would have to approve. "I am calling to see if the duchess and Mrs. Chase are at home."

"I will endeavor to ascertain that, Lord Morley." The butler bowed, and retreated into a room off the foyer, shutting the door behind him.

Michael was only alone in the marble and satin silence for a moment. He had tilted his head to examine a painting on the wall, a sweeping Italian landscape bearing the duchess's own signature, when a voice said from behind him, "Who are *you*?"

He turned to see the redheaded moppet he had glimpsed in the window. Now she stood on the grand staircase, peering down at him from over the carved balustrade. She could not be more than about four, a tiny doll with long curls and freckles. She picked up the trailing streamers of her pink satin sash and popped them into her mouth.

Michael grinned, and gave her his lowest, most elegant bow. "I am Viscount Morley. And to whom do I have the great honor of speaking? A fairy princess, surely."

The little sprite giggled. "I am Lady Elizabeth Anne."

"How do you do, my lady."

She took a step down. "I have a brother. His name is Sebastian, but he's only tiny and can't talk. Mama says it will be a long time before he can play with me."

"I am sorry to hear that."

"He is utterly useless." She gave a deep sigh.

Michael laughed. Surely it was the story of brothers everywhere, to be found useless by their sisters. He had the feeling that Violet would agree with Lady Elizabeth Anne. "I am certain he will prove more, er, useful when he is a bit older. Infants do grow quite quickly, you know."

She shook her head, her curls bouncing. "No. It will not be soon enough." She took another step, and gave him a speculative glance that quite belied her tender years. She was the very image of the duchess. "You look as if *you* could be useful. I need someone to tie a rope from that chandelier."

"Why?" he asked suspiciously.

"So I can swing from it, of course."

Michael tilted back his head to stare up—*far* up— at the Venetian glass chandelier that hung from the domed ceiling. *The little minx.* She had only known him for two minutes and she was already trying to break his neck. It was surely a harbinger of what he could expect from the ladies in this house.

Before he could answer her, the door the butler had disappeared behind opened. Michael turned, expecting to see the man there now.

Instead he saw Mrs. Chase herself. She stood in the doorway, one hand braced on the wooden frame. Gone was the sea green clad siren of the night before; gone was her wealth of red hair, the sheen of pearls against white skin. She again wore one of her caps, a hideous white muslin affair, and a morning gown of gray and black striped muslin. A plain white chemisette was tucked into her neckline, and covered her almost to the chin.

Michael almost groaned at the acute sense of loss that pierced him at the sight. For one moment, one sublime second, in Lady Portman's corridor, he had glimpsed the *real* Rosalind, a woman of great allure and an untapped fire that could burn as bright as her glorious hair.

At least, he had hoped, *desired* that that was the true Rosalind. But perhaps this woman before him now was truly her, the woman who stared at him with no expression at all on her face. Her gaze was cool.

"Lord Morley," she said, her voice equally expressionless. Her gaze slid past him, and a warm smile curved her lips, illuminating her pale face. "Elizabeth Anne, whatever are you doing here?" She swept past him and up the stairs to take the child by the hand.

"I wanted to see our visitor," Elizabeth Anne said, hugging close to Mrs. Chase's skirts. "He is going to tie a rope to the chandelier for me to swing from."

Mrs. Chase shot him a hard glare, as if she believed him capable of hurtling infants through the air. "I am sure he is *not,* dear. Now, why don't you go into the drawing room and see your mother and Aunt Emily. I will be there in just a moment."

"Is *he* going to stay, too?" Elizabeth Anne asked. "When there is a caller, cook sends up tea and almond cakes."

"We will see, dear. Now run along, and remember— no more nonsense about swinging from ropes."

Elizabeth Anne peeped up at Mrs. Chase. "Because it would be against *A Lady's Rules,* Aunt Rosalind?" Before Mrs. Chase could answer, the child hopped down the remaining steps and dashed across the foyer to disappear into the drawing room.

Michael stared after her, stunned. So now *babies* had to follow the rules? It was too much. Surely even swinging from a rope would be preferable.

But he could not think of that now, could not allow himself to become angry. He had come here to apologize. Arguing with Mrs. Chase about rules would not smooth his way at all.

She still stood there on the stairs, looking down at him. The glow that had animated her features when she spoke to the child had faded as if it had never been.

"We did not expect to see you today," she said, ever so politely. "If you would care to come into the drawing room, I am sure the duchess would be happy to receive you."

"I actually came to see *you,* Mrs. Chase," he said.

Her eyes widened. "To see *me*?"

"Yes. I wanted to apologize."

"Apologize? For encouraging my brother to make some sort of drunken raid on the Portman ball?" Her eyes were not ice now—they burned with a deep blue fire. She stepped gracefully down to the foot of the staircase, her fingers clenched on the stone balustrade. "For urging him once again to behave in a most irresponsible manner?"

Michael could feel the entire situation slipping out of his control. Of course he had wanted to inquire after Lucas after his little "adventure" last night, but really it had not been such a great thing. When Michael left the ball, Lucas's escapade had been all but forgotten. And he had certainly never *encouraged* such a thing!

"I fear I had no prior knowledge of your brother's plans at all, Mrs. Chase," he said tightly. "You can be assured that if I had, I would have done everything in my power to discourage him."

Her frown spoke volumes of doubt. "Then what *did* you come to apologize for, Lord Morley?"

"I came to apologize for—monopolizing your time at the ball last night." That seemed the most polite way to say *for cornering you in the dark*. "And to return this."

He drew her folded fan from inside his coat and held it out to her.

"My fan," she whispered. She moved closer to him, and took the scrap of satin and lace from his hand, careful not to let her fingers brush his. She spread it wide, staring down at its glistening expanse. It seemed some sort of artifact from the lost beauty of the night before, held so gently by the woman who had buried that beauty beneath layers of gray muslin.

But he could see now that she was not entirely submerged. She stood so close to him he could see the shadow of pale golden freckles under a dusting of rice powder, could smell the fresh green springtime scent of her perfume. As he watched, a faint pink flush spread across her cheekbones.

It was as if she, too, remembered their moments alone last night. Maybe she also felt the unmistakable draw between them now, his temptation to take off that absurd cap and let her hair spill down . . .

She darted a quick, startled glance at him from beneath her lashes. "Thank you for returning this," she said. Her voice was still tinged with coolness, but he fancied marginally less so than it had been when she first saw him here. Or perhaps that was just his own wishful thinking. "Would you care to come into the drawing room?"

"Yes," he answered. "I do so enjoy—almond cakes."

Her blush deepened to a rose tinge, and she brushed past him to hurry back to the drawing room.

Oh, yes, Michael thought. He was assuredly making progress with her.

She was *not* glad to see him. She was merely being polite. It would never do to quarrel with the wicked man in her friend's home.

That is what Rosalind told herself, anyway, as she led Lord Morley into the drawing room. She tried to forget the tiny, excited skipping beat of her heart when she saw him standing there in the foyer. It was probably only dismay that he had dared to appear so soon after the disaster of the Portman ball. Or it was the marmalade from her breakfast tray disagreeing with her.

Yes! she thought, seizing on that excuse. Her queasiness, her nervousness, had nothing to do with this man at all. It was marmalade.

Even if he did appear rather handsome this morning, the dark waves of his hair in disarray from the wind, his face bronzed from the sun . . .

No! Rosalind curled her hands tightly into fists and

pressed them against her skirt. It was merely that marmalade, disagreeing with her again. All would be well
once she had a sensible meal.

Or once Lord Morley took himself off and left them
in peace.

The scene in the drawing room was peacefully do-
mestic, and its very ordinariness helped Rosalind to
catch her breath. Georgina and Emily were seated
next to the small fire that burned in the grate against
the morning chill. Emily worked on a piece of embroidery, while Georgina was bent over her sketchbook.
On a footstool by her mother's side, Elizabeth Anne
wielded a stick of charcoal over her own tiny sketchbook, all thoughts of swinging from the chandelier apparently forgotten for the moment. Lady Kate slept
in her velvet dog bed.

Georgina looked up, and gave their guest one of
her charming smiles. "Lord Morley! What a pleasant
surprise to see you here this morning."

Rosalind seated herself on one of the brocade settees, watching as Michael bowed to Georgina and said,
"I trust I have not called at an inconvenient time. I
wanted to see how Mr. Lucas fared."

"Of course it is not an inconvenient time! You have
saved us from a very dull morning. And I believe Mr.
Lucas is quite well. He just rang for some wash water
and coffee, so I am certain we will see him down here
soon. Would you not say so, Rosalind?"

Rosalind, who was trying to concentrate on little
Elizabeth Anne and *not* on staring at Lord Morley,
glanced at Georgina in surprise. "What? Oh, yes.
Indeed."

"So you see," Georgina said to Morley, "no harm
done at all. I see you also found Mrs. Chase's fan."

Rosalind stared down dumbly at the fan she still
held, clutched in her fist. She had forgotten it was
there. "Yes, Lord Morley very kindly returned it to
me. I must have—have misplaced it last night."

"I thought you might be in need of it, Mrs. Chase,"
Lord Morley said quietly.

Rosalind glanced up to find him watching her, his expression uncharacteristically serious. There was no hint of his usual teasing grin, the laughing gleam in his eye. "Thank you," she murmured.

Georgina smiled radiantly, as if a great dark cloud of tension did not hover over her elegant drawing room. "Won't you please be seated, Lord Morley? Elizabeth Anne, dearest, why don't you ring for some tea?"

Elizabeth Anne leaped to her feet in a flurry of ribbons and curls. "And almond cakes, too, Mama? Please?"

Georgina laughed. "Very well, my darling, almond cakes, too. Though Nanny will be furious with me for letting you have sweets in the middle of the morning."

Lord Morley sat down on a chair uncomfortably close to Rosalind's settee. She resisted the urge to pull her skirts closer, to tuck herself away for some measure of safety. She so hated it that whenever he came near, whenever he was even in the same room, she became someone who was—was not herself. Not sensible Rosalind, who had taken care of herself and her family with no assistance for so many years, who was always calm, always competent. Always the one her friends and pupils looked to to provide an example of propriety.

When she was near him, as she was now, she became someone she could not know and did not like. Someone who felt foolish and fluttery, and very young. Which was silly in the extreme, since she was lately turned thirty, and he was probably younger than her by some years. A young man who wrote romantic poetry about love and passion and the physical world, who brazenly flirted with women in ballrooms and school drawing rooms.

Rosalind resolutely put the satin fan down on a nearby table and folded her hands in her lap. She was very glad that she wore one of her own serviceable garments, and not one of the colorful frocks Georgina was always pressing on her with the excuse that she had ordered them from the mantua-maker and now did not like them. Even if Rosalind did not *feel* like herself, she could *look* like herself, and perhaps that would be enough to fool the people around her.

If only Lord Morley would not stare at her so intently! It was as if—as if he tried to look past the yards of plain gray muslin and see into her very heart.

Rosalind thanked heaven for Georgina, who kept up a steady stream of polite chatter, and for Elizabeth Anne, who insisted on serving the tea herself and caused a great distraction by spilling it on the inlaid chinoiserie tea table.

Once the refreshments had been safely distributed, Elizabeth Anne came to sit by Rosalind, and leaned against her side. Rosalind put her arm about her, and breathed in her sweet, powdery, little-girl smell. It was comforting, real, and it reminded her of all she had to protect—her school, where girls just like this would be waiting for her when the holiday was finished.

"I'm going to go to Aunt Rosalind's school," Elizabeth Anne told Lord Morley. "That's where I am going to learn to be a grand lady. Mama says Aunt Rosalind is the best at turning little hoydens like me into grand ladies, though really I would rather be a bareback rider at Astley's."

"I will be most honored to have a future bareback rider at the Seminary," Rosalind said with a laugh. "Though you are too young right now, Elizabeth Anne. Perhaps in a year or two."

"I am sure you will enjoy it at Mrs. Chase's school, Lady Elizabeth Anne," Lord Morley said. "My sister is a pupil there, and she speaks very highly of your— Aunt Rosalind."

"You have a sister?" Elizabeth Anne looked at him with wide, wondering green eyes, as if she could not imagine he could possibly possess something so ordinary as a sister. Rosalind sometimes wondered at that herself. "Is she like me?"

"She is as pretty as you," he said. "But she is several years older. She will soon be graduating from the Seminary, and making her bow next Season."

"How is Lady Violet?" Rosalind asked, watching Elizabeth Anne as she took another cake. "I have been hoping to see her while I am in Town, but I am sure she has been quite busy."

"We have been to the theater, and to a few suppers at our aunt's home, but she has not been as busy as she would like. I am sure she would enjoy it very much if you were to call on her. In fact . . ." He broke off, and gave her an uncertain glance.

"Yes, Lord Morley?" she asked.

"I was just going to say that I am taking Violet to Gunter's this afternoon for ices. Perhaps you would care to join us, Mrs. Chase? And the duchess and Lady Emily, of course." He sounded oddly shy as he offered the invitation.

Rosalind saw Georgina and Emily exchange a significant glance between them, and she felt her cheeks heat again. In these last two days, she had blushed more than she had in the last ten years! And right now it was all due to those two incorrigible matchmakers. They spent hours gossiping and scheming about all their friends. They probably imagined there was something untoward between herself and Lord Morley. It would have been angering if it was not so laughable.

"Oh, Emily and I have an appointment at the—at the milliner," Georgina said. "But I am sure Rosalind would welcome the chance to escape such a dull outing."

"May I go, too, Mama?" Elizabeth Anne begged. "I love Gunter's!"

"No, darling," Georgina answered. "It is a grown-up outing."

Rosalind studied Lord Morley closely, trying to gauge the sincerity of his invitation. Did he truly wish her to come along? Or was he just being polite?

And what did *she* truly wish to do? She wanted to

see Violet again, to be certain the girl was faring well in Town. And the thought of an entire afternoon looking at bonnets she could not afford to buy was not appealing, though she was almost certain Georgina had just made that up as an excuse. After all, who made an appointment to see a milliner? Ices at Gunter's with Violet sounded much finer.

But the thought of an entire afternoon with Lord Morley was—unsettling, even if he proved to be sincere in his invitation.

Rosalind prided herself on being a generous lady. Surely Lord Morley deserved a chance to atone for his bad behavior, and she deserved the chance to ask him to leave Allen alone. To try to fulfill her mission in London, which was to restore the rules and the proper order of things.

Yes, she decided, she *would* allow him to make amends. With a strawberry ice.

"Very well, Lord Morley," she said. "I would be happy to join you and Lady Violet at Gunter's this afternoon."

He smiled, a wide, white grin that dazzled as the sun breaking forth on a dreary winter's day. "Excellent! I am sure Violet will be in alt when I tell her. Would two o'clock suit?"

"Yes, thank you," Rosalind answered politely. "That would suit very well."

She had surely just completely lost her mind. The moment the acceptance passed her lips, she had the wild desire to pull it back, to stay safely alone in the house for the rest of the day.

It was too late, though. Georgina and Emily were chattering again, asking Lord Morley about his newest volume of poems. Elizabeth Anne was pirouetting around the furniture. And, as if it was all not cacophonous enough, the door opened and Allen appeared.

He was paler than usual, but otherwise did not appear to be damaged in any way by his escapade at the Portman ball. He was even rather better groomed than usual, with clean boots, unwrinkled trousers, and a crisply tied cravat. If only he did not look quite so morose.

"Morley!" he cried happily, his strained, white face transformed from melancholy to avid interest in an instant. "By Jove, but it's good to see you again. Didn't know you were expected." He stepped forward to shake hands with Lord Morley, and added, in a quieter tone, "I'm afraid I made a bit of a cake of myself last night."

A bit of a cake? Rosalind almost choked. Her brother had made a veritable pastry kitchen out of himself. She held her tongue, though. It would not serve her cause if she embarrassed Allen in front of his hero Lord Morley. It would not serve her cause at all.

She would just have to bide her time—until this afternoon.

Chapter Thirteen

"Always be gracious when introduced to new acquaintances."
A Lady's Rules for Proper Behavior,   Chapter Eleven

"*D*o you really mean it, Michael? We are going to see Mrs. Chase today?" Violet practically bounced on her toes in her enthusiasm, her hands clasped under her chin. A delighted giggle bubbled from her lips.

Michael couldn't help but smile at her happiness. She *had* smiled a few times since they came to Town, and even laughed at the play they had attended. But he had not seen her eyes sparkle so in—well, in a very long time. And it was due to Mrs. Chase. Somber, straightlaced Mrs. Chase, who was not quite as prim and proper as she would like everyone, including herself, to believe.

Violet almost spun about in a joyous circle, but then, with a visible effort, brought her exuberance under control. She folded her hands in front of her, and recited, " 'A lady never displays her joy in an unseemly, physical manner.' " Then she gave a tiny jump and another smile. "*Do* you mean it, Michael? Mrs. Chase is in London and we are to see her?"

"Of course I mean it, Vi," Michael said, with a laugh to cover his irritation at her rule-spouting. "She is going to Gunter's with us. I met her at a ball last night, and she asked after you." He decided to omit the quite unnecessary details of everything that had happened after his initial encounter with her at the Portman ball.

"A *ball*," Violet sighed. "It must have been lovely." Her smile turned wistful.

Michael put his arm about her shoulders and gave her a comforting squeeze. She did not draw away, as she had so often of late when minding the rules. "Next Season, you will attend more balls than you could count," he said. "So many you will be longing for a quiet evening at home!"

Violet laughed, a strangely bitter sound, unlike her earlier happy giggles. "I cannot imagine ever longing for *that*."

Michael frowned. "Has Father been bullying you?"

"No, of course not." She pulled away from him and went to look into a mirror hanging on the morning room wall. She fluffed up her pale curls, not meeting his reflected gaze. "I have been trying to educate him on some of the rules. Just because he never leaves the house is no excuse for him not to be civilized. He took exception to one of them this morning and threw his stick at me."

"He did *what*?" Michael shouted. "Did that old barbarian hurt you?"

"Oh, no, no. I am quite adept at dodging. And I am certain there must be a rule against stick-throwing. I shall have to look it up." Violet reached for her bonnet and tied it over her hair, tucking stray curls up into its confinement. She was trying so hard to be calm and casual, but her movements were stiff.

Michael longed to storm into his father's room, grab that blasted stick out of the old man's gnarled hands, and break it over his head.

Violet obviously sensed his inner turmoil, for she reached out and laid her hand gently on his arm. "Oh, la, Michael, but you *have* turned all red! Please do not mind it. I hardly see him, really, for you and Aunt Minnie keep me so very busy. Soon enough I will be back at school. And this afternoon I will see Mrs.

Chase! Speaking of which, shall we be going? She will be expecting us."

She picked up her shawl and handed it to him for him to drape over her shoulders. Then she took his hand and guided him to the front door, obviously trying to hurry him out of the house.

Michael went along with her maneuverings. It would be too bad of him to start yet another quarrel in this house, when she so badly wanted this outing. But one day—one day soon—matters in this family would erupt.

Right now, though, they had this afternoon. And he was going to make very sure it was enjoyable for his sister, and for Mrs. Chase. Surely the woman just had to see that he was not the lout she thought him. An hour or two in Gunter's, with the warm, sugary smells of pastries around them and a luscious strawberry ice to savor, would be just the thing.

She was making a great mistake. She should stay home and work on her writing, or her embroidery, or *anything* rather than go out with Lord Morley.

But that would be cowardly, Rosalind told herself, and it certainly would not help her in her cause at all. She had to make Morley see the error of his rude ways, and she could never do that by hiding away in the house. She truly wanted to see Lady Violet, too, and be certain the girl was faring well.

She paced back to the window for the tenth time to peer down at the street. Lord Morley was not there yet, but many pedestrians and carriages crowded on the pavement outside Wayland House. She studied the passersby, fiddling idly with the braid trim at the wrist of her spencer. For just one instant, she wished she had borrowed one of Georgina's walking dresses, of vivid blue or wine red or tawny gold. Her sensible dark blue wool, with its pale yellow braid trim, was just so very—sensible. That was the only word for it.

Of course it is, she told herself sternly. *You are a sensible lady.*

She half-turned to pluck up the hat Georgina *had* convinced her to borrow, then peered down again at the street as she pinned it to her curls. It was the same swirl of humanity, but, as Rosalind's gaze moved over the crowd, it was somehow caught by the figure of a man across the street. He leaned idly against the fence that hemmed in a small park in the square, apparently just a careless man-about-town with nothing better to do than lounge about, observing passing females. There was nothing remarkable about him at all; he was of middling height, slim, well-dressed but not ostentatious. The brim of his hat concealed his features.

Rosalind would not even have noticed him, except that he had been there for rather a long time—ever since she herself had come down and begun her vigil at the window. And he was oddly intent. He gave the appearance of watching the other people, yet he never really turned his attention from Wayland House.

Rosalind frowned. She was strangely reminded of that evening at her school, when she had been looking out the window of her sitting room and thought, or imagined, she saw a movement in the garden.

"Don't be silly," she whispered aloud. "You are becoming delusional."

Perhaps what she needed was a seaside holiday, away from all the distractions of Town. Away from Lord Morley.

She gazed down again at the man. If he was there again tomorrow, she would tell Georgina or the duke. Today, though, she would just enjoy her time with Lady Violet.

As she watched, a carriage drew to a halt below her window. It was a proper open landau, driven by a coachman in livery, not Morley's usual dashing phaeton. But she would have recognized the figure who leaped jauntily to the pavement, even if he had arrived in a stuffy old barouche. His head was uncovered, his dark hair tossed about, a glossy blue-black in the sunlight. His coat fell back as he turned to offer his hand to his sister, revealing a waistcoat embroidered with red flowers and a cravat of deep yellow.

"Good heavens, Rosalind!" she said to herself. "Imagine that. You are about to go out in public with a man who wears *yellow* cravats. And forgets his hat."

That ought to fill her with horror, ought to make her run into her chamber and lock the door. But instead it gave her a tiny, tingling thrill that had nothing to do with *horror* at all.

Rosalind pushed all these thoughts away, and turned to make her way down the stairs just as the butler opened the door to admit Lord Morley and Lady Violet. Rosalind paused to be sure her hair was still pinned neatly beneath the hat, then went down to greet them properly.

"Lady Violet, Lord Morley," she said. "How delightful to see you."

"Mrs. Chase!" Violet cried, and rushed over to take Rosalind's hand. The girl was obviously trying to behave with the utmost propriety, but her eyes sparkled, and her gloved fingers curled tightly over Rosalind's own. It was quite a relief to see the girl looking so well. "I could scarcely believe it when Michael told me you were *here,* in London. I thought I would not see you again until I returned to the Seminary."

"The school is far too quiet with all of you girls gone," Rosalind said. "I am very happy to see you, too, Lady Violet. You seem very well indeed."

"My brother has been keeping me busy, taking me to the theater and such," Violet replied. "It has been very merry! This will be the third time we have been to Gunter's. I am quite in alt over their strawberry ices!"

"Well, I have never been there before, so I shall rely on your guidance in making my choices," Rosalind told her.

"You have never been to Gunter's!" Violet cried in evident horror. "Then we must go there now, at once. You will adore it, I vow! Won't she, Michael?"

Rosalind reluctantly turned her attention from Violet to the girl's brother. Lord Morley gave her a wide grin, and said, "Oh, yes, we should hurry. Some pleasures, Mrs. Chase, should never be delayed."

Before Rosalind could respond, Violet took her arm and drew her to the front door, with Lord Morley following behind. She was so caught up by the feel of his gloved hand on hers as he helped her into the carriage that she quite forgot to see if the lurking man was still there.

Gunter's was crowded with well-dressed members of the *ton,* gorging themselves on pastries and ices and glancing about avidly to see who else was there. It was exactly as if the Portman ballroom where Rosalind had first encountered Lord Morley in London had been moved in toto to the café. All the same people were there; the same snatches of conversation floated through the sugar-scented air. Only the jeweled hair combs and feathered turbans had been replaced by bonnets here.

As Lord Morley opened the door to usher Rosalind and Violet inside, Rosalind reached up to be sure her own hat was straight. It was one of Georgina's pieces of millinery, a tall-crowned, fashion-forward affair made of dark blue velvet and satin, with a flirtatious half veil of blue tulle. Rosalind had not been too sure of it when Georgina pressed it on her; unlike a proper bonnet or a cap, it left too much of her red hair exposed. But she had given in and worn the thing.

Now she wished more than ever for one of her own bonnets, preferably one with a concealing brim. When Michael stepped into the shop and offered an arm each to Rosalind and his sister, everyone turned to stare. A small hush fell over the café, but it was quickly dissipated, like a puff of smoke. Conversation resumed—yet people still watched. Rosalind saw Lady Clarke, who gave a tiny finger wave to Morley before leaning forward to whisper to her friends.

Rosalind stiffened her spine until she stood at her

full, not inconsiderable height, and tilted up her chin. She absolutely refused to let *anyone,* much less Lady Clarke, make her feel as if she did not belong here, on the arm of Lord Morley.

Morley himself seemed oblivious to the attention. No doubt he was accustomed to it, since it appeared to follow him wherever he went. Lady Violet, too, paid no heed, since she was too busy staring around with wide, amazed eyes.

"I believe I see a table over there by the wall," Lord Morley said. "Shall we?"

Rosalind glanced over at the table indicated. It was just big enough for three, in a relatively quiet corner. "It seems fine," Rosalind answered. "But do you not want to sit with one of your friends?"

A tiny, puzzled crease appeared between his velvety dark eyes. "My friends, Mrs. Chase?"

"Yes. Obviously many people here know you. I just saw Lady Clarke wave at you."

He laughed, a rich, merry sound that caused yet another wave of attention to crest in their direction. "No, Mrs. Chase. This afternoon I want only to be with my sister—and with you." His gaze lingered on hers, almost like a—a caress.

Rosalind felt her cheeks smolder again. Fortunately, Violet tugged at his arm then. "Michael," she said excitedly. "May I have one of those strawberry ices now?"

Lord Morley laughed again, and led them to the vacant table. "Vi, you may have as many ices as you like, and cakes, too."

"Truly?" Violet sighed, an utterly rapturous sound, and turned her attention to the small menu set before her.

"Anything you like." Michael turned to smile again at Rosalind. She couldn't help but think that he was well-named—Michael, the archangel. "And what would you care for, Mrs. Chase?"

What would she care for? Rosalind could scarcely consider cakes and pastries when he looked at her.

Indeed, she could scarcely think at all. She aimed her full attention on her gloves, tugging them slowly off her hands. She folded the pale blue kid and laid them atop the table.

"I think I shall just have some tea," she answered. She never removed her stare from the gloves.

"Just tea? Oh, no, no, Mrs. Chase," Morley chided teasingly. He reached out and touched her gloves, running one long, dark finger over the leather before laying his hand flat atop them. "You are at Gunter's. They are renowned for their decadent pastries. You cannot go back to the country without at least trying one."

Rosalind slowly raised her gaze to his. Much to her surprise, he was not smiling now. He was intent as he watched her, questioning—pleading? "Must I?" she murmured. The rich cakes seemed so very—decadent.

"I insist." His voice was husky.

"Oh, yes, Mrs. Chase! You cannot come to Gunter's and simply have a cup of tea. Try some marzipan," Violet piped up. Her young voice burst whatever spell of enchantment Rosalind had fallen under, and she was able to turn away from him at last.

She still felt him watching her, though, and even as he laughed with Violet she heard the darkness, the pull of him.

She needed something cold to drink. Cold, and very strong.

Michael watched as Mrs. Chase turned away from him, turned all her attention to Violet's prattlings. She even reached out and gently slid her gloves from beneath his hand and off the table, careful not to touch his skin.

He *felt* her, though, felt the warmth of her hand, the softness of her skin. She had the fairness of a redhead, with a few pale golden freckles sprinkled over the translucent back of her hand.

In his mind, he saw himself catch up that hand, pressing kisses to each of those tiny freckles, to the faint blue of the veins in her slim wrist, her delicate fingers. He could almost feel her pulse throbbing beneath his lips . . .

Michael sat back in his chair, sucking in a deep breath of the sweet air. Even then he could not entirely escape those strange feelings, for he could smell her fresh, green-spring perfume.

He could not escape them whenever he was in her presence, for these sensations drew him in, drowned him, just as they had in her office, in the dark corridor at the Portman ball. There was just something about Mrs. Chase, something mysterious and alluring and deep. He wanted to discover what that was—he *needed* to know.

But he could not discover anything here. He would have to find a way to see her again, someplace more quiet. Yet how to persuade her to see him? She was as skittish as a new colt; she did not even want him touching her gloves. He would just have to find a way, that was all.

"Morley!" someone called out.

Michael looked back to see Sir William Beene, a fellow poet who had helped to found the Thoth Club. Will was one of his best cronies; they had spent many hours discussing literature, music, and the damnable fickleness of the muse.

Michael stood up to shake hands with Will—and then saw his friend's gaze land on Mrs. Chase and kindle with avid interest.

"Morley, old man," Will purred. "Won't you introduce me to this lovely lady? It would be a great sin for you to keep her to yourself."

And, even as he made the introductions and watched Mrs. Chase smile at Will, he had the strongest urge to plant his good friend a facer.

It was rather late when Michael returned to his own lodgings. He had gone for a drive in the park with Violet and Mrs. Chase after Gunter's, had stayed with his sister until she went off to the theater with Aunt

Minnie. So the steps leading to his rooms were dimly
lit in the gloaming, and he did not see the figure
seated on the top step until he very nearly tripped
over him. Michael nearly went sprawling, his foot
landing on soft flesh.

"What the devil . . ." He automatically lifted his
walking stick to defend himself, though the light,
carved wood would actually be less than useless in
a brawl.

"Oh, no, Morley, don't hit me! It's Allen Lucas."

"Lucas?" Michael slowly lowered the stick, and
peered through the gloom to see that it was indeed
Mrs. Chase's brother. "Why are you skulking about
here outside my rooms?"

"I was just waiting for you," Lucas said, scrambling
to his feet. His coat and cravat were rumpled, as if he
had been wearing them for too long, but he looked
much better than he had after his escapade at the
Portman ball. His eyes were clear, his face not so pale.
He seemed as if he had grown up in only a few days.
"I am going back to Cambridge, but I wanted to talk
with you before I left."

"Why couldn't you just leave a card? There was no
need for you to take up residence on the staircase."
Michael pushed his door open, and ushered the young
man into his rooms. The draperies were drawn back
at the windows, letting in the last dying rays of sunlight, and he went about lighting the lamps.

Lucas sat down in one of the armchairs by the fireplace, twisting his hat in his hands. When Michael finished his task, he sat down across from Lucas, and
waited for the young man to state his errand.

"I wanted to talk to you about m'sister," Lucas said,
in a great rush as if to corral his courage, though Michael could not imagine why it took courage to speak
of *her*. "She is not at all happy with me, you see."

"Well, your behavior at the Portman ball *was* rather
foolish. I imagine she was quite embarrassed."

Lucas shook his head. "No, it is more than that. I
have not seen our true circumstances, though heaven

knows she has tried to tell me enough times. She has always been more like a mother to me than a sister, you see. Our parents died when I was very young, and she's always worked so hard to take care of me. I never realized *how* hard until recently. I got into some money trouble, you see, and then I stupidly went to a bank for a loan, and—well, that didn't work out very well."

Michael was not exactly certain why Lucas was telling him this, but he did not want the young man to stop. Michael was fascinated to hear more of Mrs. Chase, more of what she was like when she was not wearing her armor of rules and propriety. What she worked for—what she loved. What her troubles were. He nodded encouragingly at Lucas.

"So I have to go back to Cambridge and study so one day *I* can take care of *her*. But I need your help."

"How can I possibly help? She thinks I have led you into wrong thinking and bad behavior by dismissing the rules."

Lucas frowned, looking so deeply young and very confused. "I have told her that is not so, that I misunderstood you! That it was all my own doing. And I will tell her that again. But I think something is wrong with Rosie, something besides me and my stupidity, and I cannot discover what it is. She always has to pretend to be so strong."

"Wrong? Is Mrs. Chase ill?" Michael said, alarmed.

"I don't think so, but she *is* tired. How could she not be, with me, and all those girls at her school to contend with? I think—no, I *know* that there are some financial troubles, and they are mostly my own fault. Since I cannot be here with her, someone has to keep an eye on Rosie, make sure she doesn't worry herself to death. Could *you* do it, Morley? Just for a while, until she goes back to the country."

"Me?" Michael sat back in his chair. Of course it would be no great hardship to watch Mrs. Chase; quite the opposite. The more he saw her, the more he was fascinated by her. Yet he could not imagine that she would welcome such attentions from him. Not yet, anyway. Not until he could persuade her of his finer qualities. "I doubt Mrs. Chase would allow me to, er, keep an eye on her."

Lucas laughed ruefully. "She *is* dashed stubborn, it's true. Yet I'm sure you could do it without her knowing. You like her, do you not?" There was an eagerness in Lucas's eyes, in his entire manner.

Like? That was such a tepid word for what Michael was coming to feel for her. "I admire Mrs. Chase, yes."

"I do not see how anyone could *not* admire Rosie! She's a brick. If you could just look in on her while she's in Town, take her about to museums and such. She likes dusty old places such as that. Perhaps you could even discover what is bedeviling her? There must be something besides money."

"I could do that, if Mrs. Chase would allow me to. I confess to a liking for dusty places myself."

Lucas gave him a relieved smile. "That is all I can ask. You are a good man, Morley, and I am sure my sister will come to see that, too. All this misunderstanding about rules and such will be as nothing once she gets to know you."

Lucas took his leave soon after that, but Michael sat in his chair long after it was full dark, and the glow of the lamps was his only light.

Keep an eye on Mrs. Chase. Oh, yes, he could certainly do that, and keep men like his so-called friend Will Beene away from her while he did it. And he would start by inviting her to the theater tomorrow evening.

Chapter Fourteen

"True friendship is one of life's greatest treasures."
—*A Lady's Rules for Proper Behavior,* Chapter Three

*R*osalind was deep in delicious sleep, just clinging to the edges of a half-remembered dream, when she became aware that someone was sitting at her bedside, watching her intently.

She suddenly remembered that strange man she had seen watching the house, and she sat up with a terrified gasp—only to find Georgina perched on the edge of the bed, like a morning bluebird in her sky-colored dressing gown.

"Georgie!" she screamed. "You scared me out of my wits. What are you doing here so early? You never rise before ten at the least. Is something amiss?"

"Not a thing, as far as I know. I'm sorry I woke you," Georgina said, looking not in the least repentant. "But I thought you might want to see these, and you were sleeping ever so late. Late for you, anyway."

Rosalind, finally able to catch her breath, noticed what Georgina held on her lap. A bouquet of white roses and a small, ribbon-tied box. "Flowers? You had to wake me especially for that?" Rosalind wondered if she was still dreaming.

"Not just any flowers. They are from Lord Morley, as is the box. And I have not even peeped inside, though I am aching to know what is there!" She de-

posited the offerings on the counterpane next to
Rosalind.

Rosalind stared down at the flowers. Now she *knew*
she was still dreaming, if she was receiving gifts from
Lord Morley before the household was even awake.
She slowly reached out with one fingertip to touch the
blossoms, half expecting to feel the warmth of his skin
there. She felt only the cool lushness of a petal.

Georgina stretched out beside her, and for one moment Rosalind felt like a schoolgirl again. She and
Georgina and Elizabeth Everdean had often stayed up
late to talk and giggle, mostly over young men and
imagined romances. But she had never known anyone
like Lord Morley when she was fifteen. She had not
even dreamed there *could* be someone like him.

"Well?" Georgina prompted impatiently. "Aren't
you going to open the box?"

Rosalind slowly pulled at the end of the satin ribbon
and drew it off the box. She lifted the lid—and
laughed.

"What?" Georgina cried. "What is it?"

"Cakes," answered Rosalind.

Georgina scowled in disappointment. "Just cakes?
No emeralds or anything like that?"

"Certainly not. Even Lord Morley is not so wildly
improper as to send me emeralds. And cakes are fine
enough, when they are marzipan-frosted cakes from
Gunter's."

"So they *are* from Morley, then?"

"I believe so. No one else would be sending me
flowers and cakes." Rosalind was amazed that *Lord
Morley* would send gifts. She was hardly his usual sort,
she thought, remembering Lady Clarke and her daring, close-fitting gowns. But it was nice to receive them
all the same.

She took one of the tiny, luscious cakes and popped
it into her mouth. As she did this, she saw the neatly
folded note tucked among the sweets.

"My dear Mrs. Chase," it read. "I hope that you
enjoy these—they are Gunter's finest. And I hope they

recall to you our pleasant afternoon yesterday. Dare I hope you will allow me to escort you to the theater this evening? I have procured tickets to *The Merchant of Venice,* as my sister tells me you are very fond of Shakespeare. I will have my man call at Wayland House this afternoon for your answer."

Rosalind heard herself giggle—actually *giggle*!—and she pushed the paper back into the box.

But Georgina's eyes were sharp, and she saw the note before it disappeared amid the cakes. "What was that? A billet-doux?"

"Certainly not. It was merely a message stating that he—Lord Morley—hopes I enjoy the cakes, and asks if he might escort me to the theater this evening."

"The theater!" Georgina bounced up onto her knees in excitement. "Oh, how perfectly *splendid.* How delicious!"

"Delicious? It is Shakespeare. Most edifying and uplifting."

"Edifying and uplifting? Aren't you just Miss Butter Wouldn't Melt? You are such a sly puss, Rosie. Morley is sought after by every lady in the city, probably every lady in the *nation,* and here he is dangling after you. Of course it is delicious. It is marvelous!"

"It makes me feel queasy," Rosalind murmured.

Georgina dismissed this with a wave of her hand. "Naturally it would. There are no men like Morley in your quiet corner of the country, where you choose to bury yourself. You are one of the best people I know, Rosie—you always think of everyone but yourself, and you never see how lovely you truly are. You deserve a man like Morley. You deserve excitement, and love."

Love? Rosalind's bewildered gaze shot to the gloating Georgina, then fell back to the box of cakes. Was this terrible ache, this complete oversetting of her sensible, careful life—love? She did not know. She *could* not know. Perhaps it was just a surfeit of sugar in the morning. "How does a person know when it's really love, Georgie?"

Georgina gave her a smug, satisfied smile. "Oh, one just knows, Rosie. One just knows. I knew right away that Alex was the man for me, from the first moment I saw him. It just took him a little longer, the stubborn darling."

This bewildering conversation was interrupted by a soft knock at the door. A maid came into the room, and dropped a quick curtsy. "Beg your pardon, Your Grace, Mrs. Chase, but Mr. Allen Lucas is in the drawing room for Mrs. Chase."

Allen was here? Rosalind set aside the box and the flowers, and slid down out of the high bed. Practical family concerns had to push aside silly romantic flutterings for the moment. Allen had promised her he would go back to Cambridge—she prayed he was not in more trouble now. She deeply hoped she would not have to meet yet again with that reptilian banker.

"Tell Mr. Lucas I will be down in a few moments," she told the maid. The girl curtsied again, and hurried away.

Georgina watched from her perch at the foot of the bed as Rosalind pulled a morning gown and a pair of slippers from the wardrobe. "Do not think you have escaped me, Rosie," she sang out. "We *will* talk of this further. I want to know *everything* about you and Lord Morley. You are livening up my dull life."

Rosalind doubted very much that Georgina's life was ever dull, but she wished she herself could know *everything* about this situation, she thought as she sat down to pull on her stockings. But she feared she knew nothing at all. And she so hated that feeling.

Michael paused before raising the brass knocker of the Waylands's front door—and glanced up at one of the upper windows, sensing a gaze on him. Lady Elizabeth Anne stood there watching him, her long red ringlets falling over the bodice of her small velvet dressing gown. She waved to him and gave him a merry smile. He just had time to wave in return before a nursemaid came and fetched her away.

He laughed, and thought that a daughter of Mrs. Chase's would also appear very much like that, with red curls and china-doll skin. Would she also be dangerously precocious, like Elizabeth Anne, or proper and rule-following? Either way, it would be a very fortunate man indeed who fathered such a child.

And then it hit him, like a lightning strike from the gods. *He* wanted to be that father. He wanted to be the man who took Mrs. Chase—Rosalind, Rosie—into his arms and his bed every night; who came home to find a tiny, redheaded imp running down the stairs crying "Papa!" He wanted to buy his Rosie gowns of silk and satin and glittering jewels, to take his family to Italy and Greece and watch them playing in the sun and the sea. He wanted to write odes to red hair and blue eyes like the sky, to pink lips that pursed in an adorably proper way.

He had thought he just wanted to flirt with her, to enjoy teasing her out of her propriety and her rules. But, when he was not looking, it became more than that. So much more.

He was falling in love with her. But she still thought him a silly ass, a reckless poet who ruined her life by leading her brother into trouble with rule-breaking.

How could he show her that it was not true, that he was not that person she thought him? How could he even begin to persuade her of his finer qualities? Did he even *have* finer qualities? He was not sure. But at least she had agreed to this theater outing. That was a start.

The front door opened so suddenly that he was forced to take a step back. He did not even remember knocking, yet there stood the Waylands's butler, holding out a hand for Michael's cloak and hat.

"Lord Morley," the butler said. "Mrs. Chase is expecting you. She and Her Grace are in the drawing room, if you care to follow me."

Expecting him, was she? Michael thought as he stepped into the gilt and marble foyer. He could only hope that was truly so.

         *   *   *

Rosalind peered one more time into the mirror, and smoothed the bodice and cap sleeves of her gown. She had worn one of her own garments this evening, her best gown of pale gray lutestring silk piped in black satin. It was a sort of armor; she felt protected in it, as she never could in Georgina's dashing, brightly colored creations. But she had left off her cap, instead anchoring her piled-up curls with onyx combs.

She touched one of those combs, and wished for one of those caps.

"No, you may not go upstairs and put on one of those hideous caps," Georgina called from over the high back of the settee where she lounged.

"I was not even thinking of caps!" Rosalind retorted. She dropped her hand down to her side.

"Of course you were." Georgina serenely turned over a page in the fashion paper she was reading. "Since I have become a mother I have learned to read minds. I know when Elizabeth Anne is plotting mischief, or when Sebastian has a fever—or when you want to put on a cap. But you are lovely just as you are, Rosie, even if you would not wear the green satin. Come and sit down while you wait for Lord Morley."

There was no time for sitting, though, or for going upstairs to fetch a cap. The drawing room door opened, and the butler announced, "Lord Morley, Your Grace."

And there he was, as handsome as could be in an evening coat of emerald green velvet, another cravat of daffodil yellow about his throat. A square-cut emerald winked in its crisp folds.

Rosalind was very glad she had *not* worn the green satin gown Georgina offered, for then she and Lord Morley would have looked like a walking Irish meadow together. Of course, no matter what she wore, no one would glance twice at *her* when they could look at him. He was like some dark, pagan god, and his beauty only increased when he smiled at her and gave her an elegant bow.

"Good evening, Duchess. Mrs. Chase. You are both very elegant tonight." His gaze lingered on Rosalind, warm and admiring.

She could think of nothing to say, not even the little politenesses she wrote about so often. Her throat was dry, closed.

Thanks heaven for Georgina, who never lost her social aplomb. She laughed and said, "You flatterer, Lord Morley! I look like an old ragpicker, since I am settled in for a quiet evening at home. But Rosalind *is* elegant, as always."

"Thank you for the compliment, Lord Morley," Rosalind finally managed to say. "You are too kind."

"Oh, I am merely truthful, Mrs. Chase. Shall we depart? I have heard that Kean is quite fine as Shylock, and it would be a shame to miss the opening curtain."

"Of course." Rosalind picked up her gray satin shawl and handed it to him. He swept an errant curl from the nape of her neck before slowly, ever so slowly, sliding the smooth fabric over her shoulders. His fingers lingered at her bare skin for just an instant longer than was proper.

Rosalind almost forgot to breathe. "I—I do so enjoy Shakespeare," she gasped.

"As do I," he answered, a hint of laughter in his brandy-dark voice. "And I think I will enjoy the old Bard of Avon tonight more than ever."

He stepped around to her side and offered her his arm. She smiled up at him, and slid her fingers over the rough softness of his velvet sleeve.

"Good night, you two!" Georgina called gaily as they left the drawing room. "Do not stay out too late."

The theater was crowded with merrymakers when Rosalind stepped into the box Lord Morley had reserved. Every box glittered with jewels and opera glasses and silks, though it seemed no one was paying heed to the pre-Shakespeare farce playing on the stage. The level of conversation and laughter was so high that Rosalind could not hear the dialogue at all.

Not that she could have paid it much heed, anyway. Not with Morley beside her.

The box was one of the smaller in the theater, so their gilt chairs were placed close together. Rosalind fussed with her shawl, and with taking her opera glasses from her reticule.

"Are these seats to your liking, Mrs. Chase?" he asked. "There was not much choice to be had when I went to procure tickets. It seems to be a fine vantage point, though."

"It is quite fine," answered Rosalind. Fine for people to see *them* anyway, she thought, watching as numerous gazes turned their way. She lifted her chin and ignored them, focusing her attention on the stage. "I have not been able to attend the theater as much as I would like since coming to Town. I was very happy to receive your invitation."

"Were you, Mrs. Chase?" he asked, his voice oddly intent. Almost as if he truly *cared* about her answer.

Rosalind glanced at him, but it was shadowed in their box. A ray of light slanted over his brow, his sharp cheekbone, but his eyes—the windows to his thoughts—were in darkness.

But she could not turn away.

"Oh, yes," she murmured. "I was. I did so enjoy our afternoon yesterday. Lady Violet is looking well. Sometimes, when she returns to the Seminary from her times at home, she seems rather—tired."

"She was excited to see you. You are her idol, you know. Everything with her is Mrs. Chase this and Mrs. Chase that. One could hardly blame her, of course."

Rosalind gave a startled laugh. "Her *idol*? I am a poor choice for that."

"No, indeed, Mrs. Chase. I think you are the finest choice she could have made."

"I am glad, of course, if I have been of some help to her. I become so very fond of the girls who pass through my school."

"You enjoy teaching, then?"

Rosalind relaxed a bit. Here was a topic she was truly comfortable with. "Oh, yes. Mr. Chase and I never were blessed with children. I suppose these girls are a bit like—well, like substitute daughters. I am fond of them. Most of them, anyway!"

"I envy you, Mrs. Chase, having a life's work you love so."

"Do you not love your own work, Lord Morley?" Rosalind asked in surprise. "Your poetry is so very glorious! You must put so much of yourself into it."

"Have you read my poetry, then?" he asked, that dark, intent note in his voice again.

"I—yes. A few poems." In truth, she had gone secretly to a bookseller when she first arrived in London and purchased all three volumes of his work. She found his verse intoxicating, exhilarating. Only someone who truly loved what he was doing could write so very passionately. "I found them to be—interesting."

"Interesting, eh?" He gave her a very pleased smile. "I am flattered, Mrs. Chase. And rather surprised you would bother with my piddling verses. I am hardly Shakespeare, as I am sure you have discerned."

"Just as your sister speaks often of me, my brother speaks of you. I was curious about his idol. And, speaking of my brother, I had a very interesting visit from him this afternoon."

"Did you, Mrs. Chase? I trust he is well."

"Very well. In fact, he has vowed to me that he is returning to Cambridge and will stay there. I wonder whatever could have inspired such a change of heart?" She peered closely at Morley. She knew very well what could have precipitated such a change—a man Allen admired giving him a stern talking-to. And she knew Allen had gone to Morley's lodgings yesterday afternoon.

But Lord Morley merely shrugged and grinned. "Lucas is not a bad young man, he is merely—young. He just needs to be nudged in the right direction."

"I am very grateful to anyone who can, as you say,

nudge him. I have had little luck in the past few years."

"I will always be happy to assist you in any way I can, Mrs. Chase. Any way at all."

She felt his hand touch hers, briefly but so very warmly, under the cover of a fold in her heavy skirt. And, much to her shock, Rosalind found herself pressing his hand in return.

"Friendship *and* theater tickets," she whispered. "Those are fine assistance indeed."

"Then, since we are friends, may I escort you to the Smith-Knightley ball tomorrow evening?" he whispered back.

"I would like that very much, Lord Morley," she replied, forgetting every rule she herself had written about demurely turning away invitations.

This fairy tale would all end soon enough. Why should she not enjoy it while it was happening?

She would enjoy every minute of it.

Wayland House was dark and quiet when Rosalind returned from the theater. The butler, who took her wrap and then melted back into the shadows, seemed to be the only living being in the marble silence.

Rosalind was grateful for the solitude. She had so very much to think about, to process in her own mind, to hug close to her heart after her splendid evening. She knew Georgina would want to find out every detail, but Rosalind did not think she could talk about it. Not just yet.

But as she walked down the corridor that led to her chamber, she saw that she was not alone in Wayland House after all. The door to Georgina's personal sitting room was half open, spilling golden firelight across the dark wood floor. Standing by the fireplace, silhouetted in the glow, were Georgina and her husband. They were locked in each other's arms, in a passionate kiss, Georgina's brilliant hair flowing over Alex's hands.

"My darling Georgie," he groaned, sliding his lips to her temple, her cheek.

"Alex," murmured Georgina, as she swayed closer to him.

Rosalind eased the door shut before they could realize they were being observed and went on her way. Her heart warmed at the knowledge that there *could* be such love in the world—and sparked with just a hint of envy.

Chapter Fifteen

"Always wear gloves when dancing; bare flesh
should never, ever touch bare flesh."
—*A Lady's Rules for Proper Behavior*, Chapter Four

*T*he Smith-Knightley ball was every bit the crush
that the Portman soiree had been. People clad in
the first stare of fashion were crowded to the walls,
their laughter and conversation a thick cloud hovering
over the room, drowning out the lively dance music.
Couples swirled elegantly through a pavane, while observers
gossiped about the gowns and partners of others.
It was all a perfectly ordinary evening out for
the *ton*.

Yet Rosalind was more nervous than she had ever
been in her life. She had attended more routs and
fetes in her short time here in Town than ever before
in her life, and she had became rather accustomed to
them. Not exactly comfortable, yet she did not find
them unenjoyable by any means. They were—
interesting.

But she had never attended a ball on the arm of
Lord Morley. That made this evening an entirely different
proposition altogether.

Her silk-gloved fingers tightened on Morley's superfine
sleeve as they waited outside the ballroom doors
for the Smith-Knightleys's butler to announce them.
This had seemed such a fine idea last night, when she
sat so close to him in the darkened magic of the the-

ater. She had even looked forward to it, when she looked into his dark eyes as he issued the invitation.

Now things felt so very different. Now that they were actually faced with a roomful of people—people who were avidly interested in everything the dashing Lord Morley did, people who had seen them together at Gunter's and in the theater. She was abandoning years of quiet living and perfect discretion on this portal. She had imagined it would be difficult.

It was harder than any imagining could have been. Rosalind would have turned and run away, if Georgina and the duke were not standing right behind her, chatting and laughing as if this was an absolutely ordinary evening. They, and a few other couples who waited beyond them, blocked her exit utterly.

Rosalind turned back to face the ballroom doors, fidgeting with the skirt of her coral-colored silk gown. She peered down at it, watching the way the shimmering fabric draped and glistened in the candlelight. This dress was far more elaborate than anything she ever wore in her *real* life, sewn with golden spangles on the short, puffed sleeves and along the hem. She gained some superficial courage from its sparkle and flash.

"Are you sorry you came?" Morley whispered, leaning close to her. His cool breath stirred the loose curls at her temple.

Rosalind shivered at the sensations this evoked. Warm, unfamiliar, *tingling* sensations. "Of course not," she answered stoutly.

He grinned at her. "Liar."

Rosalind laughed. "I would *never* tell a falsehood. That would be most improper."

"Against the rules, eh?"

Her lips tightened at the mention, the reminder, of the rules. How could she have forgotten them so quickly, when they were such a large part of her life? Whenever she was with him, everything else just fell away. "Quite right."

They did not have time to say anything else. The

doors opened, and the butler took their names. "The Duke and Duchess of Wayland," he announced. "Mrs. Rosalind Chase. Viscount Morley."

On legs that seemed turned to water, Rosalind stepped into the ballroom. Her hand tightened on his arm. She no longer held onto him just for appearance's sake—she needed his strength to hold her up.

As she had expected, and feared, heads swiveled in their direction. She had a blurred impression of disappointed pouts on the faces of young ladies, the glint of raised quizzing glasses, waves of avid curiosity.

There was nothing for her to do but lift her chin, feign deepest disinterest, and keep moving into the crowd. At Lord Morley's side.

She was very glad for Georgina and her steady stream of inconsequential talk. "Oh, look over there, Rosalind. Isn't that Mrs. Strandling? We went to school with her, did we not? She should never wear that shade of green. Ah, champagne. Delightful. Do you care for a glass, Rosalind? Alex, darling?"

Rosalind stared intently at the pale, beckoning liquid, sparkling in crystal flutes on the footman's tray. The delicious drink called to her, but she knew she should not indulge. Champagne tended to make her giddy. The last thing she wanted to be tonight was *giddy*.

"Oh, no, not right now," she said.

"Mrs. Chase has promised me a dance," Morley told them. "I hear a waltz beginning, and she knows that is my favorite dance."

Rosalind knew no such thing—she did not think she had ever spoken two words about dancing with him. But the promise of occupation, of movement, of having something to concentrate on besides people's stares, was enticing indeed. "Of course," she said. "Thank you, Lord Morley. A waltz sounds very pleasant."

He led her onto the polished dance floor, and they took their place amid the assembled couples. When he put his hand on her waist, pulling her close, but not so very close as to incite more talk, the gawking crowd seemed to melt away. Rosalind heard no whispers. The two of them were all alone in the teeming crush, just as it had seemed they were last night in the theater box. Nothing else mattered, not even the fact that she had only practiced the waltz a few times, in classes with the girls at her school.

She had no fears of making a fool of herself, of being the object of gossip. Not when he stood so close to her, smiling down at her.

"Are you quite all right?" he murmured. "You went very white all of a sudden."

"All right?" she whispered back, thrown off balance by his question.

"I should have realized how very interested people would be when we appeared here together. I am so accustomed to being speculated over that I scarcely take note of it anymore. But you are not used to such scrutiny. I'm sorry."

"It does not matter," Rosalind answered, and realized, with some degree of shock, that it truly did not. She had lived all her life being careful, being always so painfully proper. She was suddenly so deeply tired of it all. She just wanted to dance, to forget, to have fun—like everyone else. Like people who had no school or wayward brother to worry over.

Tomorrow would be soon enough for her to worry again. Tonight, she would just dance.

"Good," he said. "I am very glad to hear it."

She tightened her clasp on his hand, and closed her eyes as the music reached its lively opening beats. They swayed together, and swung into the dance.

This was like no dance she had ever known before. Dancing classes with the girls, local assemblies with her husband—they were nothing like this. Rosalind's feet, which she had always hated as being too big, seemed dainty and graceful as they glided across the floor. She hummed along with the lilting tune, and turned and twirled effortlessly in his arms. She felt— why, she felt *beautiful*! She felt desirable and flirtatious and merry, as if deciding she would leave her real life behind until tomorrow had freed her to be someone else.

"You are a wonderful dancer, Mrs. Chase," he said, turning her in a spin that sent her skirts flaring in a graceful arc.

"I help the girls with their dancing lessons at the Seminary," she answered. "So I have had a great deal of practice. Not in waltzing, though."

His hand at her waist drew her closer, so close she could smell the faint, spicy scent of his soap, the starch from the folds of his dark blue cravat. He was so close she could lean her cheek against the curve of his jaw, feel the satin of his hair on her skin.

She leaned back a bit, trying to escape that intoxicating fragrance. But his heat reached after her, beckoning her back to him.

He did not loosen his clasp. His eyes were heavy-lidded as he stared down at her, dark, serious, intent.

"I hope they do not end up using their lessons in quite this way," he said hoarsely. "At least not until they are a good deal older."

"In what way?" she asked, mesmerized by his gaze. "This is all quite proper."

"Oh, yes, of course. Quite proper." They danced past half-open glass doors, and, before Rosalind could even blink, he twirled her out of them onto a night-shadowed terrace. They ended behind a tall, sheltering bank of potted plants.

"Proper—until now," he whispered. And then he kissed her.

Rosalind gasped against his lips, shocked at the feel of them, the softness, at the suddenness of the caress—at the feelings that crashed inside her heart. For a flash, her old, sensible self shrieked in horror, but that old Rosalind was quickly submerged beneath the sweetness, the heat of the kiss.

Her lips parted, and she twined her arms about his neck, leaning into him. She trembled as if in a wind-swept storm, and it was frightening. Almost as frightening as it was delicious. Part of her wanted to step away, to be in control again, but a larger part, that now *was* in control, knew that this was precisely where she wanted to be. Where she had to be. In truth, she had longed for his kiss, his touch, ever since he had come to her in her office at the Seminary and offered her a cup of tea.

Her arms tightened around his neck, her fingers seeking the waves of his hair that fell over his velvet collar. The locks clung to her silk gloves, warm and living through the thin fabric. He pulled back, as if surprised, and stared down at her, breathing fast.

Rosalind blinked open her eyes. Everything was blurred around the edges, soft and hot. He was so close she could see the flecks of amber in his dark eyes, the way his hair, disarranged by her fingers, tumbled over his brow.

"Rosalind," he murmured. "Rosie. You are so beautiful." One of his magical fingers trailed down her cheek, traced her lips.

She? Beautiful? She had never thought so before; she was too tall, too redheaded, too freckled. In his arms, at this moment, she was beautiful. He made it so.

"Not as beautiful as you, Lord Morley."

He smiled, and his hands slid up to cradle her face. "My name is Michael."

"Michael," she whispered. The name was dark and sweet, like a cup of chocolate, a sip of brandy, in her mouth. "Michael."

He groaned, and bent his head to kiss her again. She fell back against the wall of the house. The stone was cold and sharp through the thin silk of her gown, but she scarcely noticed it when Lord Morley—*Michael*—leaned in close to her. His lips slid from hers along the line of her throat, down to her bare shoulder.

"So sweet," he whispered, the words reverberating against her skin. She felt his hand on the sleeve of her gown, drawing it down . . .

A ripple of loud laughter pierced the haze of her passion. Suddenly, the wall at her back was hard and cold again, the hand on her shoulder shocking. With a sharp intake of breath, she drew away, hitting her head with an audible thud on the wall. Her hands fumbled against his chest, pushing him back.

Michael stumbled away, the expression on his face as dazed as she herself felt. His hands slowly fell away from her, and he raked his fingers through his hair. He was dark and tousled.

Rosalind closed her eyes tightly, shutting out the dangerously attractive sight of him. Never in all her life had she done something as shocking as kiss a man on a public terrace. Anyone could have seen them! And, if she was truly honest with herself, they had been doing rather more than kissing there.

She had spent so very long condemning her brother's foolish behavior. But she was far more imprudent than he had been. She had broken so many rules tonight, she could never be redeemed. How could she ever look at her students again, ever teach them proper behavior, without knowing herself for the hypocrite she was?

Yet, somehow, she could not be truly, deeply sorry. She could not regret kissing Michael. For those few, precious moments, she had felt more *alive* than she ever had before.

Had the rules ever made her feel like that? She had to admit that they had not.

She moaned in confusion, and reached up to press her hands against the threatening headache. In the midst of all this turmoil, she felt a soft touch on her arm. Michael drew her sleeve back up to her shoulder, gently, tenderly.

Rosalind opened her eyes to peek up at him. He also seemed confused, bewildered, pained—but he smiled at her, a wry, rueful grin. "Oh, Rosalind. Mrs. Chase. I am so sorry. I never meant . . ."

He never meant—what? To kiss a tall, awkward schoolmistress on a terrace? To almost be caught? A sour pang of disappointment added to Rosalind's chill, to her disillusionment. She turned away, patting and pulling at her hair. She wished ardently for one of her caps.

"It is quite all right," she said tightly. "There was no harm done. Perhaps we should go inside? I am sure Georgina will be looking for me."

Actually, Georgina was probably hoping that something very like this—or rather, like their kiss—was happening, and she would not be looking for Rosalind for quite a while. But for Rosalind the thought of a crowded ballroom was a haven for once. There, she would have no time to think of all this, whatever *this* was.

"If that is what you wish, of course," Michael said softly. She heard the sinuous rustle of cloth as he straightened his coat. "But I want to tell you . . ."

"Later. Please." Rosalind simply could not hear him right now, not while she was so confused. Not while the voices of the new arrivals on the terrace were coming ever closer. "We will speak later, yes?"

"Of course," he said. "But I will hold you to that—Rosalind."

He stepped to her side, and offered her his arm. Rosalind slid her hand onto his sleeve, careful not to cling too tightly, to feel the warm strength of his muscles and bone.

As they walked past the group of people, she heard a woman say, "Is that not Lord Morley? But who is that with him? I heard he was at the theater last night with some unknown redhead. Is that she?"

One of the men with her answered, "Perhaps so, m'dear. But doesn't *A Lady's Rules* say 'A lady will never walk alone with a gentleman after dark, or risk great harm to her reputation'?"

The entire group laughed tipsily, and Rosalind cringed. That was just one of the many rules she had broken this evening.

And she had the distinct feeling that it was not the last she would break before all of this was finished.

*   *   *

Michael moved through the crowd with Mrs. Chase on his arm, stopping to speak to friends, to bow to matrons, and smile and laugh. Yet it was as if he watched the entire scene from very far away, not participating at all. He had been through routs like this dozens, hundreds of times before, and could make all the correct postures, but he was not aware of them at all. He only felt the light pressure of her hand on his arm, the warmth of her at his side.

She also did everything that was proper, making all the correct responses and gestures. No one could possibly see the distraction in her eyes, the solemn downturn at the corners of her rose pink lips. No one except him.

He watched her as they traversed the edge of the ballroom. Mrs. Chase—*Rosalind.* Despite her solemnity, her stillness, she was quite the most beautiful woman in the room. The most beautiful woman in all of London. Her hair shone like the red and gold fire of dawn, caught up with coral-tipped combs and falling along the white column of her neck. She seemed serene, assured, as she took in the room with her sky blue eyes, but there, in their depths, he saw her uncertainty, her shyness.

She was as affected by their kiss as he was. He still trembled deep inside from the unexpected force of their passion, from the desire, the raw *need,* that had seized him when he took her in his arms. Never had a simple kiss affected him so deeply! There had been nothing in the world but her, her perfume, her lips beneath his, her arms around his neck, drawing him ever closer to her.

Now, as he peered down at her in the color and flash of the ballroom, he knew the truth, the truth he had only suspected when he called on her at Wayland House yesterday. He loved her. He loved his sister's stiff, proper, rule-following teacher! And he had loved her ever since he saw her alone in her office. Even then, he had sensed the bright fire beneath her restrained coolness, and it drew him in.

He *loved* her! After all the years of writing of passion and longing, of searching for it so desperately in his own life, he had finally found it where he would have never thought to look.

He wanted to shout his feelings to all the world, to seize Rosalind by her slender waist and twirl her about until they were both dizzy with laughter and joy. He could hardly do that in front of the entire *ton,* though. Even he had to follow some rules. But he did reach for her hand, drawing her around to face him. They stood still in a quiet corner, slightly apart from the social fray.

She blinked up at him, as if surprised by their sudden stillness. "Lord Morley?"

He wished she would call him by his given name. He longed to hear it in her voice, hear her whisper *Michael.* "When can I see you again?" he asked.

"You—wish to see me again?"

Had she so soon forgotten their kiss? How could she think he would *not* want to see her after that? "Of course I do. Tomorrow? We could go for a drive in the park, early, before the fashionable hour."

She flicked an uncertain glance over her shoulder, back at the crowd. She opened her mouth, and closed it again. Her fingers tightened on his for one moment before she drew her hand away and took a step back. He had never seen the cool, collected Mrs. Chase so discomposed before.

So she was *not* immune to him. But he feared she *was* about to refuse his invitation, and he tried to gather his arguments to persuade her to agree. He wanted so much to see her again, away from this blasted crowd. He *needed* to see her.

He had no need to argue with her, though. She slowly nodded, and said, "Yes. A drive would be— most agreeable. I have some things I would like to tell you, Lord Morley. Important things I think you ought to know."

He smiled at her, amazed by the rush of relief and anticipation. He *would* see her again! They would be together in the comparative quiet of the park, close to each other on the seat of his phaeton. As for whatever it was she had to tell him—well, it could be nothing so dreadful that they could not talk it over together. Could it?

As he took her arm again and they turned to resume their promenade about the ballroom, he saw two familiar figures coming in the doors. Mr. Gilmore and Lord Carteret, without Mr. Lucas tonight. So the young pup had kept his promise to go back to university after all.

Gilmore noticed Michael standing there with Mrs. Chase, and pointed them out to Carteret. Carteret gave Michael a smirk, and an elaborately polite bow. "*The rules,*" he mouthed, and he and Gilmore turned away in laughter.

Well, Michael thought ruefully. So he had some things to tell Mrs. Chase, as well.

Chapter Sixteen

"A lady should never ride unchaperoned with a
gentleman in the park."
—*A Lady's Rules for Proper Behavior*, Chapter Nine

*T*he room was dim, shadowed, with rich red velvet
draperies over the windows, hanging from the bed-
stead. The scent of wine, flowers, and woodsmoke lingered in the cool air. The only sounds were the
crackling flames in the grate—and a man's husky
whisper.

"Rosalind," he murmured. "You are so beautiful.
So glorious."

His kiss, light as a butterfly's wings, moved down her
throat, over her shoulder. His fingers drew her thin silk
gown down her arms.

Her limbs were heavy, flooded with a languid
warmth. Rosalind leaned back on satin pillows, and
opened her eyes to see Michael smiling lazily down
at her . . .

Rosalind sat straight up in bed, gasping. "It was a
dream," she whispered. "Just a silly dream."

But a silly dream that left her trembling. She rubbed
her hands over her face, and pushed back the unruly
curls that had escaped from her careful plait. It had
felt so very real, that dream. Not just the sensations,
but the emotions.

Emotions she was not sure what to do with.

Rosalind pushed back the bedclothes and slid off

the bed to the floor. She padded on her bare feet over to the window, which she pushed open to the night. She closed her eyes to savor the cool breeze on her flushed face.

When she opened them again, she felt calmer, yet still unsettled. The city was quiet at this hour, with the barest tinges of a pale gray predawn light just peeking over the horizon. Everyone was home from the night's revels, tucked up safely in their beds. Soon, very soon, it would be full light, and in only a few hours Michael—Lord Morley—would be here to take her for that drive.

Rosalind groaned. How could she face him after such a dream? How could she face him, knowing how she truly wanted him? How she—cared for him?

Loved him.

Yes. There it was. She had fallen in love with him. Truly, she was the most pathetic woman in London. Perhaps in all of England.

Rosalind had never in her life been a romantic sort. She had never had the time, between looking after her family, running the school, writing her books. There had never been a chance to sigh over poetry, to wax sentimental over flowers and moonlight and handsome young men. She had cared for her husband, true, but their marriage had been above all an eminently sensible match. His touch, his gaze, had never made her burn or tremble . . .

. . . as Michael's did. There was nothing sensible there! He was so very wrong for her—too young, too highly placed in Society, too wild and romantic. For heaven's sake, the man kissed her on terraces where anyone could come upon them! Kissed her with a fervor, a passion, she had never before dreamed could truly exist.

This was madness. It was hopeless. A man like that could have no serious ideas of a woman like her. She was a prudish schoolmistress.

Yet she did not *feel* like a prudish schoolmistress any longer. Not when she was with him, or even when she just thought about him. She felt young, and giddy, and very silly. The old patterns, the old ways of thinking no longer fit in her heart. Michael had proven himself to be more, much more than she had first thought him. He *was* romantic, but he was also kindhearted and steady, with a lovely consideration for his sister. He was a man she could almost begin to trust.

Could she herself also not be more than she had once thought? The old Mrs. Chase would never have dreamed of confiding in someone, especially a man, about her troubles. The new Rosalind wanted to tell Michael all, everything about her school, her books. She longed to put her head on his shoulder, feel his arms about her, and know, even if only for one moment, that she was not alone.

But she was scared. So scared that it chilled her heart.

Rosalind pushed her hair back from her neck, holding the heavy plait away from her flushed skin. For the first time in her life, she just did not know what to do.

Michael reached for a cravat—and paused. The cloth was of a sky blue color, a perfectly starched length of cloth just waiting for him to wrap it about his throat. Usually this was one of his very favorite colors, and it went perfectly with his silver brocade waistcoat. Today, it made him hesitate.

It made him wonder what Mrs. Chase would think of the color.

He could not remember when he had last considered what another person would think about his attire. Perhaps when his mother had been alive; she had been such a fashion plate, and had taken such delight in her child's early sartorial choices. But never since. People's opinions just did not matter.

He wanted to see the light of admiration, even of desire, in Rosalind's eyes when she saw him—eyes that were almost the color of this cloth. The light had been there last night, he was sure of that. He wanted to see it again more than he had ever wanted anything before in his life.

And Rosalind did not approve of the least hint of gaudiness in her attire. He considered reaching for a white cravat instead, something simple and stark, like a clergyman might wear. And *dull.* So very dull. He was *not* a curate, after all. His blue, and pink, and yellow cravats were a part of him, just as his writing was. Rosalind had seemed to like his colored cravat last night.

He tied it in a neat, stylish whorl, and speared it with a pearl-headed pin. As he turned away to reach for his dark blue superfine coat, his gaze fell on the papers that littered his desk. The sheets were stained and blotted with ink, some of them torn in deepest frustration. They were the beginnings of a poem he had started in the fevered depths of the night.

He could not sleep when he returned from the ball, could not stop the wild swirl of his thoughts, his emotions. They were tangled, confused, and he tried to sort them out the only way he knew how—by writing.

He picked up the top paper, the closest he had come to a final version. It was still far from perfect, but he *did* like the title—"A Kiss by Moonlight." Perhaps, one day, when it was polished properly, he would give it as a gift to Rosalind. Then she would know his feelings for her in a way that no spoken words could express.

Michael laughed, and tossed the poem back down onto the desk. Maybe by then he would know what those feelings were himself.

Right now, he only knew that that one kiss had affected him in ways he had never known before. No other woman, no matter how beautiful, how passionate, could compare to his tall, redheaded schoolmistress.

And he could not wait until he saw her again.

He caught up his hat and walking stick, and ran down the stairs to where his manservant waited with the phaeton.

*   *   *

"Lord Morley is calling for Mrs. Chase, Your Grace," the Waylands's butler announced.

"Thank you," Georgina said, and calmly turned the page of her book.

Rosalind, though, felt no such serenity. She dropped the embroidery she had not really been working on and leaped to her feet. Surely he was early! This could not yet be time for their drive.

She glanced wildly to the clock on the fireplace mantel. It was indeed the scheduled time for their outing, and she had no opportunity to go upstairs and change her gown again.

Her hands flew to her hair, which Georgina's lady's maid had arranged in a stylish tumble of curls. "Perhaps I should . . ." she began.

"No, Rosie!" Georgina interrupted sternly. "Your hair looks lovely. You mustn't change it." She put aside her book, and came to draw Rosalind's hands down before she could ruin the coiffure. "You look lovely, and you are going to have a splendid time this afternoon."

Rosalind left off with her hair, and plucked at the lace trim on the sleeves of her mulberry-colored carriage dress. "Will I?"

"Yes," Georgina said firmly. "You will drive in the park, and forget all about your book and your silly brother. What is wrong with you, Rosie? I have never seen you so—so *fidgety* before."

Rosalind did not know what was wrong with her.

There was no time to figure it out, though, for the butler was ushering Lord Morley—Michael—into the drawing room.

The park was not yet crowded, it being too early to be truly fashionable. The green spaces were mostly peopled by children with their watchful nannies, footmen walking pampered dogs, and couples who wanted a modicum of privacy.

Just like Lord Morley and herself, Rosalind realized

with a start of surprise. She had never thought to find herself seeking a quiet corner with a handsome young man, just as she had never imagined driving through a London park in a dashing phaeton, wearing a fashionable bonnet. The unlikelihood of this whole scenario happening to *her* made her laugh aloud.

Michael turned to her, one brow raised inquiringly. "Something amusing, Mrs. Chase?"

"Oh, yes," Rosalind answered. She felt oddly giddy, despite what she had to tell him today. These few moments in the springtime sunlight were unlike any she had ever known before or was likely to know again. All too soon, it would be vanished, like a sweetly remembered dream, and she would be back in her office at the Seminary wearing her caps and planning the new term. There was precious little romance there, amid all her cherished safety.

She should enjoy these moments while she had them, and come away knowing she had been honest with him. Honest about *some* things—she would tell him about *A Lady's Rules* and perhaps even her troubles over Allen and his loans. After all, he had truly proven to be a help with her brother, and seemed to have given up his utter hostility to the rules. But she would never, *could* never, tell him of her new feelings for him. Her desire to look foolish only went so far.

"This whole afternoon, no, this whole time in Town, has been amusing," she said. "It has all been so very unexpected. I will have something to remember when I return to the Seminary."

"Must you return there very soon?" he asked. He drew up the phaeton at the edge of a small pond, where they could watch ducks paddling by and children playing with their toy boats.

Rosalind sighed, both at the loveliness of the scene and knowledge of how quickly she would have to leave it. "Yes, quite soon. The new term will be starting, and I have to make sure all will be in preparation when the girls return."

"Violet will miss you very much," he said, his voice hoarse.

She dared not look at him, not directly. She feared all her emotions could be seen in her eyes. So she watched his gloved hand as he wrapped the reins about it. "But I will see her very soon, surely. Unless your father decides to end her enrollment. I do think . . ." She broke off, unable to say more.

Michael's free hand reached out suddenly to touch her arm. His clasp was warm through the muslin of her sleeve. Rosalind stared up at him, startled.

"You care about my sister, do you not, Mrs. Chase?" he said.

"Of course I do. Lady Violet has such a sweetness about her, I do not see how anyone could *not* care about her," Rosalind said. She did *not* tell him of the baby she had once lost, early in her marriage, and how she sometimes fancied that, had the child been a girl, she would have been a bit like Violet. Kind-hearted, sunny, pretty. That would sound too silly and sentimental, if said aloud. It was a secret of her own heart—one of many.

His hand slid away from her arm, and she found she missed his reassuring warmth. "Then Violet will be fine. She admires you so very much. I hope you will always stand as her friend, once she has left your school."

That seemed to be a sign that she had to tell him now—tell him some of those secrets she held. *You must begin as you mean to go on,* she told herself. And she meant to go forward in honesty now. She turned to face him, and blurted out, "*We* are friends, are we not?"

He seemed startled, but also very pleased. He gave her a slow smile, and said, "I hope we are. I would like so much to be your friend, Mrs. Chase, though I fear we started on the wrong foot. I behaved like a lout on that first day I came to see Violet at your school, and I fear I have not always been the greatest of gentlemen toward you since. I hope we can begin again?"

"Exactly!" Rosalind cried in relief that he understood her—understood her thus far, anyway. She feared that anyone as liberal-minded as he was might not understand her authorship of the *Rules*. "And friends—true friends—are honest with one another, correct?"

His smile dimmed a bit, but he nodded. "Yes."

"Then, as your friend, I must tell you something about myself."

Michael laughed. There seemed a strange mixture of disbelief and relief in the sound, with a tincture of light mockery that made her frown. This was a *serious* business! He rubbed his gloved hand along his jaw, and said, "You have dark secrets, Mrs. Chase? I can scarcely wait to hear them."

Rosalind turned away from him, blindly watching the people strolling along the edge of the pond. "I never said they were dark. I am not ashamed of them. They are simply the sort of matters that true friends share."

"Very well, then, Mrs. Chase. What are these—matters? I do truly want to hear them."

She took a deep, steadying breath, and folded her hands in her lap to keep them from shaking—and to hold herself down, so she would not leap from the phaeton and run away. "I had a very specific reason for coming to London, you see. And it was not just to visit my friend. It—well, it had to do with you, in a way."

"With me?"

"Yes. You see, Lord Morley, I wrote *A Lady's Rules for Proper Behavior,* and I had heard that you were breaking them all over the place. I had to find out for myself, because . . ." Rosalind broke off before she told him all about Allen's debts and her financial woes. One confession at a time seemed quite sufficient. She closed her eyes, and waited for his reaction.

His reaction was—silence. The other noises around

them, of children laughing, water splashing, wheels grinding on the pathway, were amplified in the strange quiet.

Slowly, uncertainly, Rosalind opened her eyes and glanced over at Michael.

His handsome face was utterly expressionless as he stared straight ahead. Then, as she watched, he began to laugh. At first it was a strange, startled chuckle, but it quickly became a deep, rollicking guffaw. He bent over, clutching at his sides as if they ached with so much laughter. The horses shifted restlessly, and children turned to stare at them.

Well! Rosalind thought with a huff. She turned away from him again. Here she had told the man one of her deepest secrets, and what did he do? He laughed. *Laughed!*

She was not sure what to do now. She was not much accustomed to being laughed at.

"It is not so funny as all that," she murmured. "Many people think I have important advice to impart."

She felt his touch on her arm, gentle yet insistent, and she stared down to see his dark glove against the lace of her sleeve. She did not yet dare peer up at his face, for fear of what she might see there. She did not think she could face ridicule right now. Not from him. Not when she had dared to let herself begin to feel close to him.

"My dear Mrs. Chase—Rosalind," he said. His voice was thick with his laughter, but there was no hint of mockery. He sounded beseeching. "Please forgive my laughter. That was unspeakably rude of me. No doubt against several rules."

So he *was* making fun of her! Rosalind tried to shrug off his hand, but his clasp was too strong. "Really, Lord Morley . . ."

"No, no, I am sorry. It is just that I feel so foolish for not guessing this before. It all makes such perfect sense."

Rosalind relented just a bit, ceasing her struggle to pull away. "What does?"

"How very proper you are, how insistent on following the rules. How you make certain every girl at your school has a copy of the book and learns to follow them, as well."

"I do *not* make the girls read the book simply because I wrote it. It is very important that they follow rules for proper behavior in Society, so that nothing ill befalls them because of their youth and inexperience. There are many unscrupulous young men who would take advantage of that."

"I know that you believe all that, Rosalind, and I admire you for it. Even a pagan like myself should behave properly, eh?" His hand slid down her arm to her fingers, which he lifted to his lips for a lingering kiss.

Rosalind shivered at the warm-cold sensations of that kiss, at the prickles of delight that went down to her very toes. He was indeed a pagan, a veritable Dionysus who tempted her to fall to his depths, to take off her shoes and run through the warm grass. To lie back in the golden glow of the sun and bask in kisses . . .

No! She could not think such things. Not right now. She removed her hand from his clasp, and placed it back on her lap. "Even pagans must behave with civility now and then, Lord Morley. Perhaps I will convert you yet."

"Before *I* can convert *you*?" He leaned closer, and whispered warmly in her ear, "Neither of us were thinking of the rules last night on that terrace, were we?"

Rosalind felt a flood of red heat spread from her cheeks, down her neck into her very soul. That was verily the truth. The rules had been the very last thing she was thinking of last night. All she had been thinking of was *him,* his taste, his feel.

"A gentleman would not bring up such a thing," she whispered back. She felt like such a ninny saying a prissy thing like that, but it was all she could think of. Her mind could not recall such mundane things as words and string them together in ways that made sense.

"Ah, well. I think we have established that I am not a true gentleman." He sat back lazily in the phaeton seat, one arm casually stretched along behind her shoulders. "But I hope I do not have an evil heart. I would never wish harm to you, Rosalind, and I apologize if my actions have hurt you in any way. Both last night, and in my dealings with your book."

Rosalind studied him closely. His dark eyes, usually alight with some mischief or delight, were uncharacteristically somber, his sensual lips downturned at the corners. He seemed truly sincere in his apology. "Thank you, Lord Morley."

"And, since you have been so very honest with me, I have a confession of my own to make."

A confession of his own? Rosalind felt the sudden chill of apprehension. Surely any confession of his would be far more scandalous than any of hers could be! "What is it you wish to tell me, Lord Morley?"

"First, that you should cease to call me Lord Morley. It seems ridiculous, when we are to know each other's deepest secrets. My name, as you well know, is Michael."

She nodded slowly, but in her mind she resolved to wait until *after* she heard his confession to decide what she would call him.

"It is really rather funny when you think about it," he said, with an attempt at his usual careless grin. "And it makes me feel quite foolish, like some bored schoolboy."

A schoolboy? That was one thing Rosalind would *never* think to compare him to. But now she fairly itched to know what his secret could be. She gave him what she hoped was an encouraging nod.

"One evening, at my club, I saw your brother and two of his friends, Lord Carteret and Mr. Gilmore. I believe you know them?"

Those two loobies. "Oh, yes. I know them."

"We were talking, and the conversation came around to *A Lady's Rules.* Your rules."

"What about them?"

"Oh, just how they are everywhere, and everyone is so very eager to follow them. You see, I fear the young men had been tossed out of a rout because of some small infraction of the rules. I stated that that did not seem like fair dealing, and someone—I believe it was Carteret—proposed a small wager. Since I had imbibed rather freely of some excellent port that evening, and was feeling rather out of sorts, I agreed."

A wager. Rosalind did not like the sound of that. Wagers always seemed to cause trouble, especially for her brother. She frowned down at her clenched hands. "What sort of a wager?"

He shifted uneasily on the seat. "That some people need not follow all the rules in order to be accepted, even admired, in Society. In truth, I have no excuse for doing such a thing! I was simply tired of seeing people like Violet behaving like automatons. Yet if I had known that this was *your* book, I never would have spoken about it."

Rosalind sat in silence for a long moment, absorbing all this strange—nay, ridiculous—information. So this was why her sales had fallen, the popularity of her rules waned, because of a wager. She could scarcely believe it. "So it was quite all right to do harm to someone when you did not know whose rules they were?"

"No!" he protested vehemently. "Of course not. I simply never considered that A Lady was a real person, with real needs associated with this book. Now I see that I was wrong about that. And I see what Lucas meant when he came to me . . ."

What Allen meant! Rosalind swung around to face him. "What did Allen come to you for? What did he say? I knew he wanted to visit you before returning to school, but surely he did not tell you . . ."

Michael held up his hand, as if to fend off her rapid-fire questions. "Nothing very great, I assure you! He was simply worried about you, and feeling ashamed of himself. He came to talk to me about his returning to Cambridge. He felt sorry for causing you trouble."

Rosalind sank back a bit against the seat cushions. She rarely allowed her temper to get the best of her— she would not let it now, no matter how much she wanted to hit him over the head with her reticule. "Tell me exactly what you and my brother spoke of."

"He simply told me he had been having some— difficulties lately, and he feared their effect on you. He told me he has a few debts, and you had been worried about them."

"And what did you tell him?"

"I simply tried to be his friend, to reassure him that these matters can be resolved, that no lives need be ruined over them. I certainly did not encourage him in running up those debts in the first place. Please believe me, Rosalind, I want only to help your brother—and you."

Rosalind gave him a short nod. She knew he *meant* no harm. They had come to know each other better in these last few days, and she knew he had no evil in his soul. But he *did* have mischief, and he did not realize that his very behavior, his very presence at that club, could influence young men like Allen.

"I know that you want to help," she conceded. "Allen is young, though, and impressionable. He should not be prattling about our private family business. I'm sorry he burdened you, especially when you were so very busy breaking the rules."

"He did not *burden* me!" Michael protested. "And I told you I was sorry about the blasted rules. They don't matter. Please, Rosalind. Let me help you, if I can. Let me make some amends for my foolish behavior."

Rosalind was confused and suddenly very tired. Her head was beginning to ache, with that telltale throb over her left eye. She did not know *how* she felt about all of this—about Michael, about all of the whirlwind changes her life had encountered in the last few days. She was used to quiet and order, not wagers and confessions and idiot kisses! She needed to be alone, to think.

"I would like to return to Wayland House now, please," she said.

He opened his mouth, as if to protest, but then shook his head. His fist clenched on the reins. "Of course, Mrs. Chase. But will you at least think of what I have said? Think of forgiving me?"

"Of course I will think about what you have said," Rosalind answered. It was all she could say; her head ached in earnest now.

He nodded shortly, and pulled on the reins to guide the horses out of their shady shelter back into the bright light of day.

That had not gone as badly as he feared it might, Michael thought, as he steered the phaeton back onto the pathway. Yet neither had it gone all that well.

Rosalind was the most difficult woman he had ever met. Most ladies let him know, through means both subtle and decidedly not so, that they either appreciated his interest or just wished he would go away. With Rosalind, he was never sure. She was always so very still, so serene, so blasted *polite*. But sometimes her eyes would flash at him with a brilliant light, or she would stiffen in a fury of temper all too quickly contained.

Or she would kiss him with heated passion on a terrace.

He had known, from the time he encountered her alone in her office, that there was much more to her than what she showed the world. Their time together in these last few days had only proven him right. She was fiercely protective of her brother, of her school and the girls who attended classes there. She was intent on being respectable and proper at all times, that was true, but there was also a yearning for *life* deep inside of her. He saw it in her eyes when they ate ices at Gunter's and watched the actors at the theater. She longed for excitement, for wonder, even though she would not admit that to herself.

She made Michael want to give her all of that excitement, to show her all the beauties that life and the world could hold. He wanted to share it all with her—and more.

He had guessed some of the secrets of her heart, it was true. Yet he had *not* guessed the one she had confessed today. He had never supposed, even for a moment, that she was the author of *A Lady's Rules.*

Michael almost laughed aloud now to think of it! He should have known. It now seemed so very obvious. Rosalind was so intent on following those rules, on making certain that everyone else did, too. She had even given *him* a copy! But he had always supposed A Lady to be some elderly spinster, dreaming up dictates in her stuffy chamber and sending them out for Society to be crazed over. He had never pictured her as a beautiful redhead.

Michael glanced over at her now. She sat beside him on the phaeton seat, her posture perfectly straight, hands folded in her lap, a pleasant half-smile on her face. He felt a great rush of pride for her, for her ingenuity in writing that book in the first place, for her courage in going out in Society to defend her principles. He himself found a creative saving grace in his poetry; she had found it in manners, and she had done what almost no one else could do—she had made the *ton* behave.

No matter how much he had, and still did, hate mindless rule-following, he had to admire her for that. And for a hundred other things, as well.

He *had* to make her forgive him for that stupid wager! He had to make her see that it meant nothing, had to undo any damage he might have caused. He had only just found her. It would kill him to lose her now.

He turned the phaeton around a corner and down the street where Wayland House sat. They had only a few more moments. He had to secure her promise that he would see her again.

"Will you be at Violet's soiree tomorrow evening?" he asked, slowing the horses to a mere crawl.

She glanced at him from the corner of her eye. "Of course. The duchess and Lady Emily also plan to attend. Lady Violet seemed so very excited about the event."

"So she is. Our father rarely deigns to entertain, and as Violet is not yet 'out' she must take every advantage of any occasion. I would not wish to excite your anticipation about the amenities, though—our father's cook concentrates only on what might charitably be called 'plain fare.' Trifles and cutlets and such."

Rosalind laughed quietly. It was a beautiful sound, one he could have listened to for hours and hours. He would stand on his head, make funny noises, wear jester's motley, do handsprings—*anything* to make her laugh.

Unfortunately, he had to keep his hands on the reins to keep them from crashing. But her one small laugh had already given him immeasurable hope.

"Oh, I can enjoy the splendors of haute cuisine every day at Wayland House, with Georgina's French chef," she said. "I look forward to your sister's company, and to meeting your aunt, Lady Minerva Fielding. I am sure it will be an enjoyable evening."

"If you are there, it shall be." They drew up outside Wayland House. Michael thought he saw a curtain twitch at one of the upstairs windows, but he could not be sure. Probably Lady Elizabeth Anne spying again.

"Thank you for the drive, Mich—Lord Morley," Rosalind said, excruciatingly polite. "The park was lovely."

Michael could not let her go like this, with a proper thanks she would give to any stranger. Boldly, he took her hand, holding the warmth of it against the lapel of his coat, uncaring that she would feel the powerful thrum of his heart.

Rosalind stiffened, and threw a startled glance back

over her shoulder, as if to see if anyone was watching them. Her fingers jerked in his clasp, but she did not pull away.

"Lord Morley, what . . .?" she began.

"Mrs. Chase—Rosalind," he said swiftly, aware that his time here with her was very short. "I am truly sorry about the wager, and about anything else I may have done to injure you. Please, I cannot be easy until I know you have forgiven me, or will at least *consider* forgiving me."

She stared down at their joined hands, staring at them as if there must be some answer written there in their linked fingers. "I—I will think about what you have said," she whispered. "Now I really must go."

"That is all I can ask for." Michael lifted her hand to his lips, and pressed a kiss to her fingertips. They trembled in his, like some wild, frightened bird. "Don't fly away from me," he begged.

He placed her hand carefully back in her lap, then leaped down from the phaeton and came around to help her alight. She backed away as soon as her feet touched the pavement, not looking into his eyes.

"Good afternoon, Lord Morley," she said, and hurried up the front steps to the door. All too soon, she had vanished behind the grand marble façade of Wayland House, more secure and distant than any vault.

But all was not lost, Michael vowed, as he climbed back up onto the phaeton. Not by a long distance. He had waited for too long to find Rosalind. He was not going to lose her now.

"So you are back!" Georgina called from beyond the half-open doors of the drawing room. "Come in and tell us about your drive in the park, Rosie."

Rosalind, her foot already on the first step of the staircase, cursed inwardly. She had so hoped to slip away from everyone, to escape into her chamber and nurse her headache—and her uncertainties—in solitude.

Now that was not to be. She would have to escape from Georgina first, which was no easy prospect.

Rosalind pasted a bright smile onto her face, and stepped past the drawing room doors. She did not go far beyond the threshold, though. That would just be inviting trouble, and she would never escape.

Georgina and Emily were playing a game of cards at a table by the window, while little Elizabeth Anne played nearby with her dolls. Georgina gave a smug little smile that Rosalind suspected had nothing to do with the hand of cards she held.

"How was your drive?" Georgina asked again. "Pleasant, I trust."

"Most pleasant," Rosalind replied in her most non-committal tone. "The park was not yet overcrowded."

"And the weather most congenial, I am sure," Emily said. Her words were all that was innocent, but the smile that curved her lips was decidedly less so.

Rosalind feared Georgina's influence was rubbing off on the poor young lady. Rosalind thought she had best take her leave from the drawing room before it infected her, as well. She already felt enough like someone not herself.

"Yes," she said firmly. "The weather was very agreeable. But it *was* rather tiring to be out so long, so I think I will go to my chamber and rest before tea."

"An excellent notion," replied Georgina. "Alex procured tickets to the opera for us this evening, so you must keep up your strength. I do think that . . ." She paused, her eyes widening dramatically. "I just had a notion! Perhaps Lord Morley and his sister would care to join us."

"It is Mozart," Emily said. "*Idomeneo*. Most edifying."

Not Michael, not tonight! Rosalind thought in a near panic. Being in his presence made her feel so muddled, so unsure. Rather like drinking a bit too much champagne and feeling the room spin about, the floor tilt. It made her want to laugh, to dance.

She loved that feeling. And she hated it. She did

not yet know what to do with such new sensations. Right now, she just wanted to lie down in her darkened room and try to figure out what to do with all the things they had talked about today. Her own confessions, his silly wager, the feel of his kiss on her hand . . . She could never sort all of that out if he was next to her in a dim theater.

She could not show that to Georgina, though. It would only urge her on in her mischief. "I think he said he and Lady Violet already had an engagement," she said. She lied, of course; they had spoken of nothing so mundane.

"Oh, that is regrettable," said Georgina. "But we will see him tomorrow evening at his father's soiree."

Oh, yes. Rosalind had forgotten about that for five minutes. At least it was not until tomorrow. That should give her some time to decide what to do next. "I think I will just go upstairs now."

"Of course, Rosie dear. I will send up some tea. You look rather pale."

Rosalind smiled at her, and turned to go. Before she could make her escape, though, she heard Elizabeth Anne's little voice pipe up.

"Aunt Rosie," she called. "Are you going to marry Lord Morley? You really should. He is *very* handsome."

Georgina and Emily burst into laughter, and even Rosalind could not entirely contain a smile. "No, Elizabeth Anne. I am not going to marry Lord Morley. I am too old for him."

"Oh." Elizabeth Anne sounded very thoughtful. "Well, then, perhaps I will marry him. I am not too old for him."

"But you are too young, my darling," said Georgina, still laughing. "And I think your father will insist on a prince for you, at the very least."

"Are there any princes as handsome as Lord Morley?" Elizabeth Anne asked.

Rosalind beat a hasty retreat before she could fall

Chapter Seventeen

"When hosting a soiree at your home, it is of utmost importance that you be certain your guests are comfortable at all times."
—*A Lady's Rules for Proper Behavior*, Chapter Four

"*A*re these flowers quite right here, Michael?" Violet asked anxiously, fussing with a vaseful of pink and white roses, moving them this way and that. They were only one of the many arrangements in the drawing room; Michael had never seen the gloomy expanse looking so cheerful. "Or would they appear to better advantage over there?"

Michael could not see any difference. "I think they are fine where they are."

"Fine? I want them to be *beautiful*." Violet's pretty face puckered in a concern far out of proportion to the dilemma.

Michael laughed, and reached out to tweak one of her curls. "They *are* beautiful. The room is lovely. You and Aunt Minnie have performed wonders here."

Violet finally smiled, a rueful little grin. She left off shifting the flowers around and pushed her curls back from her forehead. "I am being silly, I know. But this is the first time I have been allowed to attend a *real* London party."

"And the first party that has been held here since Mother died," Michael said. "I understand that you are nervous, Vi, but I promise you that all will be well. It isn't a grand ball or anything of that sort."

"No. I think I would faint if it was! I asked Mrs. Chase to come a bit early. I will not be so nervous if she is here."

Mrs. Chase. Michael's breath caught at the merest mention of her name. He had not heard from her at all since their drive yesterday, though he had sent her the biggest bouquet of red roses he could find this morning. *Would* she come early? Or had she run as far as she could from him and his wild ways and his impossible family? He could scarcely blame her if she had.

But he deeply, desperately hoped that she had not.

He had no idea where their strange new friendship, so delicate and odd and lovely, was going. Or if it was going anywhere at all. He only knew that he wanted to, he *had* to, see her again.

"Michael?" Violet asked. "Are you quite all right? You looked so strange all of a sudden."

He made himself smile at her reassuringly. "I am quite well, Vi. You said Mrs. Chase is coming early?"

"I do hope so. I sent her a note only this afternoon."

"Violet, dearest! You are not even dressed yet," Aunt Minnie cried as she bustled into the drawing room, tweaking a flower here and there, straightening a chair and some objets d'art. "Go upstairs at once, child."

"But I need to see if . . ." Violet began.

"Do not argue, young lady! Go and change your gown. Guests will be arriving soon."

"Very well, Aunt Minnie." Violet gave Michael one last harried smile, and hurried away.

Aunt Minnie laughed. "That girl needs to move in Society more!"

"She will make her bow next year. That will be soon enough."

"Indeed. She ought to become accustomed to being a hostess sooner than that, though."

"I am sure she will. She is learning a great many of the social arts at her school."

"Ah, yes. With the excellent Mrs. Chase. I understand she will be here tonight."

Here. She would be here, in only an hour or two. "Yes."

"I look forward to meeting her. I have heard that she has been seen quite often in your company of late, my dear." Aunt Minnie gave him a shrewd glance. "You know, Michael, I have attended many evenings such as this—more than I would care to count. But I have a strange feeling about tonight."

Michael felt a chill in his fingertips, a tingle of some strange foreboding. "A feeling, Aunt Minnie?"

She laughed, and waved her hand in a careless, dismissive little gesture. "Oh, I am just a silly old woman! Still, I think something *will* happen tonight. Perhaps something good? We can only hope."

Rosalind stared up at Bronston House as they stepped down from the carriage and climbed the shallow, stone front steps. It was certainly not a structure that could be called charming or fashionable. It was too dark, too foreboding, too—too *looming*. Even the golden light that glowed from its windows for the party failed to add much warmth to the chilly aspect. Rosalind shivered a bit as she took it all in.

After they handed their wraps to the footman in the foyer, Georgina took Rosalind's arm as they made their way into the drawing room. "Such a musty old pile!" she whispered. "And just look at those draperies. Thirty years out of date at least. But I do think it has potential. The lines are good, and the carvings on that panel very fine. The right woman could really make something of it."

The right woman? A woman such as Rosalind herself, mayhap? Rosalind almost laughed at such obvious machinations. If only Georgina would not say such things *here*, where anyone might overhear her! "Georgina . . ." she said warningly.

"Oh, pish! I am not saying anything untoward, Rosie. I merely mentioned that a woman of taste, with the Bronston money, could really transform this place. Beginning with taking away that awful table. Elephant legs! How perfectly horrid."

Rosalind had to agree about the table. That was certainly a horror of the first order. Yet she was not likely to be the one who cleared away the clutter, or did anything at all with this mausoleum of a house. Fortunately, there was no time to speak of this further. They had reached the drawing room, and Lady Violet was waiting to greet them.

"Mrs. Chase!" the girl said happily. "I am so glad you decided to attend our little gathering. What a beautiful gown."

Rosalind was wearing borrowed plumes again, a dark blue silk trimmed with silver beadwork and ribbons that Georgina had insisted she had ordered and then hated, so of course the gown was beautiful. It was Lady Violet who truly appeared lovely, though, in a white muslin gown edged in purple satin ribbons and trimmed with artificial violets. "And you look most charming, Lady Violet. Such a grown-up young lady."

Violet gave her a wide, pleased smile, then closed her eyes for an instant, as if steeling herself for a task. "You have not yet greeted my father, Mrs. Chase. Father, of course you remember Mrs. Chase. Mrs. Chase, the Earl of Athley."

Rosalind turned to face the earl. She had indeed only met him briefly once or twice, but she knew very well that Violet held not much fondness for him, and Michael had dropped hints that all was not well in Bronston House. Now she could see why the free-spirited Michael and the gentle Violet might be less than cozy with their father.

The earl did not rise from his chair. Indeed, he hardly acknowledged them at all. His feet appeared so swollen with gout that to stand would have been a very difficult undertaking, and it was clear that he felt a mere schoolmistress did not warrant such effort. He gave her a small nod, and no smile of greeting pierced the gloom of his wrinkled, sour, yellow-tinged visage. "Yes. You own that Seminary for Young Ladies," he said. He brightened a bit when he turned to Georgina, though. She, after all, was a duchess, even if she was also an artist.

As Georgina made her pleasantries to the earl, Rosalind stepped farther into the room and surveyed the gathered guests. It was not a large crowd; this was just a quiet evening of supper and cards for a young lady not yet out. But there were certainly a great many people, of a wide variety of ages, from the ancient Lady Day-Hamilton with her ear trumpet to the youthful Mr. Gilmore and Lord Carteret. When Rosalind saw them, lounging indolently over by the marble fireplace, she gave a prayer of thanksgiving that Allen was far away from them right now. It gave her one less thing to worry about.

Her main worry was walking toward her right now. And he looked more dangerously handsome than ever, with a claret-colored velvet coat fit perfectly over his strong shoulders and a pale pink cravat wrapped about his tanned throat. One ink-dark curl fell carelessly over his brow, and Rosalind's fingers almost itched to push it back, to feel that rough satin.

She was reminded all too clearly of their kiss on that moonlit terrace. Her gaze flickered involuntarily to the drawing room windows, but she saw no terrace beyond. Only night.

"Mrs. Chase," he said, and raised her hand to his lips for a salute that lingered just a bit longer than the rules specified. "How delightful to see you again. It has been far too long."

Rosalind couldn't help but smile. He almost always had that effect on her—if she did not fight against it. Fighting against his charm was futile, anyway, as she always found when she was in his presence. She was being drawn in by it now. Everything, everyone else in the drawing room faded away.

Oh, I am in trouble, she thought as she took her hand back. "Too long, Lord Morley? We were in the park just yesterday afternoon."

"An eternity ago. I am happy you came here this evening; I fear this soiree would be too dull without you."

"Dull?" She glanced about, searching for something positive to comment on. It was a quiet gathering, despite the varied guests, and the room did not much improve on closer acquaintance. The furniture was old, dark, and heavy, barely disguised by candleglow and copious arrangements of pink and white flowers. A carved stone family crest of spectacular ugliness hung above the fireplace.

"Your home is—very cozy," she managed to say. "Most singular."

"A moldy cave, you mean," he answered cheerfully. "Thankfully, it is not yet *my* house. I only have to visit it on occasion. But come, Mrs. Chase, let me introduce you to my aunt, Lady Minerva Fielding. She is most eager to greet you."

"Is she, indeed?" Rosalind wondered why Lady Minerva would be eager to greet *her,* and she felt a quick bolt of panic. But she had already realized that she would have to give up her usual iron control this evening. "Then I would be very pleased to meet her."

Michael held his arm out to her, and she slid her hand into the crook of his elbow. It was all very proper, yet somehow *felt* thrilling and dangerous. That was part of his power, she realized. He could make the everyday seem extraordinary.

"And I hope you will allow me to escort you in to supper later?" he asked.

"Supper?" She drew back to peer up at him. "Surely there are ladies here of far higher rank to whom you should give that honor."

He leaned closer and murmured warmly into her ear, "*You* are the most important lady I see, Rosalind. Here, or anywhere else. Please—come in to supper with me."

Rosalind could only nod; no words could press their way past the knot in her throat. No one had ever said such things to her before, and she had always thought herself immune to sweet words and flattery. She was too old, too sensible for such things.

Apparently, she had been wrong, very wrong indeed, for she felt flushed from head to toe with a strange, charmed pleasure. Her blushes probably clashed horribly with her hair, but she could not seem to care.

"Very well," she whispered. "I would be happy to go in to supper with you—Michael."

Michael. Michael. He still heard his name spoken in her soft, rough whisper, even as they sat down to supper. The conversation that swirled around him had no meaning, no coherence. The food that was placed before him seemed tasteless, bland, even though Aunt Minnie had brought in a fine caterer for the evening. Rosalind had spoken his name, had looked at him with a wide-eyed surprise that made her seem so very young and vulnerable, so very dear.

How had he not seen this the very first time he ever laid eyes on her? How had he ever thought her a humorless, rule-following matron? She might have written the rules, but now she was surely coming to see things his way. She had already gone so far as to kiss him. She just needed one small push—right into his arms.

There were such fires beneath her chill façade. He could see even now that she was struggling between following her old, safe path, and letting herself fly free. She kept giving him quick, darting glances from the corner of her eye. Her fingers were tight on the heavy silver handle of her fork, and she lifted her wineglass to her lips more often than she was surely accustomed to. She laughed freely at the admittedly weak jokes of the man at her other side. These were all very good signs that she was beginning to enjoy her life anew.

Then he noticed, tucked into the vibrant red curls

that were swept atop her head, one scarlet rosebud fastened with a sapphire clip. A rosebud from the bouquet he sent her after their drive.

Yes, he thought, trying not to be too smug. One tiny push, and a lady and her rules would be parted. Under the tablecloth, he gently, surreptitiously, pressed his leg against hers through her skirt.

She jerked and stiffened—but she did not move away. She just took another sip of wine, and gave him a small smile.

"My brother is soon to have another volume of poetry published," Violet said, breaking into his pleasant ruminations. "He is becoming so well-known. As great as Byron."

He left off gazing at Rosalind to smile at his sister. "My verses are not nearly as great as Byron's, Violet."

"It is a sister's prerogative to brag about her brother, and so I shall," Violet said stoutly. "They *are* great poems, and I am sure everyone here would agree."

A murmur of laughter and assent rose around the table, and the conversation turned generally to poetry and literature. The lady on Michael's other side asked him a question about the new volume, and he turned to answer her. Yet he was still very aware of Rosalind's warmth next to him, her fresh, soft scent. Once, she even smiled at him.

Things were all going extraordinarily well, for an evening he had so dreaded. But then his father, so uncharacteristically quiet and subdued throughout supper, finished his fourth glass of wine and tapped the edge of the crystal for a fifth.

"Demmed ridiculous way for a man to pass his time, spouting poetry," he announced querulously. Aunt Minnie tried to put her hand on his arm, to rein him in, but he shook her off. "A shame he is the only heir I have, but his mother was a bloodless woman. She had no bottom, gave out after two mewling babes. And now my daughter is the same! Inviting curates and schoolmistresses into the house. What is Society coming to? I ask you!"

He left off on a groan. Aunt Minnie had apparently just given him a quick kick to his gouty leg beneath the table. The earl subsided to quiet mutters into his wineglass.

Michael felt a rush of fury, a white-hot tide that was too familiar whenever he was in the presence of his father. The earl had never been renowned for his sparkling good behavior, but this was the outside of enough. Violet had so looked forward to this evening, and now she appeared pale and stricken.

Rosalind drew away from Michael, and would not meet his gaze. Across the table, the Duchess of Wayland watched her friend with a concerned frown.

Michael wanted more than anything to leap across the table and strangle his father, yet he knew he could not. He would not make the evening any more difficult for the women he cared about.

"My father is also writing a book," he said loudly. "On the great downfall of civilization. His theory is that art and civility are killing us. This evening, with such congenial company and fine cuisine, is hastening its demise. I say we finally send it on its way *after* cards."

There was a wave of relieved laughter, and conversation resumed its steady hum. Violet's rosy color returned to her cheeks, and she smiled at the young man—the curate—seated to her left.

Yet Rosalind still would not look at him.

Rosalind studied the array of cards in her hand, unable to fully comprehend the numbers and suits. Usually she quite enjoyed a pleasant game of piquet, but tonight it was a struggle. She had to rely on Georgina's promptings to carry her through.

She peered over the top of the cards to see the dark corner where the old earl sat slumped in sleep. He was truly horrid, just as Violet and Michael had hinted. It was a very good thing that he almost never went into Society. He could have very much benefited from a copy of her *Rules*.

Yet the old curmudgeon had been right about one thing. A schoolmistress had no place here. She should probably be grateful to the man for stopping her now, before she made an even greater fool of herself than she already had. She ought to go back to her school, before London began to gossip about the ridiculous schoolmistress widow who chased after the young poet viscount. She should cease playing dress-up in Georgina's gowns and go back to her real life.

She had not yet achieved all her objectives in Town. There were still Allen's debts. Yet she thought that now Michael—Lord Morley—would not go on trying to undermine her *Rules*. Not now that they knew each other, not now that they were—well, friends of a sort. Perhaps she could rebuild that book's popularity, finish her second edition, and go forward.

Somehow, though, that thought did not fill her with the elation it once would have.

"Mrs. Chase?" her piquet partner said, bringing her back to the reality of the moment. "It is your trick."

Rosalind gave him an apologetic smile, and collected her cards. As her partner laid down new cards, she examined the players gathered at other tables. Michael played with Lady Emily, and gave Rosalind a grin when he met her gaze. She turned away before the temptation to grin in return overtook her.

Lady Violet did not play cards, but she sat beside one of the open windows with her aunt and two other people. Of Allen's troublemaking friends, Gilmore and Carteret, there was no sign. She had actually not seen them since supper.

She sincerely hoped that meant they had gone home, and would thus do nothing to spoil the rest of this evening. Poor Lady Violet had enough to contend with in her own father.

"I am not sure this is such a good idea," Gilmore said, glancing nervously over his shoulder to see if anyone was watching. He and Carteret had slipped back into the dining room when everyone was occupied at the card tables. The supper remains had been cleared away, and tea and cakes were laid out for after the games were ended. The centerpiece was a large crystal punch bowl, filled with a weak claret cup.

"Nonsense, Gilmore! Don't be so very chicken-hearted. No one is watching, they are all too occupied with dull old cards. I vow, this is the most boring event I have attended all Season. I never would have come if my father had not insisted. This will just liven things up a bit, and no harm done." Carteret reached inside his coat and pulled out a silver flask. As he uncorked it, the pungent fumes of strongest Scotch whiskey floated out into the room.

"But I think you should . . ." Gilmore began to protest again. It did no good, for Carteret proceeded to pour the entire contents into the punch bowl.

The amber-colored liquid disappeared into the insipid pink punch. Carteret picked up a crystal ladle and stirred it in.

"They will thank us for giving them a bit of amusement," Carteret said, with a smirk. "And someone has to fight stuffy propriety, since it seems Lord Morley will not. Only a few weeks ago he was insisting no one had to follow the rules, and now he is the very pattern card of propriety! He is even dancing attendance on Lucas's sister. This will surely help him to recover."

Carteret laughed, and Gilmore did not like the sound of that chuckle at all. It was not a sound of mirth and mischief, but hollow and humorless. Yet there was nothing he could do now. The murmur of voices and laughter was approaching the dining room, and Carteret and Gilmore stepped back away from the table. Lady Violet and her aunt came into the room and went to examine the refreshments.

Gilmore could say nothing now without exposing his own role in the prank.

Violet did not feel well at all.
The room was spinning around her head in a most

odd way, and she was uncomfortably warm even when she discarded her shawl. Her temples throbbed, and everything was blurry at the edges. She turned and blinked at her brother, who stood several feet away conversing with Mrs. Chase and the Duchess of Wayland. His image wavered, and she turned away.

Perhaps some more of that punch would help. It was cool at least. She made her way unsteadily to the bowl and ladled the pink liquid into her glass. It sloshed over the sides as her hand trembled, but some of it made its way into the receptacle. She sipped at it, then gulped greedily. Really, it tasted much better than claret cup ever had before!

Violet giggled, and bumped into a chair. Where had that come from? She stumbled over the gilt frame, giggling even louder. She could not seem to *stop* laughing, even though there was really nothing funny.

"This is all very odd. I must be quite ill indeed," she whispered, and hiccuped.

A hand touched her arm gently, and she spun around. The room tilted crazily, and she would have fallen if the touch had not tightened. She blinked up at—Lord Carteret.

How odd, she thought dimly. She had met Lord Carteret once or twice before—he belonged to the same club as her brother. Yet she had never before noticed that he was really quite good-looking.

She gave him a smile, and giggled again.

"Lady Violet, are you well?" he asked. She thought he also smiled, but really she must have been mistaken, for when she blinked and looked again there was only concern on his face.

"I—I am not really sure," she answered. She pressed her hand to her head, hoping that would stop the incessant spinning.

"Come, let me take you outside for some fresh air. It will help you feel better in no time." He took her arm in his secure clasp and led her toward the doors leading out to the garden.

"I—well—" Violet murmured uncertainly. Surely it

was against the rules to go outside alone with a gentleman? Yet no one seemed to notice at all. They were all laughing, and talking very loudly. Too loudly. It made her headache worse.

Surely if no one was noticing, it was quite all right. And she did long for a breath of fresh air. She was just so *warm*.

"Thank you, Lord Carteret," she said, leaning on his arm. "I would like some air."

"Not at all, Lady Violet," he answered solicitously. "I am only concerned for your comfort."

"Michael, my dear, have you seen Violet?"

Michael turned from his conversation with Rosalind and the duchess to see his aunt hurrying toward him, a concerned expression on her face.

A cold frisson danced along his spine, which was thoroughly ridiculous, of course. What could happen to Violet in her own home? There were dozens of people about. He glanced quickly around the room, at the guests who sipped at tea and punch, milled aimlessly, chatted. His father sat over in a corner, as sour as ever despite the obsequious people who gathered about him.

Violet was not among any of the groups.

"I have not seen her, Aunt Minnie," he said, taking her arm. "But I am sure she cannot be far. Perhaps a servant came to her with some sort of refreshment emergency?"

Aunt Minnie nodded, the feathers on her turban bobbing, but she still appeared far from certain. "Perhaps. She usually tells me before she leaves. She is not the *boldest* of girls, you know. It is not like her to just run away like that."

Michael *did* know what his sister was like—terrified of appearing rude or breaking a rule. That chill instinct increased. "I will go and find her, Aunt Minnie."

"And I will help you," Rosalind said. She turned away to put her empty cup down on a table, and brushed her hands together briskly. "Surely with two of us searching, she will be found in a trice. She could not have gone far."

Michael *wanted* to have her with him. His Rosalind had an air of such efficiency that he was sure she would find any errant girl right off. And if Violet was, heaven forbid, in some sort of trouble, it would be good to have a woman with her.

But if they somehow found themselves alone in a dark corridor, or a shadowed garden . . .

He thought of their kiss on that terrace. He remembered the feel of her in his arms, the taste of her light breath on his lips, and he almost groaned aloud.

You are looking for your sister, man, he told himself sternly. *Don't forget that.*

There would be time for plotting seductions later, after Violet was safely found. And after he discovered whether or not Rosalind had forgiven him for his boyish wager. For all he knew, she might never let him set a finger on her again.

"Thank you, Mrs. Chase," he said. "I would be very glad of your assistance."

"I will fetch my husband to help me search the garden," the duchess said, already turning away. "Lady Violet probably wanted a breath of fresh air. It has suddenly become rather—raucous in here."

Rosalind slid her hand over his sleeve lightly as they left the dining room and headed for the deserted portion of the house. At least now he knew that she *would* touch him, even if in such a formal way.

If only he knew where his sister was, as well. And why it was suddenly so very loud in the dining room.

"Where are we, Lord Carteret?" Violet murmured. Her dizziness had only increased since they left the dining room, and a bright light flashed in her head even though the room was dim. She rubbed her hand over her eyes, and saw that they were in the seldom-used conservatory.

Her brother had once told her that their mother had loved the conservatory, had lavished care on the plants and flowers. Now it was neglected, overgrown with tangles of brown and green vines, littered with empty clay pots. Moonlight beamed down from the glass panels overhead, turning the whole place into a shifting, crawling, *living* thing.

Violet felt queasy, and so very warm. She stripped off her long kid gloves and dropped them onto the floor before stumbling across the room to collapse in a wrought iron chaise. The cushions were long gone, but she did not care. She just wanted to sit down. It was so very *warm* . . .

Lord Carteret sat down next to her and took her hand, startling her. She had quite forgotten he was there, and was utterly bewildered when he pressed his lips to her bare fingers.

"What are you doing?" she gasped, and tried to pull away from him.

His clasp tightened, and his other arm came around her shoulders. "Shh, Lady Violet," he said thickly. "You've been dying for my kisses since the moment we met. All the ladies do." He pushed her back so that the iron lattice pattern of the chaise bit through her thin muslin dress into her skin.

"Let me go!" she cried, and tried to shove him away. But he was too strong, and she was too dizzyingly bewildered. This all seemed too unreal, like a terrible dream she could not wake herself from.

"You are so beautiful," he muttered hoarsely. "Why have I never seen it before? Kiss me, Lady Violet!"

"No!" Violet turned her face away frantically, and his wet lips landed on her neck. His hand slid down her arm, pushing her short sleeve off her shoulder. "This is against the rules!"

Rosalind did not like this house. She knew that this was the family house of two people she cared about, Michael and Lady Violet, but she still could not like it. She was not a woman who believed in malevolent spirits, or any spirits at all for that matter, yet if she did she would say they dwelled here. The carpets and furniture were dark and heavy, adding to the gloom and the airlessness. A chill seemed to emanate from the very walls.

She shivered.

Michael glanced down at her. "Is something amiss?"

She peered up at him. His beauty was like a beacon in this gloomy place. After meeting his father and seeing this place, she marveled at his humor and kindness, at his sister's sweetness.

He appeared so like an angel now, watching over her, protecting her from this darkness. She had ceased utterly to care about the color of his neckcloths or all the rules he broke when he went about in Society. She could not even care any longer that he was a viscount, that he was younger than she, that he wrote poetry and she was dull and prosaic.

Here, in this instant, she did not care about those things at all.

"I am fine," she answered. "Or I will be when we find Lady Violet."

Michael nodded, and his angel's face darkened with worry. "Surely she could not have gone far."

Rosalind glanced about again. She half-suspected that Violet could have been snatched away by evil fairies in such a place as this, but of course that was nonsense. Violet had to be *somewhere*. "We checked the library and the morning room. Her maid is checking in her chamber. Where else is there?"

Michael frowned, and shook his head. "This is not a vast house. I think we have looked everywhere . . ." His brow cleared. "Of course! The conservatory."

"The conservatory?"

"It was my mother's favorite place. People seldom go there now. Perhaps Violet went there to find some air without going outside to the gardens."

He led her to the end of the corridor and they turned off onto a flagstone walkway illuminated by skylights overhead. At the end could be seen double doors made of glass, standing open. Rosalind stumbled a bit on the uneven stones, and as Michael steadied her with an arm about her waist, they heard a scream.

"No! This is against the rules!"

There was a great crash—and Rosalind and Michael broke into a run.

Chapter Eighteen

"A true gentleman shall never press his attentions on a lady—if this happens, he is not a gentleman, and the lady should disentangle herself from the situation by whatever means necessary."
—*A Lady's Rules for Proper Behavior*, Chapter Thirteen

$\mathcal{R}$osalind pulled away from Michael and ran the last few steps into the conservatory, with him close on her heels. She burst through the doors—and froze at the scene that greeted her.

Violet stood huddled against a long plant stand, her pale curls disheveled and one short, puffed sleeve falling from her shoulder. One trembling hand was pressed to her lips; the other held the shattered rim of a clay pot.

Rosalind heard a low moan, and her gaze swung from Violet to the man collapsed on the stone floor. Shards of the pot were scattered around him, with dirt and dried leaves dusting his hair and his elegant coat. He blinked, trying to focus, as he slowly sat up, one hand holding his head. She saw that it was Lord Carteret.

A red-hot anger bloomed in her heart, deeper than any she had ever known, or even imagined, before. This—this *cad* had taken advantage of Violet, sweet Violet! She lurched one blind step in his direction, intending to scratch out his eyes with her bare nails, but she was stopped by a choked sob from Violet.

Rosalind swung away from Lord Carteret, and stepped over his legs, lifting her hem as if he was a piece of sewer flotsam that could soil the fine blue silk. She hurried over to Violet and anchored her arms about the girl's trembling shoulders.

Violet dropped the remains of the pot and collapsed against Rosalind. "How could he do that?" she cried. "It was against the rules, Mrs. Chase! It was against the rules."

"Shh, my dear. You are safe now, don't cry." Rosalind patted Violet's back as if she were a frightened infant, and pressed her cheek lightly against the girl's hair.

She drew in a deep breath—and paused, frowning. She could smell Violet's perfume, a light violet and rosebud scent, but there was something underneath. Something sharp and sour.

"Violet, my dear," she said softly, careful not to raise her voice and alarm the girl. "What have you been drinking this evening?"

"Drinking?" Violet drew back to peer up at Rosalind, her face creased in confusion. "Only tea, and wine with dinner. Oh, and some punch."

"Punch?" Rosalind then saw the crystal punch glass, half rolled under an iron chaise.

"Yes. The claret cup."

That was *not* claret Rosalind smelled. It was strong whiskey, of the sort her husband had indulged in on rare occasions. She gently propped Violet back against the plant stand, as if she was a wax doll, and bent down to retrieve the glass. Most of the contents had been drunk or spilled out, but there were still a few dregs in the very bottom. Rosalind sniffed cautiously.

Yes. Most definitely whiskey.

She looked up, searching for Michael. She had almost forgotten he had raced behind her into the room, in all the excitement of her temper and comforting

Violet. She could not forget him now, though. He had his fists around the lapels of Carteret's coat and was roughly hauling the groggy young man to his feet. On Michael's face she saw written the utter fury she herself had felt so deeply. His sensual lips were thinned to an angry line, his jaw tight.

And a new fear took hold in her heart—the fear that Michael might fight, even challenge Carteret to a duel. As much as she wanted to see Carteret punished for his dastardly deed tonight, she could not bear to see Michael hurt. She could not see *two* people she cared about in pain this eve.

"Michael," she called sharply. "Could you come over here for a moment, please?"

He glanced toward her, frowning as if puzzled that she was there. His hands were still tight on Carteret, who was moaning and brushing feebly at Michael with ineffectual motions. Rosalind held the glass up.

Michael pushed Carteret back to the floor and came to her side, still keeping a sharp eye on the prone young man. "What is it, Rosie?" he said roughly, impatiently.

"I think Violet has been drinking strong spirits," Rosalind whispered. "There was whiskey in this glass, and she seems terribly disoriented."

"My sister has never had anything stronger than watered wine in her life!" he protested vehemently.

"I am not suggesting that Violet became foxed on purpose. She is not a girl to make such mischief. I am merely suggesting that she is in a very poor condition right now, and I ought to escort her upstairs."

"That is a very good idea. I don't want Violet here while I deal with that—that—"

He uttered a word that was most assuredly against the rules, yet Rosalind could not chide him. It expressed her own sentiments toward Carteret exactly. But she did not at all like the darkness shadowing Michael's beautiful eyes. She caught his hand between both of hers and held him beside her.

"Promise me that you will not do something like challenge Lord Carteret to a duel."

"Rosie," he answered, curling his fingers around hers. "He plied my sister with whiskey, and lured her in here to take advantage of her! How can I let these things go unchallenged?"

"They need not go unchallenged. I am sure he will pay—he is paying already." She gestured toward Lord Carteret, who still lay in a heap on the floor, moaning about his aching head. "Violet took care of herself with him, but she cannot take care of herself all the time. She needs you here, in her life, to help her. Not dead in some field, shot through the head."

"I would not be the one lying there. I am an excellent shot, Rosie."

"But what if Lord Carteret cheated? If he does not scruple at giving young ladies strong drink, he would not at turning before the count of ten." She leaned closer to him, clinging to his hand. She could not remember ever feeling more *desperate* before in her life. "Please, Michael. Violet needs you. *I* need you. Promise me that, whatever you do, you will not fight."

His expression eased a bit, the sharp crease between his eyes softening as he stared down at her. "Very well. For you, I will not fight."

Rosalind nodded, her heart lightened even if only a small bit. "Very good. I will hold you to that. And now I must take Violet upstairs before she becomes ill."

"Of course." Michael kissed her cheek quickly and released her hands. "What did Vi and I ever do before you came into our lives, Rosie? You are an angel."

An angel. Funny—that was exactly what she had thought about *him*. Smiling secretly, she went to Violet and wrapped her arm around the girl. "Come, my dear, let me take you up to your chamber. You will feel better after you have washed your face and lain down on your bed for a few moments."

Violet nodded weakly, and released her death grip

on the plant stand. She did look rather green, but at least her eyes were no longer glazed and clouded with shock. "Yes," she murmured. "I feel a bit queasy, Mrs. Chase."

"I will send for some strong tea. That will settle your stomach."

Violet leaned against her. "People are probably talking about me. Saying dreadful things."

"Not at all. No one even knows you left the party except for me, your brother, your aunt, and the Waylands. We would never tell a soul; we are concerned only for your safety."

Tears trickled down Violet's flushed cheeks, silent harbingers of misery. "I was so stupid, Mrs. Chase! So very stupid."

"Not at all, my dear. This was not your fault at all. It was entirely Lord Carteret's. He is a very bad man."

"He broke the rules!" Violet cried. "So very many rules."

Violet's words reverberated in Michael's mind long after Rosalind had led her from the conservatory. *The rules.* Carteret had broken the rules. Violet seemed quite obsessed on that point.

Michael turned to stare down at Carteret where he huddled on the floor. The man—or boy, really, as he could hardly be older than eighteen—appeared crumpled and miserable on the flagstones. But when he peered up at Michael, his bleary eyes burned with a strange resentment, a glowing, sullen fire.

For the first time, Michael had some idea of what had driven Rosalind to write those rules. It was not from some manic compulsion to control the behavior of others, as he had once imagined, before he knew her. It was to impose some order, some limits to the actions of people like Carteret. People who would take advantage of innocents like Violet—such as Rosalind had surely once been.

Women were weak, not only physically but within the dictates of Society. He had always known this, of course; it was self-evident, a part of everyday life. But he had never really *known* that, not until this moment. Rosalind had devised those rules to give the girls at her school some power over what happened to them. If all of Society insisted on following the rules, even men like Carteret and his ilk would have to fall into line or be ostracized. They were a flimsy protection at best, yet somehow Rosalind had managed to make it strong—until he came along and undermined both her and her rules.

Mindless obedience to dictates would *never* be right in his mind. But some rules were necessary, and he had been an utter fool not to see that before. He owed Rosalind a great apology.

He strode up to Carteret and nudged him with the toe of his shoe. "Get up," Michael ordered brusquely. "And cease moaning."

"Your chit of a sister nearly broke my head," Carteret whined. He held his hand away from his wound to show Michael the blood there.

"You deserved far worse. I said get up."

Carteret used the frame of the iron chaise to haul himself upright. He really did look to be in bad shape, with blood dripping from the cut on his head and his coat sleeve torn. Michael mentally applauded his sister for attempting to take her pound of flesh.

Carteret sneered at him, or at least tried to. It came out looking more like a pout. "Are you going to call me out? Demand that I name my seconds?"

"Sorry to disappoint you, but not tonight."

Carteret's sneer dissolved into surprise. "N—no?"

"No. But if anything of this sort ever happens again, I will not so restrain myself. For tonight, it is sufficient that you remove yourself and your friend Mr. Gilmore from my family's house. In future, you will never show your face at the Thoth Club again."

"No!" Carteret cried out. "Not the club! I must have . . ."

"You will *not* be a member of the club any longer. Your name will be stricken from the rolls. And you will never contact, speak to, or look at my sister, Mrs. Chase, or Mr. Lucas. Is that perfectly clear?"

Carteret gave him a sullen nod. He could clearly see that Michael meant every word he said, and would never be swayed by pleas or threats. Carteret's days at the Thoth Club were finished.

"Excellent. Now leave, before you bleed any further onto the floor."

With one last glare, Carteret hurried out of the room, his footsteps fading away down the corridor. Michael had the suspicious feeling that he had not heard the last of that young man, but for now he was gone. It was all echoing silence in the conservatory.

Michael straightened his coat and cravat, and ran his fingers through his disheveled hair. He filled his lungs with the cool evening air that flowed from the open windows and slowly released a breath, trying to let go of his raw anger.

Once he felt as if he could face the civilized world again without disgracing himself, he followed Carteret's path down the corridor. He had to make sure the cad left, and then he would send Aunt Minnie up to Violet's chamber, and tell the Duchess of Wayland that their quarry had been safely found.

And then—then he knew exactly what he had to do.

Rosalind slowly made her way down the staircase back toward the party. She had left Violet, still queasy and teary but much calmed, to the capable ministrations of her aunt. She had taken Violet's hairbrush to her own mussed curls and smoothed her gown. Now there was nothing to do but rejoin the fray.

She wondered, feared, what she would find there. Would Michael be off with his seconds, going to fight Lord Carteret with pistols at dawn? Or would he keep his word to her?

She knew that, under ordinary circumstances, Michael would always keep his promises. But she had never seen him look as he had this night, when faced with Carteret's villainy. Michael was usually so very affable, so full of jests and easy good humor. He could always make her smile or laugh, as no one else ever had before. Tonight, he had looked like a stranger, with a killing fire behind his eyes.

In that moment, she knew he was capable of a duel, but she prayed a challenge had not gone forth. If he killed Carteret, he would be forced to flee. And if he was killed himself . . .

Rosalind's breath caught on a sob. She pressed her hand to her throat. Neither of those things would happen. He had promised her.

She forced her breath past the lump in her throat and stepped into the drawing room. It was very clear from just one glance that Violet had not been the only one to unwittingly imbibe this evening. Laughter and conversation were loud, even deafening. The earl was asleep on one of the settees, snoring loudly. An impromptu game of boules was being played from one end of the marble floor to the other. Someone banged out a wild waltz on a dreadfully out of tune pianoforte while couples whirled about unsteadily.

This was like a scene from Dante, one of the tiers of hell—proper London Society gone mad, flying high on whiskey. It was almost as if the people had never had a drink before in their lives.

Rosalind laughed helplessly. So many rules were being broken she could not even count them! Yet she did not care. She just wanted to find Michael.

Ordinarily, she was sure he would be right in the thick of things, playing boules with the others. He was not there, nor at the pianoforte. He was not anywhere in the room.

"Rosalind!" she heard a voice call. Rosalind turned to see Georgina hurrying toward her through the crowd. "Lord Morley told us that Lady Violet was found. I trust that she is well?"

"Yes, she is fine. Or soon will be. Lady Minerva is with her now. But have you seen Lord Morley recently? Do you know where he has gone?"

Georgina gave her a knowing little smile. "Oh, yes. He wants you to meet him in the garden."

"The garden?"

"Yes. By the Cupid fountain, he said."

Oh, thank heaven, Rosalind thought. So he had *not* gone to duel. He was waiting for her in the garden. She hurried out of the drawing room to the doors leading into the night-darkened garden.

She was so relieved she did not even stop to think about the oddness of the invitation, or of Georgina's smug smile that was always a portent of mischief. She just wanted to see Michael.

The garden was very dark and quiet, the gravel pathways lit only by the moon and the clear stars. It was obvious that the earl cared little about horticulture; the flower beds were sparse, the borders overgrown. But there were many marble benches and statues of classical figures along the way. They shone with an opalescent glow, lighting her way to the center of the garden where the Cupid fountain waited. The music of water burbled and flowed, drowning out the remnants of voices from the open windows at the party.

The Cupid waited—but not Michael.

Rosalind spun about in a circle. She could not see him anywhere, not even at the shadowed edges of the pathway. Her slippers ground on the gravel as she strolled to the fountain. A cool wind flowed over her, and she shivered. She had been in such a hurry she left the house without her shawl.

Her stomach still fluttered with excitement, anticipation. She had never met a man in a dark garden, not even when she was young and Charles was courting her. It was such a small thing, really, especially compared with all the things she had done in the last few days. But it *felt* daring. It felt wicked. And so very delicious.

If only he was here. She began to fear that perhaps he had gone off to fight after all.

She perched on the edge of the fountain, the hard marble cold beneath the thin silk of her gown. As she wrapped her arms over her waist, a whisper came to her on the breeze.

"Rosie," it said. "Psst! Rosie!"

Rosalind shot up from her seat, glancing about frantically. "Michael! Where are you?"

"Up here."

"Up—where?" She peered up into the sky, perplexed.

"*Here*. In the tree."

She whirled around—and finally saw him. He sat on one of the thick, lower-hanging branches of a stout oak tree. His back was braced on the trunk, his legs dangling down.

"Good evening," he said, grinning at her.

Rosalind choked on a laugh. "You ridiculous man! Whatever are you doing up there?"

"Waiting for you, of course." He leaned down and held his hand out to her, beckoning with his fingers. "Come up and join me?"

Climb a tree? Rosalind inched a step back. There was probably not a rule against it, per se, but it could not be proper. And her skirts were far too cumbersome.

It was impossible. Really. Truly.

Wasn't it?

"Come on," he coaxed, in a low, tempting voice. "It is very pleasant up here. Very—private."

"My skirts . . ."

"This isn't up very high. You won't even have to climb, I'll help you up."

Rosalind glanced back over her shoulder. There was no one in the garden. They were all alone in the dark.

"Come on, Rosie," he said. "It is easy."

Rosalind took one step closer, then another, and another. She reached up and clasped his hand.

"Didn't Eve get into trouble in just such a garden?" she murmured.

"But I am so much better-looking than an old serpent," he said with a laugh.

"And not a bit conceited about it, either," she answered tartly.

"Of course not. I am modesty personified."

"Certainly. Now, how do you propose I get myself up there?"

"Do you see that large knot in the wood there? Give me your other hand and then put your foot on it. On the count of three, push yourself up. One, two, three!"

Rosalind pushed up on her foot, and felt herself pulled upward like a sack of potatoes at market. It was not an elegant procedure, but she quickly found herself seated on the branch beside him.

She did not even have time to tuck her skirts beneath her before he took her into his arms and kissed her. She drew in her breath and caught him in her own arms, feeling his solid, reassuring warmth against her.

When his lips released hers, her head fell back and she laughed from sheer exhilaration and utter relief.

"Oh, Michael," she whispered. "I am so glad you are here. When you weren't by the fountain, I feared you had gone to fight Lord Carteret after all."

"I promised you I would not, though I must say it was a difficult promise to keep."

He still held her in his arms, and Rosalind leaned her cheek against his shoulder. It felt so warm, so safe. "I know. I was so very angry with Carteret! I don't think I have ever been so very angry in my life. But Violet is fine now. I was worried about *you*."

"About me? Rosie, there is no need for you to worry about me at all. I am fine, too. More fine than I have ever been before."

Rosalind tilted back her head to stare up at him in the moonlight. Indeed, he did look fine—better than fine. All the anger, the tight rage was gone. He looked young, and happy, and free.

"What has happened?" she asked suspiciously. "An hour ago you could have killed Carteret. Now here you are, happy, sitting in a tree as if you had no cares in the world. What could have happened in that hour?"

"Oh, something very important indeed," he an-

swered lightly. "You see, Rosie, I have learned to follow the rules."

"The rules!" Rosalind was shocked. She did not
know *what* she expected him to say, but that—never.
"What do you mean? If you intend to become a
proper rule-follower now, I am not sure this is the
way to go about it. Climbing trees, luring ladies out
into the garden alone . . ."

Michael laughed. "Oh, very well, so I will never
follow *all* the rules. But I see now why you wrote
them."

"Do you indeed?" Rosalind peered closely at him,
seeking to see the truth in his eyes. Her rules had
been misunderstood by so many people for so long.
Never had she wanted someone to understand as
much as she wanted *him* to. Yet she scarcely dared to
hope. "Truly?"

"Yes. And I know one rule I can happily follow
now." He reached inside his coat and drew out a ring,
a wondrously beautiful circlet of gold set with a pearl
surrounded by small, glittering diamonds. "Mrs. Rosalind Chase, will you do me the great honor of giving
me your hand in marriage?"

"What . . . ?" Rosalind gasped. She stared down at
the ring in his hand. She feared her mouth was most
inelegantly agape, but she could not quite close it.
That pearl shone with the glow of the sea in the moonlight, an unearthly, beautiful thing. She had never seen
anything like it before. This ring was too beautiful for
someone like her.

The man who offered it was too beautiful for someone like her. Yet here he was, holding the ring out to
her like some tempting talisman, his angel's face full
of hope. She reached one trembling finger out toward
the pearl, but could not quite make herself touch it.

"What is that?" she whispered.

Michael laughed nervously. "A betrothal ring, of
course. It belonged to my mother, and to my grandmother before her. She always said it would be mine
one day, to give to my wife, and since she died it has

been kept in the safe in the library here. I fetched it just now—to give it to you. I think you are the only woman in the world who should wear this ring."

Rosalind still felt numb, dumb. She usually considered herself to be a woman of some intelligence, yet she could not string three words together. This was all so unreal, like a dream! Surely she would very soon awaken in her own bed at the Seminary, to find that she had never sat in a tree with a handsome viscount asking her to marry him.

She choked on an hysterical laugh, and pressed her hand to her lips.

Michael appeared so very puzzled and bewildered, as if he was not sure what to make of her reaction or what to say next. He peered down at the ring in his hand. "If you do not care for it, I'm sure I could find something else. A sapphire, or a ruby . . ."

"No!" Rosalind cried. She reached out and folded her hand over his, holding the ring between them. The stones pressed through her thin kid glove into her skin. "It is a beautiful ring, Michael. The most beautiful ring I have ever seen."

"Then it is the suitor you object to?"

"No, of course not."

His face brightened, like dawn breaking over the London grayness, and a smile spread slowly across his lips. "You will marry me, Rosie?"

Her head was spinning. She could not think straight, and that was a terrible thing at this moment, when she was faced with the greatest decision of her life. "Oh, Michael, I just do not know."

"Is it because of that wager? Because of my behavior in the past? I promise you, Rosie, that it is all behind me now." His other hand came up to clasp hers beseechingly and he leaned closer to her. "I am perfectly respectable now. A changed man, I vow!"

Rosalind smiled, and laid her palm against his cheek. The faint prickliness of his evening whiskers tickled through her glove. "Michael, I do not *want* you to be a changed man. You are perfect just as you are. You know that I—care about you."

"Do you care enough to accept me as your husband?"

Oh, yes. If he was a farmer and she was a milkmaid, she would accept him in an instant. But things were so much more complicated than that. "I just do not know, Michael. Everything is so uncertain."

"My feelings for you are *not* uncertain. I love you, Rosie. You are like no other woman I have ever known."

He *loved* her? Rosalind's vision blurred with tears, forcing her to look away from him, to release his hand and brush away the moisture with her fingertips. When had someone last said they loved her? Never. No one had ever said those wonderful words. Not even Charles, or Allen, or her parents. And she had never said it to them. It was as if they were dangerous words, frightening words. Yet they did not scare Michael. He declared his feelings so very openly, to all the world.

It made her dare to be brave, too. Dare to be brave—even though she was shaking in her slippers. "You l-love me?" Her tongue twisted at the word.

"Of course I do. How could I not? You are so beautiful, so very courageous. How many people could run a school as well as you do, *and* write books, *and* look after your brother? And you have done it all by yourself. But I do not want you to be by yourself any longer. I want to be with you, helping you. Please, Rosie, please let me."

Oh, that was so very tempting. To not be all alone, to have someone to walk with her, to make her laugh. To make life into a marvelous adventure, as he always did.

"I just do not know," she said. "I am so confused!"

"Here," he said, reaching for her hand. "Wear the ring for a few days, a week. Look at it, wear it on your finger and think about what I have said." He slid her glove from her arm, her hand, and placed the ring carefully on her finger. The gold band fit perfectly, as if made to go just there. "We can be so happy together, Rosie. Just give me a chance to show you that."

Michael bent his head to press a kiss to her bare fingers. Rosie laid her other hand lightly on his dark curls, felt the silk of them twine over her kid glove.

She knew so very well that he could make her happy. He filled her with such an unimaginable joy just by being near. But could *she* make *him* happy? She knew she was not an exciting woman. She had lived a quiet life, she enjoyed home and hearth and family. He loved her now, but could his poet's heart love her in five, ten years? And his family and circle would judge their match to be a terrible misalliance. He did not care for such things now, yet he very well might later.

It would devastate her to know the warmth of his love, only to lose it later in the chill of regret and contempt.

But still she yearned for him, for that sweet life they could have! A life she had never dared to dream of before.

He raised his head, peering hopefully at her from his beautiful dark eyes. "Will you think about what I have said, Rosie?"

The sensible side of her shouted at her to say no, to turn him away now, to retreat back into her old life. Yet the ring glowed at her, calling to her, whispering that it belonged to her. "Yes," she murmured. "I will think about what you have said, and I will give you my answer very soon."

He gave her an exuberant smile, and swooped down to kiss her hand again. And again. "That is all I can ask—for now."

"I should be going back to the party. I want to look in on Lady Violet again before I leave, and I am sure Georgina will be watching for me."

"Of course. You are right." He slowly, reluctantly let go of her hand, and climbed down from the tree branch. After he had swung to the ground, he reached up to lift her to his side, his clasp warm and secure on her waist. "I doubt anyone will have missed us, though. It has certainly turned into quite an *unusual* party in there."

Oh, yes, Rosalind thought fervently. *A most unusual party indeed.*

And one she would never forget.

"Well. That was certainly not what one expects when one dines out," Georgina exclaimed, as their carriage made its way through the quiet streets back to Wayland House.

Her husband smiled at her, and raised her hand to his lips for a quick kiss. "I would have thought that such raucous goings-on were exactly your cup of tea, Georgie."

Georgina laughed. "Yes, but whoever would have looked for them at Bronston House, of all places!"

"I thought it was terribly amusing," said Lady Emily. "Did you see Lady Islington singing that opera aria? Appalling!" She giggled at the memory.

"If one did not know better, one would suspect Lord Morley of playing a joke on his father," said Georgina. "Those wild young men at his club . . ."

Rosalind, pulled at last from her reverie in the dark-ened carriage corner, sat straight up and said, "Of course that was not the doing of Mi—Lord Morley! He would never do such a thing."

The thought of someone even *thinking* such a thing, after their tender scene in the garden, sent shooting pains across her brow. She fell back against the leather cushions, her hands pressed to her head.

"Of course he did not, Rosie dear," Georgina said soothingly, worry layered beneath her soft tones. "I was only teasing a bit."

"No one who saw his care for his sister would ever think he would do anything to mar her evening," Emily added gently. "He is a fine gentleman."

"Indeed he is," said Georgina. She leaned forward

to touch Rosalind's hand. "Do you have another head-ache, Rosie? We will be home soon, and my maid can make you one of her tisanes. That always helps me."

"Thank you, Georgie," Rosalind answered weakly. "It is just too many late nights." She could scarcely tell Georgina the true reason for her preoccupation. Not yet.

But Georgina might very well discover it for herself. She paused as her thumb brushed over the ring on Rosalind's finger, hidden beneath the glove.

"Rosie, what is . . . ?" she began. The carriage jolted to a halt in front of Wayland House, and Geor-gina's husband clasped her arm as the door opened.

"Come, my dear," he said. "You must leave off haranguing poor Mrs. Chase now. We are home."

"Haranguing?" Georgina protested loudly, as she stepped out into the night. "I was not *haranguing* any-one, I was merely asking . . ."

Her voice faded as she went up the stairs and disap-peared through the front door, her husband and sister-in-law behind her.

Rosalind sat by herself for a moment in the aban-doned carriage, filling her lungs with air and silence. This was the first time she had been truly alone all evening—but it did not help to clear her head. She was just as confused as ever.

"Ma'am?" the footman said softly, as he offered his white-gloved hand to help her alight.

There was nothing to do now but go upstairs and go to bed. Surely she would feel better in the morning.

She stepped down from the carriage and followed the others into the house. In the foyer, she found that, blessedly, Georgina had already retired. Only a maid waited to take Rosalind's wrap, and the butler with a letter on his silver tray.

"This came for you while you were out, Mrs. Chase," he said, holding out the tray. "I thought it might be of some urgency."

"Thank you," Rosalind said. She picked up the mis-sive with a pang of trepidation. Letters waiting at night

could not be good. Was this from that banker again?
The handwriting was not familiar, the stationery plain
white vellum.

She broke the wax wafer and read quickly.

"Not bad news, I trust, Mrs. Chase," the butler said.

Rosalind looked up at him with a smile. "Not at all.
It is from my publisher. He wishes to see me tomorrow morning."

The butler appeared a bit puzzled at the mention
of a publisher, but he was so well-trained that his expression quickly cleared to blandness. "Very good,
ma'am. Shall I order the carriage to be brought
around for you in the morning?"

"Yes, thank you. About ten o'clock, I think. Good
night."

"Good night, ma'am."

Rosalind went upstairs, her letter folded in her ring-
bedecked hand. Well, at least one thing was looking
more positive now. Her headache had even eased. Tomorrow, all would be made clear.

Chapter Nineteen

"The home and family are the lady's sphere—
she must protect them at all costs."
—*A Lady's Rules for Proper Behavior*, Chapter One

Rosalind stepped out the door of her publisher's
office into the late morning sunshine, her step
lighter than it had been in days, if not months. She
even hummed a lilting little waltz tune under her
breath as she took the footman's hand and stepped
into Georgina's waiting carriage.

This was truly a lovely day, she thought, as she
watched the scenery roll past outside the open landau.
The air was warm, the light bright, and London really
far more interesting than she had once thought it. The
shop windows held an infinite array of enticing
goods—fabrics in vibrant colors and gentle pastels,
books in rich leather bindings, slippers, parasols, bonnets. And the people—the people all appeared so very
agreeable. Rosalind sat back against the carriage cushions with a happy sigh.

Of course, what made this day so very fine was the
news that her publisher wanted a new volume from
her as quickly as possible. A guidebook specifically
for young ladies about to make their come-outs. It
was precisely the sort of thing she truly wanted to
write. Perhaps it would prevent any other unsus-
pecting girls from facing what poor Violet had last
night.

Rosalind shifted her reticule in her palm, listening to the clink of coins inside. She had even managed to talk the publisher into giving her an advance on the new volume's profits—enough to pay off most of Allen's loan.

But the coins were not even the best part of the day, as lovely as they were. The very best part resided on her finger, hidden beneath her glove.

Under the cover of a fold of her dark green pelisse, Rosalind drew off the glove and stared down at that ring. Last night, in the moonlight, it had glowed with a mellow promise. Today, the diamonds encircling the pearl caught the sun and reflected it back to her radiantly. Just like the sparkle of Michael's own personality.

"Oh, Michael," she whispered. "What am I to do? What *should* I do?"

The ring glinted in mute answer. Rosalind had stayed awake almost all the night, thinking, thinking. Every fiber of her sensible self told her that such a match could never work. Her mind urged her to go back to her school, and forget about such a life, forget about *him*. Especially since she had this new book to work on.

But her heart—ah, her heart cried out something very different. It told her to grab this man and run with him to Gretna Green immediately! It wanted more poetry, more nighttime tree climbing, more waltzes, more kisses, more—more *everything*. She had always been able to silence her heart in the past, to bury it beneath prudence and good sense. Now, it would not quiet.

"I deserve happiness," she told herself. "I deserve something for myself after all this time."

But did she truly?

The carriage lurched to a halt, caught in one of the London traffic snarls. Up ahead, a wagon was overturned, blocking everyone else from moving. Rosalind pulled her glove back over the ring, and glanced about at the people near her.

A few carriages over sat Lady Clarke, with a handsome blond gentleman Rosalind had never seen before. As she watched, Lady Clarke noticed her, and tugged at her companion's arm. She whispered in his ear, and gestured toward Rosalind. The man laughed, giving Rosalind an insolent stare.

Her cheeks burning, Rosalind turned quickly away and stared resolutely ahead. She had known, of course, that people would be bound to talk once she had been seen in public—several times!—with the famous Viscount Morley. And she had expected it to sting. After all, she had spent all of her life being a pattern card of propriety. But, somehow, the embarrassment was not nearly as grave as she would once have thought it.

It seemed a small price to pay for all she had experienced here with Michael. Yet would she think that still if she went back to her school to find no pupils to return to?

If you were Michael's wife, it would not matter, her heart whispered temptingly.

The carriage moved on once more, turning down the street toward Wayland House. She had no time to worry about such things now. Georgina and Emily would be waiting; after luncheon, they were meant to go on a shopping expedition. Rosalind actually had her eye on a bolt of sapphire-colored satin at a certain warehouse, the first expensive fabric she had thought of for herself in years.

It would make up a fine wedding gown, that subversive voice in her heart said.

"Enough!" Rosalind exclaimed aloud.

"Ma'am?" the footman who had come to assist her from the carriage asked, obviously surprised. "Did you ask something?"

"Oh, no, not at all." Her cheeks warm yet again, she took his hand and stepped down onto the pavement. The butler opened the front door, anticipating her arrival, but as Rosalind turned to go up the walkway, something caught her attention. She whirled about to see that man again—the one she had seen at least twice before, lurking outside Wayland House.

He lounged against the iron fence of the park across the way, his face twisted away from her, but she *knew* this was the same man.

He could not possibly have any business there! Perhaps he was from the bank. Or—or something worse.

"Ma'am?" the footman asked. "Is something amiss?"

"No," Rosalind muttered. "Not at all, thank you." She whirled around and walked as quickly as she could without racing to the front door.

Georgina was crossing the foyer to the drawing room, a paint box in her hand, but she stopped in her tracks when Rosalind slammed the door and leaned back against the heavy wood. "Rosie? What is wrong? Is a ghost chasing you? Was it bad news at your publisher?"

Rosalind shook her head. She could not speak; she could scarcely breathe. She did not know what was happening, but a cold knot twisted in her stomach. "That man is back," she managed to croak out.

Georgina's brow creased. "What man?"

Rosalind had forgotten that she had not told anyone about the lurker. She had thought she was imagining things, until today. "I have seen this man standing across the street a few times. I thought surely I was hallucinating, yet there he is again today. Oh, Georgie, I do not like this at all!"

Georgina'a eyes caught green fire—not a good sign. "As well you should not! You should have told me earlier, Rosie. *No one* spies on *my* house and gets away with it! Come with me. We will soon discover what this is all about."

Before Rosalind could even catch a breath, Georgina shoved her box into the butler's hands and caught up a walking stick from the stand. She threw open the front door and hurried down the walkway. As Rosalind followed, Georgina yanked the stick apart, revealing a hidden sword.

"Which one?" Georgina asked, in a hard voice Rosalind had never heard from her before.

Rosalind pointed mutely. Georgina stormed across the street, and before the spy could even suspect the storm that approached him, she had the tip of the sword pressed to his throat.

"Who are you and why are you spying on my house?" she demanded.

The man, who had appeared so very insolent and indolent only a moment before, gulped and turned a most unattractive pea green shade. He held his hands up in apparent surrender.

"I am not *spying* on anyone's house," he gasped. "I am merely out enjoying the fine weather."

"My friend tells me you have been 'enjoying the weather' here several times." Georgina pressed the blade closer. Rosalind felt scared out of her wits, yet she could not help but admire that iron resolve—and wish for some of it herself.

"I do not know what you're talking about. I simply like this park," the man said. "And *you,* madam, are attracting a great deal of attention. I suggest you put the blade down before you are arrested."

Rosalind glanced about. They were indeed gathering a gawking crowd. Georgina just laughed. "Do you know who I am? I am the Duchess of Wayland. No one will arrest me, even if I spit you like a wild boar right here. You are obviously a vile kidnapper, and my children are walking with their nanny in this very park. No one would fault me for defending my family."

"Now, just a moment—" the man began, but he was cut off when Georgina pressed the blade closer.

A man on horseback came galloping up the street, and the crowd parted to let him through. The Duke of Wayland swung down from his horse and strode through the crowd, looking neither to the right nor left, just straight at his wife.

"Georgina," he said, quietly but firmly. "What has happened now?"

"I am very glad you are here, darling," Georgina said, her sword never wavering. "Rosalind has seen this man spying on our house. He is obviously scheming to kidnap Elizabeth Anne and Sebastian."

"Indeed?" Alex stepped closer and removed the sword from his wife's hand, his dark, handsome face like implacable granite.

"No!" the man cried out, his upheld hands shaking. "I am no kidnapper. I was merely paid to watch this house."

"Paid to track my children's movements?" the duke demanded.

"It had nothing to do with your family at all, Y-Your Grace!"

"Then why are you spying on my house?"

"I was paid to watch *her*!" The man pointed a trembling finger at Rosalind.

"Me?" Rosalind whispered. Everyone swung about to stare at her.

Everyone but Alex, whose gaze never wavered from the villain's face. "That is just as bad. Mrs. Chase is a guest in my home. Who wants her followed? Speak quickly, and I may allow you to live."

The man turned even more green. "It was the Earl of Athley! He paid me. I have been following her for weeks, even before she came to London."

The Earl of Athley? Michael's father? Rosalind pressed her hand to her mouth.

Georgina laid a comforting hand on her arm. "Oh, Rosie," she murmured. "The Earl of Athley. Such a terrible potential father-in-law. It is just fortunate that his son is so very attractive. He must take after his mother."

Attractive. Yes, indeed. Michael was that.

But was he attractive enough? Rosalind thought that now, at last, she knew the answer to that question.

Chapter Twenty

"A young lady's most important decision is who she will marry—she must choose with her head, not her heart."
  —*A Lady's Rules for Proper Behavior,* Chapter Ten

*M*ichael handed his hat and walking stick to the butler at Bronston House, glancing about the foyer as he did so. The place was as gloomy as ever, dark, hulking furniture pushed back into place, dust motes dancing in the narrow bars of sunlight falling from between the velvet draperies. There were no signs of the previous night's unexpectedly raucous soiree.

That could almost have been a dream, a product of fairy spells and full moons. An aberration in the atmosphere. Yet he knew it could not be. His time with Rosalind in the garden, nestled on the wide tree branch, had felt so real. The sight of his mother's ring on her elegant finger, the diamondlike tears in her eyes—all wonderfully real. He never could have dreamed it.

Strange. He had always imagined that he would be nervous when he asked a lady to marry him, would be loathe to give up his freedom for duty. He had been as calm and steady as he had ever been when he took Rosalind's hand and asked her to be his wife, *more* steady even. He had not been loathe to give up anything—only excited to be gaining something infinitely precious.

It was right. It was meant to be. He could only pray that Rosalind felt the same way, for he had had no word from her yet today. But her kiss had not lied. She loved him, as he loved her. And he would do anything to make her see that.

"Is my sister downstairs yet?" Michael asked the butler. Hopefully, Violet would be in her little sitting room, and he could slip in there to see her without alerting their father to his presence. He had no desire to deal with the irascible earl, today of all days.

"Not quite yet, my lord, though her maid just took Lady Violet's chocolate up to her. She should be down very soon. But Lord Athley is in the drawing room and wishes to see you, my lord."

Damn and blast. "I suppose he knows I am here, then?"

"Oh, yes, my lord. He saw your carriage from the window." The butler bowed, and strode briskly away with Michael's hat and stick.

Well, it seemed he was well and truly trapped. He had to see for himself that Violet was unscathed by her ordeal last night, and in order to do that he had to stay at Bronston House.

"Ah, well," he muttered. "Might as well get it over with."

He went into the drawing room and closed the doors firmly behind him. In here, too, the signs of the night's ravages were few. Aside from some drooping roses left in the vases, everything was back to its normal aspect. The draperies were drawn, and, despite the warmth of the spring day, a fire blazed in the hearth, casting an ominous glow on the carved stone crest.

The earl sat in a high-backed, thronelike chair before that fire, a woolen shawl wrapped about his shoulders, his gouty leg propped on a footstool. He looked up sullenly with bloodshot eyes as Michael

crossed the room to sit on one of the settees set a bit
farther away from the flames' heat.

"I told your foolish aunt I would rue the day I
allowed her and your bloodless sister to have a rout
here!" the earl grumbled without preamble. "I knew it
was a poor idea. Company brings nothing but trouble,
trouble and mess. There is no one left in London
worth knowing. It is just parvenus and mushrooms.
And *now* see what has happened!"

Had Violet told their father what had happened in
the conservatory? Michael cursed silently. She had
been so agitated, but he should have warned her about
saying anything to the earl. "If you are referring to
Lord Carteret's reprehensible behavior . . ."

"Carteret?" the earl shouted. "Was it that insolent
puppy who did it? By God, but I will send the Bow
Street Runners after him to get it back! That dirty
thief."

"Thief?" Michael frowned in confusion. A cad Carteret undoubtedly was, but a thief? "What was taken?"

"Someone broke into the library safe last night and
stole your mother's pearl ring. There is no telling what
else is missing in the house. If it was that Carteret . . ."

Michael burst into surprised laughter. His father actually thought a thief had been in the safe! This was
absurd. The man was becoming bacon-brained in his
dotage—not that he had ever exactly been a clear
thinker.

The earl scowled, and swiped out with his walking
stick. Michael was too far away for the blow to do
anything more than stir the hot air about.

"You young idiot!" he growled. "What are you
laughing at? A crime has been committed!"

"I hardly think so, Father. Mother left her ring to
me, and I am the one who took it. There was no
thievery involved."

The earl turned a most unattractive shade of purple.
"*You* took the ring?"

"Yes. Did you not wonder why nothing else in the
safe was missing? Mother's sapphires are there, not to

mention her diamond tiara and a great amount of coin."

"You had no right to just take that ring! What did you want it for? To sell it for gambling money?"

"Of course not. I wanted it for the purpose Mother intended it for—to give it to the lady I mean to marry."

The earl's face cleared a bit, and he leaned forward in his chair. This was a theme he had been harping on for years, Michael's duty to wed and produce a new little heir. "Indeed? Well, why did you not say so! It is about time you did your duty. Who is it? Miss Sanderson? Lady Eveline Ferry?"

"It is Mrs. Rosalind Chase," Michael said calmly. "I am sure you will wish us happy."

That purple color suffused the earl's cheeks again, and for a moment Michael feared he might have apoplexy right here and now. He rose from his chair to fetch a brandy, but was driven back a step when his father's thrown stick hit him square in the chest.

"How dare you!" the earl shouted. "You have always been willfully blind to your duty, but this is too much even for you. Marrying a schoolmistress, a red-haired adventuress . . ."

Michael had heard more than enough. He snapped the stick in two with his bare hands and threw the jagged halves into the fire. "You will not speak of my future wife in such a manner."

"Your *wife*! A woman older than you, with no fortune, no family, a brother who gambles away what little money they have? A woman who has business with *bankers*? I know all of this and more, Michael, because I knew you and your stupid sister were caught in that woman's snare. That your sister was far too attached to her and that school. So I hired a man to follow her, even before she came here to London to entrap you."

The earl sat back in his chair, oozing with a smug satisfaction. Michael suddenly wished he had not thrown that stick into the fire so precipitously, so he could beat his father over the head with it now. How *dare* that monster set a spy to follow Rosie!

"If you thought this news would dissuade me from marrying Mrs. Chase, you were much mistaken," he said, in a low, tight voice. "I love her, and I am more resolved than ever to make her my wife. And now, I bid you farewell."

He spun on his heel and strode out of the room, before he gave in to his overwhelming desire to commit murder. He ignored the earl's shouts, and closed the doors behind him.

Violet stood halfway down the staircase, her hands clutched on the balustrade. Her face was a bit pale from her adventures of the night before, but a brilliant smile curved her lips and her eyes sparkled. She did not even seem to hear the screams and thumps from the drawing room, as she ran down the stairs to throw her arms about Michael.

"Oh, my darling brother!" she cried. "Are you truly going to marry Mrs. Chase?"

"If she will have me."

"Of course she will have you! She *must*. You are the finest catch in London, Michael, and this is the best decision you have ever made. To think—she will be my *sister*. Oh, Michael. Last night was the worst night of my life, but this is the very best day."

China shattered behind the drawing room door. Michael gave Violet a rueful smile. "As you can tell, Vi, Father is not wildly happy about my choice of bride."

Violet cast a hard glance at the door. Her look was strangely contemptuous—an expression Michael had never seen on his sister's sweet face. It was as if she had grown up in only a day. "Who cares about him? He can do nothing to you. Mrs. Chase will one day be the finest countess this house has ever seen, after Mother, of course. And *I* will dance with the greatest of joy at your wedding!"

Michael laughed. He twirled her to him and gave her a resounding kiss on both cheeks. "Vi, you are the very best of sisters! And I promise that you *shall* dance at my wedding. Now, I want you to get out of this house, go call on Aunt Minnie for the afternoon. Mrs. Chase and I will come see you later."

"What a fine idea. Aunt Minnie did have a new bonnet she wanted to show me."

Michael kissed Violet's cheek again, and framed her face in his hands as he examined her closely. "Are you truly well today, Vi?"

She clasped his hands in hers and gave him a reassuring smile. "I am fine. Never better, now that I have heard your news. Really, there was no harm done. I was saved by the rules, you know."

Michael laughed again. "My dearest sister, I think we both were."

Chapter Twenty-one

"Always marry a gentleman whose character and background you are sure of. This is the only assurance for future happiness."
—*A Lady's Rules for Proper Behavior,* Chapter Two

"*What* a truly extraordinary day," Georgina said, leaning back in her chair with a deep sigh. She swirled a crystal goblet of restorative brandy between her hands. "I vow, Rosie, you must have dragged all the excitement behind you from the country. Town was deadly dull until you arrived, and now look at all that has happened!"

Rosalind laughed, and sipped at her own brandy. Its warm sharpness was comforting. She had been more shaken by the encounter with Lord Athley's spy than she cared to admit. "I do believe it was *you* who created most of the excitement today, Georgie, drawing a sword on the man like that. You seemed like a lady pirate from a hundred years ago."

Georgina shrugged. "I am rather sensitive about people threatening my family and friends—even people who are so unsubtle in their spying that it is all rather a joke."

"Indeed. I do hope Lord Athley was not paying him a great deal. Or perhaps he could get his money back?"

Georgina snickered. "Oh, Rosie, you made a joke! You must be feeling better."

"I am feeling quite well, thank you." And, strangely enough, she was. The shock of discovering that Michael's father had set a spy on her—on *her,* the dullest woman in Town!—had faded. She felt only a still, centered calm, and an odd urge to fall on the floor laughing.

"That is good. Everyone knows that Lord Athley is truly a cranky old eccentric, but this goes beyond that. It is worthy of Bedlam." Georgina drank the last of her brandy and put the glass down on the table beside her. "I do hope that this incident will not affect your good opinion of Lord Morley, Rosie. He is a good man, and he does seem to care about you so much."

Rosalind smiled at her serenely. "Of course not. Lord Morley is not liable for his father's faults. He is entirely his own man." Indeed, Rosalind had come to a decision concerning Michael and herself before she even discovered the truth about the spy. Seeing how truly pitiful his father was had only increased her resolve. She knew truly that she had made the right decision, and she would not be swayed from it.

"I am surprised that Lord Morley and Lady Violet are the offspring of that lunatic at all," Georgina mused. "They are both so very charming."

"Perhaps their mother had a *chere ami,*" Rosalind suggested. "At least I hope the poor lady did. I am sure she deserved some happiness in her life."

Georgina stared at her, wide-eyed. "Rosie? Do you have a fever? You do not sound at all like yourself today."

"Do I not?" Rosalind tilted her head, considering this. "Funny. For I feel more like myself than I ever have before."

Georgina shook her head, obviously perplexed. "You should go to bed for the rest of the day. I am sure a rest would do you good."

"I am not a bit tired."

"Then have some more brandy." Georgina leaned across the table to pour more of the amber liquid into both of their glasses.

As Rosalind took a small sip, there was a quick knock at the drawing room door. "Lord Morley is here to see Mrs. Chase, Your Grace," the butler announced.

"Ah, yes, right on time. I do like a man who has a sense of timing," said Georgina. "Show him in."

Rosalind sat straight up in her chair, a nervous excitement that had nothing to do with the liquor dancing up her spine. She reached up to pat at her hair, and pushed stray curls back into their pins.

"I see that is my cue to depart," Georgina said. She stood and gathered her silk shawl about her as Michael came into the room. "Lord Morley, how lovely to see you again. You must excuse me, as I promised my daughter I would read to her before her nap. But Mrs. Chase would certainly enjoy a nice long chat with you." With that, she breezed from the room, shutting the door firmly behind her.

Rosalind hoped she was not listening at the keyhole. She smiled a bit at the image of her elegant friend kneeling on the floor, straining to spy on them, as she stood and held her hands out to Michael.

He was certainly every bit as handsome as he always was, with his dark hair tousled by the wind and an emerald twinkling from the folds of his mint green cravat. Yet there was an agitation about him, a nervous energy that fairly crackled in the air around him. He took her hands tightly in his, but did not raise them to his lips. They just stood there in the middle of the room, hands clasped, like figures in a *tableau vivant*.

Rosalind herself felt oddly unable to move, or talk, or even breathe. She had rehearsed so carefully in her mind what she wanted to say when this moment came. That was gone now; she remembered not a syllable. She saw only him. He alone filled all her mind.

What would the rule be? she asked herself. She had no idea. She could scarcely even remember what a *rule* was.

"Is that true? Would you enjoy a—chat with me?" he asked thickly.

"I—well, yes, I suppose. I did hope you might call at some point today."

"I wanted to come at the break of daylight! Oh, Rosie, there were so many things I wanted to say to you. I could have written an epic! Now I find that I must begin with this—I apologize."

Rosalind opened her mouth, all set to answer him— and she tripped over her tongue. That was *not* the question she was about to reply to! "You apologize? Michael, whatever for? Are you . . ." A chill settled an icy grasp around her heart. "Are you withdrawing your offer to me?"

"What!" His clasp tightened convulsively. "Never, Rosie. You shall not escape from me as easily as that. I saw my father this morning, and he told me something so abominable, so evil, I could not credit it even from him."

"Did he tell you about the man he paid to follow me?"

"Yes. But how did you know?" Michael's face darkened. "Did the bast—the earl come here? Did he threaten you?"

Rosalind laughed. "No, indeed! In fact, Georgina drew a sword on the poor hired spy and threatened to, er, 'spit him like a wild boar.' Your father was obviously too cheap to pay for a true master spy, because the man acknowledged the whole scheme to us at once." She laughed again, at the memory of his terrified expression when Georgina brandished her blade.

Michael laughed, too, though it was decidedly bitter. "And you were not angry at all?"

"Of course I was angry. No one likes to be followed about, and for him to involve Georgina and her family was truly infuriating. Yet it helped me to see something even more clearly."

"Oh? And what is that?"

Rosalind smiled up at him. "That I love you and want to spend my life with you. That you could become the man you are—so openhearted, and kind, and funny—after growing up with such a father is nothing less than a wonder."

Michael threw back his head and laughed, and this time there was no trace of bitterness. There was only a pure, crystalline joy. "Say it again!" he demanded.

Rosalind giggled. "What part?"

"The part where you said you love me."

"I love you! I adore you. And I will marry you, before you come to your senses and see what a poor choice you have made."

"I have made the best choice, for I am marrying the most beautiful woman in England, and the most clever and the bravest." Michael sat down on the nearest chair and pulled her onto his lap.

Once she would have been truly appalled. This was a most blatant violation of the rules! A lady should never behave like a tavern maid, especially not in a ducal drawing room. Now she giggled like a schoolgirl, and twined her arms about his neck. "The bravest?"

"Most ladies after meeting my father would run the other way," he answered, nuzzling a kiss against her throat. "Not you, my redheaded Valkyrie. My beautiful defender."

"Then it would seem we are well and truly betrothed," Rosalind said, with a happy sigh. All her doubts, her old weaknesses, were fallen away. This was the right thing to do—this was her future.

Michael took her hand and pressed his lips to her palm. He turned it over—and paused. "If we are truly betrothed, my Rosie, then where is your ring? Never say my father's spy stole it from you!"

"Of course not." Rosalind reached up into the tight long sleeve of her gown and pulled out the ring. She placed it in his hand. "It is silly, but I just wanted you to put it on my finger again, now that there is no doubt about either of our feelings."

He grinned at her. "Very well. Mrs. Rosalind Chase, will you marry me?"

"Viscount Morley, I will."

Michael slid the ring back onto her finger, where it dazzled in the sunlight from the tall windows. He lifted her hand and kissed it lingeringly, moving his lips over her fingers. "You are truly mine now."

Rosalind leaned her cheek against the silk of his hair. "As you are mine?"

He stared up at her intently. "I am always and forever yours, Rosie. When will you marry me? Tomorrow?"

"Tomorrow!"

"I am sure I could procure a special license. Perhaps the Waylands would let us have the wedding here?"

Rosalind was quite sure Georgina would be delighted to have the wedding here, and would immediately launch into arrangements. It was a good thing Georgina's taste was so excellent, for Rosalind's own head was spinning far too much to think of licenses and flowers and cake. "It is all so sudden . . ."

"Or we could make a dash for Gretna Green! Anything you want, Rosie. Anything—if you will only marry me. But I know you have arrangements you'll need to make."

"So I do. I have already written to Miss James, one of my teachers. She is a very competent young lady, and I am sure she will be able to look after the Seminary for the next term. I only have to let Allen know, so he can be here for the wedding."

"Next week, then," Michael said eagerly. "And not a day later! We will wed here, and then I am taking you to Italy."

Rosalind gasped. "Italy!"

"I trust there are no objections? If there is someplace else you would rather go . . ."

"Oh, no. I have always dreamed of seeing Italy. Georgina says that Venice is the most romantic place in the world. It is so full of history, so warm and sunny."

"So far from my father."

"Indeed. Another great advantage of Italy. I have no objections at all. Perhaps Violet would care to join us? Travel can be so educational."

"You *are* an extraordinary lady, my Rosie. Not many women would want their sister-in-law along on their wedding trip."

"Violet is a dear. I cannot see that she would give us any trouble, unless she falls in love with some dark-eyed Italian. And Italy *is* very far from your father. I am sure it would vex him greatly to have us all so far out of his reach."

Michael gave a whoop of laughter, and kissed her again and again. And yet again, longer and sweeter. "You *are* a sly one. In fact, I am sure such deviousness must be against the rules," he murmured, when he at last raised his lips from hers.

Rosalind leaned back against his shoulder and sighed happily. "Ah, but my darling Michael, I have discovered that there is really only one rule that should never be broken."

He nuzzled her cheek, blowing lightly on the loose curls at her temple. "And what rule is that?"

"The rule of true love, of course."

Read on for an excerpt from

The Spanish Bride

another passionate Regency romance
by Amanda McCabe

Available now in the beautiful
reissue double Regency
SCANDALOUS BRIDES
at penguin.com or wherever
books are sold.

Spain, 1811

"I pronounce you man and wife. In the name of the Father, of the Son, and of the Holy Spirit. Amen."

Carmen Montero, known in her Seville home as the Condesa Carmen Pilar Maria de Santiago y Montero, trembled as the priest made the sign of the cross over her head. Her fingers were chill in her bridegroom's grasp.

It was done. She was married.

Again.

And she had always sworn to herself that she would never again enter the unwelcome bonds of matrimony! She had relished her widowhood, the freedom to live as she pleased, apart from restrictive Seville society. The freedom to work for the cause of ridding Spain of the French interloper.

Her husband, Joaquin, Conde de Santiago, had been good for nothing in life. She shuddered still to think of his cold, cruel hands, his rages when, every month, she was *not* pregnant with a son and heir. At least in death his money had proved useful, working to help free Spain from the French.

Yes, she had sworn never to marry again.

Yet she had not foreseen that there could be anything in the world like this man.

When she had first seen Major Lord Peter Everdean, the Earl of Clifton, her heart had skipped a beat, just as in the silly novels her friends had slipped into their convent school so long ago. Then it had leaped to life again. He was just as handsome as she had heard whispered by her friends at balls in Seville—the Ice Earl, as the ladies gigglingly called him.

But it had not been only his golden good looks that drew her. There was something in his beautiful ice blue eyes: a loneliness, an isolation that she had understood so deeply. It had been what she had felt all her life, this sense of not belonging.

Now perhaps she had found a place she *could* belong, even in the midst of war. Perhaps they both had.

Carmen peeked up through her lashes at the man beside her, only to find him watching her intently, a faint smile on his lips.

She smiled slowly in return, once she could catch her breath. The only word that could describe Peter was *beautiful*. He was as elegant and golden as an archangel, his fair hair and sun-bronzed skin gleaming in the candlelight of the small church. His broad shoulders gave a muscular contour to his red coat and his impossibly lean hips looked charming in tight-fitting white pantaloons. His rare smiles enticed women the entire length of Andalucia, and everyplace he went.

Now his ring was on *her* finger. Tall, skinny, bookish Carmen. This extraordinary man was her husband, her lover, even her friend.

It was all suddenly overwhelming: the incense in the church, the emotions in her heart. She swayed precariously, only to be caught in her husband's strong arms.

"Carmen!" he said. "What is it?"

"I just need some fresh air," she whispered.

Nicholas Hollingsworth, Peter's fellow officer and their only witness, hurried down the aisle ahead of them to throw open the carved doors. "She is probably exhausted, Peter," he pointed out. "She rode all day to get here!"

"Yes," Carmen agreed. "I am just a bit tired. But the air is a great help."

Indeed it was. Her head was clearer already in the cool, dry night. She leaned her forehead against her husband's shoulder and closed her eyes, breathing deeply of his heady scent of wool, leather, and sandalwood soap.

"I am a brute," he murmured against her hair. "You should have been asleep these many hours, and here I have insisted on dragging you before the priest."

Carmen laughed. "Oh, I do not think I mind so very much."

"It was past time for the two of you to make it respectable," Nicholas said. "You have been making calves' eyes at each other for weeks, every time Carmen comes into camp. It was quite the scandal."

"Untrue!" Carmen cried, laughing. "You are the scandal, Nick, chasing all the *señoritas* in the village."

"I do not have to chase them! I stand still and they come to me." Nicholas saluted them smartly, and turned to make his way back down the hill to the lights of the British encampment. "Good night, Lord and Lady Clifton!"

Carmen and Peter watched him go, silent together in the warm starlit night, and in the sense of the profundity of the step they had just taken.

They had known each other only about two months, from intermittent visits Carmen had made to the various encampments of Peter's regiment. Yet Carmen had somehow *known,* the moment she had seen him, that he was quite special.

"I remember when I first saw you," she said.

"Do you?"

"Yes. The day I rode in from Seville to speak to Colonel Smith-Mason. You were playing cards with Nicholas outside your tent, in just your shirtsleeves. Most improper. The sun was shining in your hair, and you were laughing. You were quite the most handsome thing I had ever seen."

"I also remember that day. You were riding hell-for-leather through the camp, on that demon you call your horse. You were wearing trousers and that ridiculous hat you love so much." He laughed. "I had never seen a woman like you."

"Hmph, thank you *very* much! I will have you know that that hat is the height of fashion right now."

"I stand corrected, Condesa. But I could not believe that anyone so very lovely, so refined could be a spy."

"I am not a spy," she corrected him. "I simply sometimes overhear useful information that could perhaps aid you in ridding my country of this French infestation."

"So that is not spying?"

"No. It is . . . helping."

Peter laughed, the rumble of it warm against her. "Then, I

am very glad indeed that you have decided to help *us*. You, my dear, could be a formidable foe."

"Not as formidable as you." Carmen fell silent, turning her new ring in the moonlight to admire the flash of the single square-cut emerald. Peter had told her that the ring had been his mother's, who had died when he was a small child. "This war cannot go on forever."

"No." Peter's hand covered hers, tracing the ring with his thumb. "Are you sorry now, Carmen, that we married so hastily? Are you having second thoughts about sharing your life with mine after the war?"

"No! Are you?"

"Of course not. You are the only woman I have ever loved."

Carmen's brow arched doubtfully. "Really?"

His laugh was rueful. "I did not say the only woman I have ever *known*. You would see that for a sham immediately. But you are the only woman I have ever loved."

"Then you did not ask me to marry you out of some sense of obligation, after—well, after what occurred last week?"

"Are you referring to the fact that we anticipated our wedding vows?" Peter clicked his tongue. "My dear, how indelicate!"

Carmen couldn't help but blush just a bit at the memory of that night, when, tipsy with brandy and kisses and a dance beside a river, they had fallen into his bed and done such incredibly wonderful, wicked things. Peter's hands, his sorcerer's mouth . . .

A giggle escaped.

"No," Peter continued. "I married you because I think it is so charming that, despite the fact that you can ride and shoot like the veriest rifle sergeant, you still blush at the mention of the, ah, small preview of our marital bed."

"Small, *querido*?"

"Well, perhaps not *so* small."

"No." Carmen smiled. "Yet have you thought of after the war, when we must leave here and go to England, and you must present me as your countess?"

"Of course I have thought of it! It is almost all I do when we are apart. It will be wonderful. I have a sister and an estate that I have neglected these many years, so we must go there as soon as we can."

"You have been doing your duty for your country 'these many years.' Surely your family must understand that?"

"Yes, but it does not make it any easier to be parted from them. Sometimes, when I cannot sleep at night, I think of them, Elizabeth and Clifton Manor. I can almost smell the green English rain...." His voice trailed faintly away.

Carmen looked out over the lights of the camp. She had never been to England, or indeed anywhere but Spain. It was all she knew, warm, sunny, tradition-bound Spain. How would she fare in a new, English life?

She leaned her head against his shoulder, her eyes tightly shut. "Will they like me at your home? Will your sister like me?"

Peter tipped her chin up with one long finger, forcing her to meet his gaze. "Elizabeth will love you; you are very much like her. They will all love you at Clifton. As I do. Believe me, darling, it is much easier to be an English countess than a Spanish one, and you have done that wonderfully. You must not be afraid."

Her jaw tightened. "I am not afraid."

Peter laughed "Excellent! I knew that a woman who does the things you do could not possibly be frightened of the English *ton*." He kissed her lightly on her nose. "Are you ready to return to camp?"

"Oh, yes."

The encampment was uncharacteristically quiet as they made their way hand in hand to Peter's tent. A few groups of men played desultory games of cards around the fires. Outside the largest tent, Colonel Smith-Mason stood with some of his officers, talking in low voices over a sheaf of dispatches.

Peter glanced at them with a small frown.

"Do you think there is something amiss?" Carmen whispered. She had lived long enough with the intrigues of war to know that events could change in an instant, but she had hoped, prayed, that her wedding night at least could prove uneventful.

Outside the bedchamber, anyway.

"I do not know," Peter answered, his watchful gaze still on the small group. "Surely not."

"But you do not *know*?"

He shrugged. "We have more important things to think of tonight," he said, bending his head to softly kiss her ear.

Carmen shivered, but waved him away. "No, you must find out. I will wait."

"Are you certain?"

"Yes. Go on. We have many hours before dawn." He kissed her again, and she watched him walk away, his polished buttons gleaming in the firelight. Then she turned to duck into his tent. *Their* tent, for that night.

It was a goodly size, but almost spartan in its tidiness. The cot was made up with linen-cased pillows and a blue woolen blanket; a stack of papers and books was lined up exactly on the table, and the chairs pushed in at precise angles. His shaving kit and monogrammed ivory hairbrush were flush with his small shaving mirror. The only bit of personal expression was in the miniature portrait on a small stand beside the cot: of his younger sister, Elizabeth. Next to it was a portrait of Carmen, painted when she was sixteen, which she had given him as a wedding gift.

Carmen laid her small bouquet of wild red roses beside the paintings and went to open her own small trunk, which had been brought there while they were at the church. In it were the only things she had brought away on her journey from Seville: two muslin dresses and a satin gown, a pair of boots, rosary beads, men's trousers and shirts, and a cotton night rail that was far too practical for a wedding night.

She slipped out of her simple white muslin wedding dress, and took the high ivory comb and white lace mantilla from her hair. She brushed out her waist-length black hair. Then she sat down on the cot to wait.

She was quite asleep when she at last felt Peter's kiss on her cheek, his hand on her back, warm through her silk chemise. She blinked up at him and smiled. "What was it?"

"It is nothing." He sat down beside her and gathered her into his arms. He had shed his coat and shirt, and Carmen rubbed her cheek against the golden satin of his skin. "There were rumors of a French regiment nearby, much closer than they should be."

"Only rumors?"

"Yes. For tonight." He wrapped his fingers in her loose hair and tilted her face up to his, trailing small, soft kisses along the line of her throat. "Tonight is only ours, my wife."

"Oh, yes. My husband. *Mi esposo.*" Carmen moaned as his mouth found the crest of her breast through the silk. Her fingernails dug into his bare shoulders. "Only ours."

The bridal couple was torn from blissful sleep near dawn by the horrifying sounds of gunfire, panicked shouts, and braying horses.

Peter was out of bed in an instant, pulling on his uniform as he threw back the tent flaps.

Carmen stumbled after him in bewilderment, drawing the sheet around her naked shoulders. "What is it?" she cried. "A battle?"

"Stay here!" Peter ordered. Then she was alone.

Carmen hastily donned her shirt and trousers, and tied her hair back with a scarf. She was searching for her boots when she heard her husband's voice and that of Lieutenant Robert Means, a young man she had sometimes played cards with of a quiet evening. And fleeced regularly.

"By damn!" Peter cursed. "How could they be so close? How could they have gotten so far without us knowing?"

"Someone must have informed them," Robert answered. "But we are marching out within the quarter hour."

"Of course. I shall be ready. Has Captain Hollingsworth been alerted?"

"Yes. What of . . ." Robert's voice lowered. "What of your wife, Major?"

"I will see to her."

Carmen stuck her head outside the tent. "She will see to herself, thank you very much! And what are you doing running about unarmed, *husband*?" She rattled his saber at him.

"Carmen!" Peter pushed her back into the tent. "You must ride into the hills and wait. I will send an escort with you."

"Certainly not! You require every man. I have ridden about the country without an escort for months. Shall I ride to General Morecambe's encampment and tell him you require reinforcements?"

"No! You are to find a safe place, and wait there until I come for you."

"Madre de Dios!" Carmen pulled her leather jacket out of her trunk and thrust her arms into the sleeves, glaring at him

all the while. "I will not hide! I cannot play the coward now. I will ride for reinforcements."

"Carmen! Be sensible!"

"You be sensible, Peter! I have been doing this sort of thing for a long time."

"But you were not my wife then!" he shouted.

"Ah. So that is it." Carmen left off loading her pistol to go to him, and framed his handsome, beloved face in her hands. "I cannot give up what I am doing to become a fine, frail, sheltered lady again, simply because I am now your wife. No more than you can stay safely here in camp because you are now my husband."

He turned his head to kiss her palm. "No. Even though I wish it so, you are quite right."

"We shall have many, many years to sit calmly by the fire, *querido*."

He smiled against her skin. "And will you long for your grand adventures, Carmen, when you are chasing babies about Clifton Manor?"

"Never!"

Peter caught her against him and kissed her mouth, hard, desperate. "I will see you at supper, then, Lady Clifton."

"Yes." Carmen clung to him for an instant, an eternal moment, then stepped away. "Promise me you will fight very, very carefully today, Peter."

"Of course, my love." He grinned at her, the crooked white grin that had won her heart. "I never fight any other way."

Then he was gone.